Gillian White, a former journalist who comes from Liverpool, lives in Totnes, Devon with her journalist husband and their two dogs. Their four grown-up children and two grandsons live nearby. Three of her ten novels have already been adapted for the BBC, and *The Sleeper* is now a major BBC drama series. *Unhallowed Ground* and *Veil of Darkness* are also available in Corgi paperback. *The Witch's Cradle* is now available from Bantam Press.

Critical acclaim for Gillian White:

'This dark, spooky psychological thriller grabs you by the collar and won't let go'
Woman's Journal

'A first-rate psychological thriller – perceptive, witty and full of suspense'
Good Housekeeping

'The story of deceit and domestic infamy is very well written'
Western Morning News

'A wonderful mix of storytelling and hilarious entertainment'
Annabel

'A novelist of the highest quality . . . an intense and vividly written novel which takes you by the throat and won't let go: a splendid book for those who enjoy a psychological thriller with a deep and provocative story'
Sunday Independent

'A gripping read'
Today

'Bitingly brilliant . . . complex, witty and sinister'
Daily Mirror

'A dark, disturbing tale'
Sunday Telegraph

'Creepy and insightful'
Ms London

'This is clever, clever writing, to mix tragedy and comedy and present it as easy reading . . . it is a Martin Amis with heart'
Glasgow Herald

'Full of wonderful household imagery . . . subverts romance into a credible story of ordinary people in extraordinary circumstances'
Fay Weldon

'Gillian White is stylish enough to bring off a comedy of some poignancy'
Mail on Sunday

'Here is a marvellously exciting new writer. She tingles one's spine. She makes you think about people. She's marvellously literate and the similes really bring the writing to life'
Jilly Cooper

'She has a remarkable empathy with a rich cast of characters. Her broad but sure brushstrokes are stingingly accurate'
Independent

Also by Gillian White

THE SLEEPER

Gillian White

CORGI BOOKS

THE SLEEPER
A CORGI BOOK : 0 552 14561 0

Originally published in Great Britain by Bantam Press,
a division of Transworld Publishers

PRINTING HISTORY
Bantam Press edition published 1998
Corgi edition published 1998

3 5 7 9 10 8 6 4

Set in 11/12pt Linotype Times
by Kestrel Data, Exeter.

Corgi Books are published by Transworld Publishers,
61–63 Uxbridge Road, London W5 5SA,
a division of The Random House Group Ltd,
in Australia by Random House Australia (Pty) Ltd,
20 Alfred Street, Milsons Point, Sydney, NSW 2061, Australia,
in New Zealand by Random House New Zealand Ltd,
18 Poland Road, Glenfield, Auckland 10, New Zealand
and in South Africa by Random House (Pty) Ltd,
Endulini, 5a Jubilee Road, Parktown 2193, South Africa.

Printed and bound in Great Britain by
Mackays of Chatham plc, Chatham, Kent.

*For Jane and Garth Pedler-Palmer,
for the noble Lady Lushington and all
her pink-hatted offspring.*

THE SLEEPER

Prologue

There is stillness and there is waiting. But this is a different kind of stillness, a gasping kind of waiting.

'Is there anyone there in spirit?'

And the vapid feel of unused dining rooms where a louder than normal outrush of breath assumes the crassness of a belch. Thick, maroon curtains of Dralon hold in the smell of dry old crumbs and keep the wild weather at bay but it is still there, behind the bay window, caterwauling to get in.

'Is there anybody there in spirit?' The medium's voice is impatient, signifying firmly that she is not prepared to tolerate any nonsense from recalcitrant spirits, or dear ones present this afternoon, for that matter. She is not prepared to pander to contrariness of any sort. At all.

And everyone knows that the dear departed have a reputation for being silly.

Stern eyed, her head hangs low but attentively. She could be a turtle, the oval of wicker rising from the chair behind her the frame of a horny shell. And her eyes are the eyes of a chelonian, expectant, unblinking as she gazes into the candle flame. The cane behind her creaks acceptably, gives some comfort to the wait in the cold.

Over her head sprout the curiously pubic, question-mark curls favoured by coach-party women. Audrey's work. Audrey's in Torquay is one of the few remaining establishments that turn out perms like that. Audrey has lacquer in plastic bottles, Amami wave set and metal curlers that burn necks under dryers, and Audrey sends out customers with necks chequered in painful pinks.

The hands that the medium places on the table are old hands, older than the face above them where rouge blushes papery cheeks. Hands with the marks of time upon them, grave marks the young call them cruelly. Ten nails, invisible polish that catches the light, ten shells set apart on a shiny, oval table, bloodless from moderately applicated pressure.

This is a room you would not bother to hoover. You might run round with a sweeper once a fortnight, but there'd be no need to get out the hoover. Dry old crumbs, tempered by wet cucumber, but the scents of the room are overpowered by the centrepiece on the table. From the candelabra with two arms, branched wide in the middle, two white candles pierce the dusk in their own right, and their flames have an aura around them. Softly smoking, dripping a gentle, lily-white milk which trembles and falls with the purity of tears.

Keeping company with the candelabra is a single glass of water set before the medium and in the light it looks as though some pale species of fish is swimming below the surface – but nobody worries, they are used to this, that's how it comes, the local, privatized water.

The stillest thing in the room is the palm which stands in a lush jardinière in the corner nearest the fireplace. It came from a local garage five years ago and has done remarkably well indoors. The fire is still, too, although it appears to flicker with the candles because it is full of scrunched-up crimson paper.

A seagull screams. The medium shifts. The wicker creaks once again.

'Is there anybody there?'

If there is, it must be getting harder by the minute to ignore the undisguised threat in the medium's challenging tone. Her face shows petulance. It is hard to imagine that women like this were ever little girls in white socks. But her eyes have that watery look of hope still in them.

It is a long and patient wait, but none of her earthly listeners are worried; they have all been here before. They know that Violet Moon never fails to communicate, never fails to bring her regulars some solace on these cold, wet Torquay afternoons.

Apart from the medium herself there are five round the table, four women and a man. You can't count the faces in the photographs, those who stare at the gathering with faraway eyes, the dead in the sepia-brown of yesteryear, the grandchildren in bright, Kodak, seasidey colour.

Joining hands like flowers forming a wreath around their dead, those five present make uneasy bodily contact. Too much touch is embarrassing, too little impolite. And here they sit with straight backs, their feet square on the floor, their heads very up or very down, an individual choice for such intense concentration. For here, in this beige bungalow dining room, is the nearest any of them come to a clenching spiritual climax.

BANG.

CRASH.

WALLOP.

'Oh my God!' And they all jump back, under-arms pricking, flesh creeping. One, 'My good-ness!' is overpowered by a quietly spoken, 'Shit.' The man sweats profusely and brings out a clean white handkerchief.

'It is merely a seagull,' says Mrs Moon impervi-ously, floating a winged eyebrow which resembles the crushed bird in question. 'Dashed against the window by the storm. We who live here get used to it. Now, if everyone would calm themselves perhaps we could proceed.'

There are no exclamations from the woman in grey. The woman in grey merely goes paler and her dry lips compress. Mrs Moon knows everyone here save this one, and she sits opposite, made wraithlike by the shadowy effect of the candles. But Mrs Moon noticed her when she came in, grey from throat to hem with spectacles on a silver chain that add to the severe neatness and calm. And when, earlier on, Mrs Moon had taken her coat to hang in the hall she had been be-wildered by the lack of scent. Everyone's scent stays in their coats, everyone's essence lingers there, nuzzling deep in shiny linings or tartan fluff or astrakhan collars. When you possess a trained nose like the medium's you can detect it in leather buttons, thongs and tassels. And believe it or not there are even certain auras in zips. But in the grey woman's macintosh Mrs Moon scented nothing; she found a hanger and disposed of the coat, but she remained troubled. No past? No present? How strange. Can it be that this woman does not know who she is? That her purpose today is to find herself?

She can see the spectacle chain now, sparking across the table and giving its owner the only sign of life she seems to possess. She sits very still, like the others. She has been here three times before and still the medium isn't sure why she keeps coming because, despite Mrs Moon's efforts, no contact has been made on any occasion. She gave no clues about herself and the friend who brought her gave no hints. Not that Mrs Moon needs hints, she doesn't work like that. Just a name came with her – Miss Bates – no hint there either. Such a plain, simple name and so far, unfortunately, nobody from the other side seems to want to claim her. Mrs Moon hopes sincerely that, for her new client's sake, something will happen this afternoon. She doesn't need the money. The seances are lucrative, they provide for her needs and prevent her from having to accept charity from her son. She is not an extravagant person and the customers keep coming, she even has a waiting list. She depends on word of mouth, no crude advertising like some of them do down by the harbour. No, word of mouth and good value for money are Violet Moon's watchwords and so far they haven't failed her.

A voice in the darkness, a voice from the cold, grating into the dining room. 'Hello! Good after-noon!'

At last the medium smiles. Aha, Caster, one of

13

her favourite spirit guides. An Eskimo from Lapland, the land of ice and northern lights.

'You are welcome among us as ever, Caster, we are very honoured to have you with us this afternoon and grateful to you for being so punctual.' There is a definite admonishment in the last sharp remark which Caster appears to ignore.

The candle flames burn steadily on, waxen as wall lights made in their image. Caster is present and there was no sign of his coming save for the glimmer of recognition in the medium's eye, an off-hand recognition with little excitement about it, much as one might recognize a familiar neighbour and give a casual nod. No fuss necessary, no need to cause embarrassment, and all this reassures her customers that Mrs Moon is no lightweight, that she is at home with the spirits and nowhere near in awe of them and their eerie world. Politely, she gives Caster a few moments' grace to settle down before she continues. 'Have you anyone waiting beside you today? Anyone who desires to commune with our little troupe? We haven't got all the time in the world, you know, Caster.' Insinuating insensitively that he might well have.

The earthbound ones prepare themselves. There's a shift in the air, the lean of a neck, the rest of an arm, the whisper of one stockinged foot easing round another and the shiver of anticipation. The time is come. The loved ones are waiting. It is true what they say – Mrs Moon never fails.

Nobody here today would dream of suspecting that she was a fake. Why would they? Such thoughts would be self-defeating. Over them all she wields the kind of power normally associated with the US Secretary General. And doesn't she always get it right, a good fifty per cent of the time, anyway, and you can't ask for more than that. Spiritualism is not an exact science, more a matter of touch-and-go dependent on the moods and fancies of those who have gone over. And they don't suddenly turn into angels – if anything they are more mischievous with a kind of spritely naughtiness they might well have despised on earth.

'My dear friends in spirit,' calls Mrs Moon, sweeping her hands from the table to her chest, bestowing a kind of self blessing, and the cane crackles wickedly. This display makes the candles flutter as Caster's arrival had not. 'Where are you all today? Have you abandoned us?' And she sits back in her priestly chair and closes her eyes more tightly, breathes in, breathes out, breathes in, breathes out so the candles waver alarmingly. 'We're waiting, Caster, we're waiting.'

A voice more Red Indian than Eskimo, more likely to utter a deep 'kemo sabe' than a reindeer call, comes up through Mrs Moon's throat and spills out into the room. There are shards of ice in the back of it, a frosty implication, a wail, a wind rushing round an iceberg. And Caster speaks. 'Dear friends on earth, we have been waiting. Several of us are gathered here to speak to you today, to tell you that we miss you and wish you well and to reassure you all that we are never far away from our loved ones. Even in your most lonely moments we are with you, and watching, yearning to give you the hope and confidence that death is not the end, that one day we will be together again, and you will be happy as we are now, in this place full of light and harmony.' And the icy sound withdraws on a cold, low moan but is obviously still there, waiting, in some bleak and freezing place where the wind moans relentlessly. And they wait.

Suddenly Mrs Moon's eyes bulge, she lunges forward and takes a swig of water, disturbing the shadowy fish. Just as violently she lurches back and closes her eyes again, licking her lips and smacking them pleasurably. It is now she decides to go with the force, to hell with restraint.

'Aha. It is Minnie! Minnie, how nice to have you with us. I know that somebody here today has been looking forward to a visit from you. How are you, Minnie? And why have you stayed away for so long?'

The voice change is extraordinary. The peculiar high-pitched note of an actress playing a child pipes up and a stranger would stare at the medium closely, appalled that such a comical sound should come from such a sensible person. But those in the room already know Minnie, one of them loves her very dearly, and that's why they all smile when they hear her familiar voice.

'I have been so busy, I couldn't come before, I hope you will forgive me.'

Mrs Moon minces and pulls a prissy face. 'That's quite all right, Minnie, we're just glad to have you now and I'm sure Godfrey is overjoyed to hear from you again, aren't you, Godfrey? And have you any special messages for your brother today?'

A lisping giggle from Mrs Moon makes Godfrey smile fondly. His face is a study in gentle euphoria. Drooped, with a sad moustache, he whispers, 'Minnie, sweetheart, how are you?'

'Godfrey, Mumba says you're to wear that extra vest when it's damp outside, she knows you don't like it but she says you must and you have to write to cousin Frances before the end of the month and not keep putting it off. You've been eating peardrops,' the spirit giggles, 'I can smell them. My favourites! My favourites!'

A close, private man, Godfrey's eyes shine wetly behind wire circles of pebbled glass. Men who wear waistcoats, crisp collars and ties and do up their jackets with one button ought not to cry. With one shaking hand he moves his spectacles forward a fraction, brushes the tears with the back of the other and blinks what's left of them quickly away.

'Anything else?' The icy voice of Caster comes with all Mrs Moon's impatience behind it.

'Yes, just one more thing before I go. The angel is smiling, Godfrey. I rubbed off the face like you told me and painted in a smile instead. It looks much nicer like this, Godfrey, so nice I'm hanging it up for Christmas.'

Godfrey's face twists, anguished but safe in the gloom. He clenches and unclenches his bony fingers. For a moment he'd been a child again surrounded by those he loved. For a candle-flickering, cucumber-smelling moment. He feels that peardrop rough on his tongue. He sees his sister's face, rosy with concentration, her deft little tongue almost touching her nose on the day she drew her Christmas angel. 'That face,' he had told her, 'it's not right, you can't have an angel crying.'

Fifty years was yesterday. 'Oh, but you can,' argued the lisping child. But the serious little boy he was had insisted. Silly little Minnie, he had made her change the drawing, rub out the tears and turn the mouth the right way up. He'd said it was better like that, but it was much more likely, he thinks now, with so much of his life behind him, it was much more likely that an angel would cry.

And his little sister, who was to die so young, must have already known that.

There are other messages to come but Godfrey does not hear them. For him the voices in the room have turned into travelling voices, like the sound made by passing cars, made unreal by the void of speed. Fifty years are all around him. He ceases to hear the weather cavorting against the window. The candles shrink to pinpricks of light. Love is near, warm and sleepy.

So the gripping cold, when it comes, is shocking, dreadful to Godfrey, who imagines he hears Minnie scream. He thinks he holds out his arms to protect her as he did the day she died, but really he sits terribly still, rigid, spectacles flashing, trying to identify the source of the sound, the tinkling of the musical box. A lullaby he knows well, a popular lullaby he learned in his childhood. 'Roses whisper goodnight 'neath the silvery light . . . When the dawn peepeth through, it will wake them and you . . .' But the notes are not gentle, they are brash and tuneless and seem to be dragging him down . . .

Something is startlingly different about the room. Godfrey forces himself to return to it. He cannot remain in the place where the musical box is playing because the cosiness has changed there, it's not safe. He leaves the toneless lullaby behind and returns to the silent world of reality.

The medium's eyes are jumping like eyes behind a nightmare. Her breathing no longer sounds like that of an easy sleeper, it's gone harsh and rapid and her face has assumed a cunning Godfrey has never seen there before. In, out, in, out, and the beads round her throat seem to be tightening, one hand rises to clutch them as if she can hardly believe . . .

'Are you there?' No more than a strangled croak.

No answer. Who can this be? Whose is the voice which comes with such soft menace? What diabolical presence could fill the medium's throat so that it bulges and constricts and the painted mouth opens and shuts, the tongue flicks, reptilian inside it.

She gurgles. '*Are you there?*'

Still no response.

The words are spaced, they hiss with venom. 'Now, Chickadee, now!'

Godfrey closes exhausted eyes but finds no peace in the darkness. He opens them and stares in horror, just like the others are staring.

'Now, Chickadee, now! She is near, my darling. See. Listen. Know who she is. She is here, my darling. *Look at me!* Look . . . at . . . me.'

A pure manifestation of hatred on a cloud of freezing fog. So pure in its intensity. So pure there is a sweetness about it, the stone-sweet notes of a choirboy's song in a Christmas cathedral.

*   *   *

Afterwards, when it's all over and they're into the tea and cucumber sandwiches, Mrs Moon looks tired and wan but this is not unusual. 'It takes it right out of me, I'm afraid, it always does. It's all right for the blessed dead, but sometimes I tell myself I must stop before it does me in. At my age, you know, I'm sure it affects the heart.'

'But you never would,' pleads Godfrey, settled on the Ercol sofa. The medium's sitting room connects with the dining room by way of a curious, wrought-iron arch, and on this side of the arch hangs a plaster of Paris brigand with a cutlass in his teeth. Dainty triangles of sandwiches are arranged on a two-tier cake stand, neatly arranged on a base of paper napkins. The odd tomato, cut into quarters, gives colour to the display. No cake, though. She never offers them cake. Can't run to that.

She gives a reassuring smile, fingering her beads and the throat underneath them as if there is a sore place there that she will take a look at in private, after everyone's gone.

'Where did Miss Bates go?'

'She left all of a sudden as if she had another appointment. Quite rude, I thought,' says her companion, Nora Bunting. She'd met Miss Bates in a café and started chatting the way you do, about this and that. Nothing important. She'd mentioned the seances offhandedly, not expecting Miss Bates to take any special interest. But Miss Bates had seemed fascinated, asked if she could come with her. Nora Bunting agreed, and that is as far as their acquaintance goes. She owes her nothing, certainly no kind of defence when she's walked out in the middle of it all without so much as a by-your-leave.

'Something must have upset her,' says Gladys Carter uncomfortably, the one who never removes her hat.

'What? Did something untoward happen? I never know what's going on once I sink deep enough.'

Nobody is prepared to admit that a spectre came to the feast. It upset everyone but what is the point of distressing Mrs Moon? They all fear that one day she might do what she threatens and give up and then where would they be? Thrust into the curtained den of some crank, forced there by their needs, by their lonely despair. It is in their own interests to protect Mrs Moon and thus preserve this tenuous thread that is their only connection to the world they desire but dare not choose to visit on any permanent sort of basis.

It is not their habit to resurrect the afternoon's experiences. Well, death is embarrassing, more tasteless to bring up at the table than sex. No, they like to avoid the subject of what they have been up to behind those communicating doors, through that arch that leads to the darkened dining room.

'She's been three times now and on every occasion she's been pale,' says Godfrey thoughtfully. 'I wouldn't be surprised if the closeness of the room upsets her.'

'Or she could have been worried about the weather,' says Nora Bunting, picking the rind off a cucumber slice and settling it back on the margarine. She glances at the mayhem outside the picture window. The sky is fighting itself. The rain is so loud they are forced to raise their voices. 'Look, it's getting worse out there.'

'Now then, what about next week?' Mrs Moon consults her diary.

'There's Christmas.'

Ah. And they sit in the medium's small lounge contemplating this fact with various expressions of pain.

'We'd best leave it till after New Year,' says Mrs Moon brightly, not keen to dwell on the matter herself. She'd forgotten all about it till now. Her son is coming to pick her up, she'll be away for one whole week, one endless, tinselled, paper-chained week made sickly with brandy butter, fairy light flashing like nerve endings.

The wind roars like an unchained monster. A flock of gulls, furious about the unnatural weather, hurl themselves through the scudding grey sky. The visitors drift out in ones, their clothes pulled round them firmly. Lonely people on a wide and lonely road. A wet road, with views of the sea, and the streetlights are listless in the wind, the gleam that they give is watery pale.

Two of the medium's clients have cars, one lives close enough to walk and the fourth, battling with a rain hat, strides towards the bus stop. Hopeless to use an umbrella in this.

They'd rather not be seen together. The pool of warmth in which they have so briefly bathed now seems shameful, a little obscene, it feels as if they've exposed themselves and their hopeless-ness to each other and they know they must pay for their folly, each one solitary and vulnerable. Degraded by their morbid needs.

Wrapped in their own embarrassment, so nobody notices the woman in grey. She stands on the other side of the road, half hidden behind a lamp post, the mac that smells of nothing clutched tight around her and her face turned towards the wind. She watches the bungalow with tired, dull eyes while above her the gulls scream out their agony.

One

Deck the halls with boughs of holly,
Tra la la la la la-la la la.

They have done as the carol instructs. Christmas
down at Southdown Farm. An appropriate place
to spend Christmas with its cattle-a-lowing and
the frosty wind making moan. Although metal
troughs have replaced the gentle mangers and if *it*
were to happen here it would be a sterile nativity.

Clover Moon's Christmas list lies crumpled and
dirty on the farmhouse table, lost in a flutter of
scruffy receipts – the items either ticked, ringed or
scratched out. Clover does not have to join the
rabble at Marks for her cakes, her puddings, her
sausage rolls, mince pies, cranberry jellies, etc.,
etc. No, part of the Christmas ritual is that Violet,
her mother-in-law, brings all that with her, home
made and full of goodness just as Christmas fayre
ought to be. She has her own well tried recipes,
she doesn't need Delia Smith. And the turkey,
fresh, of course, and enormous, comes straight
from a neighbour's shed.

Lucky Clover.

But now, just one day after those shy communi-
cators with death met in that Torquay bungalow,

there is trouble afoot as a cow falls into a slurry pit. E64, commonly known as Daisy with the blind tit.

E64 for milk-recording purposes, pedigree name Southdown Bountiful. But which of these names does Daisy live up to? Which title suits Daisy best? E64, I'm afraid, because she is the only cow foolish enough to fall into the pit and she's done it twice before, so it looks as if Daisy has inbuilt destructive tendencies, like some unfortunate people are born to be accident prone and spend a good deal of their time in hospital casualty departments, tagged with a number, just like Daisy.

'That fence has been weak since the last time it happened,' moans Fergus Moon the farmer. 'I can't have mended it properly. Daisy has been eyeing it for some time now, but you'd have thought she'd have learned her lesson from the last frantic fiasco.' He sighs with resignation, commenting on her injurious behaviour as a doctor might mention a trying patient.

So Daisy falls in once again, not twenty miles from Wideacre Road where the spirits gather on damp afternoons. Clover Moon the farmer's wife receives the message by bleeper and gets straight on to Ernie Wakeham, the carrier, who has the wherewithal to pull poor Daisy out. If he can get his van to start. If the crank on his crane is working, as he so morosely informs her.

So it's neat, everyone here has a title: the farmer, the farmer's wife, the carrier and the cow, that most stoic and uncomplaining of creatures.

*　　*　　*

Curiously, over the last two years Clover Moon has suffered a personality change for the worse. It started very gradually and built itself up and up until now she has moved many miles away from the contented, loving wife and mother she was, happy with her lot.

As if she is being ill-wished.

Anxiety, anger and a sense of injustice have welled up inside her, and sometimes Fergus has seriously feared she might tumble over the precipice of madness and despair. Encouraged by her suffering husband, she visited doctors and therapists but alas to no avail. HRT was suggested but Clover refused hotly, saying, 'I am far too young at forty-three, and, anyway, when it comes I shall embrace cronism, I shall celebrate my coming of age just as Germaine Greer advises.'

But Clover Moon is not just annoyed, or disappointed, or irritated or depressed with her life. No, Clover Moon is furious. You can see this by the way she moves, talks, cooks, cleans, drives and by the way she has stopped making love to her husband. Busy with complaint, an intelligent woman who was told at school that she would go far, she never intended to settle down in the middle of nowhere and become no more than an appendage, the help-mate of a farmer, like a three-legged milking stool.

The farmer wants a wife, the farmer wants a wife . . .

Her talents have never blossomed.

In mourning for herself she feels she has failed to stretch her soul.

But Clover cannot see that she is merely going through a phase. She sincerely believes she should never have been a wife, she should never have been a mother; she could have been a hot-air balloonist, an explorer of pyramids, a singer in sleazy nightclubs . . . She doesn't know what she could have been if fate had played a more adventurous tune. But she puts the blame for this lack of knowing, for this awful injustice, squarely on the shoulders of Fergus the farmer, and her mother-in-law who is coming for Christmas – Granny.

Quite right. This is unfair, but you can't blame yourself for the traps you set.

And the only person who understands, the only one in the world who knows exactly how Clover feels, is the friend in whom she has always confided, the friend who agrees with her completely, the friend who is also arriving for Christmas – Diana. Bored, cynical, exotic Diana, with tumbling golden hair and a sharp, sad mind, who quests for fun and self-expression with a face as bland as a plastic doll's, who stokes and refuels Clover's rage as if it ever needed stoking.

An unholy bond if ever there was one.

Clover likes to moan to Diana, 'You gradually realize you've made this desperate mistake and you go round trying to tell everyone only to discover that they're all in the plot together, all in this subtle conspiracy. But worst of all are the old women, justifying their lives.'

'Oh, but Fergus is lovely!'

'Yes, Fergus is lovely and I should be on my knees at night thanking God for my blessings, a fact which makes me feel even guiltier for being such a dissatisfied bitch, but Fergus lives in a world of his own, not the real one,' says Clover

28

sourly. 'And I have been driven to this. We don't have any fun any more, we're always too worried about money or the weather and I'm nearly old and what have I done with my life?'

'Divorce him.'

'Oh, I don't hate him!' cries Clover in distress. 'I don't want to hurt him. If the farm belonged to him instead of his mother I'd persuade him to sell and we could get away from all this. I could have a career, we could lead normal lives with weekends off and holidays like everyone else, and we'd have enough money for Fergus to set himself up as something else, a consultant probably, we could do anything we wanted. Christ, Diana, you certainly got it right when you turned him down.'

'But Fergus wouldn't want to sell up.'

'Who can tell what Fergus would like? He just echoes his mother.'

'You've been hammering on about this for so long you're getting boring,' Diana replies. 'Frankly, if you really feel so strongly you should do something, take action. You are his wife, after all. Persuade him to convince Granny to sell and stop whining on all the time, demanding help and release from your friends as if it's in their power to give it.' But Diana revels in Clover's moaning.

'She'd never sell, Di. She's still punishing him for marrying me! I should be pandering to my husband's needs as I used to, as she always did. And she's the type who will live on deliberately, get a telegram from the Queen just to spite me. And by that time we'll both be too old to start again.'

This is the sort of loose talk Clover likes to

share with her friend Diana. Innocent enough. Common enough. And they both thoroughly enjoy it. Let us hope they know what they're doing with all this malicious complicity, which can easily turn so nasty and dangerous.

So here is the farmer's wife at Christmas and now, in this emergency, with a cow stuck in the slurry pit, Clover bangs down the phone and runs distraught fingers through her hair. It falls back into perfect shape. She is little and dark and quick, getting quicker by the minute as Christmas Day draws nigh. She wears neat, quick things like jeans and V-neck sweaters that slip off easily. She nips round her house in socks. All the Moons go round in socks because with all that shit outside they couldn't possibly wear shoes in the house.

There is no opportunity to wear smart clothes.

Her title, of course, is farmer's wife. On Happy Family playing cards she would appear on that three-legged milking stool gazing at the udders of a wide-eyed cow. Or perhaps she'd be standing on the doorsteps with a yoke across her shoulders, grinning. But Clover is far from a typical farmer's wife. I mean, where should she be, now? Out there in the yard giving moral support, poor Fergus, alone and in this weather, with only the sullen Blackjack to help him. And Blackjack, from the caravan, will want to be off early tonight to stay with his elderly mother in Plymouth to give him time to get round Safeway's before the Christmas Eve rush begins. But other than a giver of moral support what earthly use would she be out there keeping company with the cow? She could only stand on the edge of the pit, that dark, black lagoon, throwing her arms around and shouting. Giving advice where it's not needed. Anguished for the cow, holding it up with her own willpower, watching the light of hope drain from its terrified eyes.

'How awful to die like that,' thinks Clover Moon from the warmth and safety of her farmhouse kitchen. Struggling impossibly beneath the crust in that stinking, black porridge of excreta. She catches her breath in her throat and recoils from the horrible thought.

What right has Clover, in the grip of such bitter resentment, to see herself as a farmer's wife? The only right she can possibly have is by name – Clover. She could be one of the herd, couldn't she? But it is precisely that drear possibility that has surfaced after twenty good years of marriage to kindly Fergus – being one of the herd, becoming, for Fergus, just a help-mate, someone to turn the hay when he's busy, to pull on the end of the calving ropes, to clean out the parlour after the milking, to boil up the spuds and old cabbage leaves for the chickens. Someone like Fergus's mother, Granny, with hands all stiff and knuckly.

She'd nearly been caught in Granny's net when love was first in blossom and lay over the farm in all its pink and white sweetness. At the time she was too naive to realize what was happening; it is only now, with hindsight, that she sees through Violet Moon's little plot.

There is no good reason on earth why frozen peas should be worse than fresh cabbage. Why packet stuffing should be underrated, why anyone should cut the bottom off sprouts.

It ought to have been amusing. She ought to look back now and think of that time as funny. But it wasn't funny then and it seems even less comical now.

A bride and mother-to-be, Clover had, on Granny's advice, invited the neighbours round for a meal. All farmers and their wives, tough, grim women who could shear sheep and mend tractors and feed an army without prior warning. 'They all want to meet you, naturally. They'll be talking about you, Clover, wanting to see the kind of person Fergus has married.'

Clover struggled with common sense for she was a hopeless cook. 'Oh, I'm not sure . . .'

'They'll think you very jumped up if you don't.'

After the invitations were out Fergus calmly mentioned that Mary Tremain, the one who had said on the phone, 'Delighted,' was cookery editor for *The Farmers' Friend* and a judge at the Devon County Show. Alarmed, Clover rang her married friends to beseech them for advice on what sort of meal she should cook. She hadn't asked Granny, or 'Mum' as she had to call her then – 'Granny' slipped into common usage after the children came and, to be honest, Clover preferred the less intimate term. It didn't occur to Clover then that Mum had rigged this up intentionally. She rang Diana, who was not a good cook either, but an old and supportive friend.

'Something simple for goodness' sake. Don't try anything grand, remember . . .'

'What's simple? How d'you mean?' White and brisk with alarm, Clover clutched the receiver. 'I'm going to be the laughing stock . . .'

'Duck's always nice.'

'With a sauce?'

'Just apple. Don't attempt anything more difficult. Unless it's one you can buy and pour over, or you could go to Marks and get several packets of duck with orange and throw them together in a pan.'

'I can't possibly do that.'

'Why ever not? No-one would know. None of your guests would dream of buying a ready-made meal, I mean, *The Farmers' Friend*,' and Diana's voice rose a notch, 'you're talking Mrs Beeton here, the ultimate real food freak. They probably kill their own meat and skin it and pluck it and disembowel it. They can probably tell which farm the meat's come from like wine connoisseurs . . . you poor, poor thing . . .'

'There's six of them coming, Di, and I have since found out that Mary Tremain is the daughter of one of Mum's oldest friends so why didn't she warn me?'

'Doesn't matter now, don't waste your breath by dwelling on that. Don't start seeing it as a conspiracy. Violet might be a little protective, but nobody could be that vindictive.'

Clover, so naive, so hopeful, and oblivious of the fact that she was being ill-wished, put her mother-in-law's distant behaviour down to the fact that she wanted dear Fergus to marry a farmer's daughter, that's all, because it's a way of life, like being royal. She hadn't approved of Diana, either, when she was Fergus's fiancée. But Clover wasn't the vain, sophisticated Diana. Clover was sure that Violet would come round in time.

But the victory was Granny's.

Clover did duck. Three ducks, to be precise, hardly haute cuisine. Over-anxious, exhausted with worry, she'd put them in the Aga so early that by the time she came to serve them up the meat had fallen off the bone and only the charred carcasses were left, grinning bonily from the Wedgwood dish. And the cauliflower, warming so long in the slow oven, was black too. The stench of burnt bones and pitted saucepans filled the farmhouse. But she dished it up anyway, way beyond caring, and laughed oddly when she set it unsteadily on the table.

She was sick from too much gin.

She dropped ash on the apple pie and no amount of wiping would remove it.

Fergus merely winked at her and she'd hated him for his patronage, she'd hated his mother, the farm, his friends, farming in general, herself. It might have been a trivial matter but it was very far from funny.

'Doesn't Judy Gilmour do them beautifully,' said Mary of the apple pie in her gentle, sternish voice. Hell. Diana was right. This woman recognized the pie that Clover implied she'd baked herself and when confronted like that Clover could hardly deny it. 'She's won several prizes with these apple pies and you can see why, can't you?' nagged the merciless Mary Tremain.

With the food fiasco over, they settled down to play cards. Steadily and surely, with a kind of quiet dignity, Clover drank neat gin from a tumbler.

'You've gone blue,' said Fergus.

Clover heaved and left the room, collapsed on the stairs directly outside and was carried to bed,

34

singing her head off and farting. It was one of the two occasions in her life when she had been impossibly drunk, unable to remember what happened, even who she was. Sweat rolled off her. The room spun round. She prayed to God she would die.

And when she came down the next morning prepared to clear up the mess, she saw that Mary Tremain, cookery editor of *The Farmers' Friend*, Bob Tremain, Hilary and Mark Carter, Maggie and Joe Randall had not only washed up and put away but appeared to have spring-cleaned her kitchen. It was spanking, squeaky clean.

'They enjoyed themselves,' said Fergus evenly. 'They didn't go until after two.'

Congratulations were not in order. Did he think that her wrongs could be swept away by his smiles of forgiveness or her guests' understanding?

Clover, haunted by this for years, never tried again. She clung instead to her job in town, five years off for the children and then back to work where she was someone other than Fergus's wife, but in an estate agent's office, not the person she wanted to be, either. Far from it.

'Is the bass in?'

She should never have been a farmer's wife. Diana had the right idea, she'd turned Fergus down in the end. And Clover has never accepted the rustics' habit of entering a house without knocking, either. Here's Ernie the carrier in his grimy cap, in through her door without knocking, boots placed on the mat with care and casting his beady eyes around for tea.

'Yes, as you can see, I am in.' After all these years she still insists on this response.

Ernie, long and beany, takes no notice but sniffs at the drip on the end of his nose. It is too far gone for retrieval.

'Nasty night. The forecast is bad, very bad, they give snow for later.' And his word for snow is snooo, which imparts the feeling of falling and drifting so vivid is his intonation.

'I'm sure Fergus is waiting for you in the yard,' says Clover on a note of exasperation. 'That cow will have either died of shock by now or gone under.'

Ernie Wakeham gives his most vacant look, amazed, it would seem, to be urgently needed. 'Oh, right, then.' But he still stands there, dripping water all over the floor and shaking his wretched cap.

'I'll put the kettle on and we'll have a drink when you've finished.'

'Right, then,' says he, shocked by her inhospitality and determined to leave this vengeful prediction behind him like a curse. 'If'n it doan stop raining soon yous cellar with fill up agin and I carn vouch for my pump.'

Clover eyes him steadily and he backs slowly from the room.

The lights from the house seem very bright when it's dark outside like this.

Too soon it will be Christmas Eve. The day of the year that sounds like magic. Christmas Eve is normally still. BC, before the personality change, Clover used to come out here on Christmas Eve when the children were tiny, she used to come out

36

to stare at the stars, to listen for the quiet and search for the magic. Finding it in the strangest places, straw-filled barns of gold, misty with the breath of animals. Sometimes the innocence she felt inside herself, an innocence she clung to as long as she could, sometimes, when she sensed it again somewhere in the distance and it vanished to her touch, it made her cry. Will she find it tomorrow?

In the mood she is in, that's doubtful.

Once she danced in the moonlight, naked. It was rapturous, innocent and amazing. Fergus would have been appalled.

But the stars will probably be well out of sight because the clouds have formed into monstrous bat wings; the sky in which they fly tonight is heavy and tumultuous.

After the milking Fergus will drive to Torquay to fetch Granny. Granny, who's coming for Christmas again. He likes to collect her before Christmas Eve, get her here and settled in, tick her off his mental list just like the ham and the leg of pork. And Diana and Jonna will arrive in a minute bringing the twins as usual. For a week, as usual.

The four solid walls of Clover's kitchen signify peace and goodwill, brightness and cheer. A farmhouse kitchen with a long, pine table, window seats framed by bright red gingham, the ceiling low and beamed. The girls have stuck stars to the beams this year and a mass of cards run over and down the huge Aga mantelpiece. They clutter the pelmets. They hang in blue-tacked strips down the walls. Reassuring? There are many people out there in the world who are telling her they like her. '*Thinking of you at Christmas*.' '*Joy to the world*.' Clover is not alone. A warm room, a homely room, a Christmassy room, but Clover is wrong in it this year, pacing like a beast in a den.

What is wrong? What is the matter? Christmas was always her favourite time.

But now she has a calm moment. Blissfully calm but for the weather beating against the window. The farmer's daughters, Polly and Erin, drawn by their age to the macabre, have gone outside to watch the floundering cow. All is calm. All is bright. Everything's ready for Christmas. And Clover has cleaned the house for Christmas, been right through from top to bottom like a whirlwind. A human bottle in blue plastic. Why she cleaned the house she can't think. Who does she want to impress? Certainly not Diana, whose own house is in permanent chaos. Not Jonna.

So it has to be Granny.

And it is during this quiet moment, reaching for the sherry in the pantry in an attempt to cheer herself up, that Clover Moon spots the Christmas cake, made by Granny, un-iced, because Clover likes to ice it herself. She has forgotten to ice it! She was ready at the starting line but everyone else has passed her. She failed to hear the starter's gun, she has failed in the Christmas race.

Why this melancholy? Why this sinking dread? Where does it come from and how can she shake it off, this sickening Christmas pressure? Fancy failing to ice *the cake*, and there she was thinking she'd done it, she'd arrived at Christmas gift-wrapped and successful for once, forgetting all those good times when she came a flying first with ease. A good wife and mother, that's what Granny was. But me? What sort of mother have I been? asks Clover, more miserable by the minute. Deep down she thinks she has been a bad one, morally unfit to bring up children, within an inch of battering once when the girls were tiny and she was worn out and Erin refused to stop crying. Within an inch of being bundled with a blanket over her head from a van outside the Old Bailey, railed at by women in headscarves, a breed apart who live outside the courts in order to claw at those amongst them who have failed. Those who forgot to ice their cakes, those who battered their babies. But Clover didn't batter, did she? She'd snatched up Erin and hugged her tightly, desperate with a terrified love; how could she, even for an instant, have wanted to hurt anything so precious?

A good wife? Could Clover Moon have been referred to as 'goody' in mediaeval times? She doubts it. Clover is bad, bad inside with lustful thoughts she ought not to have. And why does she listen for the sound she's been hoping to hear all day through the rain and the wind, the sound of Range Rover tyres squelching through the mud in the yard? And why has she been trying to calm the flutter in her heart she gets while she waits?

Shit. I am a capable, successful woman in my own right, thinks Clover to herself, staring down at the cake so richly brown on the table beside her. She sips the first of the Christmas sherry. 'And I have merely forgotten to ice my cake because I have more important matters on my mind.'

When she tells Diana she'll roar her pretty head off.

Two

'Tis the season to be jolly,
Tra la la la la la-la la la.

They are trying hard to be jolly but . . .
What is this presence here in this house?
'Granny's here, everyone!'

And do they know, do her son and daughter-in-law know about Granny's little spiritual sideline? That's not very likely.

The children come out from 'the children's end' bright and warm and polite with greetings. Violet Moon kisses their cheeks and pats their backs but looks over their shoulders with searching eyes. What is this presence so pervasive it overpowers the woodsmoke? Is it here in her kitchen? Clover's kitchen. If she hopes to find something of William in the walls, in the ceiling or up the chimney then she's in for a disappointment. There's nothing there. It went with her husband, five years ago. It went when they came to tell her, 'The tractor's gone over, Violet. He can't have known a thing about it. It was quick. It was over in seconds.'

People try to be kind, but Violet Moon the medium knows different. He was lying out there on the steep three acres for a good twenty minutes before they found him. The pain, he had described to her since, was that of a chainsaw slicing his chest. Coming. Going. Revving. Tearing through bone and flesh. That's how he'd gone, chopped nearly in half by two tons of scarlet metal. The red earth he'd worked for so many years, the earth that clamoured for tears and sweat had finally called for the ultimate, had washed itself in his blood.

And her? What had it demanded from her? Well, it had demanded support and love and struggle and sacrifice and these she had given with all her heart. And Fergus, my son? Sacrifice too? Earth to earth, ashes to ashes, at sixteen years old he'd come to her and said, 'I don't want to carry on the farm, Mother. I want to be an engineer. A design engineer.' And he'd shown her the university brochure.

'Don't say anything to your father yet, give me some time to think about this.'

But her tone told him never to mention his disloyal inclinations again. And Fergus never did, nor did Violet refer to the matter. But Fergus let them both down by marrying that one – poor William, he'd never approved of Clover, neither of them considered her suitable for Fergus or the farm. Well, look at the flighty piece, I ask you.

William my dear, I'm back, but there's something wrong, it isn't the same.

'We've put you down the children's end, Mother, so you don't have to climb any stairs. We know you're not used to stairs.'

She's always put down the children's end.

41

People try to be kind. They think she is old. Fergus moved from the village into the farmhouse and said, 'There's no need for you to leave the farm, Mother. There's plenty of room for you to stay here with us and we'd love to have you. We'll do up the annex so you can be quite separate.'

She had refused. But they did up the annex anyway and called it the children's end. A tasteless place and vulgar with a rockery outside where the old waterwheel used to be. Sometimes at night, for Violet is a poor sleeper, she fancies she hears the old wheel creak and groan in the dark. A melancholy sound. The annex, hideously extended with real stone, the long, thin annex behind the farmhouse, now looks like a cowboys' bunkhouse. They were so thrilled with the natural stone that they brought it indoors as well. 'Character' they call it, my foot. In Granny's bedroom, behind her padded headboard, granite rises looking wet to meet a stippled ceiling and when she lies down she could be in a well, put there by that naughty boy who drowned that pussy cat. And the waterwheel that isn't there grinds and sounds like a pulley.

Barns and outhouses, they seldom make good conversions. They never acquire that homely feeling. They smell of owls' droppings.

They built the four-roomed annex (two bedrooms, a kitchenette and a den) so the children could play their loud music and do what they liked, out of sight, out of mind, while they themselves live in the farmhouse with all its beams and rafters. It lends itself well to Christmas.

But Granny hears what the girls get up to when the twins come for Christmas. Hanky-panky in the bedrooms, a houseful of life, or would be but for the pill. And when Fergus goes to unblock the soakaway she bets his finds are of rubber. A seeping rubber sea running through an orchard of fruit. She has walked the slippery paths with her stick so she knows. She has prodded it with the special non-slip end of her stick, so she knows.

They have buried her in Torquay, in a bungalow on Wideacre Road overlooking the bay with slopes so steep it is hard to get out. Buried away amongst seagulls' droppings and the little bits of shrimpshell they bring in their beaks and lay lovingly on the flat roof. Buried in a bungalow called Ocean View and she looks out of her picture window which lets in the sun like a great dray horse pulling a cart behind it and spilling wisps into every corner. No shade or shadow in Ocean View. Just sun. And on grey days, grey skies.

There are bungalows on either side all with picture windows and all with widows looking out. The builders sank whirligig posts into the concrete patios when the cement was wet and willing, but the half-walls between the bungalows keep the inhabitants apart even when they go to hang out their washing. Sometimes Violet can hear her neighbour, Mrs Fitzhall, humming, but only just, it could be the wind from the sea. When Mrs Fitzhall has her window open Violet can smell her cooking; she is partial to casseroled liver. She adds swede to her mashed potato. The smell of swede goes with the sea, it matches it. And Mrs Fitzhall listens to DevonAir on the wireless. She disapproves of Violet. She disapproves of Violet's 'profession'.

For years Mrs Fitzhall never knew, she wondered who the visitors were and asked in every roundabout way when they met at the bus stop, keeping her tugging headscarf on with heavily jewelled fingers. Mrs Fitzhall's hands fascinated Violet. She could tell that her neighbour's nails used to be long and curved and varnished, but now they are pale, a purply blue as if the overuse of scarlet in the past has turned them that queer shade. Violet was cautious, never gave a thing away, but then one day Mrs Fitzhall edged away and looked at her oddly so Violet assumed she'd found out from somebody else on the bus.

Violet keeps Ocean View as neat as a new pin. She tends her palm from the garage with care. She views and she views as her bungalow tells her to view, and she dreams like a soul from the underworld, a 'Gumble', perhaps, or a 'Hummit', some strange creature not quite human but of human form who lives in a lost sub-strata deep within the earth. On Wideacre Road.

Handy little buses pass by on the hour.

On Wednesdays the library van calls.

Oh yes, if Clover Moon is furious then so is Granny Violet. And there is no love lost between them.

Granny has arrived so Christmas is now officially underway.

'Have a sherry, Mother.'

Mother. Clover has always refused to call her Mother and Fergus does not call her Granny. Only when he talks to her through the children or when he talks about her. Oh, Fergus is a handsome man, tall with a resonant voice, well spoken,

capable and practical as all farmers are and as his
father was before him. He gets things done on
telephones, he commands the attention of door-
men and waiters and he drives his car with one
bronzed arm resting on the window listening to
his operatic tapes. If Violet is with him he will
compromise with Gilbert and Sullivan. When he
gestures his thanks to reversing drivers in the
narrow lanes around the farm he uses just one
commanding finger. A benign judge, too benign
when it comes to his flighty wife. And his smile is
always a solemn one.

Christmas is underway. 'That would be very
nice thank you dear.'

And she knows it will be that sickly
Bristol Cream because they think she likes Bristol
Cream, she said so once just to please them. And
Fergus will go off into the kitchen and talk to
Clover about her, they will raise their eyebrows
and groan and tell each other, 'Only six more
days.' She knows because she has heard them.
And it's awful, *because it is her they are talking
about*.

She will leave her teeth in pink sterilizer in a
glass in the bathroom to let them know who she
really is. Jaws champing, trying to get out. Oh, if
only she could leave her body as easily as her
teeth do.

What is this presence here in this house?

Violet shivers and half shudders. They call her
Granny, not Violet, not Mrs Moon, not Vi, no,
they call her Granny, inventing another identity.

They call her Granny, with all the crone-like,
whiskery qualities that loaded word implies. They

45

watch her dozing by the fire, dozing gently towards death, they think, but she never dozes at home. Only when she comes here and she's bored and unwanted, and she only comes here for Christmas.

They watch her as she watches them, especially her, Clover. That one. The wife of her son. The one who thinks she uses too much lavatory paper, the one who imagines she searches for lumps in the gravy, the one who cannot bear the idea that Violet gave *him* birth.

Yes, she sits in her chair and watches them all from under her paper hat. Clover *will* start Christmas so ridiculously early. In Granny's day they had crackers once, on the day itself, none of this reckless spending and manufactured gaiety. Clover seems to believe that crackers maketh merry, just give them a cracker and a plastic whistle, crack open the sherry and the Turkish delight and, bingo, instant merriment.

'Have another chocolate, Granny.'

'No, thank you, my dear, I've had plenty.' And she sighs and looks contented, closing her eyes to the tinsel fire for a longer time so they think she is dreaming of the meal she has just eaten and they think she eats like a bird. At meal times they put her next to Fergus her son, on his right-hand side at the table. From there she misses nothing. She watches her son's hard hairy hand, decorated by a silver-chained watch strap that sparkles like a Christmas bauble. A firm, steady hand next to hers, which looks frail on the cloth. While *she* sits and dishes up down at the other end. Punished, all flustered and stressed, wielding a knife over a pudding sacrifice. With a paper hat on her head which makes her look like a demented cardinal blessing a sacred chalice. While the children hump like rabbits in the bedrooms and everyone tries to pretend they're still children, while everyone calls her Granny, the loving old woman from the fairy tales she told them when, dressing-gowned and soaped, they sat on her knee with cheeks smooth as swansdown, downy babes with soft eyelashes.

Who's kidding who?

'I remember when I was a little girl.' No, Violet's stories never began like that, she always read straight from a book.

Violet frowns. She feels a little peculiar, not quite herself this evening, as if there is something . . . She shakes her head, she's just being silly, and she gives one of her vacant smiles.

And is she a wolf in sheep's clothing because she is not the Granny they think she is? Is she wicked because she pulls yards of paper off the false brass holder with the cherubs on the side and deliberately stuffs it down the pan knowing that Clover will run out and therefore feel inadequate? Because she looks for lumps in the gravy and puts them carefully aside on her plate? Because she talks to the dead?

Is she some devil's abominable familiar?

Hooray! It is now later in the evening, and Jonna and Diana arrive to avoid tomorrow's Christmas rush.

Granny watches Jonna and Clover and wonders.

Something has happened to the weather. They never used to have weather like this, not rain and hail, thunder, lightning and wind all scrambled together. It's enough to make you shiver just to look at it. They forecast snow. The local forecast is more accurate than the national one and Diana is saying something ominous is happening and the authorities don't want to frighten the proles. They are keeping the phenomenon under their hats – the West Country is fighting extremes of weather while the rest of the nation basks in gentle breezes. Something dastardly has happened in the west, Diana says she is certain of it.

Violet knows her type. Diana is shrewd and cunning, she worships her looks and, since the beginning, has always been a bad influence on Clover. Best friends, huh, if only Diana knew! The ozone layer, she says, has ripped open directly above them.

In this, perhaps, thinks Violet, Diana might be right.

Fergus has been out cutting channels all day to divert the water from the house. Although it is late and everyone's tired he and Jonna go back to the task, using torches and glistening in waterproofs. A deluge of water is coming down off the hill. 'Just like a river, Mother,' Fergus puts his head round the door to inform her. 'And we haven't enough bloody sandbags to head it off.'

'Can't you get the children to help you?' asks Granny, but he has already hurried off with Jonna tagging behind him and she doesn't think he heard her. Silly question anyway. By now those girls are back in the children's end, up to goodness knows what, or talking on the phone.

The trouble is that Clover reminds her of Sheena and that's not poor Clover's fault. But the likeness between the two women is uncanny. All her gestures are the same, the way she has of smiling bashfully after she has spoken, the habit of pushing her hair behind her ears. Not only by mannerism and speech does Clover resemble Sheena, but in looks, too; she could be the image of Sheena. To be smart she wears fluffy things in pastels that harbour her scent in the fur. She is dark and delicate with seagull eyes and eyebrows that hide up, sometimes, under that straight-cut fringe, so that when Granny comes for Christmas she feels like a child again, just as helpless and unable to communicate as she felt when she was four years old. Being scorned. Causing tension and distress. And she knows she is as innocent as she is guilty – she creates the atmosphere and yet she does not cause it.

Yes, it is difficult to imagine Granny as a four-year-old child. Even she can hardly remember the days when she was little.

They have put Max Bygraves on the gramophone because they think she likes old songs, because they believe she enjoys reminiscing over the past. Because they suspect that, at her age, she cannot possibly bear to contemplate the future, but the music cannot drown the might of the weather and it is the might of the weather which is part of Granny's future. And will be theirs one day, too, they ought to remember that. They are, as usual, trying to be kind just as Sheena used to pretend to be kind. The children, her grandchildren, smile behind their hands just as Granny used to imagine Sheena used to smile.

Three

A story round a Christmas fire – Christmas Day in the workhouse, or once upon a time there lived a little girl called Violet.

Alas poor Violet. So sadly depleted.

People don't *really, really* die.

Mummy never really died and neither, of course, did Sheena. But Violet hadn't known that then, how could she, she was far too young, still at the stage of believing the lambs in the fields stayed as lambs, they didn't just grow into sheep and get butchered and eaten.

But fate comes knocking on the door so simply, so suddenly. One day Mrs H came to collect her from kindergarten. In that unfamiliar environment Violet hadn't recognized her at once, she still looked as though she was in the kitchen, bending to see into the oven, and the cardigan she carried on her arm looked like the rainbow oven cloth Violet had knitted for her with love.

The black-haired child stood there, red-faced, swamped in a blazer too large for her, trying to make sense of the situation. From under the shade of her panama hat she saw that Mrs H had a bald patch on the top of her head, where she couldn't see it herself, she probably didn't know it was there. This unique view of the cook was made possible, at that moment, by Mrs H bending to re-tie a broken lace. The thin, wiry hair looked as if it needed crocheting back and Violet had just learned to crochet in Mrs Elder's sewing class. There was something repellently intimate about that naked gleam of head, like somebody showing their bottom in school; there was something worrying about seeing Mrs H out and about on the road when her rightful place was in the kitchen. Place was assuming importance in the life of this four-year-old girl, like finding your right peg in the cloakroom, turning to the right page in *Read and Learn* and picking out the right flag to stick on the shiny classroom calendar.

Violet felt responsible for the out-of-place Mrs H, and this was an uncomfortable feeling, every bit as uncomfortable as the words she was hearing.

'Where's Mummy, Mrs H?'

'Mummy's gone to hospital with a pain in her tummy. She won't be back today, my pet, Mummy's very poorly.'

'When will she be coming back?'

'I'm afraid I can't tell you that, pet. But if the Lord's merciful we should see her back in a week or two.'

Mrs H's hand was sticky. It smelt of washing up.

For a moment Mrs H stopped her urgent, kitchen-type rushing to regard the child who tagged along sulking behind her. 'They took her away this morning in an ambulance.' Ambulances and fire-engines always greatly impressed Mrs H. She'd often told how they made her feel glorious like the last night of the proms, the Royal Mail, and anything that bore the Royal crest was sacrosanct to Mrs H, who was in awe of night trains, electricity, operating theatres and important things that went on in the night while she slept. 'Emergency, your daddy said, and he should know, after all he's a doctor. So he can answer all your questions when you get home.'

'But Mummy wasn't ill this morning. She took me to school. She said she'd be here to collect me and Mummy's never not come.'

> Jesus, tender
> shepherd, hear me,
> Bless thy little
> lamb tonight.
> Through the darkness
> be thou near me,
> Keep me safe till
> morning light.

And what have they done with my mummy?

Daddy came to her bedroom unsmiling, intent. Violet was already in bed, almost asleep, when he sat down beside her looking pale and drawn. And he started by trying to talk to her in the way of Mrs H pretending she really liked burnt cakes, he went on like that, pretending, until Violet had to stop him.

'Vi, sweet, Mummy is very seriously ill.'

'But what I want to know is when she will be back.'

Daddy stared at her, silent for a while, but she could see the thoughts going on, faster and faster, behind his eyes. 'Now. Listen. I want you to try to

52

be very grown-up in these next few days. I want you to help me and Mummy by being a good girl, being sensible like I know you can be, and most of all, sweet, being very brave.' He hesitated again and Violet wanted to stick up her arm and pull the words out of his mouth. 'Mummy might never be coming back.'

But 'never' was a word Violet could not understand, like you can't get your head round eternity or a universe without end, so the implications of what Daddy said had no real meaning. She was just relieved it was nothing worse, like Mummy with an arm chopped off and left with a horrible stump, or she'd had 'everything taken away', which Violet overheard a grim Mrs H saying about somebody once. She relaxed with the idea that she had misunderstood, nothing unusual for a four-year-old, everything would fall into place in the end, it didn't matter whether she understood or not, she had such little impact on the scheme of things. It was nothing to do with her. She was often silly. They sometimes called her Scatter-brain, but Mummy mostly called her Chickadee, after a monkey they'd seen in a shop and named just for fun.

So she shrugged her small shoulders in the grown-up way Daddy wanted, and with a sense of complicity said, 'Well, we'll just have to cope as best we can.'

She wished he hadn't smiled then; a frown would have been better, less sad.

'The nightlight, Daddy, don't forget to light the nightlight.'

'You're too big a girl to need a nightlight, surely?'

And comforters are unhygienic.

The first flutterings of fear came then, like dandelion seeds blowing in her tummy because Mummy would never have said that. So Violet begged, 'Please, please light it, Daddy.' But she turned her face to the pillow and covered her ears with her hands so she couldn't know if he left without lighting it, and when she turned over it was oh so slowly with her eyes half closed. She had to know.

Perhaps it would be all right. Yes. The candle on the flower-painted chest of drawers was burning.

She didn't ask about Mummy again – not properly in that formal way. For one thing she knew that Daddy would be upset and he was worried enough already, and for another she didn't want to hear the things he might say.

But every day she expected Mummy to be there at the kindergarten gate to collect her. And every day she felt that build-up of hope, tight as a red balloon by the end of the morning, burst and go limp because it was only old Mrs H. And Mrs H, with a basket, a headscarf and a cape which reached the floor, looked as if she was rolling along on a rounded base, not two legs like everyone else.

The madness of the wake.

Ordained, considered and under control.

Mrs H came in every day to look after Violet and Daddy, and her whole world was governed by the behaviour of wasps for which she held an outraged sense of grievance. She built Heath

Robinson traps which took up much of her time, she went after them with magazines or the soles of her outsized sandals, breaking jam jars and good vases with the ferocity of her attacks. She wore sticking plasters over her ears in case the wasps crawled in. She would fall back in the kitchen chair, fanning herself and exhausted, pounding her left hand into her right to prove to any approaching wasp that she still had energy left to defeat it. And all the while her eyes were searching for further victims.

It could be the jar of raspberry chews in the kitchen which attracted the wasps but Violet kept quiet about that. She used to go round drawing rings round the spots where the day's wasps had fallen.

The wasps drew a veil over Mummy's disappearance, over the shadow of death. Even the big black cars at the door, and Mrs H told of a purple curtain. But that small, sticky wasp-infested world in the summer kitchen didn't last long.

The only answer to death is life.

So it was on an evening filled with roses – Mummy's roses. Violet and Mrs H must have lowered their guard because Sheena flew in through the french window like the wicked fairy at the christening, casting her evil spell over Daddy and over Violet, the babe in the frilly cradle.

She hadn't realized she was ugly until Sheena came along. She'd thought, yes, she'd really believed that she was a beautiful little girl.

She was beautiful and Daddy was handsome, his dark hair short, his brown eyes bright, his mouth smiled often and his shirts and his teeth smelled nice. He was a quiet and confident man, attributes useful in a doctor. Mrs H was firm and cuddly and beautiful like a heavy rabbit doorstop.

It was Mrs H, that unlikely harbinger of sorrow, who told her. 'We're going to do a special meal tonight because Dr Lewis has a very important visitor and he wants it all to be perfect. So I want you to be a good girl and have your bath early and then, if you're very good, supper in bed! How's that for a treat?' Goody, goody, supper in bed, boiled eggs and soldiers, a piece of Mrs H's chocolate cake and a mug of sweet cocoa.

Mrs H scratched her head and Violet worried, remembering the bald spot there. She ought to warn her but didn't like to, privy as she was to the awful secret. 'Now, what shall we make for this special dinner?'

'Lamb!'

Silly billy Violet. But she didn't know what was going to happen. If she'd known she would have said liver. Or heart, even more disgusting especially when Daddy named the parts. 'Roast lamb with mint sauce and new potatoes from the garden. I'll shell the peas!'

'Good idea,' said Mrs H. 'Lamb, a nice piece of English lamb. And rhubarb pie and cream for pudding. How's that?'

It sounded excellent. Just right.

Jealousy. At first it was merely a small twinge. It pricked her while she shelled the peas because she wasn't having the lamb but Daddy's mysterious visitor was. But she helped Mrs H prepare the table, put on Mummy's best lace cloth, placed the mats they had never used since Mummy . . . and Violet, in her blue dressing gown with the white teddy bear on the pocket, was clean and scrubbed and ready for bed as the first juicy streamers of roasting lamb came from the oven.

But they weren't quite ready in time because Mrs H's bunion was bad. Violet was sitting, pretending to read by the window, popping a few more fat peas in her mouth, when Sheena stepped in through the french window, jiggling a stringy fox fur round her neck and stiff in watered taffeta the lamp-light blue of poison bottles. Draped in Daddy's laughter.

She smoked a cigarette through a long gold holder. Some ash fluttered down on to Mummy's special embroidered cloth that came all the way from Madeira. Violet rose righteously from her cross-legged position and wiped it off with her dressing gown sleeve. Well, they might not have noticed it was there otherwise.

Just then Mrs H limped in, red-faced from the stove and fat in her floral pinny with her arms outstretched to take Violet away.

'I'm sorry, Dr Lewis, you've caught me on the hop. I meant to have the child in bed . . .' Agitated in a worrisome way and her teeth slipped forward with a clack.

'Sheena, this is my daughter, Violet.'

But there was an apology in the announcement, disappointment that his child was still there, a wanting to get this over with so they could sit alone at the table by the window with one of Mummy's roses, picked by Violet, smiling from a slim-necked vase.

To Mummy's gentle rosiness Sheena was a hard black tulip.

And there it was, tiny, sharp as a thorn, invisible to all but the eyes of a child, Sheena's fear, red raw, a prick of instant agony.

Sheena's thin knees cricked as she lowered herself to Violet's level. Face to face with Sheena. Teeth clenched round a cigarette holder. Yellow teeth. Receding chin. A dusty face that smelled of powder. Even a child could detect the vulgarity beneath those careful curls, and little tears in the crimson lips, cracked like a caterpillar at full stretch inching over a stone. And fuzzy hairs on her top lip, just like a caterpillar.

'I have a little girl just about your age. Her name is Kate. But she's not nearly as big as you are. Violet's enormous for her age, isn't she, David?'

'Perhaps your little girl is too small.' Well – someone had to say it and Daddy didn't defend her.

'Perhaps she is.' And a smile that wasn't a smile. One of those first frosty smiles put there for Daddy's sake. She poked her in the tummy with a long, hard finger. 'Or perhaps you eat too much.' One of the first of many, many such of Sheena's smiles. And the very first of Daddy's frowns. And the start of having to sleep without a story or a nightlight. The first seeds of a life of secrets.

But if the evening cloud shadows that gathered in the night sky, silvered by the moon, carried any sense of foreboding, it was not yet apparent to little Violet.

*   *   *

Charming.

'Roses whisper goodnight 'neath the silvery light. Asleep in the dew, they hide from our view.'

Violet played her musical box to help her sleep at night. And then, when she did that, when she tired of watching the silver ballerina and finally closed her eyes, she imagined she could hear Mummy calling. *'Goodnight, sleep tight, my little Chickadee.'*

A silly fancy. Best forgotten.

But life must go on down on the farm. One long day is over, and now it is Christmas Eve. She slept badly last night, just as she'd known she would. In her dreams she heard strangled sounds, water slushing, voices crying . . .

Granny, ignored for most of the day while Clover and Diana went to the shops, while Fergus and Jonna worked outside, sat by the fire and watched daytime TV like an old person, like a lost old lady, like most of her neighbours would be doing back on Wideacre Road. She felt a surprise twinge of longing for that wide, bleak place, for her picture window with its endless, unchallenging views, for her friends from the other side. At least she managed to fix Jonna and Fergus a decent meal at lunchtime. Proper fishcakes made with some cod she found stuck to the bottom of Clover's freezer. If Clover had been around they'd have had to get their own, probably nothing more than a sandwich and that for two busy, hardworking men.

'Would anyone mind if I abandoned you all and went to have an early bath?' asks Clover now.

Diana won't mind at all, apart from the

awkward fact that she will be alone with Granny, and Granny doesn't say whether she minds or not. It is as Fergus says, 'She's very easy-going really.'

'No, go ahead.'

'Only if I have one now there'll be enough hot water for Fergus and Jonna later and they're going to need warming up.'

Clover goes, leaving a knowing look behind her. Granny, shifting in her chair, adjusts another paper hat. This one sits on top of her curly hair, the livid blue of the paper contrasting with the darkness of her watching eyes. They shouldn't have had crackers yesterday, and they shouldn't have had them today, either; she considers Clover tasteless, silly and wickedly extravagant.

What is this presence here in this house? In spite of a glowing log fire, Violet feels cold and deeply troubled. What is this aura that gathers around her? It is clammy, cold and distant, coming and going, near and now far away, almost gone. *What is it?* Is it you, William, messing about playing seasonal games? If so, stop it now, this instant! As if Violet hasn't got enough on her plate already.

Whispering. Whispering. Humming a tune that is so familiar, Granny groans and her lips move. Diana sees and sighs. Unfortunately Clover is right, Fergus's boring old mother is slowly going off her head.

Diana, uncomfortable being left alone with Granny, stares hard at the television to avoid conversation, pretending a sudden interest in variety. The singer is awful. The juggler drops one of his balls. Tinsel tinsel everywhere and smiles on all the faces, except the juggler's.

And Granny's.

And Clover's.

And now look, the dire weather warnings are all coming true. The electric's gone, whatever next?

Four

Hark! the herald angels sing
Glory to the new-born King;
Peace on earth and mercy mild ...

But there's no mercy here.

There is no telling for how long the body has been down in the cellar, rising as the water level rises, slopping as a noxious breeze washes it from one side of the weeping walls to the other, turning it over and over gently. And lapping absurdly alongside is the torn lid of a Meccano set and an assortment of wooden farmyard animals.

The accoutrements of childhood.

Fergus Moon sinks to his knees on the high, dry platform beside the central-heating boiler. 'Oh, Christ, there's somebody dead down here.' At once his thoughts turn to Clover. Yes, even after his terrible day and the shock of his grisly find he can still think protectively of Clover. When Clover hears about this on top of everything else she might snap, her nerves are so taut.

'Turn it over.'

'I can't turn it over. I can't reach it.'

'*Is it real?*'

'Jesus Christ, of course it's bloody real, man. What else d'you think it is, some joke? It's somebody dead!'

'Shit. Man or woman?'

'I can't tell. Shine the torch.'

The water makes its own weird churchy echoes. Fergus shakes his soaking wet head, he doesn't look sober and sensible now, nor does he look benign. How much more of this can he handle? His hat is stuck to his head so that flecks of tweed match the mottled fear on his face. He cannot stop his hands from trembling, he cannot rise from his kneeling position, frozen by shock and horror. He attempts to look back at his tall companion behind him but his neck sticks halfway round, stiff from a second day's frantic exertions. In his mouth is a drenched cigar. Even his eyes are wet, and his green boots squelch as he tries to shift them.

'Bloody hell. Shit. I've only seen one person dead before and that was Father.'

When they prod the body with a pea-stick the farmyard animals circle it and weave like tresses of beautiful hair. The water in the torchlight is black like harbour water and the transformed cellar walls look as if there should be rings to tie up alongside, or seaweed, green, heavy and slopping.

A body! Hell! And on Christmas Eve of all days. And now it looks as if the body has been borne upon the flood, on a wave of muddy water which is now slip-slopping up to the tinny skirts of the Potterton boiler, threatening to engulf the system and silence the whole vibrating contraption with a bang or a phut as the system runs on Calor gas. But it can't have arrived on a wave. The cellar windows that take the inrush of water peep up just above ground level and are small and wired, not large enough for a body. The door at the far end of the cellar hangs uselessly open, watching the mayhem like a drunken man come home to chaos. Nobody uses that door any more because the steps are missing.

And now, at the exact time of the macabre find, eight forty-four precisely, it starts to snow and the electric goes, it goes like the closing of a human eye, tiredly resigned as if it just can't be bothered any longer.

Fergus shakes his torch. Oh God oh God oh God, wait until Clover hears about this.

The lady of the house, the nervous lady in question, is having a guilty bath, relieved to escape the pressures downstairs. She steams away angrily in the bath, no place for a hostess on Christmas Eve, not with everyone waiting downstairs to be entertained, and no place to be when the electricity goes either. A vulnerable place, a bath in the dark. After the first shock poor Clover sighs and lies back, resigned. She will call for help in a moment, reminding everyone where she is. But let them get organized first, let someone else find the candles and the camping gas for a change, then she will call.

Diana tries to be sensible and searches for candles in a drawerful of crumbs, shouting, 'If everyone stays exactly where they are this will be easier.' She suspects something untoward has happened because, up from the cellar with torches in their

64

hands, Fergus and Jonna start whispering, club-bing together furtively the way they did when they discovered a rat trapped behind the fender, uncertain how to break news which would herald an outburst of hysteria. Something disastrous must have happened; the boiler must have gone and Diana can imagine nothing worse. Yesterday, while she and Clover were at the shops, boozily lunching at Dingle's, Fergus and Jonna were fighting the flood with spades and picks, most of the evening also. The day before that, the day they'd arrived, that cow had fallen into the slurry pit. Thankfully the poor creature'd got out alive although bedraggled and badly shaken. Diana begins to suspect the two men are deliberately staying away, making work to avoid the stress of socializing inside, just as today she and Clover lingered at the shops for much the same reason. But the men seem oddly happy in spite of all the dramas, content to be tired and worried and doing important, busy things. Funny how men enjoy disasters while women find them boring and prefer to view other people's.

So nature has triumphed again. The natural run of water has reverted to its old course, past the waterwheel that is no longer there, along the side of the house and in through the cellar, which is no longer fortified as it was in days of old. It has ignored the neat little route through the rockery, through ponds and rushes, past the gnome they put there for a joke at the bend in the stream, with his fishing rod and his sinister smile. Well might that gnome smile to himself; they call the land-scaping natural, there is nothing natural about it.

Fergus realizes that now, now that it's too damn late.

He slaps his forehead hard. 'Christ! Christ!' he sobs out loud. And Jonna, a naturally wordy man, is speechless beside him.

Here they are being flooded. They have lost the fight with the elements. Suddenly they join the victims you watch on TV staring blankly at the cameras while water pours through their homes, lifting Formica tables and exposing oddly assorted, puny pieces of lifelike plastic salt shakers and picnic beakers to be viewed by those who are high and dry, the more fortunate. And why are these people never insured? But at least in the Moons' case their flood has so far only reached the cellar.

But their flood is no ordinary flood. Theirs has a body in it.

Nature, exceeding herself, has brought unto them a child of the flood at Christmas time. Swollen, bloated like a rubber glove filled with water and one leg caught horribly around the clay-pigeon trap. This means that somebody must go into the water and poke about to unhook the unholy limb, and the thought of that is unremittingly repellent. The water presses Fergus's wellingtons tight against his calves as he slow-moves dreamily. Anything could be floating about in this semi-darkness, any dislodged part. Hell, there is a part! It is bobbing against Fergus's leg and he shouts against all the nightmares of childhood then clenches his teeth. A black leather handbag ridiculously neat and respectable, it could be one of the children's handbags they used to use for dressing up. It looks like a dressing-up handbag or the Queen's, outdated, over-smart, but no, it probably belongs to the body and therefore this must be a woman.

Fergus stares and thinks to himself – she knows, she knows what I never will, she knows if there is life after death. Sometimes he has even stared hard at dead chickens and cows, envying their knowledge.

Leg released and the corpse is easy to push along but the clay trap tries to come too like a rusty barnacled wreck from the deep. The trap reminds him of happier days, days in the sunshine with friends shooting over the valley when life in the garden of marriage was rosy.

As soon as she is reachable Jonna takes the cadaver's shoulders and lifts her onto the dry plinth. She is heavy with death. Water seeps from her like life blood and stains the dusty floor. Fergus heaves himself up after her. It is not high, three feet at the most, but he heaves himself up all the same and wants to be sick. Jonna's torch shines on the face, marinated in the leaves and mud.

'Christ.'

'You don't ever think, do you?'

'No, you don't.'

A sobering moment. 'I don't suppose there's any chance of getting her out without disturbing the others?'

'I doubt it, but we could try. But imagine if they saw us! And we hadn't explained . . .'

Silence while they ponder. They have to get her out of here because the waters might rise even higher and somebody might come down in order to investigate. The level of the flood is quite dramatic and the children are at the age for drama. Nor can they deposit her anywhere in the house, mouldering under the same roof while they sleep in their beds, or try to. Fergus suspects that after his find he will never sleep peacefully again, not now he's seen . . . they look at each other, Jonna and Fergus, knowing they have to move her. A quiet barn where she can rest secure and dry. Stables, barns and shippens come into their own at Christmas time.

'Jesus!' Fergus's startled mind has taken him back to Clover. Clover, who was so determined this year to make Christmas go with a swing, to have everything perfect, as it used to be. Even with all the odds stacked so unfairly against her, and now this. Nature. God, if there is one, has certainly brought all the guns into play. You name it, they are contending with it. All they are short of is fire and Fergus is aware that he has a little-boy look on his face trying to be brave, a little boy determined not to cry. You have to think of these things, so much to cope with, so much, and if the snow sticks the tanker won't reach him and with the tractor on the blink he won't get his milk out either. The autumn calvers are filling the tank to overflowing and the generator has yet to be checked. Christmas Day tomorrow.

You can't give a thought to the woman at your feet, you just can't.

So he thinks, once again, about Clover, his wife. About how well it had appeared to be going until this terrible weather started, until Granny arrived and the storm seemed to increase fivefold, the darkness to gather and the unease to mount. Fergus, desperate to help her and yet unable to do so, driven outside by the cows and the weather, battening down the hatches, slipping ropes round lifting roofs, heaving the sandbags ready. But whenever he can he pops indoors to call, 'OK, sweet?' Meaning, 'Do you still love me, is everything just the same?'

'Yes, everything's fine.' Too bright, her responses were too harshly bright for comfort. 'Diana and I are coping. We've even managed to ice the cake now. We're just sitting by the fire watching TV with Granny.'

Brave smiles. Even an occasional wink. Yes, they had somehow been coping – until this.

The men are still whispering there beside the cellar door but you can hardly hear them for wind. And well might they whisper. They tell each other that a discreet emergency phone call is the answer, get the authorities to deal with it, but no such possibility exists in this house without everyone finding out. The phone is in permanent use by two teenagers whose grasp on life is dependent on constant communication with friends. It was so much easier to keep secrets when the children were small, at the time of the rat behind the fender, for instance, but now they thrive on the dramatic, the unnerving and the bizarre. And there is surely nothing more bizarre than a body in the cellar on Christmas Eve while Granny slumbers beside the fire wearing a paper hat.

Five

O come, all ye faithful,
Joyful and triumphant . . .

'One of my residents is missing.'

In spite of the double glazing, Valerie Gleeson can hardly hear for the wind. She is forced to repeat every word over the crackling line. 'Seventy-two . . . yes . . . seventy-two . . . Fit? . . . very . . . there's nothing wrong with Miss Bates. A trifle eccentric, maybe . . . I said a trifle eccentric, secretive, serious. No, no, she's never gone missing before and that's why I'm so concerned. She didn't come home last night but I didn't know until this morning.'

If the Great Wall of China can be seen from outer space then she wonders if Torquay can be seen from Heaven, for there are enough people here desirous of contacting the other side to make it heave ectoplasmically in the eyes of any attentive dear ones in spirit. She thinks of Miss Bates and her little habit.

Oh, Christmas can be a lonely time is another thought she has this Christmas Eve afternoon as she puts down the telephone, sighs and realizes she will have to report the disappearance of Miss

70

Bates not just to the police but to the owners of Happy Haven also. And Jason and Mandy Tarbuck, her employers, will not be amused.

Valerie Gleeson is Manageress but Matron would be a more suitable title. Because the small residential establishment which calls itself an hotel has only one real difference between it and the next rung in life's descending ladder: a neon-lit, stained-glass-fronted bar with a cow-bell, a gift from Jersey, on the counter. On the next rung down, a nursing home, the waitresses turn into nurses, there are three beds to one room and the decor takes a tumble from cheery imitation pine to unforgiving black metal. The only compensation on the rung below, thinks Valerie Gleeson wearily, is that the flowers turn from plastic into real ones, forlorn and parched, maybe, but real.

Tap tap. Tap tap.

'In a moment, Mrs Thompson, in a moment.'

Mrs Thompson's knock is instantly recognizable: one sequence of knocks in the morning, two in the afternoon and three in the evening, and the baffled soul spends her day going round knocking on doors, trying to remind herself of the time and prove her findings to everyone else, but she's harmless. She means well. But the Tarbucks will not tolerate her behaviour for much longer, they are keen to purge senility from Happy Haven before it gets a grip. It is not good for business to be seen shipping off the deranged and incontinent by ambulance, far better to dispatch the slightly batty by taxi before such matters get out of hand. The slide from eccentricity into madness can happen alarmingly quickly, in their experience. In fact, thinks Valerie to herself, in this day and age it is hard to draw the line between the two.

Incontinence is another matter. Perhaps that is why geriatric wards insist on real flowers, to soften and twist the smell of the disinfectant. One whiff of it, even an innocent cleaning job like Mr Tanner spilling his beer, one whiff of disinfectant and Mandy Tarbuck goes wild with the Glade.

Valerie does her pelvic floor exercises, marvellous, so simple they can be done any time anywhere just as long as you're standing up and there's no-one about to see the expressions on your face.

Up from the desk and Valerie Gleeson moves across the brightly patterned carpet to the window, where she hitches a corner of net curtain. Bleak. If she peeps to the left she can see what the Tarbucks insist on calling the conservatory, no more than a jerrybuilt leaning extension looking onto the street, made steaming hot at all times by a wall device blowing hot air from the kitchens. The wall device is of shiny pine, as is the surround under the glass. On the thin sill underneath are balanced, half-finished cups of tea and in there a sprinkle of residents loll and nod in Parker-Knoll chairs under four bunches of fat balloons. In each bunch is a regulation number, two round and one long, giving them an obscene air. And three wisps of scrawny mistletoe complete the festive effect.

Can they see the sea from here or does the kitchen steam obscure it completely, turning it into a grey, dispiriting mess which drips, eventually, and waters the scarlet geraniums? Remarkably real, those geraniums. Valerie has watched with interest as visitors run their hands down the leaves, down the warm and hairy stems, wondering. The residents don't bother. They know.

'We must keep it nice and make sure it is used to full advantage,' says Mandy Tarbuck frequently. 'Remember, Valerie, please, that this conservatory is our shop window.'

So after their meals the most respectable residents are brushed down and encouraged to go there. The mistletoe makes Valerie sad, for they will never kiss again. Or be kissed.

Will she?

Capable is the word that springs to mind when you look at Valerie Gleeson. And stolid. Today she wears a matching skirt and cardigan, a kind of suit but gentler, of blue and beige dog-tooth check, under which is a white nylon polo-neck jumper. On her feet are those white shoes with the square heels, which make her feet look larger than they are; she takes size tens anyway so she should be looking to detract from her feet, not emphasize them. She has to search in shoe shops to find a pair that will fit her, so she can never find bargains in sales. Her red hair, thick as a yard broom, is swept cleanly away from her face. It is hair that stays where it's put without the aid of lacquers and grips. Her face is round and spaced well for features so far apart, which function so independently; her mouth can smile while her eyes do not, her nose can wrinkle disgustedly while her chin remains unaffected and her mouth stays the straight thin line that it is. It is hard to know what she is thinking and this fact alone maddens her employer, Mandy Tarbuck, a woman who prefers to know where she stands. Mandy Tarbuck is certain that Valerie considers her vulgar, certain but unsure at the same time, a complex fact.

Nevertheless, a capable woman should be able to manage Christmas on a meagre budget, and she should not have lost one resident on the day before Christmas Eve. Valerie will have to raise these two contentious topics when the Tarbucks arrive at teatime whether she wants to or not.

She sighs again and returns to her chair, casting her wide-apart eyes upon the Christmas brochure. Copies of this will be placed on the tables alongside the menus tonight. 'HAPPY HAVEN' is surrounded by what looks like a wreath of holly, holly squiggles misshapenly down the side of the folded A4 sheet, down the side of the three-day event, bunching out in berries as it passes the days – Christmas Eve – Christmas Day – Boxing Day – and underneath in bold print are the words '*The management and staff of Happy Haven wish all their residents a Happy Christmas and a Peaceful New Year*'.

Happy perhaps, but peaceful? Valerie feels uncomfortable with the word, but you can't tell what she's thinking for her eyebrows fold on her forehead while her mouth keeps to its line. Somehow the message sounds sinister, as sinister and thoughtless as the birthday cards with Many Happy Returns inside because there might be a few Happy Returns at Happy Haven, but not many.

And how do we know it is peace they want? she thinks as she sits there, turning on the desk lamp for comfort and shivering at the moan of the wind. The frightening wind. There's peace enough threatening to engulf them at every turn, eternal peace, without wishing it on them prematurely. Never mind, it's been done now, too late to change it and what would you put in its place? Prosperity? Fruitfulness? Hardly. Valerie is too sensitive for her own good.

Tap tap tap.

Valerie's frown deepens so it almost reaches her eyes, for that is not Miss Thompson's knock, or if it is she's messed up the time. She gets up and crosses the room, her stockings rubbing together as they brush against her thighs. The smell of Devon violets reaches her nostrils, the perfume she's always used and everyone knows it so no doubt she will be given a year-long supply for Christmas, and the usual stiff parcel of bath salts from Father with his, 'Why can't you get away, Valerie? Must you work in that place every Christmas? It's hardly fair on me. Surely there's someone else who can take over for a change?'

'No, Dad, unfortunately there isn't.'

'But I'm all on my own here. I have my needs . . .'

'We all have our needs, Dad.'

She opens the door and looks straight into the bright little eyes of Lilian Kessel. Enquiring eyes, sharp as a bead, with a head cocked sharply ready for the question.

Valerie lowers her shoulders, so busy worrying over the Tarbucks she hadn't given Miss Kessel a thought. Of course she would want to know. Miss Bates and Miss Kessel are inseparable, or were inseparable until twenty-four hours ago. But what can Valerie tell her? She has no news to give her. No good tidings to pass on to this awkwardly stiff little person who comes to her door so eagerly, so politely, for news of her missing friend.

They call her Miss Kessel, not Lilian or Lil or Lily. Ah, and long ago she stopped behaving like a Lily; that name only follows in shadow, a memory trailing behind. But she is still Lilian to her friend Miss Bates, they are on Christian name terms in the bedroom they share, more formal in front of everyone else. Lilian is worried about Miss Bates, who rarely leaves the premises without telling her where she is going, just in case – they always joke this way with each other – just in case something unforeseen should happen.

She wasn't sure whether to knock or not, she hates to be pushy but she is so very concerned. Here in Miss Gleeson's office there are no decorations and after the festive atmosphere in the rest of the hotel the distressed Miss Kessel finds this rather restful. So are the special, personal items Miss Gleeson keeps in here: a Mexican throw over the sofabed disguises its serviceable features, hiding the hard wooden arms, there are freesias in the jug on her desk, real ones, you can smell them, and the cups she uses are clearly her own, not at all like the unbreakable Melamine matching sets with the border of black interlocking Cs which Miss Kessel is used to.

'Miss Kessel, have you thought really hard about this? Did she give the slightest clue as to where she might be going?'

'She didn't tell me where she was going. I've

76

asked everyone in the hotel and nobody even saw her leave.'

'She should never be out in this. What could be the purpose in setting off in this? She has no friends or relatives in the area that I know of.'

'No, nor me.'

'She'll probably be back in time for tea,' says Miss Gleeson, bending low to press the switch on the private kettle she keeps on the floor. 'She'll be soaked to the skin if she hasn't already caught hypothermia.'

And as she passes the window Miss Gleeson lifts the corner of net once again, as is her habit. Seeing the state of the weather, watching a passing car thrashing through the water with full headlights on in the afternoon, she turns to Miss Kessel and their worried frowns meet. They shake their heads together. 'They've closed off the promenade because of the ferocious waves,' says Miss Gleeson softly, and then adds quickly to counter her pessimism, 'The police told me that. I've contacted the police, of course. They're coming to see me and it might be a good idea if you spoke to them too, if you wouldn't mind, Miss Kessel.'

'Of course I wouldn't mind. I want to help.'

'Of course you do, we all do.'

Neither of them takes a biscuit, but they are there, four on a doily, should Miss Kessel want one. Over their cups of tea Miss Gleeson makes mild enquiries about her residents, merely polite interest, made with a caring face, the expression hard to define. Miss Kessel is no mole and is careful with her answers; it is hard to tell which side Miss Gleeson is on. Miss Kessel suspects she dislikes the Tarbucks as much as everyone else does, but she is in an invidious position, dependent on them for her job. In their various ways they are all dependent on the Tarbucks. There are not so many efficiently run small hotels that offer the comforts of Happy Haven. Over the years so many of Miss Kessel's fellow residents have gone from the frying pan into the fire, hopeful, down the steps with their cases, dog-eared brochures in their hands, gone to join the competition. Sometimes a card comes a week later, sometimes not. But nothing to say the grass is any greener, nothing to encourage them all to defect lock, stock and barrel. Perhaps there is somewhere better than this and the finding of it is kept secret. Miss Kessel doesn't know.

Once, giggling like guilty schoolgirls, Miss Bates and Miss Kessel made discreet enquiries. Miss Bates was reluctant at the time, saying, 'I'll come with you out of interest but I have no intention of leaving here.' Miss Kessel hoped she might persuade her if she saw somewhere that appealed. They went to view the competition but felt anxious all the time, knowing that Torquay is a small place and that there are times and functions where hotel proprietors meet. They felt disloyal and wicked as if they were running away from school. They didn't tell another soul lest their crime be reported and expulsion follow. In the end loyalty won. Extraordinarily and un-expectedly they did feel a sense of betrayal as if they owed some allegiance to Happy Haven and were letting the side down by looking elsewhere. They did not take the double room offered them at the Beaumont. They didn't approve of the smells coming from the dining room, or the hard-faced girl who showed them round.

At least here they know where they are. The rules are straightforward, the food well cooked if basic. Miss Bates and Miss Kessel share a room, a neat little room which overlooks the conservatory, overlooks the rooftops leading down to the sea. They dare not remove the embroidery seagull for fear of upsetting Mrs Tarbuck. The framed embroidery seagull on the wall has one distinct wave underneath it but it doesn't really look like a wave, it looks as if the seagull is relieving itself. You have to be spry and genteel to be accepted at Happy Haven and then all that matters is staying spry. They club together to be seen to be spry and consider they've failed if somebody gets carted away. So Miss Kessel is particularly prudent this afternoon with her answers to Miss Gleeson.

'Could it be my imagination or have you noticed Miss Bates becoming a little absent-minded of late?'

Miss Kessel feels a defiant flush rising to her cheeks and she'd thought she was over that sort of thing. She pauses and bites her lip. 'No more than normal. Miss Bates is a thinker, she goes round with her head in the clouds, but I wouldn't call her absentminded. Definitely not.' Is Miss Kessel being over defensive? Is there something she'd rather keep quiet?

'No, probably not. I merely wondered . . .'

You wondered if she'd gone wandering off and forgotten where she lived. That's what you wondered . . . There is a sense of truancy here about every expedition.

'She couldn't have had an appointment with that medium of hers?'

'All things are possible, but I think she would've told me.' Miss Kessel is uneasy with this answer because Miss Bates might not have confided in her. Miss Bates, a peaceful soul, would rather avoid another argument on that painful subject.

Miss Gleeson stares at her massive shoes. 'The police will need to be told about that.'

Does Miss Gleeson believe in spiritualism? Miss Kessel sips her tea, nice Earl Grey out of a pretty container, sweet and strong just as she likes it. She would rather not discuss Miss Bates's strange habit with the police. Miss Kessel does not approve of such things and she never will. She tried to dissuade Miss Bates from going the first time she suggested it, but her friend was determined, refused to listen to reason. She'd even tried to persuade Miss Kessel to keep her company, but Miss Kessel said, 'There are two reasons why I refuse to go. The first is that I do not believe one word of it, mumbo-jumbo such as it is. If any of this nonsense was true they would have shown it on TV and let the whole world judge for themselves, like they did with that fork-bender, Geller. And secondly, there is nobody on the other side in whom I have the remotest interest, quite the reverse in fact. I would rather not be in touch. And I must say you surprise me. You never struck me as the superstitious type.'

That's when Miss Bates opened her heart, told it all, brought it up. Everything came out in a terrible rush and what she said went a great deal towards explaining much that Miss Kessel, up until then, had misunderstood.

Miss Kessel stares hard at Miss Gleeson. Can she trust her, should she trust her? And risk her friend being thrown out of here with nowhere to go. For no self-respecting hostelry would consider Miss Bates as a resident if they knew the shocking truth, if they found out where she came from. It was hard enough for Miss Kessel to accept and she was her best friend.

Obstinate, determined to go in spite of her friend's misgivings, it was Miss Bates's habit to come and go by taxi. She would return from her dubious encounters on Wideacre Road smelling strongly of cucumber; apparently they were provided with cucumber sandwiches afterwards. Miss Kessel never asked what happened or whether Miss Bates had been contacted. She didn't want to encourage such unhealthy indulgence, and so Miss Bates never told her. She wishes she'd asked her now. She knew how much these sessions meant to her friend and as far as she knows Miss Bates never discussed her experiences with anyone. But up until now she always said where and when she was going – just in case.

Miss Kessel shakes her small head. No-one would ever guess what she was.

The past tense upsets her. Just because it is dark and wet and Miss Bates is still not home it doesn't mean she should use the word *was*. Was was was . . . she must take courage and use the present tense, *is*. Yes. That's much better.

'She'll be back,' repeats the anxious Miss Gleeson, reading unease on Miss Kessel's face. 'And the Tarbucks will be annoyed with me for calling the police and making a fuss, diverting them from more urgent tasks. Rescuing motorists stranded on the prom, for a start.'

Miss Gleeson is trying to be positive, they are both trying to be positive. Christmas is almost upon them and it is essential they all do their utmost to make it go with a swing, to be joyous and glad. Mr Tanner will help if he can be prevented from getting too morose in his cups, for he truly loves this time of year. He is just like a child again and his eyes mist up when young Donna, on the stepladder, wires the fairy to the top of the tree and he blubs like a baby when he listens to the carols from King's.

They have all been down to the kitchen to view the turkey. There are cardboard boxes full of bottles tucked behind the bar in the hall, not enough shelves inside it to set them all out properly. A strand of tinsel round the cow-bell makes it wink for attention. And tonight the Christmas brochure, gaily decorated, will be placed beside the menus. Perhaps Miss Bates will be back in time and she and Miss Kessel will read it together and giggle, making sure nobody sees. They won't pay bar prices, they have their own supply upstairs hidden carefully under the shoes in the wardrobe. The Tarbucks are ever alert to that little ploy.

Miss Gleeson is right. Miss Bates must come back. She has to come back, for how can Miss Kessel endure Christmas without her friend Miss Bates?

Where is poor Miss Bates? Where on earth has she got to?

Six

Silent night, holy night,
All is calm, all is bright . . .

If only. If only.

Lurching through the fast-accumulating snow, driving through the blizzard, Fergus and Jonna struggle to hide the bloated body without being spotted. You think you are snug and secure in your house with its sturdy walls safely round you but dammit you're not, and how easy it is to lose that civilized veneer, how quickly you cease to care how you look or how your hands burn or your back cries out for relief, dribbling, cursing, grunting like an animal in your efforts to protect your house, your family, your life.

How easy it is, thinks Fergus now as he thrashes through the rubbish in the barn searching for a piece of wood he can use as a stretcher, and how quickly you would kill if needs must.

'Why the hell doesn't it stop?'

But the wind and snow absorb his furious shouts. There's no point in yelling out here. Above the roar Jonna can't hear him. They are reduced to communicating through gesture and expression, huddled men with horror on their faces. They've kept the body a secret so far, now they aim to get the stretcher to the house. Snow gusts in through the holes in the barn roof, corrugated metal clatters in the wind. Those holes really should have been mended properly during the summer.

Southdown Farm is a comfortable size – five hundred acres, which carries a dairy herd of one hundred head, thirty followers, corn and bullocks and only the sullen Blackjack and Marvin from the village to help. Hard work, a hard life and he owes it all to Father and Mother. Mother, whom he hardly saw in his childhood unless he donned his overalls after school and went outside to find her. Work, work, always more work, unlike Clover, who will occasionally feed the chickens and collect the eggs from the coop.

No sons to carry on, although Father regularly hoped and hinted. Mother still does, to Clover's fury.

Faint through the gale the house lights twinkle, pale candle lights, not the shimmering illuminations of a normal night. So must men have returned to their pale cave fires in days of yore, Fergus thinks fancifully. He has never known weather like this. He suspected the lines would be down before he attempted that emergency call. There was only the ghost of a chance, but even so his heart dropped when he heard the stretching silence. The vaguest breeze and the lines go dead in a place so far from civilization. 'You must expect it, sir,' is the common retort of the BT engineer. The excuses they have been given in the past have ranged from shot on the line to falling birds.

'But the nearest public phone is four miles away in the village, you should be firmer,' nagged Clover. 'You should have told him, insisted! Something has to be done! We can't function without a phone.' Weak weak weak, she forever accused him of being weak, the same argument she liked to use over Father and the farm. 'You never stood up to William, did you? Hell, you never dared! I doubt the old man even knew you wanted to do something else.'

'It would've killed him. He lived and breathed for the farm, so did Mother, why don't you try to understand? They worked themselves into the ground so they could hand it on.'

'Oblivious to the fact that you weren't interested and neither are the girls and it's cruel for them to have to live buried away out here. What sort of social life do they get when we have to drive them everywhere? It was bad enough in the village, some village, a pub, a postbox and a pebble-dash garage with one oily rag and a poster. I'm forever in the dratted car, never a moment to myself.'

He might have argued, 'They're seventeen and eighteen, they can drive themselves now.' He might have said, 'You didn't complain at the time, in fact you seemed to enjoy it.' But Fergus rarely argues back because, since Clover's tragic transformation, it's not worth it.

Fergus cannot admit to unhappiness as easily as Clover can, he hasn't the time, or he's too proud, or maybe he simply doesn't feel it.

But he feels guilty about hers. Clover's not

happy in her job. She says she drifted into it, it was never what she wanted to do, but if Fergus asks what she would enjoy, encouraging her to return to college and train for something new, she merely gives that fierce look and closes her eyes against him. Fergus is guilty of something but he's not quite sure what. But the amiable Fergus accepts his burden of guilt as he would a sack of beet nuts and gets on with his life.

Perhaps he should have offered to take her away for Christmas. Given her a break.

There is never any chance of leaving the farm over Christmas, even summer holidays are rare and have to be planned way in advance. And when Fergus suggested Christmas away one year the children complained loudly, 'We can't possibly! It would be awful. Not the same at all. And Christmas is one of the few times we get to do things together.'

My God. Fergus grimaces, not from the cold this time, or from the pain of the jagged splinter that has just rammed itself into his thumb, but from the audacity of Polly and Erin, who have hardly shown their faces since the twins arrived, and won't, unless they are forced to at mealtimes, or when, half dressed, they make an appearance in the kitchen for more coffee to add to the collection of mugs already mouldering away down in the children's end. My God.

And Jonna's twins are as bad. He'd said, on hearing they were coming, 'Oh no, you haven't invited them again, Clover, not after what we said last year.'

She'd closed her eyes exhaustedly. She'd said, as if pandering to a fool, 'Would I have invited them, Fergus? I mean, would I? Think about it! Anyway, they invited themselves as they always do.'

'What happened to the list of excuses?'

Clover shook her head. 'They'd know and be hurt. They'd know.'

'Do we actually care what they think?'

'I don't want to upset them.' Clover turned sullen.

'I wouldn't give a damn if you upset them, not in the slightest. Not in the most minuscule way.'

'Well, you should've said so earlier.'

'I thought I had. I thought we'd agreed. I thought I'd made my views quite clear.'

'Well, you obviously didn't make them clear enough. I can't understand why they never want to spend Christmas in their own house, why they always assume they'll be welcome here.'

But she let them come, of course she did, she couldn't endure Christmas without her best and dearest friend Diana, and Diana's husband Jonna. Clover is not the type to be harangued into doing anything against her will, in spite of her fervent protests. Clover loves to moan. The long phone calls to Diana start a whole month before, long, whispering conversations behind closed doors. Making arrangements, Clover calls it, it is more to do with moaning about the grim inevitability of Mother's annual pilgrimage. He'd tried to placate her about that, too.

'We really do not have to have her. She'd be perfectly happy at Ocean View. She's told me so often enough.'

'Of course we have to have her! We can't leave

her there to spend Christmas all alone. Violet is your mother, Fergus, after all!'

What does Fergus the farmer honestly believe? What does he really want for himself? A man of few words, he rarely says. He tends to stare at the sky instead. To be truthful, he would like nothing better than to be allowed to have Christmas alone, in some golfing hotel on the Helford river with a bar and a garden of snowy rhododendrons and a boat on the river. But alone. Quite alone. So that when he woke up in the mornings he could order a paper and an early coffee and actually get to drink it undisturbed. He could plan out his day without taking so many others into consideration before he moved his arm or his leg or his brain. He has scanned his personal horizon with gritted teeth and anxious eyes but there is no sign of his boat coming in, no prospect of that sort of freedom, not until he's in his nineties and stuck in a wheelchair and dependent, at which time he would probably rather not spend Christmas alone.

'If you insist on inviting her, Clover, why do you need to spend so many hours on the phone to Diana moaning on about it? There's only one decision to make: leave her at Ocean View. If you decide to have her here why can't you just accept it and get on with it? She's not interfering or nagging, she's not demanding or difficult, you have to admit that a person her age could be far, far worse. Mother is fairly easy if a little strange at times, more so just lately.'

'Fergus, your mother has been difficult ever since I've known her. And no matter what else she says she hates that damn bungalow. What can she do inside it, cooped up there all day knowing no-one? Poor thing, I can't imagine.'

'So you sympathize with her, do you?'

Clover stared at her husband steadily. 'Well yes, in some ways I do. I can't count the times I've asked her over, offered to go and pick her up, but she just refuses to come. She hates me as she always has, she resents me, that's more to the point. But even so, I do care and I don't like to think of her lonely or miserable.'

'Violet is quite harmless.'

Clover sent him a withering look. 'That, Fergus,' she said with a hiss, 'is just what your mother is not. She talks to herself all the time, she's vicious, mean and manipulative.' And then she added more gently, 'It would help if you were less afraid of her.'

Baffled, Fergus gave up the struggle. But the phone calls to Diana went on and he wished his wife would agree to undergo some counselling or at least agree to the HRT. Damn Germaine Greer. Secretly Fergus worries that Clover is too far gone already, unstable with so many paranoid ideas and nerves that are constantly shredding. It's probably all down to hormones: she must be approaching the change, and if this instability is going to get worse, now is the time it will rear its head.

Dammit. He has never been afraid of his mother. Trying to please somebody close, trying to do right by them, is part of the human condition, nothing to do with being afraid and other such dramatic ideas. Violet has led a hard life. She deserves a little respect, that's all.

But the children don't always help. 'Your girls get on so well with the twins.' 'It's amazing to see childhood friendships lasting so long.' Oh yes, it is amazing, thinks Fergus, viewing his friend Jonna over a stack of body-sized planks they have gathered in one darkened corner of the barn. But Fergus has never been sure. The incredible fact and one that haunts him, one he can hardly bear to consider, is that they could . . . *it is perfectly possible* that he is the father of his friend's twin sons.

Clover was pregnant at the time. It couldn't have been helped, really, thrown together in that damn Scottish croft, one of their more fateful holidays in those early days when they were able to leave the farm, when Father was still alive. It was only the hand of fate, anyway, that moved between them and declared that Jonna and Diana should end up together, and Fergus with Clover. It had started the other way round. The two girls were inseparable, had been since schooldays. Diana the sophisticated, Clover the overgrown child. Both boys made a play for Diana and she led them a merry dance while Clover hung around whining in jeans and a childish haircut, demanding to make up a four at the pictures. It was all rather odd when you think back. Their rivalry had been extraordinarily amicable and when Fergus gave Diana that ring she took it, and Jonna slapped his back, shook his hand, bought him a beer. She changed her mind at the very last minute, there were terrible tears, sighs, desolation, she said she'd loathe life on a farm, but for Fergus there'd been no way out, he couldn't let Father down. Conveniently (too conveniently?)

Clover was there to console him in her sweet but artful-little-girl way and that's how the situation was sorted, no bitterness, no regrets. Weird, it's almost as if the two girls dealt with the problem between them as if the men were a bag they were sharing. But then came that fateful holiday, that blasted punt, or currach, the locals called it. And Jonna so jolly: 'You take Diana, I'll stay at home with Clover today if she'd rather rest. Off you go, you two. Enjoy yourselves!'

What was wrong with the fool? Jonna was well aware that Diana was an attractive, sensual woman whom Fergus had once desired. Fergus also suspects, although this is something they never discuss, that, at that same dizzy time, Clover and Jonna were lovers. Perhaps they have stayed such good friends because they rid themselves of that sexual stumbling block so early in the relationships. They've had it away with each other so now they can relax and bury the serpent's tempting head, leave it as a joke, a continuous but meaningless flirtation which everyone can safely enjoy. Happy innuendo that never turns into anything more dangerous.

Or is there still something going on between Jonna and Clover?

If the twins belong to Fergus then this begs another important question, a terrible, worrying question which Diana should feel as uneasy with as he does. They should not be closeted away upstairs in the bedroom of his two young daughters. The girls should not be alone with the twins. Sam and Dan, lusty lads, he had hoped they would stay away this year, too independent to accompany their parents to Devon every

Christmas. Not so, it would seem and no wonder. Polly and Erin, seventeen and eighteen, with boyfriends of their own, seem to consider intimate relations with their Christmas visitors as natural a process as exchanging gifts. But perhaps Fergus need have no qualms. Perhaps his suspicions are misplaced. If only he knew the truth.

The twins have always enjoyed the farm and love to help when he lets them. 'They should have been farmers' sons,' Jonna said once rather sadly. 'They're certainly not academically inclined, no interest in carrying on in the business. They call the newspapers rag mags and have never shown the slightest enthusiasm.'

They should have been farmers' sons. *They are probably Fergus's sons.*

A wardrobe drawer, the very thing, the ideal stretcher, lying on the floor half covered in snow. Fergus and Jonna spot it together and move towards it quickly, chums who are easy working together, playing together, mates since childhood. They scrape off the snow with frozen hands, easing the wood off the ground. Heavy. It will be heavier with the body on board and Fergus shivers, unable to contemplate further this whole frightful mess.

When they reach the cover of the yard, when they tip the wardrobe door on end to ease it through the deserted kitchen without allowing the blizzard to follow them into the house, all he can say is, 'Whatever happens, Jonna, don't tell Mother.'

For yes, in spite of his defence of her, Fergus is worried about his mother.

'Why ever not?' Poor Jonna is trying to kick off his boots with his hands still full. He needn't bother, he'd be wiser to keep them on. Luckily, because of the power cut, the Christmas party is more or less confined to the sitting room.

'Because Violet is old and frail.' And peculiar? He does not add peculiar.

'Rubbish,' says Jonna impatiently, tiptoeing forward to make sure the rest of the party are out of the way. 'You and Clover have the oddest ideas about your mother. She's only seventy-two, for God's sake, and that's not old these days. Violet is as strong as an ox, she can take anything life throws at her. That woman is more resilient than the rest of you put together. It's OK. All clear. They're still in the sitting room.'

Fergus stares at his friend for a moment. Extraordinarily, he is probably right. He takes off his hat and shakes his head, spraying water. It's funny how you get certain images in your head, put there by others or conjured up by yourself for convenience. Once seeded there they take root and grow in the face of logic. You see what you want to see and that is often quite the opposite of what everyone else is seeing.

'Drink? Before we . . . ?'

'No.' There is something irreverent about dealing with bodies with Teacher's on your breath. 'Let's get this ordeal over first and then have a drink.'

'Right,' says Jonna, and Fergus follows him quietly. Thank God there is no-one about. So the pall bearers drip their way gravely through the darkened house towards the door of the cellar. There is no alternative route, for the cellar steps are missing. Let us hope, for their sakes, that the rest of the party are still in the sitting room with the door firmly closed before they retrace their steps, bearing their grisly load. If Clover should spot them in her state of mind she would probably crack up completely.

Fergus would dearly like to see inside Clover's head. But selfish Clover never considers what might be happening in his.

Clover should be playing hostess. She is the lady of the house, the missis. Isn't she?

They gave Granny an encyclopaedia last Christmas because she told them that's what she wanted. Clover couldn't imagine why. She said to Fergus, 'She'd much rather have a warm dressing gown or a set of nice towels. She's no need of an encyclopaedia, she's just being perverse.'

But Fergus said, 'That's what she's asked for so that's what we'll get her.'

So Clover watched Violet unwrap the book on Christmas morning but she couldn't make out her expression, and then Granny went off into a distant reverie. Clover noticed the book left on the arm of the chair when Granny disappeared off to bed, so she didn't enjoy the present and she didn't enjoy the children's, either.

And Fergus says there's nothing wrong!

Seven

Once upon a time there lived a little girl called Violet.

Violet's fifth birthday and it's downhill all the way. Where on earth will it end? Don't you look at me like that, Sheena Lewis. *Don't you dare look at me like that.*

> Happy Birthday to you,
> Happy Birthday to you,
> Happy Birthday, dear Violet,
> Happy Birthday to you.

Five years old today, hooray! Black-eyed Violet glared back at her wicked stepmother, Sheena. Poor Sheena, still striving to falsify some kindness in those eyes of dolly-blue.

Now that she was five years old and grown up, her black hair in thick plaits tied with tartan ribbons, Violet kept many secrets from Sheena. So that by the time she was ready to kill her she was quite a specialist in the art of deception. In the art of concealment and guile.

Some secrets she kept in her head, others on pieces of paper which she hid in places she calculated Sheena wouldn't look: behind the gollywog's eye (she pushed the little black bead firmly back on top of it); under the cardboardy sole of her slipper; deep in a torn piece of lining in her little tartan handbag. Rude poems mostly, and drawings of Sheena being hurt, Sheena torn limb from limb, in a Roman amphitheatre surrounded by lions, and the boldest statement of all in big print, every word worked carefully in a different colour: I LOVE MUMMY. I HATE SHEENA.

And sometimes, on her knees on the cork-topped laundry box, watching her face in the bathroom mirror, fascinated and frightened by the intensity of her own spite, Violet would bare her teeth and say 'SHEENA', spitting out the detested name through the foam.

Nobody really wanted to be at Violet's party. The little friends present that day were brought to the Lodge by their mothers, satisfied that their precious offspring had friends and a social life of their own, proud to see them developing in a way that was acceptable. But most of the children were not enjoying it and neither was Violet. Sheena had made her colour in the party invitations. She used the same crayons with which she did her hate-writings so they were mostly blunted down, and the picture on the front of each card was a chubby child with a puppy by Mabel Lucy Atwell. It said, abruptly, 'Please come.'

Violet's eyes moved to the gramophone plenty of times during pass the parcel, willing the parcel to stop on her lap when the music stopped. But Sheena was working the gramophone, so short of a miracle the birthday girl knew that the parcel would not stay with her . . . unless she cheated.

Violet was the only child to be aware that in the middle of that parcel, under all the layers of paper, was a fairy doll in a silver dress meant for the top of a Christmas tree. She knew because she'd been allowed to help Sheena wrap the unwieldy paper bundle. The doll was a magical surprise to have in the middle. She didn't want to win the sweets or the rubber babies with painted hair, certainly not the lead soldiers put there for the boys she'd been forced to invite. Although to win one of those, she supposed, would be better than nothing at all. What Violet longed for most in the world was that fairy doll, and Sheena knew it. She'd never ask 'them' for a doll because that would give her needs away, she felt too vulnerable for that. Instead she asked for gifts she didn't much like . . . and got them . . . but if she won that doll it would be different, she could accept it. And she would never allow it to decorate the top of any old Christmas tree, lonely and exposed like that, she would keep it safe and private in her own little room, and give it comfort. If Violet won it she would not share it. She would hoard it. She might even hide it.

> *This old man*
> *He played one.*

Squeals and shouts and the ripping of paper and Sheena in the middle of the circle with her Bear Brand stockings and her hard-edged skirt of powder blue which reminded Violet of talcum powder, trying to collect the string, trying to impose order on chaos, even in a game, even now, tidy tidy tidy, and Violet could see the slither of white between Susan Webster's legs because the girl was showing her knickers in her eagerness to tear out the prize before the parcel moved on, and the slither of white annoyance down the centre of Sheena's forehead because the voices were too shrill and likely to bring on one of her heads. Sheena wrapped the string round her hand to add to the ball in the kitchen drawer. Thrifty Sheena. Tight Sheena. She would save what bits of paper she could for use on another day.

> *He played knick-knack on my drum*
> *with a knick-knack paddywack*
> *give a dog a bone . . .*

Sheena was particularly cross because some of the boys were throwing the parcel and that wasn't the way to behave at parties. That was being greedy. And all the little girls were dressed to be pretty and feminine in smocked dresses from Gamages and Liberty's, they were dressed like the royal princesses. They were certainly not dressed to withstand this rough throwing of parcels. But Violet? She was different. She'd insisted on wearing that kilt with the pin and the poppy-red twinset all the way from Scotland. She was proud of her shiny red shoes with buckles. She was not dressed to be pretty because she knew she could never be pretty, although, when she walked, she tried to swing out the kilt behind her like the pipers did.

Violet had asked for a sporran, but was told by Sheena, who pretended she knew, that girls did not wear sporrans. Violet didn't believe this.

Sheena disliked sporrans because they were rude and hairy. She sucked the end of a plait as the music struck up again and wiped hot hands down the pleats of her skirt. The parcel was growing thinner and thinner. She watched out for the blue piece of paper which meant that the fairy doll was next and she studied Sheena's face. If she were being fair she would have her back to the room, but Sheena was choosing exactly when to stop the music.

And then Daddy came home carrying the most enormous box in his arms. For a moment Violet thought that someone had turned the light on. Now there was somebody here who loved her so she pretended not to notice him and watched the slimmed-down parcel instead as it came round the circle for longer than ever because Sheena was kissing Daddy and saying how glad she was that he had managed to make it home in time. Daddy was trying to attract Violet's attention, but she couldn't help herself those days, she ignored him on purpose and went on watching the parcel, but her cheeks turned red with the effort. Pretending she didn't care he was there and hurting herself when she'd like to hurt him.

Kate was wearing her fluffy bolero. She hadn't won a prize yet, she was certain to win the fairy doll.

> *The farmer's in his den*
> *The farmer's in his den*
> *Ee-i adeyo*
> *The farmer's in his . . .*

Violet blushed redder than ever. She could even see her own cheeks. They had puffed up as fat as fairy cakes with hundreds and thousands on top. The wonderful parcel, smooth and blue, was in her lap and her hands were on it. The music had stopped. The paper was hard and ungiving as clean sheets. She tore at the paper with all her might, feeling the jealousy of those around her because they all wanted to win the prize, but they were polite enough to pretend to be pleased. They mimicked the manners of their elders when they called with ecstatic eyes and affected glee, 'Oh, Violet, quick! Quick! Open it. Let's see what you've got!'

But Susan Webster's face couldn't keep up with her words. Her face still said, 'It's not fair, it's Violet's birthday, one of the guests should have won the prize.'

Violet had no need to look down because she knew what was inside the paper. She took time with the unwrapping, savouring that blissful moment, scanning her circle of friends, and Kate. Careful not to rip the paper in the greedy way of everyone else because she knew that Daddy was watching. She wanted to please him so badly. She wanted to hurt him. She wanted to love him. Kate's blue eyes were hard and angry. Oh yes, she'd expected to win this doll.

'Well, well, well,' said Daddy when Violet reached the sequinned netting of the fairy's dress. It sparkled. It glittered. 'Hold it up, birthday girl, let's all have a look!'

And she longed to run to him and be alone with him and sit on his knee while she cradled the fairy, she would put the doll under his chin to see how it fit. She wanted to please him and be lovable. To be a good, sweet, outgoing child, like Kate or the Princess Elizabeth.

A high, cold excitement leapt in her, and when she heard her own cold laughter she could scarcely believe it. It was as if some other unwholesome child, someone Violet didn't approve of, was pulling her strings like a puppet, putting shameful words in her mouth like Sheena did when Violet felt sick and she'd drag the girl to the bathroom and thrust two cheesy fingers down her throat until she retched and Sheena shouted, 'Right, our Lady of Sorrows. So you feel sick! Well, be sick, then! And stop seeking attention all the time. Go on! Go on! Be sick! Get it over with!' And then she'd say, 'Here, have a plaster if you must demonstrate your life's great calamity.'

Couldn't they all see what had happened? The reason Sheena stopped the music when the parcel reached Violet was because Daddy was there. Sheena was cunning and scheming. Now Daddy would be more unlikely to believe Violet's sullen tales of Sheena's unkindness.

Her own voice betrayed her. 'I don't want this silly doll, let Kate have it.' She gave it with no generosity of spirit, just a sneering contempt and she felt the hot tears behind her eyes and her heart was hurt and outraged when she saw Daddy's stern, troubled air. She had betrayed herself and him with her own perverse lack of grace. She wanted the doll more than anything on earth but she refused to let herself have it. Perhaps a five-year-old ruse to attain some sense of purification.

Daddy's patience was sorely tried but it was his

101

daughter's birthday and so he strove for tolerance. 'Never mind, old thing, perhaps you'll like this better.' He gave her the massive parcel and smiled at her invitingly. But Violet knew he considered her spoilt.

But now, at last, she was where she wanted to be, sitting on Daddy's knee with the others gathered round and Sheena banished to the kitchen to bring him a plateful of party food and a gin and tonic because this was Violet's special day. The birthday cake stood proudly on a plate in the kitchen. Sheena had baked it herself so its intentions were not good. Violet might blow out the candles but otherwise she'd refuse to touch it. From her newly elevated position she gave Kate a condescending look, but Kate was too busy rubbing the fairy's netting dress against her fluffy bolero, loving the feel of it. Watch me! Violet wanted to shout. Whatever else they tried to do, Sheena and Kate could not stop her having a birthday.

Violet undid the string round the box, smiling at Daddy as she did so. She knew what was inside the box because it would be what she'd asked for. She felt a stab of pain for Daddy because of what she had made him do. And then anger, because he ought to have understood the workings of her troubled mind. He had gone to the shops on his own, specially to find the best Meccano set in town because Violet told him she wanted one. She didn't, she didn't, *she didn't*. She hated Meccano sets, they were as boring and dull as the Post Office set Sheena had given her last Christmas. Why not a sweet shop like Kate?

For Daddy's sake she had to pretend, so she

clasped her hands together and put a gleeful look on her face and snuffled into his chest where he smelled so warm and she said, 'Oh, thank you, Daddy! Thank you!' And then she turned to everyone else, she held up the set and said, 'Look what I've got!' But they all looked fairly dismayed because none of them would have wanted that, except the boys and they didn't count. And because they weren't all envious, Violet, in a tumultuous grief, knew that somehow, and this was so complicated she couldn't understand, she had betrayed her father. A hopeless little victory gone sour.

But they'd all wanted that fairy doll.

From over the top of the Meccano set Violet watched Kate. The silver of the fairy's dress showed through the fluff of the bolero in which she had wrapped it. Kate sauntered off to the kitchen in triumph to find Sheena, her mother, and show her.

One day, for sure, Daddy would wake up and see through them. One marvellous day he would come into Violet's bedroom, draw back the curtains and announce, 'Come on, old thing, we don't need them, we're going home!'

She fiddled intimately with Daddy's tie so they all could see the special influence only she had over her handsome father. Because she was so special to him, and he was hers since Mummy died. Sprung from his loins, Kate said.

A man of a neat and orderly mind, he snapped and knocked her hand away. 'I've told you not to do that, Vi, it's so annoying. Come on, get down, you're too big for this, let's see if we can build a house.' So he got on the floor with the boys.

Daddy smelled pink. The coral pink of Sheena's Kissproof lipstick.

That night, in bed, 'Mummy tells her friends you're common.'

Whispering. Whispering. Kate was forever whispering. She picked up the habit from Sheena. Kate took Violet's friends away, too, with her little whispers and help from Sheena. But Kate didn't hate Violet like Sheena did – not then.

Kate was porcelain-pale like her mother with sharp blue eyes which peeped and hid like bead eyes do, and people used to say to Kate, 'You'll drive the boys crazy, you will, when you grow up.' But they never said that to Violet. And Violet suspected that Daddy heard the compliments that went missing and was hurt by them, for her sake. How could anyone think Kate pretty? Sheena and Kate, they both looked hard and varnished like an ornament and their skin was morbidly white, like that wicked American Mrs Simpson who snared the Prince of Wales.

'Daddy, what's common?'

Sidling up, cuddling up, too big but trying to be kittenish, knowing full well what 'common' meant but wanting to hear it all the same, needing to introduce the subject so she could pass on Sheena's unkind remarks.

'Why d'you want to know, sweet?'

But Sheena came into the room so the matter could go no further. She gave Violet a hard look to let her know she had been listening. Daddy turned the radio on while Violet chewed her nails and staréd, cat-eyed, at Sheena from under Daddy's arm.

'God knows I've tried, David, I've done my utmost damndest to try and make her feel like my own, even to the detriment of Kate sometimes. Oh yes, don't turn away, don't try to pretend there's nothing happening. It's absolutely true. Kate has suffered a good deal since Violet came to live here.'

Violet cared enough about what they said in private to climb, at night, onto a chair, pull herself up through the attic hatch in her bedroom ceiling and crawl along under the eaves until she was positioned directly over their bedroom. She insisted on calling this Sheena's room because there was little of Daddy's in it. Except for Daddy's sturdy brown one, the wardrobes were full of Sheena's clothes, the dressing table littered with her creams and lotions. Even the bed was covered in Sheena's slippery style of sheets. Up there, in her little crow's-nest position, Violet would rock as if on a great sea, legs crossed, listening, while the wind blew the wisteria rigging hard against the roof, tearing at the claws of ivy. She knew what nights to go there. Any small incident during the day would provoke Sheena into another vindictive, whispered attack on Daddy as they sat in bed together with the light on and Daddy was trying to read. Oh yes, Violet knew exactly what tales Sheena was telling, what lies she was constructing.

Daddy never really wanted to hear. You could tell that because he answered mildly as if he was bored with all this messiness of emotion. Violet could hear the edge of his page being rustled. Sometimes, if Sheena was really upset, he would try to placate her by saying, 'Darling, I'll have a word with Vi about it, I promise, yes, tomorrow. But it's not been easy for her either, you know that, since Wendy died . . .'

'I know, I know, I know,' Sheena would answer impatiently. 'Don't you think I realize that? And before you say it, yes, she is very young. But, dear God, I'm not Solomon, you know, and I really believe that Violet is quite seriously disturbed, David. She needs some professional help.'

Violet felt glad when Daddy said he was going to talk to her because this gave her a chance to have Daddy alone, not to accuse Sheena, she'd learned by now that that never worked. She'd developed her own methods for dealing with Sheena. Daddy, all day at the hospital and most weekends, didn't know the half of what went on.

Violet insisted on keeping a photograph of Wendy beside her bed, just as Kate kept a picture of Michael, her father. Michael was dead. Wendy was dead. Wendy was dead but Violet could still see her, she could still talk to her mother.

Violet felt sick because if Sheena was saying she was common that meant that Daddy was common too, and that Mummy had been common. Worse than this, Violet suspected that might be true. The house they lived in when Mummy died, the house she could only just remember, had been much smaller than this one, more homely, with elderly furniture, cushions and rugs, not the brash, new, uncomfortable stuff that dominated Sheena's home. They had not needed a special maid to polish and dust it each day, or chandeliers to light the hall. And they ate most of their meals in the friendly kitchen, not stiffly in the dining room like they did at Sheena's house.

And in her dear old home Violet used to be carried to bed all wrapped up in a blanket, and after her bath Daddy always came upstairs to tell her a story.

Those were the days she was Chickadee. She clung tenderly to the memory.

Common. But one day Violet would marry a prince, Cinderella-style, and Sheena, like an ugly sister, would come begging at the palace gate, not for food and shelter, but for 'mixing with the right people'. Kate would be trailing along behind in that silly little white bolero. Violet would not drop the drawbridge. She might manage to be gracious about it, she might say, disdainfully, 'Oh, I am so sorry, Sheena and Kate, but you are far too common to be allowed in here, only Daddy, I'm afraid.'

Then Violet would swing her kilt behind her and shake a huge sporran in Sheena's face as she banged the palace gate. And a golden key would turn in the lock.

How long it takes for nail polish to grow off the end of one's toes.

You could use your toenails as a clock, a terrible slow-moving timer. While that scuffed pink is still there, while you can see it so clearly, you are somehow still linked to the events that happened so many months ago.

Nails and hair, they both grow so slowly even when you are dead, they say. For three weeks or three months? Clover wonders. How long does it take to grow that nail polish off?

Clover sits in the bath and wishes she had broken her leg like she has been hoping to do for the last three weeks. Yes, recklessly trying to break a limb, either one, it didn't matter. Not a serious break, of course, not a serious thought, she supposes, but it was there, in her head. With difficulty she lifts her two healthy legs from the water and frowns at their pink and rubbery treachery. She remembers how Diana warned her, 'The risk is far too random, you could break your neck by mistake and end up a cabbage in a cot. And I would have to waste my time coming to visit you with little gifts, cursing because I knew you had injured yourself on purpose. Really, Clover, you are going too far. Christmas can't be that bad! Anyway, what good would it do to break your leg?'

'Fergus would have to cancel Christmas and I wouldn't feel guilty about it.'

'Cancel Granny is what you mean. Well, why don't you stop playing childish games and do something sensible about it?'

Clover took no notice but continued to walk on the dangerously wet sloping grass of the orchard without looking down to avoid the slippery apples. All she experienced was one nasty slide on the slime, and her heart nearly stopped beating. But even so she continued to close her eyes when coming downstairs with the hoover, determined to fall on the wretched thing, or tumble down with a pile of ironing, or trip on the toilet rolls lurking on the stairs waiting for her to take them up.

But nothing happened.

She even ran, once, with her eyes closed, across a hard, ploughed field, hoping she might twist her ankle but her guardian angel was at her side. 'I have to do something,' she muttered to herself. 'Diana is right. Things cannot continue as they are.'

'What is it you really want?' Jonna asked her that last weekend.

She told him while relaxed in his arms. 'To be joyous, that's what I want.'

'Joyous? What an odd word to use. You are being obtuse deliberately in order to confuse me.'

Jonna is careful with his words. He owns a chain of local newspapers, edits and runs them himself, loving every minute of it in spite of his moans. He searches carefully for cryptic headlines, cuts out the slack, reduces the copy to its bare minimum in order to fit it all in. If he knew how desperate Clover felt he would reduce her to four words: *Woman in Xmas Crisis*.

So now here she is lying in the bath, yearning and longing and hating and trapped by the darkness and Christmas, waiting for a candle or a torch. But far better to be here than down there sitting amidst the dates and the nutty sloth. She longs to arrive at an unnamed day in the *Radio Times*; even the most ordinary days are now labelled, Christmas Tuesday, Christmas Wednesday, etc. Now and then the kids will appear and insist on playing some mindless game, Christmas as it ought to be, as it was such a short time ago before she got ill. And then they will disappear down the children's end to play with the twins in their own way.

'We all want some figgy pudding . . .'

'I know you damn well do,' thinks Clover from the safety of her bath, and every year she is that pudding and if everyone keeps delving in there will soon be nothing left but crumbs on a plate to be cast out eventually, to the chicken trough to be pecked at and scratched. Oh God, I sound as dismal as my mother.

Diana is Clover's very best friend and her arrival is the only bright thing about Christmas these days. God, they used to have such laughs, they'd cling together laughing hysterically. She'd hated it when, at thirteen, Diana suddenly went boy crazy. Her mother called her friend a trollop and wouldn't let Clover wear make-up. Diana was always wanting to go up town and hang around drinking coffee. She got quite petulant and started walking in an embarrassing way, started to use an oddly deep voice which made Clover uncomfortable. She bought *Misty* and *Photo-Love* while Clover was still reading 'babyish books', she bought records and went to parties. Why did she have to spoil everything? Different from other girls, hair growing under her arms and the first in the class to wear a bra, boys noticed Diana. *Adolescence*. It sounded disgusting. And when it started to happen to her Clover found it disgusting, too.

She wanted fairies and princes.

Now look at them both, boring, married, middle-aged women. Clover supposes she will get old, she will probably even die one day, it's no good denying it like she tried to deny her *adolescence*, never believed that such an appalling thing would ever happen to her.

Men.

Lucky she didn't end up with Jonna, who, Clover has noticed, is becoming neurotic in his old age, refuses to drink from a cracked cup and once she went into the kitchen and found him obsessively scrubbing those black bits round the base of the taps with a withered Brillo between his fingers. Perhaps he's developing some cleanliness phobia which will worsen as he ages. Are we all going slowly mad? And Clover wonders if she should mention Jonna's condition to Diana, then wonders why Diana hasn't mentioned this worrying trait to her. Maybe his wife hasn't noticed.

Clover is not in love with Jonna, he cannot fulfil the yearning within her, although his attraction to her provides some sense of self-worth. There are many small reasons for Clover's prolonged affair with Jonna, though none of them satisfactory.

She should not be languishing here in the bath, not with everyone else downstairs trying to cope in the dark, waiting for her arrival. She dreams of the life of a bag lady, doesn't everyone dream, sometimes, of walking out of the house with nothing and never coming back? But what boots would be best to wear? She would worry about which coat to take. Which coat would be most suitable to protect her from an icy night in a ditch? And would Fergus rescue her if she phoned for help, would he save her if she deserted him so cruelly like that? No, no, as Diana says, that is not the way forward.

She'd read a story in the local paper a couple of days before Christmas, about some middle-aged woman going off. Quite out of the blue. They were searching for her with helicopters, frogmen were scrambling about in the river. Clover showed the story to Fergus, who said, 'I know, they were talking about it at the market. The police are certain she's dead. She was on pills for depression and there's little hope of finding her alive. Her family are beside themselves. She's only a few years older than you.'

'Oh?'

'Poor soul,' said Fergus.

Yes, poor soul indeed.

Tap tap tap.

'Who is it?'

'I've brought up a candle. Shall I come in?'

Granny! Christ no! 'Just leave it outside the door and I'll pick it up in a minute.'

'Are you sure you're all right in there? You'll be able to find your way out of the bath?'

She is trying to open the door. Thank God Clover locked it. She rises noisily from the water, staring at the lock in alarm. 'The water's gone a bit cold but otherwise I'm quite all right, thank you.'

'Right, I didn't want you to think we'd forgotten you.'

Silence. A reassuring, dark silence save for the wind outside. But as Clover steps gingerly from the bath, shivering, eyes searching blindly for a towel, it is not the cold in the bathroom that causes her hackles to rise. It is the thought of Granny out there on the landing with a torch, in the dark.

Is it that, or is it the darkness inside her that frightens poor Clover so?

Clover listens till she's certain Granny's gone.

Then opens the bathroom door with caution.

Eight

The first Noel the angels did say
Was to certain poor shepherds in fields as
*   they lay . . .*

And is poor Miss Bates lying in some field awaiting the angels?

We must sincerely hope not.

Valerie Gleeson shares a pot of tea with Miss Kessel, wrapped in lamplight against a darkening evening. She waits for the police and the Tarbucks to arrive, resenting these intrusions into her carefully regulated day. When Miss Kessel leaves, Valerie will not budge from her desk, she will not pick up anything to read, or write any messages, reports or accounts. For a good half-hour she will sit alone and do absolutely nothing and if anyone comes in without knocking and catches her expression they might think she is sleeping, so deep are her thoughts, so blankly will she have set her face.

Because she is desperately worried.

Because she knows that all is not right. There are things going on at Happy Haven with which she is not happy. But dare she risk her job? Should she, for the sake of someone she hardly knows, put her future on the line? What, after all, does she owe Miss Bates or Miss Kessel? Not only must she support herself but she has to pay the mortgage on Father's two-bedroom flat. And what about when Father gets worse and needs to be looked after? Valerie needs to save all the money she can, while she can. When Father's needs get more demanding Valerie must give up work and return home to live. After a lifetime of struggle, of trying to escape, she will have to go back after all.

She must concentrate on number one, after all she cannot be sure that her nagging doubts have any real substance. Couldn't her fears be the result of an over-active imagination, or too little stimulation caused by mixing almost exclusively with elderly people with their quirks and little fancies? She might despise the Tarbucks, but are they really as sinister as she has come to believe? Shouldn't she merely assume, as the police certainly will, that Miss Bates has suffered a fall, or got herself lost, or taken it into her head to go on some spurious journey? Valerie Gleeson shakes her head, for Miss Bates is one of her youngest residents, quiet and shy, a little odd but certainly with all her senses about her.

Father would say, 'Too vivid an imagination, that's your trouble. Leave it alone, Valerie, let things be, don't interfere. The world has always managed to turn without your help and will do so long after you've gone. Who d'you think you are, anyway?' Oh yes, Father, you're right, who do I think I am?

There was something just as curious about Miss Bates's arriving as there is about her departing.

And on two occasions this last month alone Valerie has seen Mandy Tarbuck coming out of Miss Bates's room.

So what? The police would smile scornfully if she confided that fact to them. 'What's so strange about that? Why shouldn't the hotel proprietor take an interest in a resident? Isn't that perfectly natural?'

And yes, under normal circumstances it might be, but not in these. Not when Valerie knows full well that Mandy and Jason Tarbuck not only ignore their residents completely, as much as any folk can ignore the source of their bread and butter, but even appear to despise them, blaming them, in some obscure way, for the fact that at the end of their lives they have risen no further than Happy Haven. And Valerie knows that Jason, at his expensive golf club, and Mandy, at the gym, would dearly love to be the owners of the Grand.

Maybe she should have told the Tarbucks earlier so they could deal with the law, but something stopped her from doing that. They are not going to like her decision, she knows that, but she doesn't understand why.

The police arrive in a panda car. 'I am the manageress. Miss Gleeson.' She smiles and shakes hands when she greets them in the hall. They meet as if in a party game, round the back of the Christmas tree. Some irresponsible person has turned the fairy lights to flash so she bends to turn them off; they are dangerous to some of the residents who incline to fits. Sergeant Pollard, with the sparse red whiskers of a music hall comic and rueful blue eyes, asks to see Miss Bates's room, so the little party go upstairs with little Miss

116

Kessel, unnoticed, trailing behind wringing her hands.

The news on the TV makes a background hum and the firebuckets match the carpets. Mr Tanner has obviously been using them for ashtrays again, in spite of Valerie's warnings. She wishes the residents would not smoke, for smoking is the worst, most worrying hazard she has to face. As they pass through the lounge the residents look up and nod. Donna has organized a pre-dinner game of bingo but nobody is seriously listening to the numbers she calls. 'Downing Street. Downing Street. *Downing Street*.' Donna is a girl without much patience, although she is willing and basically kind. But like so many young people of her age she lacks a certain respect. A trickle of voices call, 'Number ten.' It is disturbing for the residents to see the police in the hotel. It is disturbing for everyone, let's face it.

The men are so large in their dripping uniform macs, and they joke as they go. You see them dressed like this more often on the roads; they shine and reflect disaster at traffic accidents when they wear those luminous bibs. And now they are trying to be gentle in order to humour Miss Kessel. Valerie did wonder if she should offer them a seasonal drink but decided against it. It would mean making conversation and she finds getting on with men a strain.

'How long has this lady been a resident at your hotel?' asks Pollard, florid and clearly in charge.

'Two years,' says Valerie without hesitation. 'And she's shared a room with you from the beginning, hasn't she, Miss Kessel?'

Miss Kessel is unduly flustered by seeing her

knitting bag out on the bed. She rushes past to pick it up and thrusts it in the wardrobe. She knows they won't find any clues, she's removed anything worth finding. But she overlooked the Christmas sherry hidden deep in her knitting bag.

'Would you know if the lady took anything with her?' The tall men bend to address Miss Kessel, who is pressed against the wardrobe with guilt all over her face. They bend and they raise their voices.

'Yes, I would know. But she hasn't taken a thing.'

'Not even her handbag?'

'Well, yes, of course she's taken her handbag. And her coat.'

'May we have a shifty?' He opens the wardrobe anyway and Miss Kessel is forced gently aside. Rummaging amongst the shoes he pulls out three bottles and holds them aloft. 'Secret boozers, hey?' He thinks he has cracked a joke but Miss Kessel's face is agonized.

'Not at all, not at all, we clubbed together! We're going to use them as raffle prizes!' she lies.

'It's all right, Miss Kessel, calm yourself,' Valerie reassures her. 'Sergeant Pollard is only making a joke.'

'Oh,' says Miss Kessel, as one childish hand flies to her mouth.

The red-haired one, who has large hands that look as if they've been held under a tap for too long, looks odd perching on the end of Miss Bates's narrow bed. How little you can tell of anyone who lives in a rented room like this, he thinks. He picks up a library book and glances at the date. He turns to Miss Gleeson to ask,

'Medication? Miss Bates is a senior citizen. Did she take any regular medication?'

Miss Gleeson shakes her head. 'This is not a nursing home, Sergeant Pollard. The residents' health matters, unless they need a special diet, are entirely their own affairs.'

'She didn't take anything,' Miss Kessel says quickly. 'She didn't believe in doctors, she steered well clear of them and I don't blame her, I'm not too keen myself. Miss Bates was more a follower of homeopathic remedies and only took those if she needed them. She took nothing regularly as far as I know.'

'You know that for a fact?'

'Yes, I certainly do.'

'She must have been registered with a local GP.'

'Unless they have any objection all our residents are registered with Dr Turner in the Crescent. I assume Miss Bates was his patient, although I can't say if she ever used the surgery.'

Miss Kessel, who knows that Miss Bates is not a patient of Dr Turner and never has been, stares at the ceiling and concentrates on a cobweb she spies there.

The sergeant takes notes. 'We shall, of course, have to talk to him. Now,' he says, 'how about personal correspondence?'

'Anything like that she kept in her bedside cabinet.'

The sergeant looks at the wicker cupboard beside Miss Bates's bed. He edges along the counterpane until he reaches the handle. He pulls it open and bends to peer inside. Miss Bates's mail is all there done up with a rubber band, but surprisingly little, nothing personal, some post-cards from fellow residents on holiday, a couple of brown envelopes, receipts, statements, that sort of thing. He looks up from his bent position. 'Relatives and friends.' It is not a question, just a statement requiring an answer.

'Nobody,' sighs Miss Kessel, who can feel sweat on her brow. 'She had no-one at all. She never married, Sergeant, and when she worked she was in London . . .'

'What did she do?' It seems that the sergeant is chary about giving Miss Kessel her head, thinking that old people can't be stopped once they start.

'She stuffed birds for museums,' says Miss Kessel proudly and not at all insulted by the interruption. 'That's what she told me she did for a living. Apparently she was good at it.'

'We'll take this little lot away with us if we may.' It's not clear who he is asking but he pushes the thin bundle of letters deep in his gabardine pocket and gets up to go.

'But . . . what do you think has happened . . . ?' There is desperation on Miss Kessel's small face, she thinks they must know something, these men so used to dealing with crisis and missing persons. 'Do you think Miss Bates is all right?'

Again Miss Gleeson notes the concern on the sergeant's face. She recognizes one of the common concerns of the young – that the old, like Miss Kessel, might cling, might beg . . .

'Far too early, my dear,' he says.

'Too early for what?' Miss Kessel will not be dissuaded.

'Too early to worry, of course,' says he, block-ing the doorway with his bulk and replacing his

120

cap only when he is back on the wider landing. 'We'll check all the hospitals right away, that's the most likely outcome. Your friend has probably had a fall, that's all. I don't doubt she'll be back, right as rain, tomorrow or the next day. We'll find her. And as soon as we do, Miss Gleeson, of course we'll inform you.'

Miss Gleeson leaves Miss Kessel in her room and follows the policemen down the stairs in order to show them out politely.

'No need for you to come any further.'

But there's nothing for it, she has to go. When she closes the front door behind her she gasps at the force of the howling wind. It tears the words from her mouth.

'No need, really, Miss Gleeson.'

The tall man, clinging to his hat and splaying his legs to stay upright, can't hear her properly. Valerie's skirt, already wet, is slapping painfully round her legs. He turns to face her impatiently, struggling to remain polite. Already the driver is down the steps and on the kerb, battling with the car door.

'There's something you should know,' she says.

'Pardon? I'm sorry? I can't quite catch what you're saying. Shall we go back inside?'

Valerie shakes her head uncertainly. 'I think something dreadful has happened to poor Miss Bates.'

Sergeant Pollard stands erect and smiles with relief. 'As I told the old lady in the hotel, it's far too soon to worry.' He has to shout to be heard.

Valerie glances up at him cautiously.

121

'Something is going on here that makes me very suspicious.'

There! She said it! Her conscience is clear. Sergeant Pollard thinks he hears, he frowns and searches her face but decides he must be mistaken. She's just another hysterical spinster worrying unnecessarily. One of a kind, a pest, frankly, to busy people like the police. She senses he shares her father's views, and she's not prepared to push it. She lacks the confidence for that. She fears she has said too much already. He can't stand here any longer. He's eager to be gone.

She'll say no more and neither will he. She must not be so hasty in future, she's gone too far at this early stage. But he'll take the nagging doubt with him and it'll surface at the oddest times, when he gets into bed that night, when he takes the top off his egg the following morning, when he sweeps the snow from his drive in order to get out. Yes, her suggestion will surface and worry him until he starts wishing he had asked her to repeat it.

And she? She might wish she had never spoken.

Valerie Gleeson returns to her office, relishing the warmth, listening as the car starts up outside. She sits at her desk with her legs stretched out in front of her, waiting. Waiting for the Tarbucks to arrive, waiting for the phone call from Father, waiting for Christmas to begin, waiting for Mrs Thompson's taps as evening comes to Happy Haven with its smell of onion soup and yesterday's gammon.

Nine

See amid the winter snow,
Born for us on earth below . . .

Uhhh.

BIFF.

THWACK. Flailing at the chaos. Clover lies still at the bottom of the stairs, getting to grips with her destiny.

How very perverse. A dire calamity, the sort of fall she had planned in her dreams, but uncontrolled, not deftly and prettily and, therefore, not quite the kind she intended as the house spirals backwards and upside down, clattering with the colours of pain, blue-black and red roaring behind poor Clover's eyes.

Clover lies still, streaming with painful sensation, with her dressing gown awry, slippers scattered, calling with a weary fatalism, 'Fergus! Oh, Fergus!'

The children! The children are unexpectedly wonderful. Rallying as they usually do to the untoward, the disagreeable, displaying degrees of wisdom and sensitivity which you wouldn't think they had in them.

'Am I still alive? Am I alive?' She can just

about feel her toes twitching.

'Yes, you're alive. At least I think you're alive. Here, let me help you.' Fergus's large bulk moves comfortingly over hers. He leans forward and stretches out his arms and the flimsy Clover, her eyes large and bright, half tumbles, half falls towards him and all his wonderful strength, sobbing and sniffing. His voice is deep and powerful, and she, so full of sorrowful appreciation, can hardly detect the vague reproach, 'Oh no, oh no, d'you think you've broken anything? Can you still move your legs?'

By now his is a desperate face, long, lean and harassed.

Of course Fergus's face was distorted by distress long before he came inside to be faced by his wife's feeble screams. Getting the body out had been a nightmare. He'd never imagined he could feel so afraid of being caught in deceit by his own family. Hell, he'd even felt his right eye twitching as it did when he used to lie as a boy, as if he'd done something shocking. He could have been the murderer trying to dispose of his victim. Sweating with a mix of exertion and relief, he and Jonna had eventually managed to haul the dripping corpse into the only barn with a door.

'You'll have to lock it,' spluttered Jonna. 'We can't risk somebody coming in here and falling over the wretched thing.'

'How can I lock it when there isn't a lock?'

Both men glanced round nervously. No soft corners in here, just a huge, galvanized hangar overshadowed by two massive grain bins. High above them criss-cross planking made fragile inspection walkways underneath the roof. The bins are full to their brims with grain because Fergus hasn't sold any yet; he dried it himself and is storing it on the farm waiting for the price to rise. There are no nooks and crannies in here, just an assortment of machinery.

The wind rattled the mighty structure, tearing at the riveted sheets, shrieking with weird and discordant echoes like some mad and wild-haired organist in a metallic cathedral.

Dazed with disappointment, Jonna stood with his hands prayerfully clasped, gazing up and around him. This was an inappropriate mausoleum. 'I'd imagined somewhere cosier.'

'The sheds are full of animals,' Fergus apologized. 'Come on, there must be somewhere in here.' The Massy Ferguson, missing from its place, was out in the milking parlour already attached to the generator. Fergus hoped like hell it would start the system in the morning. A hundred Friesians to be milked by hand was a thought too awful to contemplate. But other large implements were stored there in the barn, the hay-turner, an assortment of ploughs, the fertilizer drum. Looming over all these, its great bulk nearly blocking the door, was the muck-spreader, a vast sarcophagus of cylindrical solidity, an empty container, an empty drum that nobody would dream of climbing up and looking inside. Fergus looked at Jonna, who raised enquiring eyebrows.

'It's the one place I can think of where she'll never be found.' And then, aware of the terrible irreverence of his suggestion, 'I can't think of anywhere else that would be more secure.'

'Damn it, man, we can't put her in a muckspreader.'

125

But Fergus muttered, 'She's well wrapped up. It wouldn't hurt.'

'It's the principle of the thing!'

'The dead don't know.'

'I suppose you're right. It's just a rather insalubrious place to find oneself, even on a temporary basis. I wouldn't be happy for Diana to be hidden in a muck-spreader. I wouldn't want anyone I cared about . . .'

Both men looked down and contemplated the body. Wrapped in sacking, they could no longer see her face. Did someone love her once? Does someone love her now?

'It's imperative that nobody finds her. Clover is having a tough enough time already coping with Mother and I must admit Mother does seem to be getting more awkward. She's never approved of Clover but in the past she made a pretty good attempt of not showing it. And if you're highly strung, as Clover is at the moment, it's easy to imagine things are worse than they really are.'

'What things?' Jonna wasn't listening properly.

'Oh, I don't know. All sorts of odd little inconsistencies. Signs of eccentricity.'

'And? Is it Clover's imagination? Or do you think so too?'

Fergus lifted his sopping cap and scratched his forehead. He held Jonna's eyes when he answered, 'Hell, I just don't know, Jonna. I honestly don't know any more.'

Uneasy, Jonna changed the subject. 'Come on, then, let's get this over with. Let's get back indoors, it's like a bloody freezer out here.'

'She'll not go off, at any rate.'

And neither man quite smiled.

*   *   *

And now here is Fergus bending over his prostrate wife, unsure what to do with his hands. He touches her shoulder nervously. He runs his hands through his wet hair. He is big in a comforting way, a solid man with solid features and an easy smile. He wears his hair in the same style as he wore it in childhood, just an ordinary cut administered by an ordinary barber, no unisex salons, no specialist clinics for Fergus, who has never been moved by fashion. Perhaps this is why people take to him instantly, why they so often confide in a man they see as trustworthy and sensible. A constructive man, who has had a constructive passage through life, he has never looked truly young and Fergus will never look truly old.

'Leave me! Leave me! Don't make me move, not yet. Everywhere hurts, oh God, Fergus, I'm aching all over.' And then, more from shock than pain, Clover weeps in the way that fallen people do weep, jerkily, embarrassed, trying to smile, and with dry tears. And of course, for her own illogical reasons, Clover is furious with Fergus, she blames him for her accident.

Predictably, perhaps, Fergus's anxiety turns to anger. 'Who left that damn box on the stairs in such a dangerous place? Who could do such a crass, stupid bloody thing? And in the dark! It's incredible! Absolutely incredible!'

'It doesn't matter who left it there, Dad. Who-ever did it must feel bad enough anyway without going through the third degree. Whoever left it there is hardly going to do it again after this. Poor Mum.' And this is Polly trying to placate her father, seventeen-year-old Polly with her pale face and her long, dark flowing hair reaching halfway to her waist, head to foot in shiny black plastic, chains at the waist and two crucifix earrings dangling from her left ear.

Clover, limp as a rag, now weeps copiously, stretching an accusing arm towards the cause of the accident. Trivial Pursuit. What was that blasted game doing at the top of the stairs? Who the hell would bother to cart it up and dump it there? Who, in this house, would bother to move anything anywhere? Her gestures and her nervous frowns tell her audience this and they see and understand her bewilderment.

Diana stands watching the scene with her arms behind her back, occasionally rising off her heels and going slowly down again. Her expression is complicated, difficult to define, smacks of the same contempt she sometimes used in childhood.

Diana is an exotic woman, rather Joanna Lumley, bold and tall with an abundance of black-rooted golden hair tied carelessly on the top of her head. Her voice is loud, her laughter raucous and despairing. At most times she is nervous and tight, she does not spread ease and calm around her. Compared with Clover, still lying on the floor, heavy and sprawling with all decency abandoned, Diana oozes sophistication, her high, wise cheekbones are shaded in with care and skill, her eyelids blue as a summer sky and her heart as deep and sad as sin. Just now, in that silky red jumpsuit, she has the look of a mandarin gazing down with an inscrutable smile on her face. A most indefinable smile, with a touch of admiration in it.

Understandably suspicious after Clover's silly, dramatic threats, Diana asks quietly, 'Are you hurt, Clover? Really hurt, I mean?'

Fergus's glance to Jonna beseeches: how the hell can we tell them about the body now?

'I won't know till I move,' spits Clover peevishly.

'And can't you move at all yet?' As if we haven't got enough problems without you putting on this act, Diana's question implies, damn her. Christmas is upon us already, it can't be cancelled so there's no point in faking it now. 'Could this be a case of hysterical paralysis?'

And is she laughing at her?

'Diana! Don't jest.' Clover resents Diana's attitude. Oh, the absurdity of it all. This is a genuine accident and Diana should see that and treat it as such, not sneer at her from above. 'I will move when I can. But don't touch me! Whatever you do, don't touch me.'

If only they wouldn't cluster round her like this. Still, it would seem, everyone expects something from her, if only the reassurance that she is all right. Yes, even as she lies here in agony, distraught, pulsing pain from head to foot, a hammering in her temples, even like this they are waiting and needy, all except one. *For where is Granny?*

Granny is no leech. Granny is sitting beside the fire still wearing that paper hat, a spider in the centre of its web.

When they carry Clover in Granny says, 'Goodness me. I heard a bang, a series of bangs, actually, but I never imagined . . . What on earth has happened to poor Clover?'

'She's had a bad fall, Mother, but no lasting damage done. She's just terribly bruised and shocked.'

'She fell right from the top of the stairs to the bottom,' says neat, pretty little Erin, the image of her mother, Clover, but with a refined fascination for the morbid. 'I doubt she missed out one stair. Look, Granny, one side of her face is all red and swollen.'

And puffy-eyed Clover thinks, she is proud of me! For the first time in years I have done something to impress my oldest child.

'How dreadful,' says Granny gloomily, holding up the candle, a flint-eyed Florence Nightingale under the paper hat. 'That could have been very nasty. You could have been killed, Clover. What made you so careless?'

Fergus interrupts quickly. 'Oh no, I don't think there was ever any question of the fall being fatal.'

But it is already too late. Clover is suddenly aware of a cold dead breath coming from somewhere, some essential corruption, so different from the warm exhalations of the living. Unease and dread join the pain and surprise written on Clover's battered face.

They plump up the cushions to make Clover comfortable. They bring in a knitted blanket along with the camping lantern and set it on the coffee table which they draw up beside her. Polly, a vision in her black plastic and creaking like a bin liner when she walks, holds back the curtain and wipes a hole in the steam. 'Just look at that! All the rain has turned to snow. I've never seen it coming down so fast or so thick. We're trapped already, aren't we? We couldn't get out in this even if we wanted to.'

'We could always get out on the tractor,' says Clover, all anxiety now.

'I can't move the tractor from the parlour. It's been on the blink these last few days and I daren't risk it for anything except the milking.'

Jonna's twin boys are large and they fill the furniture the way they sit, slumped all over it. Tall and lean with long curly hair, their acne has gone; these boys are good looking and they know it. Their eyes follow the girls wherever they go. Sam and Dan, at single-sex schools, are easier with Polly and Erin than they are with other girls, they have known these two from childhood. They have always been lovers, from the age of ten when it seemed like a game and Polly and Erin, giggling and experimenting, shared their beds with their fumbling guests and fooled about with a bar of soap. Sam and Dan have Polly and Erin's photographs pinned to the dormitory wall at school. 'Wow,' say their friends, impressed.

And Sam and Dan, they smile.

They are boys with secrets tonight. They mention one secret now.

'Well? Aren't we going to tell them?' It is Sam, rangy and athletic, who can't bear to sit around with the adults doing nothing but talking. Someone will suggest a terrible game in a minute and that's the last thing he wants. And the tellies don't work. To be honest, he'd prefer to go back to the children's end but, with the storm raging outside, and with Clover's dangerous fall down the stairs, they all have the feeling that they should stay and offer support.

Fergus is pouring some well-earned drinks. 'Tell us what?' He panders to the boy who might well be his.

'About the ouija board. After the lights went we got it out.'

'I didn't know we still had the stupid thing,' says Clover, accepting a double gin with a trembling hand. She feels a tooth with a tentative tongue; the one at the back on the right feels wobbly. Surely she can't have knocked it loose. 'I thought we threw it out years ago, Fergus, when there was all that fuss.'

'You didn't, Mum, it was there in the cupboard, with all the other games.'

'All hell broke loose,' Sam says easily. 'The board jumped right off the table.'

'That was Erin pushing it.'

'I swear I never pushed it.'

'You must have pushed it.' Dan narrows his eyes. The grin on his face is supposed to be sexy, he thinks he exudes sexuality, that's why he sits like this. Polly, coy but responsive, apparently finds him so. 'It wouldn't do that on its own.'

'It doesn't do it on its own, jerk, the spirits made it do that.'

This is getting dangerously close to a childish tiff. Still, with her daughters at seventeen and eighteen, Clover has to endure childish tiffs. She longs for the level of conversation to rise in her house as she imagines it rises in other houses with teenagers in them, surely? A state of grace, and about time too. Why must hers still bicker, why must their conversation remain so trivial? And if,

Heaven help them, they ever manage to get on to anything remotely interesting, the rows between Fergus and his daughters are more exhausting than the trivial matters that flow past her ears.

Diana senses the tension, too, because she says, 'Come on, then, go and get it. We'll watch and referee. We'll see if anyone's pushing it. Look, the atmosphere's perfect and Christmas Eve is probably a significant night for the spirits.'

Clover thinks there's a breathless sparkle about Diana tonight. Can it come from the soft lights and the candles? With the lantern they make a celestial light. Can it come from the loss of electric light, the way it turns the air to wicked black velvet? And Clover wishes she, too, could find some excitement, that she didn't just feel totally weary. And sore. And unseasonable. And ugly. And angry.

What is wrong with Clover these days? Has the devil got into her soul? Is he souring her mind, tormenting her brain, sucking her bodily juices?

She can smell the magical Christmas tree standing there so broadly behind her, that smell that used to send her reeling into the realms of Christmas, the most evocative part, delving in the old school trunk for familiar-sweet decorations. She doesn't hold with new ones, tradition is what it's all about. The whole point of Christmas is to dust off and bring back . . . what? Is there only, now, a gentle, lost nostalgia?

Hell, perhaps after all she will buy some new decorations next year.

Here come the children, animated, and they set up the ouija board under the camping lantern on

the table beside Clover. Trying, kindly, to involve
and distract her.

'Granny? Granny?'

Is she nodding again, muttering away in her
sleep? Surely not. Polly goes over and shakes
her gently. 'Granny? Wake up! D'you want to
take part?'

The paper hat sits at a rakish angle. It will fall
off in a minute and out of habit Granny will try
and reclaim it, chase it down her back with her
arm as if it is something important and not merely
a slip of blue tissue.

Granny blinks like an owl. 'Take part in what,
dear?'

'A seance!' Polly's complexion is always pale
against all that black, but when she pulls that
sinister face and widens her eyes to help explain,
when she does that she looks gaunt and ghostly.
'We're about to commune with the spirits.'

What is this presence here in this house?

Granny glances urgently at Fergus, who sits in a
chair directly opposite with a fresh cigar in his
mouth and a warming brandy in his hand. He has
changed out of his sodden clothes and now wears
a Guernsey sweater, bottle green with leather
patches on elbows and shoulders, and stout
corduroy trousers. Thick grey socks, as always,
hang off the ends of his feet, socks that Granny
unfailingly knits to put annually under the tree.

'I don't think that is a good idea,' says Granny
firmly. 'You should have more respect.'

It is so long since she expressed an opinion,
let alone a controversial one such as this, that
the adults in the room sit silent, half smiling,

nonplussed. But the children don't even notice, they answer as they would answer Clover being silly, Fergus being difficult, they answer with good-humoured patience.

'Of course it's a good idea. It's fun. No-one really believes in this crap.' So they get the board out and make ready.

And really, Clover has to agree, they mustn't be small minded over this. 'I don't think it'll hurt, Violet, not if it keeps them happy for a little while. We can't do much else in the circumstances.'

'And we've got to keep our eyes peeled for fraud,' announces Diana with glee.

'I don't believe in any of it,' says Granny, and the paper hat falls off. She brings her hand to her head to catch it but it's not there, it's on the floor. It has landed on her slipper.

'Well, if you don't believe in it, Mother, then there's no harm in it, is there?' Fergus comments easily.

'Those boards can be dangerous,' Granny insists.

'Mother, really! Don't be ridiculous—'

'I have heard,' Jonna interrupts, 'that the Yanks are thinking of introducing recorded messages in cemeteries. A button on the grass which you press as you approach.'

'Saying what?'

'Well, I imagine something like, "Hi, folks, this is Elmer – or this was Elmer, who died . . ." '

'Stop it, Jonna,' says Diana strictly.

'This ouija board business is a tasteless idea,' sniffs Granny.

And Clover wonders if this reaction is anything

to do with William's death, with the fact that his broken body was brought here immediately after the accident. He spent the night in this very room. 'Spooky,' Clover had called it. Fergus called it tradition.

'Is there anyone there?' giggles Polly, one finger on the board and the other hand teasingly clutching Sam's jumper.

'Watch Erin,' says Sam. 'Watch her like a hawk. I don't trust her.'

'Don't worry, I'm watching,' Diana reassures them and Erin squeaks with laughter.

Granny gets up stiffly.

'You're not going, Mother?'

'I am. It's late, Fergus. It's gone ten o'clock. I'm off to bed.'

'But it's nothing to do with the game, is it, Mother? I hope we haven't driven you off.'

'I'm going,' Granny repeats, her face set firm, her eyes shining fiercely.

'If you feel this strongly of course we'll stop.'

'No, no, Dad! We won't stop! Not now! Jesus, look at it moving!'

Fergus gets up to console his mother, but by the time he finds his lost sock she has already gone.

'Oh, do sit down,' says Clover indignantly. She is hurt. She has fallen down the stairs and everyone seems to have forgotten. And, what is worse, they seem to have conveniently sidetracked the main issue of the day, which is that she didn't just fall, she was deliberately tripped. And she tripped over something that should not have been there, something that under normal circumstances would never have been there, couldn't possibly

136

have been there. If her family pile up stuff on the stairs they pile them neatly, at one side, at the bottom, never on top and never right in the centre. And never anything like a game that doesn't need to be taken upstairs or put away, like towels or soap or loo paper.

So Clover turns and watches Granny's sudden departure. She and the candle disappear into the darkness of the hall, leaving Clover shivering, suddenly cold, hunching her bruised shoulders and pulling the blanket of knitted squares high up round her neck, huddling into it.

'All right, sweet?' asks Fergus. Tried by circumstances, his is a forlorn entreaty.

But Clover is not prepared to play this love-me, love-me-not game any longer. She stares at Fergus long and hard, with a coldness she did not know she possessed, before she gives a small shake of the head.

Trouble brewing. Diana sees the exchange of glances and smiles to herself.

'Look!' shouts Erin. 'Look at it move!'

'But what is it saying?' asks Diana.

'C . . . H . . . I . . . C . . . K . . .' They all chant together as the marker swishes across the board looking as if it's alive.

'Chick?' What can that mean? Jonna has too much in his head to be truly interested in such superstitious nonsense. So much has happened today he can hardly take it all in, and he is an indoor man, not used to physical labour. Every bone in his body aches.

'Wait! Wait! It's still going. Look!'

'Erin? Are you sure you're not pushing again?'

'No, no, I swear I'm not.'

Silence and intense concentration overtakes them all once more. 'D . . . E . . . E . . .'

'Chick. Dee. Doesn't make sense.'

'Did you honestly expect it would?' And so, at last, Fergus settles into what's left of the evening, a drained and tortured man with a presage of disaster.

It is cold tonight down in the children's end, and much quieter than usual. Of course the girls aren't playing their music and the waterwheel which is not there is blocked by the snow.

Softly, softly, the snow falls softly now there's a lull in the wind, banked and blown so that outside Violet Moon's window it almost touches the sill. By morning it will have risen much higher.

Violet is tired, so tired she doesn't undress but slips underneath the eiderdown and stares at the stone wall directly behind her on which the candlelight flickers. She feels herself falling, falling down into the depths of the well, a round, brick well with oil-black water at the bottom and something else that frightens her. Is death down there? Is this death she can smell, rank, odious, or is it the fact that Clover never airs her sheets properly, gets them off the line, folds them up and puts them straight in the cupboard. She doesn't bother to iron them, nor pillowcases.

In her day Violet ironed towels.

But Clover's got better things to do, not useful things, oh no, not busily outside helping Fergus. Southdown has never been Clover's priority, she couldn't care less about the farm that William gave his life for, the farm that will be hers one day, hers and Fergus's. But not until Violet passes

138

over. No, Clover prefers to drive to Plymouth each day to that dreary estate agent's office, anything rather than dirty her hands.

Fergus is too weak, he has always been too weak. He'd have been a damn sight better off with Diana, who at least produced a couple of sons.

Violet sinks a little deeper into the spiralling well where death waits at the bottom. Death is wet. Death is soggy. Ugh. Oh no. Why this ominous dread, where does this revulsion come from, why should Violet be frightened of death, she who casually nods to it on everyday terms? She knows better than most that people don't really die, doesn't she?

Somewhere a musical box is playing and Violet Moon is asleep now, a sort of sleep without smiles.

For nobody ever really dies and some are always watching. Life by proxy.

Ten

'*Sleep in heavenly peace,*' a line which should be
sung softly, rises to Miss Kessel's room in the
Happy Haven hotel, born on the raucous voice of
a well inebriated Mr Tanner. The pianist, keen to
encourage the camaraderie, is wantonly indulging
Mr Tanner's tearful sentimentality and moves to
those emotive carols which haunt the senses like
tinsel ghosts of Christmases past.

Most of the guests are either too tired or too
embarrassed to join in, that's what gives the
feeble effect of congregations in half-empty
churches. Those who do sing out, like the emotional Mr Tanner, sing extra loudly to make up
for the rest, a kind of defiant, discordant despair.

One floor up, Lilian Kessel sits on her bed this
Christmas Eve and stares at the picture she has of
Miss Bates, the photograph taken by the red-
nosed man last summer as they strolled with the
tourists around the harbour. 'Enjoying your holiday in sunny Torquay, ladies?' the man with the
camera asked them. So after that, for the rest of
the afternoon, they pretended they were on holiday, they rented two deck chairs, they bought
shrimps and ice creams and Miss Bates had a
candy floss.

But now Miss Kessel picks at the cashew nuts she has stolen from the hotel bar, a handful in each pocket of her skirt. This nibbling calms her. They seem to have picked up the habit of hiding and storing like squirrels. The last time they went on an organized outing to the country by coach, she and Miss Bates picked blackberries to bring back, to hide in the wardrobe. Of course they'd known they were bound to go off. The fruit seeped and grew a fuzzy white mould which smelled rankly alcoholic by the time the two women got round to smuggling out the mess, but this small and rather silly behaviour made them feel they were still in control.

Miss Kessel will go downstairs in a minute, she won't abandon her fellow guests and sit sulking on her own upstairs. But she needs to be here for a little while longer, just to sit alone and consider.

She gazes at the photograph. The harsh colours used and the shiny surface do nothing to flatter poor Miss Bates. She hated the photograph, she would have thrown it out, she said, but Miss Kessel wouldn't hear of it. Instead, she bought a cheap silver frame and keeps it on her dressing table, just to the right of the swing mirror.

'You don't have to display it in such a prominent place,' said Miss Bates briskly. 'I wouldn't be hurt, you know, if you put it behind the curtain.'

But Miss Kessel said, 'I like it, there's something hopeful about it. Don't you remember how silly we felt that day, when we pretended to be on holiday? What a shame we can't always believe that's what we're doing. What a shame we can't always feel as lighthearted as that.'

Miss Bates's appearance hardly varied. She

kept her hair twisted and pulled sharply back to a knot behind her head, never allowing one wisp to stray, and the real reason Miss Kessel is so fond of this particular photograph is that some of her hair has escaped and flown across Miss Bates's forehead. The lens must have clipped shut cheekily before she could push it back. It softens her, makes her look younger and her eyes don't look quite so lost. But even so, it is far from a flattering likeness, and the lips, they seem buttoned tight against some foolish utterance she might be about to make.

Apart from those few strands of wayward hair, all Miss Bates's terrible grey neatness was accentuated in the processing. You wouldn't have believed that Miss Bates could possibly look neater than normal, but in this picture she does. Every button on that cardigan is fastened, right up to the neck. There is not one crease in her skirt. Her neck is held straight and the rest of her body aligns itself, as if on a plumb line, down to where two short legs appear in sensible unscuffed shoes. Miss Bates could walk with a spirit level on her head and not move it. And grey, always grey, and defiantly upright as if she is protesting about some terrible, terrible mistake.

In spite of Miss Bates's age, the face in the picture is almost unlined, as if it's been ironed with the same care she takes with her blouses, steamed damply flat, not a crease, not much expression there either. Calm. Blank. The eyes which stare back look at nothing.

Searching for some illusive truth, Miss Kessel lifts the picture to the light, for perhaps, with the light behind it, Miss Bates will show some sign of recognition, her eyes will glint life at her worried friend or the corners of her mouth might move. But no. Completely still. Totally flat. A picture person protected by glass.

'*The rising of the sun, and the running of the deer . . .*'

Surely that verse should not be sung so frequently, or with such wild gusto.

Miss Kessel slips the photograph she had cunningly removed from its spot on the dressing table before the arrival of the police into her wicker bedside cupboard and pulls out, instead, the information about Miss Bates which could, in the wrong hands, mean that her friend would be forced to leave the hotel with her bags and baggage, which could sentence her to tramp the streets of Torquay begging for sanctuary, while keeping very quiet about her background – about where she has been for the last fifty years.

The information had come in a rush of dry-leafed memories, the result of one of the few serious disagreements Miss Kessel and Miss Bates ever had. It came after the fight when they were sitting, determination stiff in their backs, back to back on their own beds, tight-lipped and staring at the floor, at the little rainbow-coloured mats on the floor on their own sides.

Eventually Miss Bates broke the angry silence by muttering, 'And I do not see why you should take it upon yourself to criticize anything I do. You have no right.'

Miss Kessel thought hard before she answered. 'I feel I can criticize because I care about you,' she said dryly, her chest all a-flutter after taking the plunge.

'You don't even know me,' replied Miss Bates after one more uneasy half-minute. 'So how can you say you care?'

'I know all I need to know,' said Miss Kessel, behind her. 'We have shared this bedroom for almost two years now. I know the things that matter. And anyway, what is knowing? Who ever knows anyone else, if you want to take it all the way?'

'There are things,' started Miss Bates with a jerk, pausing to neaten her shoes on the floor beside her mat, as neatly together as they could possibly be. But she fiddled all the same. 'There are things that can change friendships. People have firm views, particularly when they reach our age. I mean, look how disparaging you are about my little spiritualist sessions, look how you disapprove of my visiting a medium and yet you know nothing about it. You sulk, or you go downstairs without me, and you make unkind remarks. You even called me a crank.'

The last thing Miss Kessel wanted was to start the argument up again. She said, 'That sort of mumbo-jumbo has always disturbed me. People get caught, because of their needs they get hooked. There are skilful hoaxers about, always alert to people with needs, and, as I have said so many times, if there was the slightest truth in any of it the scientists, the philosophers, someone would have proved it by now.'

'Not everything is provable, you can't measure everything by probing and testing, you know. There's God for a start.'

144

The ticking of Miss Bates's bedside clock clanged into the following silence. A seagull watched from the windowsill, begging, head on one side, eager eyes staring in, trying to shame them for a piece of chocolate. Miss Kessel rightly ignored it. The birds are becoming a menace, especially in St Ives where they are a downright danger. She is not a seagull lover, she does not like their cruel beaks or their glaring eyes. 'I'd rather not get on to religion, not now, dear. Not after our argument. All I want to say is that I am concerned for you and that's what made me angry, and I was concerned because I care.'

And then, when Miss Bates turned round to face her, Miss Kessel saw with pity that her face was stricken and taut, tense and shiny as a seaside awning battered by the weather, hanging on against hopeless odds.

That is when it all came out. And when Miss Kessel heard about the hospital her face drained, she went quite pale. All those wasted years. At first her thoughts had naturally turned to some terrible physical illness, some wasting disability that had mercifully been cured. Although Miss Bates was fitter than she and never had, as far as Miss Kessel knew, been to the doctor for anything.

'You poor, poor soul! Your whole life – since childhood! How absolutely tragic! My dear . . .' She was lost for words after hearing such a sad, sad confidence. She thought of all the changes, how in fifty years even the landscape had changed, fashions, shopping, transport, houses and coinage. And poor Miss Bates must have watched all this helplessly from her hospital window. Miss Kessel's soft grey eyes had filled with tears as she turned to comfort her friend. 'And no-one, you say, absolutely no-one to call your own?' This was unendurable. Miss Kessel could hardly conceive of such terrible circumstances.

'I tell them all I worked in London stuffing animals for museums.'

'Well, of course, you would . . . You have to tell people something,' said Miss Kessel quickly, eager to agree with anything Miss Bates said. But then, recovering slightly, she asked, 'But why do you tell people that? It seems rather a strange tale. Why don't you just tell the truth?'

'Because I am tired of telling the truth. I am tired of seeing the look on people's faces.'

Then came the description of Parkvale Hospital and the fact that the ward was a locked one. How disgraceful and how mortifying. They talked and talked, even missing dinner. They could smell it drifting up from downstairs, softening the atmosphere of the hotel, the swede and mashed potato smell which overpowered the beige carpets. They heard the gong but neither had felt hungry. And anyway they had some breadsticks hidden in a napkin in the wardrobe.

'It couldn't happen now, of course,' said Miss Kessel brightly, patting her hair as you'd pat a pet, trying to reassure herself. 'They'd never lock a child away for that length of time. Not any more, they wouldn't.'

'Yes,' Miss Bates had agreed. 'Life was very different then. People's attitudes were very unsympathetic.'

'And how hard it must have been for you. How

strange you must have felt, the adjustment must have been terrifying. And why Torquay? Why here? Presumably you could have gone anywhere when you . . . when you . . . came out.'

'I heard that my sister had settled here. My step-father made a will, he kindly left me a small bequest. They gave it to me to sign and that's when I caught a glimpse of the word Torquay under my sister's name. So that is why I decided to come here and I'm still attempting to find her.'

'And have you discovered anything positive?' This was exciting. Something for Miss Kessel to get her teeth into.

'I think I might be getting closer.' But Miss Bates became more reticent and the last thing Miss Kessel wanted to do was push. Well, naturally not, on such a sensitive issue. But she had begun to understand Miss Bates's need for a medium. If there's no-one in life someone in death must be better than nothing, Miss Kessel supposed.

'So you see,' Miss Bates went on, 'if the Tarbucks found out . . . they have such a terror of anything to do with the mad.'

'But you're not mad! You're one of the most sensible people I have ever met in my life. A bit distracted sometimes, rather introverted, but then you like reading, and you enjoy sitting thinking, don't you, dear?'

'I never was mad,' said Miss Bates defensively. And Miss Kessel was far too sensitive to follow that up with, 'So why did they put you there, then?'

Ghastly.

Tap. Tap. Tap.

Miss Kessel has wandered too far in her thoughts so the rap at the door gives her a start. Valerie Gleeson puts her cheery red head round the door, raises her eyebrows and asks, 'Mr and Mrs Tarbuck have arrived, Miss Kessel, and wonder if you'd mind having a word . . . ?'

'In here? In my room?'

'If you wouldn't mind.'

The door closes quietly behind Miss Gleeson and Miss Kessel feels like a criminal about to be tried for withholding important information or deceiving the authorities or wasting police time. It could be that her information could save Miss Bates from some danger, after all. Perhaps she has returned to her old hospital home, perhaps she has some worrying illness that only the hospital knows about and any relevant information might be essential for Miss Bates's own good. The police have already asked for a photo but Miss Kessel had shaken her head and told Miss Gleeson she hadn't got one. But what possible harm, she asked herself afterwards, could a photograph do? Once you start on this lying game it easily takes you over so you're too confused to know when to lie and when to tell the truth. Conspiracy. Double dealing. And, oh dear, all those personal papers Miss Kessel has stashed away, what on earth will become of her if her deception is discovered?

Miss Kessel is scared of the Tarbucks. She suspects they are more likely than the police to see through her poor little web of deceit. And if they do, then what will happen? She'll be thrown out of Happy Haven, that's what, and end up in that wretched Beaumont.

Eleven

Happy Christmas!

'Do me a favour. Have a quiet word with Clover
for me, calm her down, find out how she's feeling.
I'm worried and she won't speak to me. She's
suggesting that Mother deliberately left that box
on the stairs. She says she went up there with
some candles while Clover was in the bath. It
beggars belief, Jonna, and it's all part of Clover's
strange paranoia.'

This stealthy conversation takes place on
Christmas morning in the wet and heaving chaos
of a darkened milking parlour. What a way to
spend Christmas morning when the rest of the
world lingers in bed, or seethes under wrapping
paper, or gathers round cosy TVs listening to
carols. Even before they started, deep in the dark
and cold, Fergus was forced to defrost the pipes
and valves with a blow lamp because everything
out here is gripped by the cold, seized up by
it, frosted with it, disappeared underneath it.
Buckets and basins are frozen with ice one inch
thick and still it snows, persistently, ceaselessly,
causing the dark to be darker, movement to be
more perilous. And at the best of times, thinks

Jonna, this yard is a dodgy place.

Fergus the farmer and Jonna the lover, how he would enjoy that label.

But Jonna feels the symptoms of a cold coming on, a little fever, a runny nose and sore eyes. Luckily he brought a selection of medication with him. These days you can't be too careful, but is he up to a session with Clover, so distressingly prone as she is, at the moment, to emotional demonstration?

In all this desperate urgency even a body can be forgotten for minutes at a time. The milking machinery pressure is worryingly low, the clusters drop off the teats with a weary regularity, the cows, so fleshy and overpowering, sense much amiss and are restless, likely to kick. They turn their great heads and their deep eyes rest on Fergus and Jonna. They are not used to Jonna or his sons. Where is the familiar Blackjack this morning? Where is Marvin the YTS boy?

Swish swish swish goes the milk as it jets into the bottles and colours them bubbly-cream. The cows at the door jostle for position, they skid on the snow, their eyes look wilder this morning as they crane their wrinkly necks over the top of the stable door, eager for relief.

The twins work the gates and wash the swollen udders with disinfected cloths. They fill the troughs with nuts according to yield, according to need. Some scrawny beasts get little, those most fat and sleek can hardly eat their quota. They stuff their mouths and munch and scatter the feed which turns to a greying mulch, slippery on the floor.

The twins, they're quite fearless, thinks their father, Jonna, marvelling, he who cannot move in here without one nervous eye on the cows and another on the door. What if the herd burst through and took over? He'd be torn apart and trampled. Those women who clamber to get at the sales, if the cows wore hats there'd be little difference, that same acquisitive gleam in their eyes, that same sense of the kill.

Fergus sits on the sharp, wet step beneath a cow, stripping a teat with one hand and holding a capsule in the other. In a minute he will shove this capsule into the hole and up, despite the protests of the beast, rendering the animal helpless with an experienced shoulder. The milk he strips is smelly and yellow and flecked with blood. It lands on the concrete and sets like junket. Mastitis.

E24, with the red band on the tail, gets a hypodermic syringe of such impossible proportions thudded into its haunches that Jonna flinches while the cow merely twitches. It turns its chained head and rests an accusing eye on the editor who feels guilt, shame, embarrassment, for this treatment of the female. Female, feminine, Eve and snakes, unclean, perhaps it is this perception of the cow that makes him so uncomfortable, all these shes seeping and leaking, and the cow lifts its tail and craps, a long slow slime of noxious liquid taking an arched slide. Fergus skips over it like a dancer in overalls and wellington boots, making a strange grace out of it.

Surely they should not discuss Clover like this, not in front of the boys. But Fergus is saying, 'She is certain poor Mother left that box on the stairs, she was on about it all night so I hardly got any

151

sleep. Talk to her, Jonna. She might listen to you. Tell her she's crazy.'

Shit shit shit. Clean clean clean. Jonna prefers the neat and the clean, neat rows of print, clean white paper cut to size, black and white, crisp and fresh. And he likes his facts to be correct, he cannot stand to have things wuzzy in his head. When he gets home he cleans his house because Diana won't do it, not properly. Not to the standard he now requires. He's getting fussier, he admits to himself, and the older he gets the more of a perfectionist he becomes. Sniffing loudly, Jonna looks round this milking parlour, at the buckets, the broom and the mess of torn kitchen roll, at the bottles and salves and syringes in the cobwebby cupboard nailed to the wall. No, he could not work like this, not in this chaos.

'Well,' says he, stepping aside to escape being splashed by a sourly fermented torrent of urine, 'well, of course I'll try, but I don't know what good it'll do.'

Does Fergus know? More and more frequently Jonna asks himself this question. Way back, when it started, the whole affair was much easier. A rush of passion, pure and simple, to be dealt with furtively, yes, but more agreeably than now. Because what is it now, this thing that Clover and Jonna have going between them? There are no words which describe it accurately and this annoys Jonna. With the correct words he can tidy up his emotions.

This is how it is for Jonna – he needs Clover most when he is not with her, that's when the passion floods him the fullest, that's when his need is greatest. In his head his relationship with

Clover is quite different from the one he has with the woman he kisses. And it is also a good deal to do with the fact that this goes on behind Diana's back, and the confidence this knowledge gives him. It's a shield against growing old, against Diana's many slights. 'What's the matter with you, anyway? You're getting so damn fastidious it's like living with a fussy old queer.'

But fussy old queers don't make secret assignations with women, don't go on dirty weekends, don't make eyes over candles or flirt over early-morning toast.

Sometimes, when things go wrong at work, Jonna will stop and close his eyes, lean back in his chair and think about Clover, how he sees Clover, and he rolls up his sleeves as the energy returns, sees the strength in his wrist veins, watches the blood flow through as he clenches his fists, determination again and the will to carry on. Self-confidence. Clover gives him all this and he plays squash twice a week to keep himself fit for Clover.

But does Fergus know?

And what about Fergus and Diana? Jonna is not a fool, there was something once but has it finished? Jonna, not wanting to know, does not look very hard. If there is something still there they are discreet just as Clover and Jonna are discreet. Well, hell, they are best friends, aren't they?

Jonna is inadequate in Fergus's milking parlour just as Fergus would be in Jonna's office. But Fergus's milking parlour smacks of manliness and the macho which offices lack, even news-paper offices. Strength and vigour, virility and masculinity, and the twins often ask him to sell up and buy a farm. They could train for the job, they tell him, at Bicton or Seale Hayne, and Fergus would help to get them started. They are young and strong and have no interest in carrying on Jonna's business.

'I couldn't if I wanted to. I wouldn't have the money for the kind of set-up you need to make a living in farming these days.'

'You could borrow. We could borrow.'

The countryside is offensive. Nature, here, unlike the neat green parks of home, just doesn't care. She is blowsy and whorelike, not clean, and forever exposing her darker parts, open and willing to be taken by someone like Fergus, taken by strength and power and arrogance. She smells like a woman on heat, but Fergus can cope with this, he is easy and he dominates as men are meant to dominate. Jonna can't dominate Diana and, anyway, she'd hate that. Jonna, so tall and thin and, he thinks, rather effeminate with his narrow face and his long white hands.

He watches now and sees how the twins leap to Fergus's every command. Here they become immediate men while at home they are boys just pretending. While Jonna feels duty-bound to come out here and labour with Fergus, the fact he would rather be back in bed or sitting with a coffee beside the fire is all too obvious. No, Jonna would loathe to buy a farm and go into competition with Fergus. What he does with Fergus's wife is bad enough, is taxing enough, is worrying enough.

Is fucking Clover a way of stealing a tad of virility from Fergus?

'Sam, take this cup of chlorate inside and put it in the kitchen for me. I'm going to unblock that sink that's worrying your father so much. And for Christ's sake, lad, don't get it on your hands, it'll burn the skin to the bone if you do.'

The boy seems pleased to be asked, anything to please Fergus. If Jonna's is a vengeful adultery, if Jonna is sneaking virility, could it be in exchange for his sons?

Happy Christmas.

Back at the farmhouse and those within would look ordinary to anyone who happened to peer through the windows.

'It's still coming down like curtains out there,' says Diana, wrapped in a snow-white dressing gown and slippers like furry ski boots. Her morning hair, untended, looks more alluring than when it's been done, whereas if Clover doesn't brush hers it stands up like crazy hair and the only dressing gown she possesses is a tatty old candlewick that looks like a bedspread. As a farmer's wife she is used to getting dressed first thing every morning in case she is needed, an emergency person like a scout, ever prepared. 'Look at that. It's coming down thicker than ever.'

'The tanker won't get through and Fergus daren't move the tractor. He'll have to throw all this morning's milk away.'

'And you'll lose all that money?'

'No, thank God, we're insured.'

Granny, in the kitchen with the girls, is busy making chestnut stuffing. Clover has packets of sage and onion in the pantry and she bought those chestnuts to roast by the fire. But when Granny suggested they be turned into stuffing the girls seemed eager to help so Clover pursed her lips and said nothing.

What's so special about chestnut stuffing? How can it fill your heart with anger and malice? Granny is alienated, just as Clover intended, but her malice still wells up and spills over.

The Aga is a traitor. Stoic and resilient, it has stayed alight when everything else has failed and this means that Clover must still cook her turkey. If they hadn't got an Aga she could have got away with a few tins of soup heated up over an open fire, soup and toast and two fingers up to Christmas. Bliss. The end result would not have mattered, would not have turned into something so threatening, and she would have been called a brick.

So she and Diana peel sprouts by the fire, getting it ready. They love to be together like this, they have no secrets, well, hardly, theirs is a dark complicity, sly looks, amusingly exchanged, the flicker of unkind smiles. No-one will open their parcels until Jonna and Fergus come in. Shiny parcels wait in dark, exciting piles beneath the unlit tree. In the dismal light, without colour or form, they could be boulders raised and toppled at tortured angles by hundreds of growing roots. But this tree has no roots, it is as rootless as Clover, the only child, whose parents both died in her teens. This house is dark when the lights go out with its tiny, peeping windows and low ceilings but the firelight burns so much brighter in snow, the fire crackles merrily with a definite Christmas vigour.

When Granny enters the room Diana catches

Clover's eye but neither enquires about the stuffing. Granny watches to see if Clover is cutting the base of the sprouts properly, with a cross. She is not. Clover does not consider this necessary. She wonders who thought of such a time-wasting ploy in the first place. She holds up a sprout, peels off the dirty leaves and drops it in the colander. How can a sprout take on such meaning? How can anger be caused by a sprout? Clover asks, 'Did you sleep well last night in spite of the gale?'

'I had strange dreams. I think I slept, but my dreams were terrible.'

'Yes, you do look tired this morning.' And cross. And bad tempered. Your face is hard, as hard as nails, thinks Clover. But perhaps it's just the poor light.

Diana shivers. 'Is it too early for a drink?'

'Shouldn't we wait for the men?' asks Granny.

'Certainly not,' says Clover, refusing to get into that. 'We'll have one now. Perhaps it'll help us all get into the Christmas spirit.'

All together in the kitchen now and Clover pulls out the turkey and bastes it. Is it time for the sausages yet, and what about the bacon? Should she boil the potatoes first, would that make them crisper? And how d'you cook chestnut stuffing anyway? Granny has left it like a threat spread out on a tray looking lumpy. Clover prods it with a finger. Ugh. It looks most unappetizing and she's overdone the herbs again.

Drinks on a tray. 'Shall I take yours through, Clover?'

'No, that's OK, leave it there on the side and I'll bring it when I come.'

'I'll stay and help,' says Granny.

'No, no, you've done enough and you're tired. You go through and sit down. There's not much more to do now, really . . .'

Oh oh oh, how Clover hates her.

It is dark here in the kitchen. The decorations and the hundreds of cards make it darker and the snow outside turns the colours to grey. It is particularly difficult to read the recipe book, to read what to do with chestnut stuffing. She puts out her hand for the glass, for the gin and tonic she needs so badly. Touches it. Recognizes it with the tips of her fingers. She lifts it, yes she does, she lifts it up and holds it to her lips while she muses, while she finds S for stuffing. She pauses. She sips it. Drops it.

Opens her mouth.

Grimaces, runs to the tap, calling.

Holds her head under, letting the water run over the burning, searing, charring, ripping that happens to her tongue and her throat and the soft, sensitive sides of her mouth.

Did she . . . *How much did she swallow?* Oh God, let her not have swallowed any. And there on the floor her wild eyes watch as the tiles turn from red to white, blistering as the corrosive eats away at the top layer of colour, eats away the skin and seeps like a thing alive deep in the solid heart of the matter.

Her drink – the one they poured – it is there on the table, innocently waiting. But nobody puts drinks on the table, they leave them for her, the cook, on the side, on the windowsill next to the Aga.

Clover licks her rusty mouth. Everyone, Fergus, will say, 'Don't be so paranoid. Think! Please think for a moment about what you're saying. Mother is not insane! She might be annoying but she's far from mad and she doesn't hate you this much, Clover! For God's sake, what's happening around here?' He will put his hands to his head and say, 'Has everyone in the world gone loopy?'

And to give her her due, for a moment Clover imagines Fergus's oh-so-sensible attitude, she stands there and thinks, pushing at a mouth with a tongue that is furry, swollen and dry. She stands like a piece of washing in frost, rigid, cold, corrugated with thoughts which she knows are ludicrous. She knows what she will sound like telling Fergus, telling anyone, especially when you remember how strange she's been getting of late. More than once Fergus has suggested that she must be going through the change, or going senile prematurely. 'What else can I think when you come out with this sort of crap?' And he laughs at her, as if she's another Grace Poole.

Clover cannot laugh any more.

But she can tell Jonna. Jonna is on her side and she's sure she can convince him. She knows she can, and she knows that it is essential that she succeed.

The men come indoors. *Happy Christmas. Happy Christmas!*

Rubbing raw hands. Boots off. Overalls left to steam by the Aga. The twice-wounded Clover, backed against the sink, watches and listens.

'Where did you put the chlorate, Sam?'

'On top of the fridge where you told me.'

159

'Where is it now?' asks Fergus, searching. 'I'll clear that sink before I do anything else.'

This is no coincidence. To try and speak is agony. It feels as if her whole mouth is bleeding. 'Somebody put it in a glass' – her voice is quite dead – 'and I tried to drink it.'

And all the eyes that turn towards her are horrified eyes with no Christmas in them.

Twelve

While shepherds watched their flocks by night,
All seated on the ground . . .

Clover watches, too. Clover shoots dark looks at Granny full of far more than a mere distaste. But Granny doesn't want to be here, Granny would far rather have stayed in her bungalow home listening to Mrs Fitzhall's DevonAir Christmas next door, cooking her own small chicken, making proper stuffing and cutting crosses in the base of the sprouts. They always did things properly when William was alive, there were none of these sullen meals cooked then, no short cuts taken in this farmhouse kitchen, no, not in those days.

Dear William, I can't get near you this time. There is something dark in the way. I would have loved to wish you a Happy Christmas.

Distaste, expressed in wrinkles and the lowering of an eyebrow and a kind of horror behind the eye, concealed as yet, but it's there waiting.

Attention-seeking again, thinks Granny, and how can it be that no-one sees through this shallow, pampered woman? But everyone's rushing round making a fuss of dear Clover. 'A ghastly mistake,' groans Fergus, who has washed her

161

mouth out with more water and observed the livid white blisters with exclamations of pity.

'You'll have awful ulcers, Mum.'

'Shit! Who poured the drinks?' demands Jonna.

'I did,' says poor Diana, frazzled. 'But the glasses were already out in a row and it was so dark I could hardly see what I was pouring. That lethal stuff must have already been in the bottom of one, it just wasn't possible to see.'

'And who took the glasses out of the cupboard?'

'I did,' says Granny. 'And I just assumed they were empty. I presumed they would be, as anyone would.'

'So how the hell did the acid get into one of these glasses? You did leave it on top of the fridge, Sam, as I told you? You didn't decide to tip it in a glass for some extraordinary reason known only to yourself?'

'Of course I didn't.' Sam is rightly annoyed. And all the men close their frost-nipped faces.

Fergus glances at his mother worriedly. Jonna sees and follows the glance. So does Clover. Distaste, yes, it is there and Granny knows about distaste. She remembers distaste on a thin, narrow face, she remembers the fluffy white jersey, like the very one Clover wears now. Only Clover's is slightly different because of the embroidered star on the front.

And Granny can smell it, too, she can smell herself and she can smell the wet leather of the car they rode in that day. She hadn't wanted to be there either, very badly not.

*   *   *

162

Violet smelled wet leather as she rode in the back of Sheena's car the day they drove to the Lodge to see it for the first time. Sheena's home. There to meet the formidable Kate.

She'd wet it. It was either that or be sick because she'd never experienced Sheena's driving before and she was frightened, Sheena took the corners so fast and tried to overtake on bends. Violet was used to Mummy's steady driving, to the shops and back, to school, to the park, always somewhere safe. She was nervous about meeting Kate, too, because she'd heard so much about her. Kate could read better than anyone else in her class. Kate wasn't fussy, she liked greens and the skin off rice puddings. Kate was learning to ride a pony and she enjoyed playing games at parties. Kate had friends in a new place, a place Sheena knew and admired which accepted only 'the right sort of people'. Violet was sure she wouldn't like Kate, and she did not understand why she was being forced to meet her.

Kate had 'spirit'.

Something, apparently, which Violet lacked.

Party games were a nightmare. What she liked best was reading her *Teddy Tail Annual*, listening to music on the wireless, playing ludo with Daddy and dressing her dolls. Safe things, like eiderdowns. Even to herself this list sounded boring and childish, as if, at five years old, she had already turned down some vital challenge which would influence the rest of her life. Sheena made it sound like that and in Daddy's eyes Sheena was right.

Kate would be good for Violet.

Sheena was driving Michael's car with Daddy

beside her. Now that her husband was dead it was Sheena's. Everything was Sheena's, even Mummy's roses and this Lodge they were visiting today.

The warm wetness took its time to seep into the leather. For a while the puddle stayed on the seat so she slopped in it and when she pulled up her sticky legs they made a sucking sound. She thought she was a mussel on a rock at the seaside, maybe they'd have to prise her off the seat with the edge of a sharp spade. She wished she'd left that poor mussel alone last summer but she'd wanted to see what was underneath.

She was surprised by the vast amount of pee underneath her, in the loo it never seemed much, the water level never rose as far as she could tell. Violet was five years old and Sheena was right, five was too old to do 'dirty things like that'. It was disgusting. The stain would never come out. Sheena was right about that, too, because, to Violet's eventual satisfaction, it never had. Hah. She'd left her mark on Sheena's back seat for ever.

'You should have told us you needed to go to the lavatory. We would have stopped the car at once. And fancy trying to pretend that nothing had happened in that sly way, covering up and saying you'd rather not sit down.'

That's what Sheena had said when the sin was discovered.

It was a sorry business.

Violet hadn't meant to be sly, she didn't want to let Daddy down but how could she tell Sheena that? When the car stopped there'd been a hole in the conversation and Violet knew she was expected to fill it with an exclamation of some sort. 'Oh, what a lovely house!' Because it was a lovely house, she supposed. But she didn't. For a start she was too small to see out of the window properly, even when she hung on to the strap, and secondly she hadn't even noticed the Lodge, so worried was she over what to do. And she didn't want Sheena to know, or Kate. Most of all Kate. So she whispered to Daddy when they walked through the hall.

'What did you say? Do speak up, Violet. This is not a church, there's no need to whisper.'

Abandoned in her hour of need. So she'd let go his jacket and said out loud, 'Please can I wash my hands?'

Sheena drew herself up, then, as if Violet had said something not very nice. She never liked bodily functions, but she laughed easily to cover this initial distaste. 'Upstairs,' she said, 'turn right at the end of the landing and we'll see you back down here in a moment.'

Poor little mite.

Up the stairs in this quiet, smart house full of pictures, and Violet could feel the wet edge of her coat slapping the backs of her legs. Her knickers were swollen and heavy, so heavy they slipped down her legs which already felt sore. She wanted to cry but there was no point because no-one was there to help her. She made a mistake and opened the door to a room which must be Kate's because it was full of rosettes and pictures of horses, and a monkey pyjama case with a tail so long it came over the edge of the counterpane, its face looked like Chickadee's.

The unfamiliar, frightening belongings of a

stranger. They said so much. This ordeal would have been easier if Kate had been a few years younger, or even a little bit older. Being the same age made this meeting with Sheena's daughter all the more competitive and threatening. Violet imagined Kate would be a smaller version of Sheena, just as sharp and brittle, just as strident and insincere.

So this first sight of Kate through the medium of her bedroom was alarming. Violet closed the door quietly in case they accused her of snooping. She found the bathroom at last and discovered with dismay that she couldn't turn the key in order to lock the door. Again she felt like crying. She wanted to go home. She wanted Mummy to kiss it all better and call her little Chickadee.

But she leaned against the door of this room that smelled of Pears soap, not the familiar Lifebuoy of home. She took off her saturated knickers and found that her socks and sandals were soaking wet too. She pulled a towel off the rail and rubbed herself dry. Then she removed her sandals and socks, drying her feet carefully before putting them on again. It was tricky, trying to do this and keep her back to the door at the same time in case someone came in and discovered her and her wicked deed. She stuffed her knickers in her coat pocket then breathed very deeply to find the courage to go downstairs.

And it did take courage to walk down that wide open staircase in this strange house, without knickers, damp and draughty. In the hall she stopped and took off her coat, tiptoeing to reach up and drape it over the banisters.

Sheena must have been listening for her because she poked her head round the drawing room door and said, 'Oh, here you are! I didn't hear the chain.' As if she knew, as if she'd been waiting for clues. As if she'd been trying to catch her out from the very beginning. And now what did it look like? Sheena was suggesting to Daddy and Kate that Violet was the kind of person who went to the loo without pulling the chain. A dirty, disgusting, ill-mannered girl.

Someone who uses too much paper . . . someone who has to be put in a bedroom next door to the bathroom because they have such little control. Someone who might even leave wet marks on the seat . . .

'Violet, this is Kate. Well, aren't you two going to shake hands and be friends?'

Violet didn't dare shake hands in case hers was damp. So she held both arms tight down beside her and looked Kate hard in the eye, defying her to hold out a hand when she said quickly, 'Hello, Kate.'

Kate wore a party dress with a white cardigan over the top, she wore white shoes and socks. She had yellow skin and a parting down the middle of her head with two brown bunches at each side. Had she dressed like this specially to meet her? If she thought Violet was impressed she was wrong. The ribbons in her hair were blue. By the way Kate stared at her Violet felt she was all in black. In fact she wore a pleated skirt and one of Mummy's hand-knitted jumpers with a Fair Isle border round the neck and wrists. She towered over Kate and for this she blamed her wretched legs. She twisted them all ways as they grew, stretched into Daddy-long-legs' legs and wrapped

167

themselves round the entire room.

'Sit down, Violet, and would you like some orange squash before we have lunch? Kate will pour you one, won't you, dear?'

Their drinks were in a cupboard which Sheena called a bar. They didn't keep theirs in the kitchen like Violet and Daddy and everyone else did. There were cigarettes on the bar in a silver casket, some were all colours, some were black. Since when had Daddy started smoking?

'I don't want to sit down at the moment, thank you.'

'Violet, don't be silly, there's no need to be shy. Here,' and Daddy patted a cushion beside him on the silvery sateen sofa. 'Come and sit by me.'

'I want to keep standing up.' She sounded so silly, just the sort of petulant child Sheena and Daddy would despise. Her face burned red. Never mind Sheena, she was beginning to hate Daddy, too. She wanted to go home, she despised the house and everyone in it. She hated Kate, but above all others, with a loathing that made her whole body shake, Violet detested Sheena.

But Kate brought a glass obediently and set it on a mat on the glass coffee table. 'Perhaps Violet is shy, Mummy.'

It was a shock to hear the spidery Sheena called that, such a safe word up until now.

'What?' exclaimed Sheena. 'A big girl like her, shy?'

'I think that must be it,' said Daddy and Violet sensed his disappointment. How easily he took the side of these two hostile strangers. How glibly he abandoned her to their sport.

Violet remained standing up during the

pre-luncheon drinks, and they were on their way through to the dining room, summoned there by Lizzie the cook, when Sheena passed the offending coat draped untidily over the banisters.

'Oh, Lizzie,' she started to say, 'would you mind hanging this up in the . . .' Her expression changed. She scrunched up the coat with her long nailed fingers, feeling it before she declared, 'But this coat is soaking wet!'

'It's not raining, m'um,' said the stranger the cook.

Sheena grimaced, scandalized. 'Feel it, Violet, it's all wet round the back.'

Violet felt it and backed into Daddy. Surely he would save her now, now she needed him so desperately. But Daddy pushed her out into the room. As far away from him as he could.

His voice was stern. 'Violet, how did your coat get so wet?'

Violet stared at Daddy then, her lips tight together, sealing her secret.

'She's wet it,' said Kate incredulously. 'Violet has wet her knickers.'

'Kate. Please!' Sheena stared at Daddy and shrugged her bony shoulders, her eyebrows raised into pained arches.

Daddy bent down so that no-one could hear him. 'Is that what happened, Violet? Did you have an accident?'

It was time to give up, so she nodded fiercely. She nodded to Kate, she nodded to Sheena and she nodded to Lizzie the cook. She grew dizzy with all the nodding and shame, overcome by a shivery sickness.

'Where did this happen? Upstairs just now?'

169

'No,' she said. 'In the car.'

'Oh no! Surely not in my car?' Sheena recoiled. Presently, she said in a cool, measured voice, 'Lizzie, fetch Gwendoline, please, and ask her to take Violet upstairs. David, why don't we go through to the dining room and make a start. Violet can join us when she's clean.' And in her eyes was a quiet exultation.

Why couldn't they say their goodbyes and go?

So then it was back upstairs again and strip in front of Gwendoline the maid, and it was into a shallow, lukewarm bath while Gwendoline went to find some dry clothes. 'Although I really don't know what I'll find of Miss Kate's to fit a great strapping lass like you.'

And the great strapping lass was bigger than ever, and cumbersome in the bath, and she almost slipped when Gwendoline tried to help her out. And what was that razor doing on the washbasin shelf, along with the Shave-eze that Daddy used? Perhaps it was Michael's, and they had forgotten to put it away.

Ten minutes later and nobody spoke when Violet crept into the dining room, bulging out of a dress of Kate's, the kind of dress she would never wear. Mummy would have called it silly. She smelled of a strange, strong soap and wore no shoes, just a pair of tiny white socks, and the heels dug into her monstrous feet.

'I'm drying the shoes by the Aga, m'um, though I don't know if they'll ever be right. They stink to high heaven.' She left them to get on with the meal having first announced to the world how ugly and smelly Violet was.

*   *   *

Whose fault was it that the world was ruined?

Sheena's! She wore her hair in rolls round her head, rolls that curved and shone like pieces of dog dirt and Sheena had black hair on her arms.

'*But why do we have to leave this house?* Why can't they come and live with us? Why do we have to live with them? And what will Mummy do when she comes back here and finds us gone?'

Daddy, tired, exasperated with this child who was being deliberately obtuse, explained once again. 'I have tried so hard to make you understand. Mummy is dead. Mummy is not coming back, but you know that already. You need a mother. Kate needs a father. And Sheena and I love each other, sweet. That's why we're going to get married. One day, when you're older, you'll appreciate what this all means.'

It was Daddy who refused to understand. Mummy knew what Violet felt like and Violet knew Mummy was there whenever she opened her musical box. Mummy came whenever you called her, she recognized the tune.

'But why can't you love each other from your own houses? Why must we go and live at the Lodge?' There must be something Violet could say to stop this from happening. She stood there, rigid as stone in the pool of light from the standard lamp, her legs burning from the heat of the fire behind her. 'Well, I refuse to live there! I am not going to leave this house and go and live in that terrible place with Sheena and Kate. I hate them! *Daddy, don't you understand? I really, really hate them!*'

'Oh, Vi, don't. I was so hoping you were going to be grown up and sensible about this. You are the most important person in my life and I need you to understand that Sheena and I have to be together. Yes, I know it's all strange and rather unsettling for you just now, because it's such a big change, and new, and you feel safer in the home that you know, that's understandable . . .'

'I'm not going, Daddy!' Her own voice, so frightened, frightened her. 'You go on your own and I'll stay here with Mrs H.' Couldn't he see? 'You go, Daddy, I really don't mind.' She felt big and grown up when she said that, as if she was giving up a great deal for his sake, and was far, far wiser than he.

But Daddy shook his head and his eyes moved off her and went on a tour of the room. 'Vi, I hate to see you behaving like this. So spoilt. So selfish. So unconcerned about my happiness.'

Sheena was a witch. And Sheena had cast this devilish spell to make Daddy distrust her like this. The fire felt hotter. She wanted to bend and rub her burning leg but she was stuck in this position of defiance and if she moved an inch Daddy might think she was giving in. And so she endured the pain. She would never move. Never!

'Lord knows, I've tried to discuss this with you reasonably. I've tried to make you understand. But now I see that Sheena was right and I should have treated you as the child that you are and ordered you to obey. The plans are made. There is nothing you can do to stop them. We are moving from here on Tuesday.'

Violet knew the secret because she had listened and had heard them talking. She'd listened while peeling a scab from her knee and sucking the

172

coppery blood that oozed from the new soft skin before turning red and dripping down her fuzzy leg, following the path of a great crimson bubble, down towards her sock. If the bubble reached the sock her father would not get married on Saturday and Violet would be saved. She sucked her knee while she watched its progress. The bubble stopped half an inch short, changed course, and slid round the back of her leg. She pulled the scab off bravely, enduring the pain. Whether it reached the sock or not she knew they were getting married on Saturday and that she could do nothing to prevent it.

Unfair! Unfair!

Daddy had gone so far away. Even if she'd walked across the room with her arms outstretched she could not have touched him. Her brain waves could no longer reach his. If they had, they would have scorched his with their desperation. She could have made him understand. She bit her lip hard to stop herself crying. She squeezed her small fists together. And when she spoke it was softly. 'Daddy, I don't want to live with Sheena and Kate. It's the thing I want to do least of all in the world. I would rather be dead than do it.'

Dr Lewis was quite shaken. 'I am not prepared to discuss this any further with you, Violet. This is for your own benefit as much as it is for mine. You are far too young to see it as such, but you will understand my motives when you get older. Now, you can consider the whole matter closed. We are moving from here on Tuesday and that's all there is to it.'

Never had he spoken to her in that unfeeling manner before. Never! She was a stranger and so was he, and they'd never been in this room before, never played ludo, never told stories, never shared a moment of life together. He was reading his paper again. It no longer mattered if Violet moved from the fire or stayed there, suffering. He wouldn't see her. He didn't care. She was five years old and he didn't care about her at all. Her agony never abated.

She ran to her room. Confusion, anger, fear and misery. She kept the sounds she made hidden in her pillow. She kicked and she struck at nothing, she ripped her bed to pieces. What was happening to her? She was a stick person made of crayons, small and staring over the edge of some mighty chasm, the depths of the fall before her were, like death, further than she dreamed existed.

Sheena had put this precipice there, she wanted Violet to fall over. And if she didn't fall on her own, then Sheena would be happy to push her.

An hour or so later, calmer but freezing cold and shivering, Violet brought out the musical box. The one Mummy had given her. And to the strains of the cold lullaby the ballerina revolved with a silver perfection.

'Choose a carol, Granny! Come on, choose a carol!' For God's sake, thinks Jonna, the atmosphere in here is more to do with death than life.

Granny blinks and watches a huge wasp, a queen, scorched from its winter stupor, crawl from a log and make its way towards the ashes under the fire dogs. 'That was lucky,' she mutters softly, 'someone could have had a nasty sting.' And louder, 'I think I'll have "Silent Night", if you can play that one, Polly.'

Thirteen

Oh Christmas tree, oh Christmas tree,
Thy leaves are never changing . . .

It has to be said that at Happy Haven the needles are falling already.

Who would want to be a Christmas tree at Southdown Farm or Happy Haven for that matter? Who would choose to celebrate Christmas at either of these two places, the first unsafe and spiked with fear, and the sign outside the doors of the second completely obscured by snow. Snow-chained tyre marks, almost disappeared, draw yellowly up to the verge outside and it looks as if the Jaguar, crouched like a camouflaged beast outside Miss Gleeson's window, is the only vehicle that moved in the whole of Torquay this morning.

But at least there is electricity here. At least they can turn their tree lights on.

Jason Tarbuck, proprietor, forty-five this year and boasting a fat man's moustache, stands beside the tree benevolently, handing out gifts to his elderly residents who accept and bow their way back to their chairs like servants to their master. A fat man's moustache and a fat man's colours, but Jason Tarbuck is thin as a rake and looks like a smothered coat hanger. The little presents he hands to his serfs have the same utilitarian style as the presents dolled out in big houses of old, nothing bizarre or silly which might give a cheery feel to this stiff occasion. But no, it's towels, ties and handkerchiefs and some of the residents are so bemused that they sit with them unopened on their laps, staring at the ceremony as if it is something on the TV. As if they are part of a game show audience but unsure when to applaud, and uncertain whether it is really right to claim this personal prize.

A spiv's black shirt, red tie, white jacket and brogues, that's what Father Christmas Tarbuck is wearing and beside him is his help-mate Mandy, reading the labels and delving daintily into a pigskin suitcase, wearing a clinging, sparkling dress that hugs an hour-glass figure. Bangles jangle on her wrists and designer perfume fills the air, competing with the resiny smell of the tree. Her hair is a fair honey-blonde and feathered to her head as her accent is feathered to her mouth. Her words come out fluffily, contrived and careful.

'Mr Gerald Parker.'

A roar of applause would be appropriate, better than this polite silence as Gerald Parker, dwarfed in the smart new cardigan sent by his sister, goes forward playing with his conker buttons, accepts his gift and backs away, a confused smile on his face.

This morning the conservatory is empty. Here in the lounge the mantelpiece above the fire is covered in the thin old cards with glitter that the elderly send to each other, spidery writing inside. The streamers that reach from corner to corner have not been twisted sufficiently so they curl and uncurl amongst themselves, every so often, like snakes sunning in the balmy heat.

'Mrs Eleanor Tickle-my-fancy.' Jason Tarbuck enjoys a joke with the ladies as much as the next man, but Mrs Tickle has no sense of humour and scowls at him as she backs away, as if she has been contaminated by the touch of his hand alone.

And so the awful dance goes on until Mandy Tarbuck delves deep once again and arrives at Miss Bates's parcel. Vain, she won't wear glasses although she needs them and so she is forced to raise the silver package to the light, screwing up her eyes as she reads the label, half out loud. She wraps her upper lip under her lower, slides her eyes towards her husband and coughs politely as she puts the gift to one side. It seems to sting her fingers. But Jason merely shrugs.

Last night Miss Gleeson gravely informed her employers about their missing resident. They had followed her heavy tread to her office not half an hour after the police left.

'We should have been the ones to speak to the law,' said Jason Tarbuck worriedly, sweating and throwing frowns at his wife. 'You should have informed us first.'

Miss Gleeson watched them carefully with no expression on her face, interested to gauge their reaction to the news. They did not disappoint her.

'And her things?' Mandy asked at once,

fiddling with the gloves she carried, slapping one down on the other. 'I suppose the police have already been through her things?'

'They asked to be shown her room,' Miss Gleeson informed them. 'So naturally I took them there. They also spent some time with Miss Kessel.'

'And what did that worthy have to add?' Jason Tarbuck ranged the room like a wild beast pacing, from desk to fire and back again. But his eyes were fixed on Miss Gleeson, eager for her answer.

'Very little, from what I heard,' said Miss Gleeson placidly. 'It seems that Miss Bates is a retiring character. Even her best friend knows little about her past or where she hails from. And she has no other friends, no relatives in the area. She receives very little mail.' This last remark was made pointedly.

'I see.' Jason mused, chin in hand. 'I think that perhaps my wife and I should go and have a look round.' He coughed to cover this odd request as he marched towards the door.

'In Miss Bates's room?' questioned Miss Gleeson with surprise. 'You want to look round her room? When the police have already searched it?'

'I think we should,' put in Mandy. 'She was – she is – after all, our responsibility.' But Mandy, in spite of that tight woollen dress, looked cold and dismayed.

'Not yours, but mine, I fear,' said Miss Gleeson, staring sadly at the Christmas menu, feeling a powerful urge to doodle, to do something with her nervous fingers. 'It is my responsibility and I feel it is all my fault.' But was her look one of accusation? Mandy Tarbuck, still slapping with one glove, could not tell.

'It's nobody's fault, Miss Gleeson, this is not a nursing home,' snapped Jason. That fact was never far away from his protesting consciousness. 'And it would be pointless for any of us to take part in that sort of self-indulgent nonsense.'

And so, after obtaining Miss Kessel's permission, the Tarbucks had disappeared upstairs, had spent a good twenty minutes up there, confirming Valerie Gleeson's suspicions that this missing resident had something to do with the Tarbucks' unstable financial existence, that they had been using her deliberately for some nefarious purpose.

A woman alone, no past, no family, no chance. The Tarbucks are happily unaware that Valerie, quite by accident, once caught sight of Miss Bates's bank paying-in book, and that gave the curious impression that the Tarbucks pay all her bills, cover her keep at Happy Haven and contribute one hundred pounds quite regularly into the woman's account.

Why?

Why?

Why?

Something ominous. *Something sinister*. The Tarbucks are up to something shady, no doubt, some dastardly operation with Happy Haven as a cover. How else can they afford their glitzy but tawdry lifestyle?

Drugs? The handling of stolen property? Probably nasty pornography, that sort of disgraceful thing. *And they need to launder their illegal gains*.

180

This must be where the hapless Miss Bates comes in handy.

Miss Gleeson wishes she'd never seen that dratted bank book. But Miss Bates had accidentally dropped it after fiddling with her handbag to retrieve a violet-scented handkerchief, and by the time Miss Gleeson rounded her desk, picked it up and reached the hall, Miss Bates had disappeared up the stairs. Sighing, Miss Gleeson had glanced at the neatly filled-in stub before her, stared at it and then returned to the office to study the rest at her leisure. It contributed one more clue to the mystery of the resident who was, incredibly, being paid for by the Tarbucks.

So many entries from the not-so-mysterious donor, JT. The dubious Tarbuck himself. That resident in grey with the quiet, slow voice, she came from nowhere, had been picked up and brought to the Happy Haven by the Tarbucks on one of Valerie's days off, and now she has vanished into nowhere. No doubt disposed of with the same sort of stealth, no use to her benefactors any more.

Or perhaps Miss Bates has gone off in fear, unable to take any more, worn down by the pressures of some shady collusion.

Dear God, am I dreaming? asks Miss Gleeson. Please let it be so. And who do I tell, if I tell at all? There's not much substance to her suspicions. Nothing with which to accuse her employers.

If she loses her job what happens to Father? Father, who telephoned only this morning, whose dire 'Happy Christmas' was couched in the form of a threat. Of course Miss Gleeson had called the police before informing the Tarbucks, of course she had willingly shown them the room, tried to suggest something untoward, but if Miss Bates's disappearance is down to the Tarbucks they would have made sure that no trace of involvement was left behind. And look, there was nothing for the police to take away, no relevant documents, no useful papers. No, she's afraid that the Tarbucks did get there first.

Even so, they were keen to go up and check. And they spent more than an hour with poor little Miss Kessel this morning. She came out shaken, looking wan.

Father would tell her, 'Valerie, if you spent more of your time worrying about the obvious instead of the ridiculous everyone would be much happier.' Father would say, 'You're quite neurotic. The Tarbucks are probably acting out of the kindness of their hearts, taking in a resident who cannot afford to pay their prices. Some people do that sort of thing, you know, people put themselves out for charity. Why do you always look on the black side? You always have done and you always will.' Yes, yes, Father would say all these things but Father, astonishingly indifferent to the distress of others, would really mean, 'I need you, Valerie. Give me more attention. How can you do so little for me and yet spend such energy on others?' Yes, that's what Father really meant when he accused his daughter of negative thinking.

And Valerie would reply, 'Everything I do is with your welfare in mind, Dad. When I work late at the hotel, when I do weekends and bank holidays, when I volunteer to organize outings, at the end of the day it's all for you.' She dreads losing

her job here and having to go back to that flat
with Father.

The bird! A steaming vision in aluminium. And
the dutiful Miss Gleeson, weighted with worry,
goes down to the kitchens to inspect it.

'No need to hide the sherry, Mrs Gartree. It is,
after all, Christmas Day.'

The cook, a sweet, bashful woman, uncovers
the Enva Cream from its hiding place in the
mixer, uncorks it with a squeak and offers,
'Would you, Miss Gleeson? Would you join us
seeings how it's the season of goodwill?'

'Oh no, I don't think . . . *Hell, why not!*'

The cook inclines her head. 'How's it all going
up there?'

'Same as every year. The Tarbucks are dishing
out their annual largesse so I thought I'd get away
for a break. All that nodding and smiling gets
tiring.'

'Thank God it's only once a year.'

'What about you, Mrs Gartree? Wouldn't
you sooner be somewhere else than slaving away
in the kitchens on Christmas morning?' Miss
Gleeson takes a sickly-sweet gulp of the proffered
sherry and feels almost restored.

'No,' says the cook with certainty. 'Nowhere
else to go, to be honest. Nobody home. Might as
well be here as anywhere, at least the food's
appreciated.'

'The thing is,' starts Miss Gleeson, with her
very stiff hair that looks like a yardbroom but is
surprisingly soft to the touch, 'you always imagine
that somewhere, some people, somehow, are
having the most riotous time, don't you?'

Mrs Gartree looks at her pityingly. 'I am seventy years old in February,' she says. 'And you'd never guess it, would you? But what I must tell you is this is a myth. If anyone's having a wonderful time they'll be drunk or male, probably both. To my mind women should give up on Christmas after their twelfth birthday, call it a day, disinvent it. There's more suicides, more marriages go down the pan and more folks go right off their rockers than at any other time of year, so I like to stay safe in my kitchen.' She sniffs and puffs at her hair. 'I know where I am, and there's Hilda to help me.'

'And where is Hilda this morning?'

'Having a fag outside. Trying to kill herself. No dear, at Christmas time I'm just relieved I haven't got a family,' states Mrs Gartree flatly.

Fourteen

Good King Wenceslas looked out,
On the feast of Stephen . . .

Unlike Mrs Gartree the cook Clover Moon does
have a family, so she has to have a Christmas. The
two go together like peaches and cream, like holly
and ivy, like sage and onion.

Only this particular Christmas is turning out
to be worse than all the others she has ever
experienced in her life. Everyone thinks she is
being neurotic but she's not as neurotic as they
like to imagine, certainly not as neurotic as the
poor soul on the radio, the caller who shrieks into
the void, 'Thank you for being there, oh God,
thank you for being there. I don't know what I'd
have done without you and your reassuring voice.
I'm an old-age pensioner and live all alone miles
from anywhere and my roof has just caved in.'

'Well, that's what we're here for, my lover,' says
the DJ chirpily, 'and can I just ask the rest of our
listeners one more time to please, please, stop
jamming our lines for news. We'll give it as soon
as we receive it. Only telephone if you have useful
information relating to the immediate emergency.
And another thing, would you all mind not lifting

your receivers in order to check you are still connected. This is causing problems for the telephone engineers.'

Visions of listeners wandering nervously past their telephones, eyeing them warily before pouncing to check, waft bizarrely over the airwaves.

'This is just like the war,' Granny murmurs comfortably. 'We used to huddle round the wireless in the semi-darkness, just like this, waiting for news.'

'The batteries are going,' says Erin. 'Turn it over to Radio One while there's still time.'

'Don't be ridiculous, Erin, we need to hear the forecast, we have to know what's coming our way. People are getting killed . . .' And Jonna looks knowingly at Fergus, who twiddles the radio knob. Jonna thinks of the body freezing outside in the barn. At least high up in the muck-spreader the rats are unlikely to reach it.

'The emergency services are still working at full stretch but with further disruptive weather expected they are fighting a losing battle. Many remoter villages are already completely cut off and navy helicopters are ferrying the sick and injured to hospital. Eighty thousand homes are now without electricity this Christmas Day, but the progress of the services is being hampered by the ferocity of the blizzard, snowdrifts and fallen trees.'

'Hopeless,' groans Fergus, shaking a mournful head. 'Absolutely hopeless and no end in sight. I've just had to let three thousand litres of milk run away, it could break your heart.'

'It's the greenhouse effect, it has to be,' says

Diana, pulling at her earrings in the way she does when she's nervous. 'We're going to have to get used to extremes all the time now.'

'I've never known worse,' says Granny. 'Never.'

Clover has a headache. She raises a fragile hand towards the source of the pain. Tension. Stress. She's covered with bruises and her mouth stings. Spiritless and withdrawn, she sees how Fergus's attention jumps from one subject to another like a man in turmoil. Even one eyebrow has started to twitch, he's got so much on his plate. The last thing he wants to hear are Clover's dark accusations. 'You're always imagining something,' he'd said earlier, dabbing her mouth with salve.

'Dammit, I am not under some morbid illusion,' she'd mumbled back, voice high and rough with anger. 'Christ, it hurts. Your mother has finally cracked completely, she put that lethal stuff in that glass deliberately to hurt me.'

'Clover! Calm down and listen! It was an accident, simple as that. No-one in their right mind would do such a thing, certainly not poor Mother. Give me one good reason why she should! Now do be quiet. Hell, for God's sake, don't let her hear you.'

Clover can be embarrassing at times once she gets these bees in her bonnet, and over the last couple of years what had been an endearing trait had become an increasingly worrying trend. He watched his wife standing there in the kitchen, carefully inhaling and exhaling, struggling for the patience to deal with his complacency. She closed her eyes, she dabbed at her swollen mouth with a cloth wrapped in ice, glaring at him as if it was his

187

fault. She'd composed her face before moving back to the sitting room where the children were waiting to open the presents. He'd watched her. Over the weeks he had watched her becoming more and more nervous as Christmas drew near. It's something to do with Christmas that's causing this heightened persecution complex, must be to do with the tension, and the weather doesn't help.

And nor, of course, does poor Granny.

But Jonna is not quite so sure. He sees Clover with different eyes, not a neurotic, certainly not an emotional ruin. At their secret assignations Clover is strong, confident and assured, a different woman from the one he sees when he visits the farm and she's battling against herself in the kitchen. He prefers the Clover he knows and loves, he's afraid of the incompetent woman who lies on the sofa, bruised and hurt with that anxious look in her eyes. Jonna keeps at his best for her but at home Clover gives up.

Jonna smiles inside. They must organize another weekend, preferably some time in February, a cold and miserable month. Yes, the thought of a weekend with Clover makes Jonna feel brighter already. How remarkably easy it is to lie. He's often pleased and surprised by the ease with which he can hoodwink Diana, a woman normally so shrewd and astute. His weekend assignments he arranges with ease. Perhaps Diana is glad of the freedom, happy to get him and his phobias out of the house for a while.

In an atmosphere stiff with unease they sit in the gloom of this twilight morning contemplating their presents. The children are bright-eyed, ten years younger, childhood magic still lives on in this crackling, papery side of Christmas. The wonder might have gone, the innocence certainly has, but for a while the children are children again, trying not to open their parcels too greedily, acceptable in the under-fives but distressing at any age later than that.

Will the twins be pleased with the shotguns? Diana persuaded Jonna to give in to them this year but it went against the grain. Will the girls like their skis? They are off to Verbiers in March, but if the weather improves outside they'll be able to ski on the steep three acres where William died . . . that's if Granny wouldn't be upset . . .

Diana catches Clover's eye but Clover just frowns. 'Let me get you a real drink,' says Diana briskly. 'It might act as an anaesthetic, deaden your sore mouth a bit. And shall I have another look at the turkey while I'm up?'

Clover nods and looks pathetic. 'Only don't keep opening the Aga door,' she manages to lisp. 'Or else the dinner will never cook.'

Fergus watches Diana's exit with a gleam of approval in his eye. She looks good in the dress Jonna gave her this morning. The soft wool fabric strains against her breasts, her waist is small and her hips curve appealingly. Her lustrous hair tumbles from the knot on her head and tendrils of curls touch her face. Diana could be a model, she has style, and Fergus clenches his fists. Not only is she a beautiful woman but a sensible, competent individual not given to the kinds of sulks and traumas Clover has suffered of late. Funny how fate takes a hand, how, even though he went to school with Jonna and knew him from early childhood, he ended up with Diana and Fergus chose Clover. If it wasn't for their wives he and Jonna would probably not have kept in touch.

Oh yes, Jonna believes he has more of an intellectual bent than Fergus, he's better read and he often makes harmless jokes about the difference in lifestyles, referring a little too often to his university education. In his turn, Fergus maliciously gives Jonna the most arduous jobs around the farm so he can stand back and smile and take over. He likes to see Jonna inept, enjoys his nervousness around cows. These two men are in competition as their women are not. Does Jonna still worry about Fergus's relationship with Diana? Both men harbour suspicions that seem to increase over the years, become more threatening with age, not less.

'The trouble with you two,' Diana and Clover sometimes say after a session of secrets, hours in discussion about nothing, 'is that you are both too serious.'

Fergus considers this a compliment. Serious, fine, but stupid – never. Does Clover secretly see him as stupid? This fear has always dismayed him. His wife is clever, has done well in her job, could have done better, she always says, if she hadn't got stuck with a farmer.

He never intended to hold her back, to stand in her way, to make life difficult. When they first married it didn't seem at all like that.

He could have chosen a university education like Jonna if it hadn't been for the farm. His teachers had encouraged him, but how could he let Father down like that? In spite of the lack of books around the farm, in spite of the fact that thumbed copies of *Farmers' World*, manuals and pamphlets from the Min of Ag were the only written material to find their way into the house, Fergus excelled at school, but there's no point in looking back, a stupid and profitless exercise. Father, a bull-necked, strong and handsome man, was never impressed by exam results. 'What's worth knowing you learn by instinct, you don't find it in books,' Father said.

Father was always the boss and Mother supported him completely. A good wife? A good mother? Fergus wouldn't know, he saw so little of her. It's different now with all the latest machinery, but Mother and Father built up the farm with their toil and their sweat, by giving no inch to anyone and owing no-one.

'Your mother and father were both too strong, they made you weak,' Clover told him witheringly once and Fergus has never forgotten, neither has he forgiven her. Following in Father's footsteps was a strength, not a weakness. His destiny always lay with the land, he turned his back on the life that he wanted and accepted his fate because it was in his nature to do so. He is not the rebellious type. Oh, he sometimes thinks about freedom and the way it might have been, but then who doesn't?

Jonna stirs these feelings up, makes Fergus resentful. Back in the old days it was so simple, Jonna was merely someone to play with.

Divorce? Like suicide it's an option, and therefore lurks in the subconscious. But Fergus has never desired a permanent break from Clover, has he? The possibility has hardly entered his head because a divorce from Clover would mean losing half of his farm. Like royalty, you lose a wife and your kingdom falls round about you.

So no, Fergus Moon has never seriously considered divorce, just as he has never seriously contemplated suicide.

He is not that sort of man. He is stable.

Unlike Clover, who has, at times, seriously considered both options, but then Clover is an emotional wreck, behaving extremely foolishly at times as her best friend, Diana, is always telling her. Fergus is the stabilizing influence in poor Clover's life and how sad it is, thinks Fergus, that Mother and Clover have never hit it off.

The humble voice of a vicar comes over the radio saying prayers for Christmas and introducing carol number fifty-one to an eager congregation in a poorly attended church that has never been chosen before. You can tell. There is an amateur echo. They have failed to get the speakers quite right.

Jonna, concerned, leans over and asks Clover, 'Are you all right?'

Those whom God hath joined together let no man put asunder. Clover, gazing back thoughtfully at Jonna, huddled here on the sofa with a gin in her hand, remembers how she thought of those words the first time she cheated on Fergus, and it had been that churchy voice, so firm, so forbidding, that added the spice to the venture, that thrilling touch of fear that made it so awful and so good. That voice and Jonna's hands, smooth, clean and delicate. Sensitive hands.

'You're smiling. Good. You must be feeling better.'

But under her breath Clover whispers, 'Jonna, I need to talk to you later. Alone.'

Under cover of the crackly carol Jonna says, 'Sure, at the first opportunity,' and feels his spirits rise almost to Christmas heights.

'Come on! Come on! How long is it going to be before we're allowed to open our presents?'

'You know what you've got, Dan, so what's the hurry?'

'Knowing doesn't make it less exciting,' says tall, good-looking Daniel, with his dark curling hair unbrushed but still silky. 'It's just a sod the weather's so bad so we're not going to be able to use them. As soon as it's clear let's get out the trap and shoot down the valley.'

'I doubt there'll be much chance of that this week.'

The boys chose the guns themselves. They went with Fergus the last time they stayed; back in the summer he took them to choose. So by rights these are Fergus's presents despite the fact that Jonna paid, and it will be Fergus who teaches his sons how to shoot, who takes them with him, man and boys, with their boots and their waterproofs. Jonna will be present, of course, trailing behind as usual and laughing at his own ineptness. Fergus will hit the clays every time, it is he the twins will emulate.

When they were boys Jonna and Fergus were close. They used to go out with a light at night after rabbits. Since those days Jonna has grown away from the country, grown away from Fergus.

Could Jonna be jealous, not of Fergus but of his own two sons? The other way round, in fact. The other way round indeed.

Fifteen

Ding dong merrily on high,
In Heaven the bells are ringing . . .

Alarm bells ring in the farmhouse tonight. They
could be any normal family, thinks Clover, knowing they're not. But there is peace in the very
idea.

When Clover and Fergus moved into the farmhouse five years ago they brought their own
furniture with them, threw out the old stuff that
Violet and William had used. And they installed
central heating, redecorated, knocked two rooms
into one and, of course, added the annex. So it's
quite different now from how it was.

Is that easier for Granny? Or does this make it
worse? Does she resent it, or consider them insensitive? And how can anyone tell?

The old farmhouse was unfashionable, full of
serviceable things, nothing there for aesthetic
reasons. Well, Violet and William had more to do
than spend their time sitting round indoors contemplating their navels. On the rare occasions
when they did sit down they stayed in the kitchen.
William's chair is still here beside the Aga and
sometimes Fergus sits in it but never, ever Clover.

And the carpets didn't go from wall to wall like they do now, there were rugs over old lino. In the sitting room the useful Park Ray has been replaced by an enormous copper-fronted fireplace. They reopened the fireplace to its original size, the size it was when the range was still there. They painted the beams and stripped the shutters, they filled the room with lamps, they covered the walls with pictures.

You can hardly see any of it because of the darkness. Now there are just lots of shadows and a presence – not William's.

Granny frowns.

'Don't you like your Magimix, Mother? It is what you asked us for.'

'I can't think why,' mutters Clover under her breath.

'Yes, I do like it, Fergus dear, and I'm sorry, I was miles away.' Another inappropriate present. What a complete waste of money and effort.

The twins are ecstatic about their guns. Erin and Polly are sporting extraordinary bobble hats with massive tassels which make them look like Christmas helpers, give them a sharp and elfin look. But their faces are flushed and happy and they adore their skis.

The presents pile up on the floor, all the gifts from friends and relations are here. Higher and higher goes the pile of paper in the centre of the room until Granny, tucked over there in the corner, looks as though she is disappearing.

Fergus wears his new padded waistcoat, but it's dark so Jonna can't read his new book. Diana exclaims at the beauty of the ring in the velvet box while Clover inspects the lock on her journal.

196

Dare she keep a journal? Under the circumstances?

And risk anyone discovering the truth.

'Granny? Are you still there? You're almost completely cut off by paper.'

What fresh hell is this?

'Mummy says you're adenoidal.'

Violet should have listened to Kate. She knew where the rumour came from.

Sheena believed that Violet enjoyed having earache. Laying on the agony she called it, My Lady of Sorrows ploy again. But the pain was hardly bearable and those times she missed Mummy most, weeping into her pillow for the loss she felt while the pain in her ear plunged her into such a dark world there was nothing between her and the moon.

'What a fuss! What a fusser! Kate gets earache too, you know, and she doesn't make a drama like this.'

Relentless daggers of agony. And at those times Violet said little, asked for little because she couldn't. Once Sheena made her get up and go to school. All morning she rocked at her desk with her head down, sobbing, until the janitor took her home.

'Attention-seeking all the time,' said Sheena, pale and furious, when Violet arrived wrapped in a school blanket. 'I can't think why David doesn't whip out those tonsils and be done with it.'

Violet stayed home from school on the day Daddy planned to come home early to remove her adenoids and her tonsils. Violet stayed at home and Kate was envious.

Not only did she stay at home, listening to Sheena's car pull out bearing the disgruntled Kate, but she was allowed, for once, to stay in bed. So she listened to their departure from the cosy comfort of her covers, knowing it was cold outside. Hah.

But to her chagrin she wasn't allowed any breakfast. And she'd had to go without supper the previous evening. Life was not quite so perfect, and she was frightened.

Gwendoline came in to light the fire, bearing an armful of towels. She started by moving the ornaments from Violet's chest of drawers, including the musical box from her bedside table. She packed them all in a cardboard box. Everything went, the shepherdess, the blackberry dish, the cane basket and the china shoe. 'Not my musical box,' called Violet. 'Gwendoline, don't take that! Give that to me, I have to keep it beside me.'

Fear made her watch, eagle-eyed, every sinister thing that Gwendoline did. Daddy had tried to explain to her exactly what he was going to do but she didn't believe him entirely, especially the bit about no pain. She suspected there were secrets here, secrets of a grown-up kind, and if there were it would be the indiscreet, gossipy Gwendoline who would give them away. So Violet watched and listened carefully.

'I'm doing what I've been told to do,' said Gwendoline huffily. 'As is my wont.'

'But why are you moving my things?'

'Germs. A sterile environment. Doctor's orders.' And Gwendoline shook out the sheets of newspaper in order to wrap the knick-knacks, stuffing them into the heart of the box with such enormous energy you'd think she was claiming them for herself.

'But why?'

Gwendoline, goaded into answering, repeated herself impatiently. 'Germs, I told you. We can't have germs lurking where there's blood and open wounds. And all these bits and pieces are bound to be riddled with germs.'

Violet fell silent as she watched Gwendoline's bent back, the crisscross of her apron straps where they came together and buttoned. She lit the fire with the quick, deft movements of the highly experienced, adding a lump of coal here, another there, whenever she spotted a likely flame, while with the other hand she swept the tiny hearth with a silver brush from downstairs.

'Daddy says there'll hardly be any blood.'

Gwendoline stopped what she was doing, looked over her shoulder and gave a pitying smile. 'Well, perhaps the towels I've lugged all the way up here are just for effect, then, madam.' She creaked as she rose to her full height, shook her apron and regarded the patient with a knowing eye.

'Daddy says it'll just be like going to sleep and when I wake up with a sore throat I can have as much ice cream as I like and everything will be over.' There was a challenge in Violet's voice, daring the maid to say otherwise, willing her to rise to the bait and say more . . . the real truth, perhaps.

'Well, far be it from me,' said Gwendoline. 'Daddy knows best in this house. Daddy can do no wrong. We all know that.'

She bustled about the room, laying out towels

on the surface of the chest of drawers, sniffing them first, for freshness.

'Yes,' said Violet, beginning to crow. 'He told me there's nothing to worry about. He does this operation all the time, he's done it so often he could do it with his eyes closed. Daddy's a very intelligent person, everybody says so.'

'I daresay. But you know what clever did.'

'What did clever do?' Violet rose on one arm in order to watch Gwendoline better.

'Come on! Up you get! Out of there, and sit yourself down on the chair. I've got to make this bed with clean sheets before they all arrive. It does seem a shame, bearing in mind the mess they'll no doubt be in afterwards.'

'You didn't tell me what clever did.'

'He tripped on his own shoelaces,' said Gwendoline, puffing and bending over the bed, flapping the sheet like a huge bird's wing so that Violet felt her loose hair move in the turbulent gusts.

'Well, Daddy never makes mistakes!' She thought about this positive statement, she questioned it in her worried mind. He'd married Sheena, hadn't he? If that was not a mistake, what was?

'Everyone makes mistakes,' said Gwendoline firmly.

'Surgeons can't afford to.'

'Ah, that's where you're wrong, m'dear. And the easier the operation is, the less they're likely to concentrate. That's when accidents happen.'

'You don't know that.'

Gwendoline sniffed. 'No, I don't. What could I know about it?' She patted and neatened, the flinging done. 'But my sister certainly knows.'

200

'How does your sister know?' Violet climbed back into bed. It was cold, but she loved having it made up around her, feeling the weight of each blanket as it fell upon her with a heavy puff, the tightness as she was tucked in, the bed forming around her.

'My sister lost her youngest, God blesser,' said Gwendoline darkly, picking up the used sheets and tying them up in a bundle. 'Margery would be, let's see, fifteen now, if she'd lived. But she died when she was only five, having her tonsils out on the kitchen table. My sister never got over it. You don't when you lose a child.'

'But it's different now,' said Violet. But already she felt like a sacrifice and her clean, cold bed was a slab, the top sheet a shroud.

'If that's what they say I'm sure you're right.'

'That's what Daddy says.'

'A messy business in those days,' Gwendoline went on, blithely impervious to the effect she was having. 'And of course out in the sticks where my sister lived there was no proper anaesthetic and no clean surfaces. The chickens used to live in the house . . .'

'It's totally different now.'

'I'm sure you're right,' said Gwendoline, with a quick, dismissive smile. 'I'm sure you have nothing to worry about. And one thing's for certain, whatever it's like it'll soon be over. God willing.'

But what if God wasn't willing? What if God wanted her to die? Violet was alone all morning compiling an endless list of sins, most of them involving Sheena. She watched the birds on the roof outside her window, she watched them and she envied them, wishing she could fly like that, fly away from here and never come back. Daddy would not have considered removing her tonsils if it wasn't for Sheena. Sheena had made this happen with her vicious naggings and complaints. How relieved Sheena will feel when Violet's skin goes deathly cold.

She tried to read a book but she couldn't concentrate. She flopped her velour rabbit around on the pillow, watching the way his ears fell, sometimes right, sometimes left and sometimes still upright. If they fell to the right she would die, if they fell to the left she would live. They stayed straight up in the air, which suggested some place in between. She shook him hard. His ears fell to the right this time – but that wouldn't count. She knew she had made that happen.

Once she dropped to merciful sleep and woke up believing her ordeal to be over. But no, the fire glowed just the same, the towels were ranked in their pristine piles and her bed was the same shape as when Gwendoline had made it. When it was really all over the fire would probably be dying, the towels would be gone to the wash and maybe her bed would be different. Rumpled. Bloody. Empty. Violet turned over to see Mummy regarding her sadly from the photograph Gwendoline left behind. Rueful, knowing, but powerless to help her child.

Then she heard Daddy's car on the gravel. The butchers had arrived.

She'd not been aware that her room was so small, but she was usually the only one in it. This afternoon was different. There was Daddy, the anaesthetist and Daddy's nurse. And Sheena. And a nasty medical smell.

The smell was not only in their gowns but in their hair and on their faces. Their hands were big and rubber and powerful. Even Sheena wore a big white apron. Could they see her at all? She was small lying there.

'Now just relax, old thing, and this will soon be over, no more earache after today,' said Daddy, sounding like a liar. He unpacked a sealed box and pulled on his stretchy gloves. He took a green face mask from the pack and started to hook it round his ear. He paused, looked at Dr Wilson and gave him a nod.

Dr Wilson was Daddy's anaesthetist, a virtual stranger to Violet, and she tried not to look at him at all. Nor did she look at Daddy or Sheena. Instead she turned her face to one side, opened her eyes again and stared hard at Mummy.

'Now I'm just putting some drops of chloroform on this towel,' Dr Wilson said in his crackly voice, 'and then I'm going to place the towel very gently against your nose and you are going to drop off into a beautiful deep sleep. When you wake up you'll be able to tell me what you dreamed about. So I want you to count up to twenty very slowly with me, slowly, taking deep breaths . . . deep breaths . . . see how far you can count . . .'

This was a plot! *They were killing her!* She caught Sheena's eye and she knew it! Sheena saw this as an ideal way to rid herself of her obnoxious step-child and had influenced Daddy somehow. She would choke to death if she didn't get air, the smell was thick, cloying, intolerable. She couldn't bear the towel on her face, she was drowning in green dreams, held under the bath water until the bubbles reached all the way to her lungs.

'NO!' screamed Violet, fighting wildly, ripping away the towel and struggling to get up . . . She was nearly there, one foot almost free of the bed, when Sheena caught her.

'NOOO!' She fought like a trapped rat, clawing, biting, tearing. 'DON'T DO THIS TO ME!'

Horrible! Horrible. Sheena and that nurse. One on either side.

Holding her down.

Smothering her.

Grasping hands.

Squeezing, pinching.

Violet couldn't fight them. And that look on Sheena's porcelain face, smiling through sharp teeth, excited eyes sparking. Violet's head was still free but the towel came down, blotting out the world for ever with its baggy clamminess. Making everything hollow and heavy. Dr Wilson's face came down behind it, yellow-eyed and anxious under his evil mask. Saying again, 'Count with me, Violet, there's a good girl, count with me . . . one, two, three, four, five . . . There's a good girl, there's a good girl, there's a good girl.'

She thought she was still waiting. She opened her eyes warily and looked round the room. The towels had gone and the fire was dying. The birds had left the roof. It was dusk. How long would it be before they came for her? Kate would be home from school by now and she didn't want her to be around when they . . .

And then she swallowed, caught herself, and attempted to do it again. There were razor blades stuck in her throat. The room reeked of anaesthetic. She tried to call but could not make a sound. There was a towel under her head, pink with watery saliva, not crimson, not thick with the sludgy, livery pieces she'd feared. Someone had opened a window, the curtains were blowing and she felt a cool breeze on her face. She lifted one arm, tried a leg. *She was still alive!* They had done it to her but she had survived. Violet lived!

Mummy must have saved her.

Violet wept with pain and relief. But Sheena had nearly won, had seen her cry, seen her terror, conspired with Daddy to render her helpless. Violet's teeth chattered with shock and she shuddered with rigours of futile rage against the woman who held her down so that her father could come, white-coated and steely-fingered, to cut her throat and inflict his pain.

To do what he did to Sheena at night? Oh yes, she'd heard them.

Carefully she turned over. There on the table beside the bed between Violet and Mummy's picture was the little glass jar with the screwtop lid, the kind Sheena pickled onions in. Inside were Violet's tonsils and adenoids, preserved in alcohol so she could keep them for ever, Daddy had said. Round-eyed, Violet stared through the jar at the watery, distorted photograph of her mother. Inside the jar was herself, reduced to blooded matter, the remains of herself, an offering. She wondered who had placed the jar there.

This is how she would be if she let them have their way. This is how Sheena wanted her and she must have placed the jar there between mother and daughter to show them both what she planned to do.

Slowly Violet rolled over and picked up the musical box she had hidden under the bed during one of Gwendoline's absences. She tried not to swallow because it hurt too much. She lifted the lid and let the tune come. *'Roses whisper goodnight 'neath the silvery light.'* She closed her eyes, comforted, and lay flat on the pillow, the towel rough under her head.

'This is the last time, Chickadee. They won't hurt you again, I promise you that. The time is coming, it's almost here. Wait and listen, Chickadee. Mummy will tell you when.

'Remember that Mummy loves you and will never, never leave you.

'Just do what Mummy tells you and Sheena will never succeed.'

Chop chop chop.

Granny lays her scrawny hand on the shiny new Magimix she will never use and says to Fergus, 'It's very nice, dear. Just what I wanted. It will be very useful indeed. Maybe, before I leave, someone could read the instructions and show me how to use it.'

Sixteen

I saw three ships come sailing in,
On Christmas Day, on Christmas Day . . .

'Three cheers for Mrs Gartree! Hip hip . . .'
  'Hooray!'
  'Hip hip . . .'
  'Hooray!'
The cook rises rheumatically, uneven as a dumpling, sweating profusely and bubbling with a thin wooden spoon in her hand. The Christmas pudding refused to flame, not long enough to get it from hatch to table, more brandy was the obvious answer, blowing on it was not. The effort has worn her out and Hilda her helper, for once without a fag in her hand, only a stub behind her ear, hovers behind her superior, bright eyes shining under this little bit of acclaim.

The separate tables have been pushed together for this special occasion. It is essential that nobody feel left out, or lonely. The elderly can be very spiteful, Miss Gleeson knows this full well, look at Father. They have their little cliques, they run their little spite campaigns as much as anyone else. But they lack the patience of everyone else and no longer bother to pretend.

It is a depleted little group who dine in the hotel today because those with friends and relatives are spending the day with them. Some have gone for as long as a week, and Mrs Masters is away for a fortnight, staying with her daughter in Hull.

Long before the start of the meal Valerie decided to close the curtains against the violent weather. They are heavy and lined and red. The dining room is a red room with a livid maroon carpet. The cranberry sauce, if spilled, would match it. The turkey legs are much the same hue, and Mr Tanner's speckled nose. Not that it isn't seasonal outside because it certainly is. No Christmas card could compete with such whiteness, no brand of washing powder get near it, but there's something wrong about it this year. It is not the soft dreamy snow of innocence and purity, amiable to council snow ploughs and boots with rubber soles, but persistent, gale-blown and lethal with a sting of ice in its frenzied tail. Behind the thick curtains you can still hear it like gritty claws against the windows, biting in all its malevolence as it clings, as it sticks.

Surely Miss Bates isn't out in that, under a hedge or in some ditch, and if she is, and if she is, is she alive or dead?

The Tarbucks opted not to stay. 'Not this year, Valerie, we were here all day last year and we need some time to ourselves. You know what they say,' quipped Jason Tarbuck, his whisky breath fermenting the air, 'all work and no play makes Jack . . .' And they presented her with a 'little something, just a gesture'. A box of hankies with a V on the corners.

What are those two villains up to?

She was relieved to see them go. The atmosphere is always tense when the Tarbucks are on the premises. And in these worrying circumstances she can hardly look them in the eye, especially now she harbours the suspicions she harbours, yet nothing definite to go on.

'What nonsense, Valerie,' she hears the jarring voice of Father. Is it really nonsense?

In paper hat and plastic pinny (she will eat later at Father's if she can get through the snow), Valerie's face is flushed and shiny from the exertion of waiting at tables. At least pushed together like this there is not so much walking involved. Thank goodness for her sensible shoes. Jason Tarbuck stayed long enough to carve the enormous turkey. The electric carving knife he insisted on using grated horribly against bone as he sought to utilize every scrap. Valerie feared there would be some dangerous splinters. And meanwhile his wife eked out the complimentary wine – a Safeways offer, quite nice.

Mr Tanner still does his exuberant best, reading out the cracker jokes in his loudest, most jocular Christmas voice but nobody understands them, there's a tendency to seek a deeper meaning, an inability to believe anything in print could be so crass. But the ritual calls for raucous laughter and so they attempt to mimic the sound. Once they are laughing and the wine does its work some of the peals turn real and there's every chance this ordeal will turn into success. It would be useful if the meal could linger into the afternoon, to save the stress of more forced entertainment. Donna is coming in to help out and she's always chirpy, she does mimes to pass the time, she plays chords on her guitar and the livelier members will sing along. Protest songs, most likely. Not the most appropriate, but Donna's into sixties stuff. Miss Gleeson would not like to see another afternoon of slumped lethargy, that descent into everyday life that can be a threat after Christmas lunch, some in the lounge, some in the conservatory, slippers off, mouths open, nobody particularly enjoying themselves.

She'd often considered asking the Tarbucks if she could buy a hotel dog.

No, somehow this jollity must extend until after cabaret time tonight or Valerie will feel that she's failed.

And then of course there's Boxing Day.

Miss Kessel looks pale. She is quieter than usual and not joining in with her normal gentle enthusiasm. Preoccupied, she fiddles with the keyring that came in her cracker, first crushing it in her hand and then drooping it from her fingers. The smile on her face has been carefully put there. Anyone can see it means nothing.

'What must you know to be an auctioneer?' goes on the stoic Mr Tanner. But his cigarette has fallen from the ashtray and is burning a hole in the paper cloth.

Everybody pretends to ponder.

'Lots!'

He takes another sip of wine. 'What horse can you put your shirt on and make sure you get it back?'

'A clothes horse.'

So this is the level they're on this Christmas afternoon as Miss Kessel rises, steadies herself with one hand and moves to Miss Gleeson to murmur timidly, 'I must . . . I must just have a word with you.'

All the documents which, in her panic, Miss Kessel had pounced on and hidden are now on Miss Gleeson's desk. She spreads them out and reads them, and all the while her unease increases. Not only does it increase, but becomes more exaggerated than ever, made massive as the truth is revealed.

No wonder the Tarbucks were able to use Miss Bates like a pawn for their own dubious reasons. They plucked her from a mental hospital that was closing down, took her in, how ideal! How very convenient for the pair. Miss Bates has been a virtual prisoner in the two years since her release because how could she possibly leave Happy Haven, how could she find an alternative home with such an incriminating tale of woe dragging along behind her?

And the poor creature, so unused to the ways of the world after her years of containment, muted and battered by experiences so ghastly the mind can only boggle, submitted and obeyed. The Tarbucks gave her her freedom, gave her care and a home, she must have regarded them as her saviours and gratefully did all they asked of her.

Eventually Miss Gleeson falls back in her chair. 'So you deliberately held all this information back from the police?'

Miss Kessel's eyes drop as if she's in court. She answers with a quick, 'I did.'

'Because you were afraid she'd be turned out of here if anyone ever found out?'

211

'That's why I did it, yes.'

Miss Gleeson leans forward once again to stare at the notice of release from some institution called Parkvale, signed by the sturdy, unmistakably childish hand of Jason Tarbuck himself. By what authority? She glances towards Miss Kessel, who has obviously gathered up all these papers without studying them properly. They are still in a large brown envelope. Miss Gleeson sorts through the paying-in stubs once again and, yes, there they are, regular as clockwork, payments into Miss Bates's account from the Tarbucks, sometimes a little more than usual, sometimes less, cunningly done, because everyone knows that the catering trade goes through its seasonal ups and downs. The payments over these last two years, nefarious gains from shady dealings, mount up considerably despite the hefty withdrawals which follow. Miss Bates has a tidy sum put away. Another few years and she'd be a respectably wealthy woman.

Laundering money. But why would the Tarbucks dispose of Miss Bates and leave any behind? Miss Gleeson almost asks this puzzling question out loud, it's Miss Kessel's worried face that clamps her lips just in time. Perhaps there is a will somewhere. Perhaps there are investments. Perhaps those vast withdrawals of cash passed straight back into the Tarbucks' hands to be used to open some secret account under some other name. In Jersey. The possibilities are numerous but the facts are hard to pin down.

Something has happened to poor Miss Bates and somehow the Tarbucks are involved.

'Oh, what shall we do?' wails poor Miss Kessel, in a voice worried and small, and Miss Gleeson, deep in her twisted ponderings, has almost forgotten she's here. 'And now that I've told you the truth, if Miss Bates does come back will you put her away again? Will you inform the Tarbucks? Will you snitch on us both and tell them where she's been all her life? Oh dear . . . I'm a nark.'

But Miss Gleeson shakes her head. 'Of course I won't tell them anything. Why would I? It's no skin off my nose. Miss Bates, in spite of her past, is now as sane as you or I. Well, isn't she?'

But Miss Kessel's eyes drop once again and she stares down at her shoes. 'I don't know. I truly don't know.'

'You sound uncertain. What do you mean?'

Miss Kessel is uncomfortable. She shifts in her chair. She plays with the keyring still in her hand. 'Things she told me. Things she did. Oh, I don't know, you start to look for things once you find out . . . And sharing a room with someone, well, you become very close. There's her visits to that medium for a start.'

'Lots of people believe in spiritualism. That's not to say they're out of their tree.'

'I know. I know. I used to tell myself, I used to say she would be peculiar just living in an institution for so long, she wouldn't be quite the same as you or I, would she? She couldn't be, not after all that time.'

'Miss Kessel, what are you getting at?'

'Well, that story she made up about stuffing animals for some London museum. That wasn't true, of course. I know she needed a story as a cover but why tell anyone that? I wouldn't. Would you? Something like that just wouldn't occur to me. And then her attitude was definitely odd about finding her step-sister, that's what took her to the medium in the first place. Apparently she believed that somebody from the dead would show her where her sister was.'

'Well, if you're a believer in that sort of thing you might well convince yourself . . .'

'But,' Miss Kessel hesitates, takes a breath and continues with effort, 'she didn't love her sister, Miss Gleeson, there was nothing like that. The way she spoke, the expressions she used, she didn't love her sister at all. I would say that she hated her.'

'Are you sure? A sister she hadn't seen for years? Why would she waste her hatred on anyone as obscure as that?'

Miss Kessel finally makes a decision and draws a photograph from her pocket. When she passes it across the table she keeps her eyes firmly on Miss Gleeson. Miss Gleeson holds it at a distance, keeping her face well under control. The photograph is ragged at the edges, creased with white folds across the centre. Two little girls in a garden on a glorious summer day. Hollyhocks rise up behind them and the borders are neatly trimmed. Both children are pretty and smiling. One wears a dress with a smocked bodice and puffed short sleeves, the darker child wears a kilt and a blouse. The manageress catches her breath, purses her lips and stares from the photograph across to Miss Kessel. Two lights shine through the photograph where someone has put out one child's eyes.

'Horrible. *This is horrible.* You think this is Miss Bates and her sister? And she's kept it with her all these years? Dear God, Miss Bates must have despised her. But why would she try to trace someone she must once have loathed with such intensity that she actually defaced her picture in this terrible way?'

'I haven't a clue. She only mentioned her step-sister once, never talked about her again, which disappointed me rather because I imagined that finding some natural place in the world would have helped Miss Bates with her insecurity. But you're right, Miss Gleeson, and this is precisely what worries me so. If she detested her sister, why did she come to Torquay especially to find her?'

'People are hard to fathom, it's true,' sighs Miss Gleeson, bemused. She does not feel comfortable, and here in her office, normally a haven of peace and tranquillity, the wind still wails against the windows with an unnerving intensity. Why the hell doesn't it stop, and when will this wretched snow stop falling? When will life get back to normal, and what is it that makes Miss Gleeson so anxious? The effects of Christmas, the weather and Father thrown together like some grotesque parcel?

Miss Kessel seems eager to talk, in the way of the recently bereaved. Trying to conjure back the person as if it's as easy as that, attempting to paint them back into the picture and blot out that terrible empty space. 'Sometimes I'd walk into the bedroom and find her chatting away to herself,' she says. 'Pacing the floor, wringing her hands. She'd stop when she saw me, of course. She'd stop and wear that bewildered smile, she'd sit on her bed and watch me. Or she'd pretend to read. But I knew she was still pacing inside, she wanted me to leave the room so she could start doing it again.'

There's a pause as Miss Kessel remembers. 'And in bed at night when she thought I was asleep, I'd wake up sometimes and hear her crying, moaning, sobbing, muttering, thrashing backwards and forwards as if some demon was trying to escape. I was never sure whether to put on the light and sit up and offer to talk things over, but I didn't. I thought, this is one of the drawbacks of sharing a room and Miss Bates is entitled to think she has privacy even if she doesn't. So I kept quiet and turned over, tried to get back to sleep. But, Miss Gleeson, I'm afraid that there were times when she went on all night like that.' Miss Kessel, badly agitated, twiddles her cracker keyring, a bull terrier on a plastic tag.

The old lady looks exhausted after that abnormal outburst. She says limply, 'And I am so very concerned. She wasn't completely right, you see, not really. But I couldn't speak out, not then, not knowing that if the Tarbucks found out she'd be homeless.'

Miss Gleeson can't help a wry smile. How cunning, how devious. The Tarbucks could manipulate such a poor confused creature at will. But Miss Kessel's original question still stands: what are they going to do? What is Miss Gleeson going to do, knowing the truth of the matter?

So the telephone is an intrusion, an insensitive visitor barging in uninvited. Wearily Miss Gleeson picks it up.

'Happy Haven, how may I help you?'

'Valerie?'

'Oh, Father.' She raises a tired eyebrow, she glances at Miss Kessel and whispers, 'Just a moment.'

'Of course.' Miss Kessel quickly leaves the room, sadness and betrayal in every footstep. For can she really trust Miss Gleeson, who is not one of the residents? Has she let her best friend down? For Miss Bates is her friend, despite her odd little tendencies, and she just couldn't keep mum any longer. She had to share the burden, but now she has she feels no better, no more relieved, just a traitor.

She had felt far nobler, far more heroic last night after the Tarbucks' inquisition. She'd not given a thing away. She'd felt like a resistance fighter in front of SS interrogators. She had not buckled or given way in spite of the fact they'd gone on and on, with Jason Tarbuck stamping about and continuously asking, 'But where are all her papers? The police took only a handful away according to Miss Gleeson, so where are the rest? Everyone has documentation and you lived with the woman in this small room, you must know where she kept hers.'

'No,' Miss Kessel insisted. 'Miss Bates was a most private person. I never knew where she kept those things. Perhaps she used the bank, maybe she used to carry them with her and they're still in her handbag.'

And then he veered to the other tack. Jason Tarbuck was a bully and so was his voice. 'But she must have confided in you. Told you about herself. And yet you insist she didn't, you say you know nothing about her. That's damn hard to believe and the police will certainly find that suspicious when they take up their enquiries again after Christmas is over.'

'She'll probably be back by then.' Miss Kessel kept her chin up. She eyed the proprietor hard, refusing to be intimidated. 'We don't know for certain that anything disastrous has happened to Miss Bates, there's no way we can be sure.' And all the while, ridiculously, she worried about the sherry in the wardrobe.

He poured himself another drink with a vaguely shaking hand. He had needily brought a bottle of gin and two glasses from the bar to the bedroom. The ice had melted by now. It felt strange to have a man in the bedroom. His size made the room smaller. His wife sat silently on the bedroom chair with her smooth legs crossed, staring morosely out of the window. There is no view, Miss Kessel wanted to say, it's no good staring out of there unless you want to see roof-tops. Mandy Tarbuck's fists were clenched, there were sweat marks on the patent leather where she had gripped her handbag.

'So you still persist in this story of yours that you know nothing about these papers?'

Why on earth were they so concerned? Surely the documents she had taken were not that important? How come the Tarbucks were so involved? Her little crime seemed magnified. Perhaps when the law found out what she'd done they would put her in prison, or is she too old for that? Do they lock old people up? Miss Kessel does not know.

Jason Tarbuck would have picked her up and shaken her if he could, but Miss Kessel was staunch. 'I would say if I knew,' she lied. 'And I would have told the police.'

But after a sleepless night of worry Miss Kessel had finally broken down and gone straight to Miss Gleeson.

And now she feels ashamed.

Seventeen

On the first day of Christmas my true love
sent to me
A partridge in a pear tree . . .

Clover could do with the sensible no-nonsense,
food-friendly Mrs Gartree in her kitchen this
morning.

So how is the dinner coming along? This annual
dinner which requires planning and preparation
for one whole month in advance.

Very well, considering. Considering you can
hardly see what you're eating and the kitchen, in
spite of the Aga, is freezing cold without the
additional central heating back-up. In this chilly
atmosphere vapour rises from the plates.

The candles do nothing, nothing at all.

Clover leaves her chestnut stuffing to one
side on her dinner plate, along with the shard
of glass in her pudding bowl about which she
says nothing. Unearthed from the darkly spiced
Christmas pudding the glass catches what light
there is in this dark room and glints like a lucky
charm by her spoon.

Granny would have done the same with the
lumps in the gravy but in this dim light it's imposs-

ible to see, so this year that nasty gesture will prove pointless. Nobody bothers to read the jokes inside the crackers. They're fed up of jokes and fed up of paper hats by now, but they have to wear them just the same. If they're there you have to wear them.

'That was smashing!' Fergus pats his stomach and compliments Clover as he always does no matter what she has presented. Everyone joins in: 'Gorgeous,' 'Delicious,' 'That was a super turkey, pity there's not much left.'

And after the coffee and After Eights Fergus says, 'Now, you women go and sit down. It's our turn to take over, the kids can help.'

Without the electric there is no dishwasher and the kitchen already looks dirty, the sink is crowded with mugs and glasses because nobody in this household is in the habit of washing up.

'No,' replies Clover, relieved it's all over and dabbing her mouth with a reindeer napkin, 'I'll do it and Jonna can stay and help me out here. He needs to make sure it's all properly cleaned, so he can supervise, can't you, Jonna?'

Nobody argues with this sensible suggestion, after all Clover knows where everything goes. There's a staggering amount of washing-up but Diana is tipsy, and Fergus and the twins, freed from this drudgery, can bed up the animals early with Polly and Erin to help.

So alone at last by candlelight. The snow climbs up the windows. The gusts sound like sighs of longing. The wind moans as Jonna comes up behind her and gently takes her breasts in his hands. Clover cuddles back into him, her hands

221

limp at the sink. 'The water's warm,' she says, 'at least the water's warm, thank God.'

'You feel cold,' Jonna whispers in her ear so close and so hotly she shivers. She feels good under Jonna's caresses, and when she backs right into his body she knows exactly how much he wants her.

She removes her hands from the water and turns. 'Wait. There's something I must show you,' she says simply, unemotionally. In this light she looks childlike with her straight-cut fringe and her wide eyes. She reaches for the pudding dish that she'd put to one side. 'Will you please take a good look at that and tell me what it is.'

His eyes show uncertainty. What new drama is this? A moment on their own, the moment he has been waiting for and now, look, she's going to waste it. But he obeys her all the same, peering down at the sticky bowl, facing the scrapings of brandy butter. She lifts up the spoon and shows him.

'Well, what is it?' she demands. But she knows what it is, just as he does.

He touches the shard of glass with his finger. Short and sharp, it is no longer than a needle and almost as slim. A dangerous object if swallowed.

'Well, it looks like glass,' he says wonderingly.

'Yes. Quite so. It does look like glass, doesn't it? And yes, Jonna, it is glass, a piece of glass that was wedged in my pudding. I didn't say a word, and you are the only one I am telling, that's why I'm showing you now and I want you to look hard at that, think hard about the other near-calamities that have befallen me in the last two days and tell me if you think, like Fergus, that I am making everything up.'

She puts her hands on her hips as she waits for Jonna's answer.

His words come slowly and carefully. 'This is quite extraordinary. First the fall, then the drink. At a pinch they could have been accidents, but not this.' He shakes his head wearily. 'This couldn't be an accident, could it?'

Clover's voice is caustic. 'Well, yes, I suppose a lethal shard of glass could have fallen into the pudding while Granny was mixing it, it could have arrived, funnily enough, on my plate today, all wrapped up in the mixture, hidden away from the human eye. Yes, I suppose, it could be called an accident.'

This hysterical sarcasm annoys him. 'I am on your side, you know.'

'And Fergus?'

'Fergus hasn't seen this. His attitude is bound to change when he realizes . . .'

'And if this is not an accident, Jonna, if someone deliberately placed this glass here, then who, out of all of us, do you think is doing it? My kids? Your kids? My husband, my best friend, or you, Jonna? Now you think about this and you tell me who would do these things, or have I flipped completely and burnt my own mouth, bruised my own body, placed this piece of glass in my bowl for attention?'

Jonna stares at her blistered lips. 'You're saying it's Violet, aren't you?'

Clover bends to tip the plate, to scrape the contents off with a spoon into the rubbish bin. She turns back to the sink, hooks back her hair and stares at the mounting snow. 'Granny? Yes! I am saying it's her. I'm saying it couldn't be anyone else and I'm saying that Fergus would rather deny it than face the inescapable fact that his precious mother has lost her mind.'

Jonna gives a timid laugh. 'That's perfectly understandable. I'd take the same convincing that my own mother . . .'

'*How much convincing, Jonna?*' Clover's back is rigid as she whispers the question softly. 'Just how much convincing would it take?'

'It just seems too incredible.'

'She's always hated me. I know that now.'

'I realize that. But there's one hell of a leap between hating someone and trying to . . .'

'Go on, then, Jonna, say it.'

'Trying to harm them. Like this.'

Clover sweeps around for the cloth in the scummy water. 'She's insane. She is quite, quite mad. It's losing William and living alone that's caused it.'

And there's a body out there in the muck-spreader. Jonna runs fingers through clean brown hair. 'My God, I think I'm about to join her. And if she has gone crackers what can we do?'

'Start handing me the plates,' says Clover. 'We might as well get on while we're talking.'

But Jonna is silent, lost for words. Do people discussing murder continue to wash up? Do they talk in conversational voices as if it's the time of day they are passing, and is this because it's so hard to believe, so hard to imagine that such a drama can be so downright ordinary? That an elderly woman, not yards from here, sits dozing

224

in an armchair wearing a paper hat while she constructs her devilish plots.

There are no set methods of talking about such dire experiences. You are forced into using the same words and phrases and that's what makes for absurdity. Makes for the disbelief.

'If the phone was working I'd already have called the police by now,' says Clover matter of factly. 'And after this last thwarted attempt I'd leave here, if only I could.'

What would Clover be feeling like now if she knew about the body in the barn?

'I'm going to talk seriously to Fergus,' says Jonna.

'Good. It's high time somebody did,' Clover replies, rinsing the glasses too carelessly under the tap. 'Somebody's got to do something.'

He had wanted to touch her, but Jonna has changed his mind. All that earlier lust has been replaced by a gnawing anxiety. If he really loved this woman wouldn't he want her in his arms, wouldn't he want to comfort her rather than feel this anger towards her? It doesn't make much sense. But Violet? Oh no. People do lose their minds, they behave strangely, they crack in certain circumstances. Hell, he writes about them each week in his newspapers and thinks nothing of it. But it's different when it's someone you know, and murder, and such an unlikely suspect. And Christmas makes it worse. What do you do if you discover a lunatic at large in your midst? Perhaps Violet should be locked in her room and left there until help can be fetched. That's if what Clover suspects is true. If she's right, Violet must be restrained.

'We should warn Diana,' Jonna says. 'If we believe this is really happening then everyone has a right to know.' Tall and stooped and worried, the bones in his face tense up tight.

'I'll talk to Diana, you tell Fergus. But for God's sake don't let Granny hear you.'

He is tempted to look over his shoulder. He feels they ought to be whispering. She could be listening behind the door as they speak. 'What about the kids? Shouldn't they be told?'

'Wait and see what Fergus says. We don't want to get them involved if we don't have to.'

'Quite,' says Jonna, inspecting a badly washed glass. He rubs and rubs until it shines but it's still not clean. There're all sorts of little madnesses, some more harmful than others.

They finish the job in an efficient but uneasy silence. Clover wipes the surfaces with a cloth. Jonna doesn't want to leave, he doesn't want to confront Granny. How can he look at her now? What can he say? He feels there is something he should say to Clover, but all he can think of is that everything will be all right. If he told her that she'd be angry. He needs to be off on his own so he says, 'I'm off upstairs to find something warmer to wear. I won't be long, don't worry.'

'Fine.' And Clover watches him go with a sigh.

'How's it all going?' Diana whispers drunkenly, coming in with a trayload of mislaid glasses.

'Fine,' says Clover distractedly. 'Fine. I've had three lives already and mercifully I'm still here.'

Soft voices. Secrets, whispering, telling tales.

Granny can hear them whispering out there in

the kitchen. They think she is asleep in her chair but she daren't go to sleep only to face those dark, saturating dreams again. First it was Clover and Jonna muttering away together. Granny's not so stupid, Granny knows what's going on. And now it is Clover and Diana, women whispering together, women are far more spiteful than men.

When Fergus first brought Clover home life was good and full of hope. William and Violet had long been expecting a serious relationship. First it was those silly girls from the village. Fergus, a member of the Young Farmers, was never short of a pretty companion because he did sociable things. He went to barbecues and barn dances, balls and beach parties, as any young countryman would.

'A country lass with her head screwed on the right way, that's what the boy needs,' said William.

'We can trust Fergus to make the right choice when the time comes,' said Violet, who had never told William about Fergus's brief aberration, about his ideas of becoming a design engineer. Well, it was a flash in the pan, a childish whim not worth considering.

When Fergus first brought Clover home William and Violet had finally paid off the last of the mortgage. Lock, stock and barrel the farm was officially theirs and no-one could take it away.

'This is Clover Manning, a friend of Diana's. She's a student in Plymouth, a local girl.'

Hands out to shake, William, in the firm way he had, having first wiped off the muck on the leg of his overall. While Violet was left standing behind

227

him, horrified and staring because of the uncanny resemblance between this slip of a girl and Sheena. Gasping, shivering and sweating, she waited, breathless, for the smile, because it couldn't possibly be that same false, glazed expression . . . but it was, oh dear God, it was. Even the dimples were perfectly placed and her mouth went straight at the corners, just like Sheena's.

'Yes, Mrs Moon, I certainly would like to see round if you've got the time.' *That voice!* Shivers ran up Violet's spine and settled in her stomach like newts.

This was far, far worse than Diana, that unlikely creature he'd first brought home.

So off went William followed by Clover, tottering behind him in high heels, mincing through the puddles and holding her skirt past the dirty bits. Turning up her nose and sniffing. Violet watched Fergus as he followed them both, all that silly adoration written all over his face, filling his eyes and even making his walk over-eager.

He was making such a fool of himself.

And later, in the kitchen, the girl, at ease, took over. It felt as though she had visited before, as if she already knew her way round and when the teapot was empty it was she who leapt up to fill it again. 'You just sit down, Mrs Moon, I'll put the kettle on, I'll work it out.' Cocky as you please, just like Sheena.

She had taken Violet's kitchen away.

Afterwards, when she'd gone, when Fergus, all moon eyes and simpering, had taken her home in the car, William said, 'She's all wrong for him. She's wrong for the farm. She'll never make a farmer's wife, she's even worse than that other one.'

'He's about to make a terrible mistake.' Violet rested her hand on his arm.

'Well, then,' said William, a practical man, 'we'll have to do something about it.'

'I'll talk to him,' said Violet. 'He's more likely to listen to me. He has to do right by Southdown. After all, when we're both gone it'll be his.'

But the talking failed and the visits increased. Fergus took time off, far too much time, time that he could not afford. He started complaining. 'But I can't live for my work the way you do, Father.'

'If you can't live for your work, then you're not worth your salt,' said William.

'There's another life, Father, another world out there, not just this one.'

'It's a life that's not worth having,' said William. 'The trouble is, that takes a lifetime to learn, you'll learn the hard way, I can see that, but in the end you'll learn, mark my words.'

Then the girl came and showed them her ring. So suddenly. No warning given, not even from Fergus. 'Isn't it just charming?' She held it to the light which shone greenly through the emerald, sweetly greenly like grass after rain. The finger that held it was long and white and smooth and shapely with a clean, curved nail on the end. Those hands had never done a decent day's work, that much was obvious.

Fergus went out to milk with his father. 'Come with me and watch,' he told his fiancée.

'No, no, Fergus, I'll be all right in here. I'll stay in the kitchen and talk to Violet.'

Will you now, you madam, thought Violet.

Even back then Clover never pretended to show any interest in the farm or the stock, not the slightest.

And then Violet had told her exactly what she thought. 'You're wrong for him, wrong for this life, you'll never be accepted. Fergus is smitten like a silly young puppy and it won't last. He already nearly made one mistake and regretted it. Diana, I believe you know her? At least she was honest. She admitted she couldn't live on a farm. Fergus needs a help-mate, you see, a big strong maid that's able to pull her weight about the place, not you, dear, I'm afraid that's just not you.'

And all the while the sulky girl fiddled with her ring, listening to Violet's passionate outburst with quizzical eyes and a little frown furrowing her forehead. And then she said in her small, quiet voice, 'It's true what you say. I'm not interested in the farming side of things, but I am interested in marrying Fergus.'

'My dear, that just won't work.'

'It would work if Fergus could be persuaded to give up the farm. Do the job he's always wanted, three years and he'd be qualified. He wants to be an engineer, Violet, a design engineer. He's only working on the farm to please you both, can't you see that?'

'Don't talk such unadulterated nonsense! It's you, it's your influence that's brought all that silliness to the surface again.'

'He's terrified of letting you down. He'd talk to you about it if only you would listen, show some concern for his needs—'

'But he doesn't mind talking to you, I suppose—'

'Of course he talks to me. We're engaged to be married.'

But Fergus was stubborn, turned away when she tried to confront him, turned away from his father, too, for the first time in his life.

'It's my decision,' he started saying. 'I choose who I marry and I know that Clover is the right girl for me.'

'I might change my will,' said William. 'I might not leave you the farm.'

Fergus smiled a slow, sad smile. William's childish threat made no difference.

So they bought the newly-weds a cottage in the village only ten minutes away, so he could get to work easily.

'We'll play along with it for now,' said William. 'It's doomed to failure, they won't last the course, that one has no stamina. One day she'll force him to choose and Fergus will never give up the farm.'

Violet kept silent. The girls were born and she still said nothing, well, just a hint that boys would have been useful. Clover went off to work, a boring job with long hours, no time for the house or the children. But Violet kept silent, just waiting for the split. She waited and waited but it never came.

Violet watches Clover, gimlet-eyed, just as she's always done. She sees her inadequacy round the house, the way she fails to discipline her children, her hopeless battles to fold sheets, the fact that her freezer is full of fast food, she never dusts the sitting room and leaves the ashes for the next night's fire. Poor Fergus gets his own breakfast.

231

She never folds his shirts properly, never darns, never folds socks.

Yes, Violet watches hard but says nothing.

And now the little minx is whispering with that unsuitable friend, a bad influence, Diana, too strong and confident, too full of aggressive ideas about rights and with a peculiar sense of humour, given to giggles and secrets. As a wife for Fergus, Diana would have been worse than Clover. When Clover is with Diana she seems to gain strength, laughing with her at life, religion, the Queen and God and men.

If Diana only knew what Clover gets up to with that effeminate husband of hers, my goodness the fat would be in the fire or the shit would hit the fan, as Clover would coarsely put it. Jonna was always such a nice, polite little boy but now he's as bad as the rest of them.

And now it sounds to Granny as if they are talking about her . . . whisper whisper whisper.

Eighteen

Little Jesus, sweetly sleep, do not stir;
We will lend a coat of fur . . .

Like a careering sledge gone crazy, Valerie
Gleeson skids and slips her way across the top of
the snow to see Father. She is blown into the low
crouching run of women at Crufts, and with the
same sensible kind of shoes.

She has only a ten-minute journey and all the
time, in the distance, she can see her destination
rising above the higgle-piggle of ordinary roofs
and chimneys. The flat block is red and oblong
and cuts the sky and dominates it like an olden
day castle. And the people inside could be said
to be defending themselves against invaders.
Father certainly is. Someone is always looking out
of the blank bank of windows, just standing,
staring.

They say that the building is designed to sway
with the wind and Valerie has to sway, too, when
she reaches the tunnel between the stanchions.
The presentiment of coming pain touches her far
more coldly than the icy fingers of wind. She
removes her gloves and blows on her fingers from
habit, looks for the out of order sign on the lift.

The nail is there, but no sign hangs upon it, so she takes the lift and goes trembling upwards.

The door to 6B is of the strange silver metal of a butcher's cold room, you might imagine carcasses on hooks behind it and men with hambone arms cutting. But Father is behind it, and contrary to expectations the heat behind that door is intense, double-glazed, under-floor-heating-intense, so that all the various smells get trapped and hover halfway up the walls.

Valerie has her own key. She calls, 'Cooee, Dad, it's only me.'

Flaked tobacco, wet clothes scorching and the sour dregs of beer. All Father's homes have smelled the same for as far back as Valerie can remember, so these are the scents of her childhood – though today they are overlaid with the smell of singed turkey. Valerie lost her mother when she was eight. The scents are like a wall to be passed through or to scramble over like a marine, because they all bring trauma, the trauma of life with Father, who keeps himself to himself so that no other aura can sneak through.

'Happy Christmas!' Head on, words to fall into, but they have to be said, you can't delay them or vary them to soften them. You can't say, 'Have a nice day,' or a gentle, 'Good afternoon.' The joyful hysteria of Valerie's greeting bounces off the smell in the flat and comes back to hit her on Father's expression. Wry. Gnarled. Unshaven and unforgiving. For how can he have a 'Happy Christmas' abandoned like this and alone?

'I'll put the kettle on,' says Valerie brightly.

But this afternoon there's a secret in Father's face. He is smug with it, his lips smack toothlessly over it and his eyes drape it like a pair of net curtains.

Valerie sees the secret there as she spoons two teaspoons of tea out of the caddy and into the pot. She knows that Father, all alone, won't be able to keep it in spite of his efforts to do so. It is merely a matter of waiting. Father's secret will come out eventually.

The little plastic tree, which Valerie decorated last week (Father said why do you bother?), stands on the table beside the window looking out on nothing but sky. Sailors might see it from the horizon as they sail back into the harbour. The cards are up on the mantelpiece. They look so sorry, these cards, blasted by comment on arrival. 'Well, I didn't think I'd ever hear from Joyce this year.' And, 'Fancy that Mrs Reid bothering to put a card through the door, coming all the way up here, what a waste of money.' 'The Harrisons are still together, then, that's a surprise.' Why does Father hate the people who send him Christmas cards? Why does he have to be so vicious? If Valerie's there when he opens his cards she has to close her eyes, she wishes she could close her ears and not listen. Sometimes her heart starts to palpitate and she wants to fly from this bitter place, she gasps with the heat and the hate of it all. Is she the cause of Father's chronic vindictiveness? Father is always telling her so.

Valerie Gleeson sits, balancing her tea on the wooden arm of the sofa, waiting for the secret to come out. Father slumps opposite, the blanket round his shoulders falsifying the image and making him seem frail. Is the blanket a deliberate ploy, a play for sympathy, then? For Father cannot be cold in here. Old Mr Gleeson has sparse grey hair cut short and his head sprouts directly from his shoulders. No neck any more. A small, thin man, he is dwarfed by his chair and the cushions stuffed behind and beside him. Seventy-five years old this year and yet he is nothing like the garrulous, well-meaning Mr Tanner. He has put on a waistcoat for Christmas. The shiny front is stained and worn, the shirt underneath buttoned up wrongly and his slippers are on the wrong feet again. No socks, and his ankles are scabby and blue. When he lifts his eyes to regard his daughter they are watery dull, not angry or bitter, but there is no questioning in them, no interest, nothing, as if they have stopped looking out and are now content to look in. The sparkle in them is the secret. When that's out the sparkle will go.

He should keep his secret, thinks Valerie sadly. Whatever it is it's a better present than anything I can give.

'I put the turkey in like you said,' says Father. 'It's already done. It's burnt. It's keeping warm in the oven. I thought we'd have it about four.'

'Lovely,' says Valerie, she must do the spuds and the sprouts, and then, 'I had to fight every step to get here. It's unbelievable out there today. I can't remember ever being out in this sort of weather.'

'I thought you looked flushed. I wondered if you'd been drinking.'

'I had some wine with the residents and a sherry with Mrs Gartree.'

'Oh, that one,' growls Father. 'She's still there, then, is she?'

Valerie rises and moves towards her basket. Is forced to say those words again as she hands Father his parcel. 'Happy Christmas!' Has to bend and kiss him, and feels, as she moves away, that she should have made an extra effort, she should have touched her father's hand.

'Oh, you shouldn't have bothered about me.'

'Well, of course I would bother about you! You are my dad.' There is terrible anger in his words, an anger that does not pass unnoticed.

'If you look in the right-hand drawer of the dresser you'll find something in there for yourself.' In spite of my age, in spite of the effort, in spite of the fact that you are a bad daughter to me, in spite of all these handicaps, I have gone to the trouble once again, but you'll damn well have to fetch it yourself. I will not show my love by actually presenting my gift to you. I have never shown my love and I am certainly not going to start now. All unsaid but well understood by both father and daughter.

Valerie prepares the smile for her face, more than a smile, an expression of pleasant surprise. It is surprising, sometimes, how hard this is to do. A thousand muscles have to be worked, inside more than out. Breathing has much to do with it and she breathes in and out as she goes. Calmly and regularly she pulls at the sellotape.

Devon violets. A presentation pack. 'Love from Dad' on the tag. He bought it the last time she took him to Boots.

'I can't afford anything much,' says Father.

'This is just perfect,' says Valerie. 'You know how much I love Devon violets.'

'Yes, well.' Father unfolds the cardigan, a nice

warm soft one with a front zip. It will match most of the grey clothes he wears. He unfolds it and holds it up for size. 'Nice,' he grunts, 'very nice, thank you.' And he lays it on the table beside him, lays it on top of the hairy comb and the *Radio Times*, the Wedgwood dish of used cotton buds and the half-empty box of crystallized fruits.

So that's that, then. Apart from the meal and the secret.

'Have you been watching television?'

It's always on in Father's flat, never quite loud enough to hear but its flicker is just enough to intrude and allow Father to slide his eyes towards it during conversations, to suddenly concentrate hard as if on something he has been longing to watch.

'I watched for a little while,' says Father dourly. 'Kids in hospital, rather depressing on Christmas morning. Why don't they pick something more cheerful?'

'There'll be sport on later. You should write to *Points of View*.'

'All those letters are made up.'

'I doubt it.'

'Of course they are, Valerie. They're not interested in the opinions of ordinary people like you and I.'

Are you an 'ordinary person', then, Father? Do you really consider yourself one of us? God help us all. But Valerie says nothing.

The whole ordeal drags on endlessly. Two more hours and she can get up, brave Father's wrath and depart. Now the violence of the weather appeals, it calls to Valerie with all its freezing clarity and she longs to fling herself in it and be cleansed. Like she once tried to throw herself into the arms of Jeffrey Vincent, but Father put a stop to that. 'He's using you, can't you see? Men like that are only after one thing. Men who wear white socks and trainers, thin men in jeans with shifty eyebrows. He's half your age. And a poofter.'

'Not half, Father. He's only five years younger.'

'Well, he looks half your age and he jogs.'

If Valerie had jogged, if she'd kept herself fit, would Father have approved of the match?

'There's something soft about men who wear tracksuits, and a travelling salesman, Valerie, I ask you.' Father used to work in a bank.

But it wasn't Father who took him away, he went of his own accord. She really can't blame Dad for that. It was exactly as he warned. 'I told you so, only one thing. Wham, bang and thank you, ma'am.' Prying. Forever prying. But Valerie had been more than happy to give that 'one thing' he was after, she gave it joyously, sweetly and shyly and now, sometimes, she thinks that the memory of that one thing is possibly the happiest she has. And the saddest.

'I haven't been all on my own this morning,' says Father smugly. And pauses. Crosses one slippered foot over the other while exercising one stiffened shoulder. His shin bone is brittle and blue.

'Oh?'

'I've had visitors. They brought me a present. I thought you might have noticed by now. Look.'

Valerie regards the bright pot plant. She thought the flat was slightly more cheerful. It is big and broad leaved with bright red flowers.

'A poinsettia,' says Father with triumph. Waiting for his daughter's reaction.

'It's very nice,' says Valerie, 'and it looks lovely just there.'

'Yes, that's what I thought. I thought it looked better there on the table rather than by the door. There's more light for it there. But of course it'll die. They breed these plants for Christmas, they're programmed to last over Christmas and then they die, and they hope you'll go and buy another one. Huh.'

But you won't do that, will you, Father? Oh no! You're not so naive! And are you going to tell me who gave it to you or am I really going to have to ask?

'The Tarbucks called on me this morning. I was hardly up, not expecting a caller, of course. They caught me in my dressing gown. They caught me before I could shave.'

'*The Tarbucks?*'

'Yes, decent people. I've always thought they were decent. They have time for others, unlike some. As they said, they were passing and they wanted to make sure that I was all right, knowing, I suppose, that you couldn't get away until now.'

'*The Tarbucks brought you a poinsettia?*'

'Yes.' But strangely this is not the secret. The plant and the Tarbucks could well have been, but Valerie knows they are not. There's more, she can see that the gleam in Father's eye has not been put out by his announcement.

Valerie is stunned into silent surprise. What on earth has come over the Tarbucks? Why would they call round here, and on Christmas day, with a gift? It is too incredible for words but apparently

240

Father does not find it so. Father has met the Tarbucks on two or three occasions, certainly no more frequently than that, and on those occasions Valerie is sure the proprietors hardly noticed him sitting in a chair in the office filling his pipe and leering in the way that he does when in the presence of his betters.

'They're in business.' Father would excuse himself with a kind of crawling awe. His position at the bank was lowly. 'And they live on Wellingborough Road.' It was hopeless trying to point out to Father their callous, nit-picking ways, their coarse sense of humour, their tasteless behaviour. Father would chant the same old mantra, 'They're in business,' as if this fact granted them immunity from any moral or social codes.

Valerie cannot sit still any longer so she gets up uneasily and goes to stand by the window. Outside the wind moans and propels grey snow against the bright flat windows. But up here on the sixth floor it doesn't stick, the height is too much for it and it melts and drips to the ground as ice. The sky matches the distant sea. Looking out over the rooftops from here it is impossible to tell where one ends and the other begins.

'They've offered me a room,' gloats Father, climaxing on his secret. 'They have offered me a room at Happy Haven, all in, expenses paid. All I will be expected to contribute is a small amount from my pension, but that's just a gesture. They say they're doing it for your sake, Valerie, because they're concerned about the pressures of your demanding job and the worry of me here on my own. "We're doing it for selfish reasons, really," that's what Mr Tarbuck told me. "It'll benefit us in the long run if it means that Valerie can relax more over her work." They say I can move in after Christmas. They said it was the least they could do.'

There! At last the real secret is out.

Cold fear grips Valerie's throat. She turns from the window and stares hard at Father sitting there before the gas fire, a challenge on his upturned face. Because he is expecting Valerie, his only daughter, to turn this magnificent gesture down, he is expecting the terrible, hidden truth to come out after all these years. I don't want you there, Father, I love living away from you and I dread the day when I have to come back here and nurse you.

'I find it hard to believe,' Valerie starts slowly. 'And what if I chose to leave Happy Haven and get a job elsewhere?'

'I asked them that,' says Father quickly. 'I said, that would tie poor Valerie down. But Mr Tarbuck laughed and told me my fears were unwarranted. Told me it would make no difference if you were there or not. "No strings," he said. "You have my word, Mr Gleeson. I am not that sort of man, and nor is my wife." That's what he said when I asked him.

'Say something, Valerie! Don't just stand there looking more gormless than usual. Aren't you as thrilled as I am? You know how often I've told you I'd like to move to a hotel, be around other people, have my meals cooked for me and a little bit of respect at the end of my life. Treated like a king. *Sport on Sky*. I've had a hard life, Valerie, God knows. I've struggled most of the time on my own to bring you up and make sure you lacked nothing. And now that I'm a senior citizen don't I deserve some of life's little luxuries? Don't I deserve something special?'

So.

Head bent, Valerie fiddles with the ornaments on the windowsill, the same old ornaments that have always adorned their homes, mostly brass, a bell, a gnome, those pear-shaped dishes, relics left to a widower. A layer of dust sits on them now. Father never bothered with cleaning and now the home help refuses to do it.

So it has finally come to this. Blackmail. The exchange for her freedom lies in a brown buff envelope. In return for her silence she can escape from Father because Jason Tarbuck knows only too well that if Father moved into Happy Haven Valerie would move straight out. They are not fools. The Tarbucks know that much about her.

Valerie is the fool. She should have known they would guess where those incriminating documents were. Miss Kessel, unused to lies, had not fooled the Tarbucks for a moment. Truth and honesty shone at all times from that small bemused face as firmly as the black beret on her head. Pinned there, it could never be accidentally knocked off.

So it's freedom in exchange . . .

What would Valerie do with her freedom? She would take a job as far away from Torquay as possible. Without the need to earn a living she could use her small savings and go on an archaeological dig, a dream she never ever imagined would come anywhere near to reality.

And all for a brown envelope.

Valerie catches her breath . . . but wait . . . she

mentioned to the sergeant . . . no, no, she had said nothing definite, had she? He had scuttled off into the snow preferring not to know her suspicions. It is doubtful he will return asking awkward questions, and if he did she would deny that she'd meant anything untoward.

So when she turns round to confront her father there is a genuine beam on her face. Her expression is open and easy to read, for the first time for years there is joy in her smile. Christmas joy. Anytime joy.

The Tarbucks must be into something extremely murky to offer such generous terms. For a moment her heart lurches, sinks before it rises again. Poor Miss Bates. What can have become of her? What have the Tarbucks done to her and why?

'Well, Valerie, say something. I thought you'd be pleased for me.'

'I can't guarantee that I'd stay at Happy Haven, Dad, not if you were there.'

So! This is nearer the truth than anything that has passed between them and Father, recognizing the fact, hating it but grasping it with both hands, says, 'I realize that. And maybe you should get on with the dinner before that turkey dries up completely.'

As our love did. A very long time ago.

Nineteen

Away in a manger, no crib for a bed,
The little Lord Jesus laid down his sweet
head . . .

Although Granny had not been brought up in the
country – she wasn't born a farmer's wife – when
William came along she needed him, adored him,
clung to him desperately and worked for love of
him and the farm until she became as obsessed
with success as he was. Blindly obsessed, for
obsession keeps all else at bay and makes it
possible for some to survive. And by this time
young Violet had quite a few memories she would
rather keep at bay.

Now Clover leans against the doorframe peeling
soft rubber gloves from her fingers, one two three.
She adopts an expression of placid acceptance as
she nods to her mother-in-law and walks forward.
'That's done, thank goodness. Now who's ready
for a cuppa?'

'I should have helped you,' says Granny, 'all
that washing-up. Instead of just sitting here nodding.'

Spiteful spiteful.

'I'd far rather get it done on my own.' In my own kitchen, not yours.

'Are the men still outside?' asks Granny, uneasy being here alone with Clover but not understanding quite why. Little minx.

'They're still bedding up, be in in a minute. Now I'm going to lay the table for tea while there's some daylight left, such as it is. At least it's better than floundering about in the dark.'

She says it with such gracelessness. How Clover loathes providing food. She feels it is more than food they are after and she doesn't want to share her body like Christ. They exceed themselves with their demands. They ask for more than she can give.

Granny always enjoyed cooking. 'Plain and simple, that's the answer,' she used to say when Fergus and Clover came here for a meal. 'William's not keen on anything fancy.' She strove to please the men. 'Man-sized portions,' she'd say, when dishing up straight on the plates. When it came to Clover she got the scrapings and very often Granny went short.

Once Clover said, 'At home I eat as much as Fergus.'

'You have your ways, we have ours,' was how Granny dealt with that.

All this give give giving can get to be like an illness. Clover'd stood and watched Granny taking the top off William's egg, putting a plaster round a scrape on his finger and for all her care she was seldom thanked. Nobody said, 'That was lovely,' when they finished a meal. Perhaps she'd see compliments as insults, suggesting perfection was rare, that sometimes she made a mistake.

But nothing, in Granny's ordered existence, ever seemed to go wrong.

Now Granny replies, 'I'd love a cup of tea, Clover, if it's no trouble. Why don't you sit down and I'll do it?'

'No!' Clover is not prepared to take any more of this false giving. She's had it up to here. She goes to put the kettle on. She stands silently in the kitchen for a moment, mesmerized by the falling snow.

Jonna has gone to confront Fergus with the unpleasant but obvious facts of life. Jonna will talk to Fergus and Diana will back him up. They will all discuss it together and Clover will keep silent while they all arrive at the right conclusion.

Granny sits beside the fire without a paper hat. *What is this presence here in this house?* It is impossible to get properly warm and her head is buzzing with voices. She tries to blink them away. The pressure inside her head is intolerable. Perhaps it's still light enough to read. She reaches for her library book and touches Clover's rubber gloves, clammy cold on the table, reminding her once again of Sheena and her Marigolds.

Roses whisper goodnight 'neath the silvery light . . .
Violet kept tags on Sheena and Daddy by climbing into the attic and creeping along the eaves to listen, crouched there in her hiding place. 'She's odder than ever, David, and I'm seriously worried now. She's not recovering as should be after such a simple operation, she's pale and listless and very hostile, and she's lost her appetite. I don't know if this is another bid for attention or what, but the pick-me-up you

prescribed has made no difference. Most of the time she won't even speak to me.'

There was a long silence during which Sheena flicked a magazine angrily. She was trying to keep her voice from trembling. 'She seems to consider the whole thing my fault.'

Daddy was uncomfortable. 'Can Kate talk to her? Would that do any good?'

'If Kate tries to talk to Violet the poor thing ends up in tears. And why should Kate have to involve herself in this? She's a child herself, remember.'

'Violet is tired and run down and I know she's not sleeping properly. I was up for an emergency call last night and found her wandering aimlessly about listening to that damn musical box Wendy gave her. To begin with I thought she might even be sleepwalking, but when I sent her back to bed she responded quite normally. I know that she heard and understood me.'

'Well, I can't account for it, David. I suppose, given time, she'll come round.'

Daddy said, in his coolest voice, 'I know you find it hard to relate to her . . .'

'Hard?' Sheena gave an icy laugh. She snorted. 'That's one way of putting it. She doesn't want me to relate to her, David, she's not interested in a happy home life. All she wants is to disrupt any kind of harmony we manage to create. She's so bloody destructive. And her strategy seems to be working, doesn't it?'

'I wonder whether a holiday might help. I can't get the time off but if you three went away, a complete change of scene, maybe there'd be a better chance of lightening the atmosphere. Perhaps Violet would relax a bit more with me absent from the scene, nobody to play to. You both might find it easier to unbend.'

Sheena's tone was weary and bored. 'I'm in a cleft stick, aren't I? If I say no I'll be accused of being negative . . .'

'If you say no I will understand.'

'Oh yes, and we'll bowl along as we are now from one trauma to the next, Violet slouching about the house with that hard, closed face, black round the eyes as if she's been beaten. As if I'm abusing her in some way! Even her fists are clenched defensively most of the time. Have you noticed that?'

'Won't you consider my idea?'

Sheena sighed and said tonelessly, 'I suppose anything's worth a try, but I don't hold out much hope, quite honestly. I think a few sessions with a psychiatrist would do one hell of a lot more for Violet now than any amount of holidays.'

And then they put out the light. But Daddy didn't do anything to Sheena, he just turned over and went straight to sleep and Violet, listening, smiled.

Sleepy and secretive.

She did not want to go. She had to be persuaded. They had to make the cookie crumble.

They went to Wales by train. Sheena bought them colouring books to help pass the journey. Violet accepted the colouring book but refused the packet of Rolos. She accepted the hard-boiled egg, but not the apple or the orange. Denial is exhilarating, pain and pleasure, it brings a feeling of power.

It was winter. The sea was grey, the clouds were

low. You could watch the sea from the hotel dining room and all the lights the weak sun made on it. The hotel itself smelled of tweed and brown Windsor soup.

Violet wanted to be left alone, to stay in her room and crayon or read. She was told this behaviour was unnatural. Kate and Sheena were always making her go out walking. They could never bear to be still, while Violet dreaded to break the chalk circle in which she felt trapped like a caged bird. If she went with them, if she left the warmth and safety of her bedroom, Kate and Sheena would walk on ahead and she would dawdle along behind kicking stones and sulking, forlorn and neglected.

On stony tracks, on springy turf, she wearily plodded on, past slate barns and cottages, the carcass of a sheep killed by ravens, and once a chorus of dogs imprisoned them against a gate. When Violet got too far behind Sheena fumed and tapped a foot. They were so alike, Kate and Sheena, petite and thin with small bones and delicate hands while she was stocky, plain and coarsely built. Also, it was cold and she got wet, walking in wellington boots in the drizzle was horrid. Dreamy, uncertain and awkward, she knew how much they both disliked her, but walking sharpened her feeling of isolation and made her feel duller and more stupid. Her eyes smarted childishly. She dashed away the tears with her fists as she blundered on through bramble and gorse.

In the dining room a great fire blazed and crackled.

Violet was hungry for once. Must be all the

exercise. The waiter started to dish up the spinach.

Violet told him, 'No thanks. I don't want any of that. I don't like it.'

Sheena looked up with a shrewd smile and said, 'Take no notice. Just put a little on her plate. She needs her greens and she's just being awkward.' For the waiter she used a curious ultra ladylike voice. She leaned over to Violet. 'Spinach is full of iron,' she said. 'Just what the doctor ordered.'

In the ashtray was a bent cigarette with lipstick on the end.

The following day it was venison pie, potatoes and braised celery. But not for Violet. Because her plate came out of the kitchen swing doors quite separately from the rest, with a metal dish on top, and when the waiter removed it the spinach was revealed to her in all its shaggy greenness. The same tormented spinach, one day older. The waiter's face held no expression, but was that a wink he sent her? Were they fellow conspirators? Violet couldn't be certain. She stared down at the plate. The spinach was patted in the same shape she'd left it. She felt it with her finger. It was springy and warm. She cleared her throat unhappily and said, 'I don't eat spinach.'

She tucked her napkin in the neck of her dress and Sheena slapped her hand. 'Don't do that!' With a ring of cold anger in her voice.

Over the days the spinach changed colour and Violet was well aware that everyone else in the dining room was watching with amused distaste when her plate came out on that special tray. She felt self-conscious and absurd. But it was interesting to see what had happened to the spinach in the space of a day, how it had matured. It had formed a speckled crust and wept a yellow mucus onto the plate beside it. It clashed with pink carnations and the pink bottle in the pail of ice. Over the days Kate and Sheena had all Violet's favourite foods, chicken, ham, salmon. Violet was allowed a pudding, even second helpings of pudding, but for the main course she was made to sit and stare at that spinach. Of course she couldn't eat it. It smelled like a dirty cloth.

'Try it,' urged Sheena. 'Go on, try it! Just one mouthful and the rest will be taken away.'

'I don't need to try it, I know exactly what spinach tastes like and this is old spinach, gone bad, I might die.'

And Kate stifled a silly giggle behind her hand.

Violet watched Sheena eat. Saw how she cocked her little finger when she handled her knife, her glass. Even if there was nothing to eat except soup and a pudding for the whole fortnight, Violet would not touch that spinach, for she was a child with an 'obstinate will'. In the end the waiter refused to serve it up.

'See you tomorrow,' said Daddy on the phone.

The day before they were due to go home Sheena decided on a trip to Harlech. She was surprised to find Violet so uncharacteristically keen, Violet, who normally showed little interest in anything. She showed an almost extraordinary elation. Her dull eyes shone and her face was almost animated. But, strangely, Kate was reluctant.

'There'll be dungeons at the castle, Kate,' cried Violet in ghoulish glee. 'And towers and steps.'

'We'll go by train,' said Sheena, 'for a treat. There's a little train which will take us straight there along the coast.'

Gloves swinging on elastic and hats with bobbles on top, the cold put colour in the children's faces. Violet in her rosy red coat and Kate, so fair but pinched and whiter than usual, in her green. Snow White and Rose Red. And Sheena the Snow Queen. They looked like two little pixies and people smiled to see them. They ran all over the green sward, smooth as worn velvet, they clamoured over the battlements, their voices echoing off the stone. The walls were high and grey and grim and the swirling clouds put caps on the turrets. The sea was green and menacing, the wind was wild that day.

They went down to the dungeons but Kate got upset by the litter smell so Violet stayed there on her own until Sheena called out vigorously, 'Come on, morbid, let's go and see the view from the top.'

'I will lift up mine eyes to the hills . . .'

They climbed a circular tower, dark, twisty, menacing, especially when you realized how many steps you had climbed, how high you must be. Bats probably lived here, one might fly out at any moment and touch her as she passed. Her gloved hand stroked the hard metal rail, catching occasionally on the rivets. Ahead of her was Sheena and behind Sheena was Kate. Violet's socks started to slip.

The wind howled when you reached the high ramparts, shrieked deliriously through the door of the tower. You had to push hard, you had to struggle in order to move against the force of it.

'I don't like this,' Kate shouted. 'What if we're blown off?'

'Don't be silly,' called Sheena, 'just hang on tight and don't go too near the edge.'

If you went too close to the edge you looked down and down and people on the grass moved like insects. You felt like jumping off because the walls seem to slope back under you, propelling you into space. You had to close your eyes to stop yourself jumping off because the only way to overcome temptation is to yield.

'From whence cometh my help.'

Violet's ears were aching again. She pulled her hat down hard but it didn't make any difference. Once they'd started aching, in her experience they stayed aching until she moved out of the wind and up here nothing could be done, there was no sanctuary. She found little shelter from the battling wind in a turret room, cold and crumbly. How cruel and lonely castle life must have been. Winters were colder, pain was sharper, death was quicker, and men were savage. No love, probably, no comfort, no mercy and little gentleness even for children. Violet watched Sheena. She watched Kate. Her ears were singing, singing, singing. They ached. Oh, how they hurt her. She covered them with her warm woollen hands but that was not enough. The cold was trapped inside her head. Her ears ached so the very stones tilted before her eyes and the sky was spinning with speed. She flinched, clenched her teeth, wanting to call out, 'Somebody help me,' but Sheena and Kate were still out there, inches from the drop.

'When the dawn peepeth through God will wake them and you.'

'Mummy, my ears hurt again, take the pain away, please . . .'

'When the dawn peepeth through God will wake them and you.'

'I want to go home, I'm afraid in this place . . .'

'Watch them carefully, Chickadee. I warned you the time was near. Watch and listen, watch and wait. NOW, CHICKADEE, NOW!'

Her expression was one of solemn rapture. She was floating in some wonderful element entirely detached from life. She knew instinctively what to do. Violet darted out from the turret, pushed at Sheena's back, kicked at the bend behind her knees, felt the chunkiness of her coat, smelled her rancid perfume, felt the tension and weightlessness that followed, knew the exact moment of no return and fled back into the turret, sped down the stairs on thin, thin legs. Like a bat. Like a bat out of hell.

'No, Chickadee, no need to run away. You know what to say and Mummy's here to help you. Turn back, Chickadee, you have to go back and finish it properly, you know you do.'

A great sob stormed up inside her, but Violet stopped dead obediently, turned like a ghostly sleeper and climbed slowly back up the turret steps onto the parapet.

Kate, who'd seen everything, shrank into the stone behind her. Stunned. Terrified. Violet looked down to see Sheena broken, head smashed, crooked neck, legs pulped to pieces. Even from right up here you could see her dolly-blue eyes still open. And the name of Jesus was certainly not the last word on her geranium lips.

Kate's eyes.

They were bursting.

Why should they burst when Violet had merely put the world back to normal?

Kate, having watched her mother's descent from the top of the grey, granite walls, was stricken, struck dumb with horror. She yawned, she trembled and her knees began to buckle. More so when Violet started that high-pitched screaming. 'Help! Please, somebody come! Kate pushed Sheena off the wall . . .'

Violet yelled, she bawled, she shouted, she shrieked. People rushed and pushed and listened, open-mouthed. Kate shuddered and nodded and gaped idiotically, pushing her knuckles into her mouth, overcome with panic. When they brought them out there were tooth marks on the top of her hands.

'I saw you I saw you I saw you. *How could you do that? Why did you push her like that?*'

Kate continued to gape out of wide, horrified eyes, and to mumble from a mouth that was soundless, and on her face there was no expression, no emotion at all.

'What has happened here? Dear God, what has happened?'

The man in the uniform turned towards Kate who shrank back guiltily into the stone, paralysed with terror and apprehension. Determined to be utterly ruthless, Violet sobbed even louder, everyone saw that her heart was breaking. But Kate was another matter. And the man's puzzled glance swept up from her little socks where the bony knees shook, to her wide, wary eyes and up to the bright green bobble on top of her hat. 'My God,' he said to the shocked little crowd. 'My God. I don't know what's gone on here, but without doubt something very bad and tragic has happened here this afternoon.'

'Do something! Oh dear! Take her fist out of her mouth,' said a woman with a shooting stick, pointing, as if to impale the offending limb. 'Oh dear, how awful. The poor thing's biting herself, look.'

Twenty

O come, let us adore him,
O come, let us adore him . . .

No longer a cage without a gate, now Valerie
Gleeson regards Happy Haven in a totally
different light. Freedom shines like a brilliant star
at the end of a long, black night. The decorations
of gaudy foil might not be the most tasteful, but
they're a damn sight better than nothing and
Donna has decorated the tree so charmingly this
year. How comforting and seasonal is the smell of
cigar smoke mixing with pine and she feels a
tolerant fondness towards her residents she was
never aware of before. Yes. It's pleasant. Even Mr
Tanner's drunken cries, overriding laughter from
the lounge, are familiar and endearing.

Valerie has been bought off. Cheap at the price.
Where oh where has her conscience gone, and her
moral obligations?

What does it matter what means I use? she
thinks as she opens her office. Other people are
ruthless in order to achieve their desires. Immoral
or realistic? Forty-two years old, if she lets this
opportunity go there may never be another.

She sits and stretches down to pop the switch

on the kettle. She sighs and relaxes, and that's when she sees, to her great alarm, that somebody has been in before her and forced open the drawers of her desk. This is enough of a shock to cause her heart to double-beat and the pale red hairs on her arms to stand to attention. Hell. Goose pimples all over. Up until now Valerie has led a sheltered and restricted life and in lives like that strangers never interfere with your private drawers. They don't even dream of it.

Nervously she draws the curtains. Locking the door with a trembling hand she crosses the room to her cupboard and takes down the biscuit tin. She removes the custard creams, lifts the layer of greaseproof paper and her heart leaps when she finds the brown envelope still in place. Despite their efforts the Tarbucks have missed it, thank the Lord.

For the first time since Miss Bates's disappearance, Valerie pauses and faces the unnerving fact that her life might actually be in danger. So afraid is she, at that moment, that with no further ado she turns on her copier and swiftly and determinedly she makes a copy of every document, every photograph in the envelope. Then, to be sure, she repeats the process. The copying, conducted under a pale blue light, is mesmerizing in itself, this is all so unreal, so dreamlike. Her actions feel soft, slow and far removed from herself. She puts the copies in a drawer. The original goes back in the tin. She is no longer behaving like the manageress of a genteel hotel, she has all the cunning of a crook.

So that when Miss Kessel comes knocking she almost faints with fear, and it is with wet, clammy hands that she goes to the door and unlocks it. It is with a pink face and eyes too bright that she exclaims with relief, 'Oh, it's you. Oh dear. Come in.'

'It's no good, I just can't rest,' Miss Kessel begins, her head cocked, alert, in her sparrowlike way. 'I had to come and speak to you. I have been worrying all afternoon and I feel we should go to the police immediately and tell them all we know.'

'Calm yourself, Miss Kessel. I've just made some tea. Would you like a cup?'

But Miss Kessel's enormous decision makes it a nuisance to answer. She only nods vaguely, raises her anxious eyes to Miss Gleeson and says, 'What do you think about this idea? Surely we must take action now? It's the only way to go forward. I have to confess and face the music. It is the least I can do for a friend.'

'But, my dear Miss Kessel. Confess? To what? You've done nothing wrong. You merely did as you thought best, and we all do that.' And Valerie feels a prick of conscience which she waves away with disconcerting ease.

'It's no good. There's no need to try to make me feel better.' Miss Kessel's mouth fights a battle with tears. 'I know you're trying to be kind, and I might well have got you into trouble by asking for your discretion, but now is the time to come clean. There's no point in trying to protect Miss Bates from her past, however horrible. I see that now, how I wish I'd seen it before. What possessed me to lie to the police and take that envelope?' She twists a shredded tissue. Miss Kessel brushes her skirt but there are no bits on it.

'I can't think why I acted as I did. I have never been so dishonest before, I am a most law-abiding person, and now what will the police think of me?'

'They will think that you are kind and concerned, misguided, perhaps, but merely trying to protect your friend in the only way you knew how. But I have to tell you, Miss Kessel, that I have already taken that decision upon myself. The police already know about Miss Bates's sad background. The matter is out of your hands. And the police were most understanding. They realized why you took those steps and they won't need to bother you again.'

'Oh, what an enormous relief!' cries Miss Kessel, her thin hands clutched together in prayer. 'I wish you'd told me earlier, Miss Gleeson. I could have been spared an entire day of self-recrimination and worry.'

Valerie sets her face to calm. It is essential Miss Kessel be reassured. 'I should imagine that by now the police have already contacted Miss Bates's hospital and that they have circulated the photograph. Everything is being done that can be done to find her, so you have no need to concern yourself. I'm quite sure they'll find her safe and sound. But if, God forbid, they don't, that will be through no fault of yours.'

Miss Kessel looks unconvinced. 'I feel I let her down. By not co-operating immediately.'

'You really must not feel that way. No harm has been done, I assure you. Go and enjoy the rest of the day without dwelling on the matter.'

'But I can't possibly enjoy it. I can't enjoy anything until I hear about Miss Bates. You might have removed one worry, the one that was making me ill, but I'm certainly not able to relax until my friend is back in her bed alongside my own. By the way,' starts Miss Kessel, getting up, 'I would like that envelope back. It contains all the photographs, all Miss Bates's personal papers, and I wouldn't be happy to part with it in case . . .' and Miss Kessel looks lost, 'in case she doesn't come back.'

Valerie has to think quickly, not in her normal methodical way, but a wild kind of thinking, born of a galloping guilt. What harm would it do to give her a copy? Miss Kessel's the type to pester, the bulldog type who won't let go. If she honestly feels that this envelope is part of Miss Bates she should keep, then she'll nag and nag until she gets it. But in the greater sphere of things Miss Kessel is fairly harmless.

So Valerie opens the desk drawer and takes out one of the copies. She slips it in an envelope and slides it towards Miss Kessel.

'Oh,' exclaims Miss Kessel with surprise. 'The police have finished with it already?'

'They took the original, I'm afraid. This is just a copy. You will see from this that the Tarbucks signed Miss Bates out of hospital, an act of charity on their part. The police have checked on this and it all tallies. That's what they told me.'

'Good Heavens, pigs might fly,' says Miss Kessel, calmer now with the envelope in her hands. 'So they knew all along. They must have told the police straight away. You just can't judge people, can you? Who would have dreamed . . . and yet I'm certain Miss Bates couldn't stand them.'

'I don't suppose feelings came into it much,' says Miss Gleeson steadily. 'You don't have to like your benefactors, in fact, people often resent them. And the Tarbucks are not as superficial as they might appear on the surface. They often do good works around town. He's a member of the Rotary. Perhaps this was a Rotary project, who knows?'

'Well,' says Miss Kessel, 'fancy that.'

'And you must remember that Miss Bates was not herself. We can't judge her behaviour in quite the same way we would other people's. Goodness knows what got into her head to make her go off like this. You were quite right with your concerns. Now, keep that envelope safe and out of sight,' warns Miss Gleeson. 'These matters are confidential and not something that Miss Bates, wherever she might be, would like put about. Don't let anyone know you've got it.'

'Oh, I wouldn't,' replies Miss Kessel. 'It's given me quite enough cause for concern. I shall hide it, mum's the word.'

So Miss Gleeson winces, knowing that whenever she passes Miss Kessel in the next few weeks, that odd little person will wink and repeat the jingle with that same knowing spark in her eye.

What other attitude could she have taken? How else could she have played it? Miss Gleeson hardly has time to finish her tea and ponder before the phone rings. Expecting this call, she is slow to respond. She does consider leaving it, just letting the damn thing ring, after all, it's Christmas, she might well be out of her office. But she thinks to herself, I have to face it, and it might as well be now as later.

She's right, it's Jason Tarbuck himself. He shouts into the telephone and she has to remove it from her ear. She bites hard down on her lip, it's essential she gets this right from the start.

'How's it all going? Swingingly, I hope.'

This isn't the reason for his call, he'll get round to that in a minute, and Valerie finds herself fascinated to see how he's going to approach it.

She follows his cautious start. 'It's all going very well indeed. Everyone is enjoying themselves, there's laughter coming from the lounge. But I'm only just back from my visit to my father.'

'That's the ticket,' says Jason Tarbuck, but Valerie is so aware she can sense the tension in his voice. He lowers it slightly, he sounds like one of the criminal classes. 'And how was Mr Gleeson this afternoon?'

He has never enquired about Father before. 'Very well, surprisingly happy, thrilled with your gift, Mr Tarbuck, and delighted that you bothered to call.'

'He's a very brave man.'

Brave? Father?

'And did he mention anything else, anything I might have suggested?'

'He most certainly did. He told me of your generous offer and I must say, Mr Tarbuck, I was astonished, such a magnanimous gesture, and all for my sake. I must say I find it hard to believe I am worth such a . . .'

'Miss Gleeson, both you and I know why I made it.'

The silence between them hums loudly. It spirals up the phone wires on undiluted energy.

Up until this moment Miss Gleeson depended on speculation, there was always the hope, the shining doubt, the smallest possibility, that her suspicions were unwarranted. She knows she is given to fantasizing. She's been told what thought did by Father only too often. 'You put two and two together, Valerie, and come up with five.' But five is so much more interesting a number than four, and only unimaginative people can be cruel. And if you didn't have dreams and fantasies what are you left with? But all the same, up until now she had hopes that she might have been wrong, that Jason Tarbuck made his offer out of the kindness of his heart.

'I think I know why you made your offer, Mr Tarbuck, but you had no need to force my desk, I had already made my decision.'

He is holding his breath, she can tell. 'And what might that be?'

'Father is very keen indeed . . .'

'Are you going to take me up on it?'

'This is very important to you, isn't it?'

'Of course it's bloody well important to me. And I thought your future freedom was equally important to you.'

A threat? Another pause which lasts an age. So she has concluded correctly. Mr Tarbuck certainly assumes she has. And Valerie feels oddly flattered.

'It is. I am surprised that you understood my dilemma so well. I never thought you so astute. I shall certainly accept your offer of a bed for my father, but I feel we should discuss this further, face to face rather than by phone. I want to tie up any loose ends. I don't want Father thrown out on his ear if I decide to leave Happy Haven. And you and I both know that I will.'

'You have the papers?'

'Oh yes, you know full well that I do.'

'I'll come by this evening to pick them up. And then we can talk.'

'I shall want something in writing,' Valerie puts in carefully.

'Naturally,' says the proprietor. And is that a note of admiration? He has never used that tone before.

'Then I'll say goodbye until later.'

Can it be that Valerie Gleeson has been hob-nobbing with a murderer? Yes. She believes this is possible. Is she a collaborator?

Of course she is, and a concealer of evidence, and a party to blackmail.

Miss Bates? *Who is she?*

She regards her cold tea, sniffs, walks to her cupboard and brings out the brandy kept for medicinal purposes, saved for emergency. Well, this is an emergency situation if ever there was one. She pours the liquid into the glass and feels like a con herself, listening to the comforting gurgle in the neck of the bottle; it is in the mean way she pours it. She bangs down the bottle and gulps. How strange, to discover the easy mannerism of the boozer hidden inside herself, she's never poured drinks before with such abandoned aplomb, and she's never tippled it down so fast. Knocking it back, she smiles and supposes.

All of a sudden this ordinary woman with a horror of picking something up inadvertently at Safeway, with such a horror of cheating that she daren't return faulty goods, all of a sudden this person has descended into the depths of depravity, the lowest of the low. She smiles again, but wryly. And she has sold her soul to the devil not for the good of Father, not for the benefit of the residents, not for anyone's good but her own. And the awful part is that she feels so satisfied! She honestly feels like singing, dancing, kicking her legs and throwing her hat in the air with relief.

She faces the future instead of the past. As soon as Christmas is over she is going straight to the travel agent to pick up an armful of brochures to dream on. And perhaps she can trace Jeffrey Vincent. Perhaps, without Father in evidence, he can love her again.

She will not think of Miss Bates.

Thank you God thank you God. After all these weary, careworn years she has the prospect of Father off her back. She has freedom, she has a new future. And the guilt she will carry will not be that of an undutiful daughter – that was a guilt she couldn't have borne – but the guilt of a criminal kind, a blackmailer and a collaborator. Far, far less weighty. In fact she can hardly feel it at all.

She is not Miss Bates's keeper.

There is ecstasy in Valerie's heart. All that hopeless sorrow has gone from her eyes.

For the crime is not directly hers. The crime, whatever it is, belongs to the Tarbucks. Valerie Gleeson just happens to be going along with it.

Twenty-one

God rest you merry, gentlemen,
Let nothing you dismay . . .

The wind is a ferocious demon breathing ice around the farmhouse. The snow turns hard as it falls and icicles can be seen hanging from windowledges, a phenomenon unknown since the Moons installed central heating. Granny tells the girls how Fergus used to snap the icicles off and suck them when he was a boy, and Polly sneers, I expect that was way before they invented ice lollies.

The only way to see outside properly is from the bedroom windows, even to wipe them is unpleasant, the vapour burns unwary hands. That's what it's like inside the house now and 'This is what it used to be like when winters were winters and summers were summers and you could count on every day being hot and you slept all summer on top of the sheets.' Granny seems to be perking up, appears to be enjoying the drama.

She sleeps less, sitting instead, staring into the fire, her eyes fixed and round.

A glassy pathway splintered with pieces of straw and dung leads through the snow from back door to milking parlour and shippen. This is the only beaten track. Seen from the outside the house peers through snow-laden, frosted eyebrows, the ghostly look of the fairy-tale cottage inhabited by the witch. In the orchard trees lie ravaged, torn from the ground by wind and weight. There they slump, grotesquely positioned bodies on sheets of pure white. Soon the snow covers them up and they lie, arms waving, beneath the bedclothes.

If this continues, Clover will never need to feel guilty about wasting the apples again. Granny's orchard is devastated. There are very few trees left standing. Clover informs Granny of this, slyly gleeful, but Granny doesn't appear to mind.

'She's battier than ever this year – jittery, distracted, she probably isn't even aware of the mischief she's up to.' Diana whispers this to Clover. 'I wouldn't be at all surprised if Fergus decides she's not well enough to go home after Christmas. I wouldn't bat an eyelid if I heard that Fergus wanted her to stay here at the farm.'

'Don't even jest,' Clover replies. 'That would be quite impossible. He'd never suggest that once he realized how dangerous she has become.'

'Well, we'll just have to see about that,' says Diana.

'If she comes I go,' says Clover firmly. 'And that's flat.'

'You should have left long ago,' says Diana. 'There's nothing for you here anyway. You should have gone instead of moaning and playing games. After all, it's a simple decision, you've got a good job, it's not as if you'd starve.'

'You know very well that while Granny owns the farm I wouldn't get a penny from Fergus,' Clover repeats herself tiredly. 'I have to wait until Granny dies, or signs the whole thing over to us.'

Jonna, miserable in frozen, wet socks thick in his boots, is constantly amazed by Fergus's endless capacity for endurance.

'I want to talk to you seriously,' says Jonna.

'About what?' Fergus is fighting the elements, cutting silage from the pit. The lethal cutters churn out the beery brew to the waiting cows who circle it with their tongues and drag it into their juicy mouths. If you got yourself trapped in that machine you'd end up as mincemeat, one of the many daunting aspects of work on a farm which Jonna finds so disturbing. And Fergus is always calling, 'Watch your back!' 'Look out!' 'Keep clear!' No, Jonna can never relax out here.

'Are you sure?' asks Fergus incredulously when told of the shard of glass.

'Of course I'm sure. I saw it myself, I touched it, it was unmistakable, it was sharp, it could have been lethal. Fergus, it was meant to be lethal.'

Fergus gives a frowning smile. 'Are you trying to tell me you agree with Clover's outrageous suggestions that Mother is trying to kill her?'

And it does sound ridiculous, put so simply like that, out here where everything is so black and white, so animal, so crude.

'What other reason could there be for so many incredible accidents? And you have to admit this conflict between them has existed for years. Oh, we all know Clover can be over-dramatic, but hell, Fergus, this is something else. You have to

270

take this seriously now, we all do. My God, we have to do something about it in case there's a disaster. I know you'd rather pretend it's not happening, but we can't just ignore the ugly facts.'

'I just can't understand why Mother would . . .' And Fergus wears a hunted look.

Jonna, impatient with his old friend, is cold, uncomfortable and afraid. He is shocked by Fergus's lack of response. Perhaps he's as weak as Clover suggests, not the strong, capable man that Jonna always imagined but inadequate when faced with human conflict on this sort of scale. Jonna is put in an awkward position. 'There doesn't have to be a reason, not a logical reason, anyway. When someone starts acting like this they've cracked and gone off their heads. When somebody tries to kill someone else you can't stop and grapple with reason.'

'Are you standing there seriously telling me that my mother has gone mad?'

Jonna shifts his stance, stares at the happily munching cows. Their expressions just couldn't care less. 'Yes, Fergus, I'm afraid I am.'

'And you honestly expect me to believe you?' Fergus angrily works on. Underneath his sweaters and overalls his arms are knotted with powerful muscles. Clover regularly sews buttons back on his shirts, as if the strength and broadness of his chest – his manly chest – pops them off. Fergus's hands are tough and calloused. Jonna is not built like this. Jonna is tall and thin and wiry. Fergus, he thinks, is built like a bull and doesn't feel pain like ordinary mortals.

'You have to bloody believe it. If we don't take

action right now we'll end up with another body on our hands.'

For an extraordinary, awful second, Jonna thinks of Clover's breasts, small and neatly nippled, the comfortable feel of his hands around her naked waist and the sweet place under the neat brown triangle where he likes to bury his lips. Try as he will he can't shift the image. And what is the biblical punishment for screwing another man's wife? And what makes him think of that now? The farmyard, even with the latest mod cons, is a most biblical place, biblical beasts and emotions. My God my God, sighs Jonna out of the depths of his misery, are we all being driven insane? Are we all being punished?

Fergus says gravely, 'Sometimes I get the feeling that this is a dream and I'll wake up in a minute. To be quite honest, Jonna,' and he wipes his hands on his overalls, 'I don't think I can take much more of this. You see, do you understand, I have to hold on to reality because I have to carry on here . . .'

'I think we should have a meeting,' says Jonna, for this is his way of dealing with trouble, he's a great believer in words. Fergus, being a farmer, is more used to dealing with problems alone, taking the initiative and the ultimate responsibility. So now Fergus doesn't know what to do, he has to agree with Jonna.

'We'll have to be careful that Mother doesn't hear us,' he says, shaking his head with some force as if to shift the storm from his brain. 'Imagine if she suspected, if she knew what some of us were thinking.'

'She's going to have to know sooner or later.'

'What does Diana say?'

'She's more worried than I am, and she knows Clover so well, better than anyone apart from you. She thinks we should lock Violet up.'

Fergus blanches. 'That's hard to grasp.'

'We have to grasp it, that's the trouble.'

'We'll talk this evening after I've milked.'

Jonna feels no easier. He wishes he'd never agreed to come again for Christmas. He never truly enjoys himself but the prospect of spending Christmas with Clover overrode his common sense. It's never how he imagines it will be. It is reliably cold, dirty, uncomfortable, claustrophobic by the end. Clover is stressed or throwing a sulk, and even Diana, at Christmas, seems to abandon him.

And now he feels like an old wife, nagging. He feels like the sort of person Diana accuses him of being, but he has to ask, he can't stop himself, it's no good circling the horror. 'Have you checked on it recently?'

'The body?' Fergus works vigorously on.

It is Jonna who feels ashamed, as if they've betrayed it by not saying 'woman', or 'our friend'. She's dead anyway, no more than an it, but even so Jonna's uncomfortable.

'No, I haven't had time. But it's OK, it's not going anywhere.'

'I just thought we ought to, perhaps.'

'You go and check if you'd feel easier.'

But Jonna is reluctant to approach that irreverent chamber on his own. He had a terrible dream last night. He dreamed of Granny revving her way across the fields, her small frame springing up and down on the tractor, her mottled hands gripping the wheel, changing gears, while chunks of body from the spreader behind her flew this way and that, splattering redly on the snow. When he woke up he was sweating. He'd stayed awake for hours. His second dream was no easier. He saw the body floating, face upwards in the milk tank, and when Fergus pulled out the bung it slipped, changing shape, becoming liquid, fluidly splashing down the drain. An eerie voice seemed to call from the earth, a throaty sort of singing, he hadn't been able to catch the tune.

'I don't feel too happy with where we put it,' says Jonna lamely, unable to explain his unease.

Could the body, he thinks absurdly, could the body that came on the flood have anything to do with Granny? Oh God, no, could she, in her madness, have done it? One murder down, another to go?

Fergus rises from his task and stares. 'There's no safer place than the one we chose, I promise you.'

'I've been having strange dreams . . .'

But Fergus turns away, uninterested. He's got more to do than listen to Jonna's latest neurosis.

After supper Granny goes down to the children's end for a rest. Her absence is a great relief. Pretending there's nothing wrong is a strain. And now, however briefly, they can relax and breathe again.

Everyone assembles in the sitting room, Fergus with his back to the fire so he confronts them all. 'But no-one has actually seen her at it.' Her son is on the defensive.

'So what d'you want me to do? Wait until she loses her cunning?'

'That aggressive attitude isn't going to help anyone, Clover,' says Diana tiredly.

Polly sprawls on the sofa stuffing currants in her mouth although how she can possibly be hungry after that enormous tea is beyond belief. And the twins are messing the floor with those nuts. Funny how people behave when there is no electric light. If you can't see it then it's not happening, thinks Clover dourly.

It is also interesting to note how quickly the children accept the possibility of a deranged grandmother. Because after their initial reaction – disbelief, horror, fascination – soon after that came humour. They actually consider the whole thing amusing. And that weird kind of acceptance, thinks Clover, is a symptom of youth today, far from the defiant anger of Clover's own generation.

'There's no longer the slightest doubt about it,' Diana tells Fergus, the only one left to need convincing. 'The fact that your mother is up to these tricks is no longer in question. What is in question is what we intend to do about it.'

'She needs treatment,' says Jonna.

'Of course she needs treatment,' says Diana, 'but we're hardly going to get an ambulance here through all this, are we?'

Fergus is thoughtful. 'I think what we all must do is keep a close watch and make sure that Clover is never alone with Mother. And, Clover, you must be careful with anything you eat or drink. Don't move about in the dark alone. Stay with Diana whenever you can, or me, or Jonna, or the kids.'

'Evasive action,' says Sam. 'A policy of non-aggression.'

'And is that enough?' asks Diana.

'We can't lock Mother up,' says Fergus solidly. 'We can't possibly lock her up. Not in her own house.'

'I will,' says Erin. 'Let me do it. I've done psychology.'

'You wouldn't do any good. You might even make her worse,' says Polly, crackling in her black plastic.

'Jesus Christ!' Clover's face is a picture of impatient fear. 'If you two can't contribute anything sensible then why contribute anything at all?'

'I thought I was being sensible,' says the injured Erin, losing her smile and sinking into a moody silence.

'You could talk to her, Fergus,' Jonna suddenly suggests.

The thought, the very thought of having to do this is so appalling to Fergus that he can hardly contemplate it. 'I couldn't possibly do that,' he says quickly. 'Where the hell would I begin? And anyway, if this ridiculous notion is true, then talking won't get us anywhere. If Mother's as mad as a hatter then there's no point trying to communicate. She'd deny everything. Of course she would.'

'Are you saying that, after all this, you still don't believe it?' asks Clover, incredulous.

Fergus sighs wearily. 'No,' he answers at last. 'No, I'm not saying that any more. But it does take time, believe me, to absorb such an incredible truth. I keep looking for other explanations, but then I'm her son, I suppose I would. We'll have to deal with this, I suppose, as soon as this weather breaks. As soon as we can get her some professional help.'

'She'll have to be committed to a nut house,' says Polly, her gaze direct. 'I wonder if it's inherited. Madness often is.'

'Well, she can't be allowed to roam free with murder in her heart,' states Diana. 'Clover would never feel safe again. She could never relax in her own house.'

'It isn't Mum's house,' says Polly. 'It's not Dad's house, either. It's Granny's.'

'Don't be silly,' says Fergus, 'we all know what Diana meant. And unfortunately it looks as if she might well be right.'

Twenty-two

In the bleak mid-winter
Frosty wind made moan;
Earth stood hard as iron,
Water like a stone . . .

Granny, down in the children's end, cannot rest
this evening. Under the floral eiderdown she
insists on using – she will not hear of a duvet,
preferring to feel tucked in – she tosses and turns
and listens to the wind which has turned from
the north and taken a warmer, south-westerly
course. They say the weather will change tonight,
a milder airstream will cover the country.

It is not, however, this change of direction that
is undermining poor Granny. Her head is split-
ting, raging with roaring thoughts and sounds. She
imagines she hears a familiar song, so faint it
could be the shifting snow, or the stream water
moving under the ice, but whatever it is it comes
from out there, from across the courtyard, from
the direction of the granary. So Granny, toothless,
huddled like a child in her eiderdown, hair hung
in a loose hairnet, gets up and peers outside,
wiping the window, tracking the sound. Only
darkness, but you can just make out the shapes

out there, banked shapes, snowy shapes. It is not quite so dark as it is inside, down in the children's end. When the candle blows out the blackness is total.

Granny would prefer to be outside, away from the turmoil she senses in the house. She hasn't been out since she arrived and she loves to roam the yard and buildings, bringing back the memories of William. Perhaps it's because she's been stuck indoors that she experiences such restless unease, perhaps that's the reason she longs for escape into the natural elements, an aloneness she is easier with. She can't stretch her mind or breathe in here. The annex, and her bedroom, are cages in which she is cruelly trapped.

The music she hears from somewhere out there is comforting and it beckons to her, it flows smoothly upon her senses. But Fergus would have a blue fit if he found her outside in the dark in this weather. He considers her old and frail but she's not. William's death has not left her frail, just lost, bored and bewildered.

If only she were back at Ocean View. She would be if the weather were normal, she would have confronted Fergus by now, withstood his arguments and demanded to be returned to her home. She cannot remember a more uneasy Christmas than this, for something tormented has come between her and William, something wet and unearthly, strange, because here at the farm is where his aura is normally at its most powerful. *What is this presence here in this house?* It's not William, but there's somebody here, and the music comes directly from the granary.

It's just no good. She can't settle. So Granny puts on her hat and coat, she buttons the coat right up to her chin and wraps her scarf tight round her neck. Now where did she leave her gloves? Ah yes, they're here in her coat pocket. It seems years since she experienced really rough weather, during her earliest farming days, the lean years when nothing short of real sacrifice was called for. Then her hands were constantly blistered, festering sores that never healed because of the wet and the cold . . . Now she feels excited, catches her breath like a child, and her tongue curls in anticipation. She bangs her cold hands together. There are boots beside the kitchen door, if she can reach there unobserved, and the torches are on the shelf in the porch. Why does she feel as tense as a prisoner making a desperate escape? If she wants to go into her own farmyard, by God she will, and nobody's got the right to stop her.

So Granny creeps furtively along the narrow corridor of the children's end, she comes to the kitchen and glances about her. Empty, a stroke of luck. She feels her way along past the sink, past the freezer, towards the back door, where she finds the boots. She is so used to putting on boots she does not have to see to do this. She's careful with the latch, listening, listening all the time. She knows it so well, it will click when it's halfway open, so Granny doesn't let it rise that far. She squeezes through the door and closes it quietly behind her. Then she feels for the torch, presses it once just to check it, and clicks it straight off again.

She stands for a moment in the freezing night air. The sounds of dripping are all around her, creaking and dripping as the earth turns over under its frozen blankets, the creaking of old iron bedsteads. She sniffs and smiles as she smells her farm, just as it was when William was here. She slips, curses, steps out once again, more cautiously this time. No moon. No stars. The sky is blanked out completely on this magical Christmas night.

She knows that the others are whispering together somewhere back in the farmhouse. What are they saying about her now and does it honestly matter?

And did it honestly matter what people said back then? She'd achieved what she'd wanted, hadn't she? Daddy was back, Sheena was dead and Kate was locked away for her own safety and everyone else's.

They remained at the Lodge because their lovely old house had been sold but the whole atmosphere quickly changed because, joy upon joy, the balding Mrs H came back and soon her own scents of steak and kidney and mince obscured the polite pink polish of Sheena's day. The place took on a scruffier but more homely feel, and Daddy needed her more than ever after the tragedy and all its awful repercussions.

'You poor little soul,' said old Mrs H, regarding Violet with fondness and pity. 'Two mothers lost within two years of each other, and a father who's a broken man after so much pain to contend with.'

'He should never have married her,' Violet insisted.

'Well, I thought it was a mismatch at the time, but what can you say? And that girl of hers, she

281

was always the strange one, but who would have dreamt . . . ?'

'And I saw it all,' murmured Violet. 'I was there, I watched it happen.'

'You poor mite. No wonder you have nightmares.'

And she'd go and help Mrs H make a batch of jam tarts, lemon curd, marmalade and blackcurrant jam.

Much pondering needed to be done by the adults and those in authority as to what would cause an otherwise normal, well rounded child to turn on her mother so fiercely like that and commit such diabolical outrage.

Violet was questioned again and again, but stuck to her story which was uncannily backed by several witnesses, probably auto-suggestion, who said they had seen the child in green step forward and push the woman off the battlements. During these inquisitions Daddy's eyes were always so sad, sunk with unanswered questions. Violet hung on to his hand tightly and pressed it to make him believe her.

'But there was never the slightest sign . . .' groaned Daddy, grim, thin-lipped.

'The girl was obviously unable to accept her mother's second marriage,' said one psychiatrist assigned to the case. 'And unlike her step-sister here she failed to let her emotions out, kept them tightly locked inside her until they burst out in uncontrolled violence. It happens, I'm afraid, Dr Lewis. As you yourself must well know.'

Poor Kate, still deeply in shock, seemed unable to provide any kind of convincing explanation, save to say she remembered nothing, the whole incident remained a blank in her mind, and everyone agreed that this was the consequence of her severe mental condition. There was to be no trial, of course, because Kate was far too young, but until the experts reached their conclusions Kate was confined in a private nursing home, kept sedated for her own sake and visited regularly by Violet and Daddy.

'When can I come home?' she would ask pathetically, not even understanding what she'd done or of what crime she was accused, not even bothering to deny it.

'Soon, darling, soon,' Daddy assured her kindly, while Violet ate her grapes and drank her Lucozade.

'I'm not ill, so why do they keep me here? And I'm always so sleepy.'

'It's not for long,' Daddy promised. 'Soon this whole nightmare will be over.'

'But what will really happen to her, Daddy?' Violet asked archly as they set off down the nursing home drive with Kate's small bag of washing for Mrs H.

Daddy shook a sad head. 'Who knows, sweet?' he said tiredly. 'We'll have to see what the doctors' reports tell us. Kate's not well, I'm afraid. She's very poorly indeed, and it's hard to say what's best for her at this stage. She's so young, and there really are no suitable places . . .'

'But she won't be able to come home, will she?'

Daddy stopped walking, gave her an odd look. 'Don't you want Kate to come home, Vi?'

'I do in one way.' Violet crossed her thin legs and mused. 'But I watched what she did and . . .'

'I know, I know, and you're frightened,' said

Daddy, opening his warm, safe arms and hugging his daughter tight. 'That's understandable, God knows.'

'So when are you going to tell her . . .' Violet insisted.

'Tell her?' They continued on their way to the car.

'That she's never, ever coming back?'

'I don't think there'll ever be a need for quite such a simplistic explanation. I think that understanding will come as more of a gradual process for Kate.'

When they reached home Violet took the laundry back to the kitchen.

'Oh dear, just look at the state of these nighties,' said the cook, now turned housekeeper too, and general manager, living in. 'Kate's been picking at these hems again, the sleeves are all frayed, I don't know what that little tyke's up to, behaving like this with her clothes. Chewing them. Fiddling. It's no good, we're going to have to go and buy her some new ones, something with a little bit more stamina.'

'Oh, can I come, can I choose something really pretty for Kate?' Violet skipped up and down with excitement.

'Well, of course you can, you dear child. If you're so concerned about your sister, of course you can help me choose. And we'll pick out some nice, colourful comics . . .'

'And some crayoning books . . . ?'

'And some sweets. Yes, if you like.'

Nothing was too good for Kate. Violet could afford to be selfless and everyone liked her the better for it.

'Eternal rest grant her, O Lord, and let light perpetual shine upon her.'

Sheena's funeral was good fun, except that Daddy was so unhappy and everyone said complimentary things about her. *The dead*. Sheena was one of the dead. Had anyone else been murdered here? Violet, her knees trembling in the ancient quiet, was struck nevertheless with a sense of exultation and courage, a kind of bigness in her head. It was weird, standing there beside the little grave in the sunshine, a grave almost lost between massive, flamboyant Victorian tombs, seeing the fresh grass that Sheena would never, ever see again, the flowers she would never smell, the earthy soil, so full of squiggly life. Soon, Sheena's body would be full of life, and all sorts of creepy crawlies would live in her heart and her liver and her kidneys until she slowly turned into soup, probably the colour of mushroom.

Ugh. What would she taste like?

The headstone already beside the grave was white and incongruous. It was easy pretending to be sad because Violet knew so well what it felt like, it was only a question of remembering some of the times when she had felt her heart breaking. The only problem was holding back laughter. The sadder she tried to be, the more she felt threatened by the kind of hysterical giggles that come, even when you're crying. How appalled everyone would be if she snorted, no-one would understand that the vicar's nose had a hair on the end, that Sheena's mother's knickers were tucked into the back of her dress, that one of the strict old men in black, whose sparse hair was at play with the wind, had a spider on the side of his neck.

Sheena's mother, an older version of Sheena herself, was cool, snobby and brittle. She refused to visit poor Kate, she found anything mental far too disturbing and could never forgive her only grandchild for bringing such disgrace on the family. A cloud of shame. The press. They had visited the castle and told a tale of dank, dark shadows on stone, of a raging sea and a crow-filled sky, a little excitement to sell in the market place. They had visited the school and spoken to teachers and pupils, who with hindsight said that Kate had always been quiet and peculiar. Yes, the publicity had been horrific, although still back in the fifties when the tabloids were not at their vitriolic peak. No wonder Sheena's mother was appalled. But Violet would find Daddy frowning, abstracted and angry, the paper on the table before him.

Kate wasn't allowed to go to the funeral. Only Violet and Daddy. He tried to persuade her to stay at home. 'A funeral is no place for a child, particularly one who's recently been through so much.'

'But I want to come! If I don't see her buried, how can I believe that she's really dead?'

She cut out some of the roses from the many cards of sympathy and stuck them in her scrapbook with Uhu.

'Will Sheena meet Mummy now?' she asked with casual interest.

'Oh yes, they'll be the best of friends by now.'

But Violet doubted this. It was Mummy, after all, who masterminded her death. Strange how often these days she felt so much wiser than Daddy.

'I blame myself for all this,' said Daddy, on the way to his breakdown, during the times Violet would find him sitting in the darkened study with the windows open and the cold air blowing in.

'It was Kate's fault, Daddy, not yours. It was Kate who pushed Sheena.'

'You're much too young to understand. I should have known. All our concerns were for you, when all the time there was Kate trying to cope, needing so much more of our attention.'

Violet clenched her fist on her knee. 'But how could you know?'

But Daddy didn't answer, just sat there with his restless conscience, gazing at space and being frightening, being remote, being unhappy and getting thinner.

He stopped being able to go to work, too occupied with his dark thoughts. They gave him pills to help him, but he started crying around the house and at those times Mrs H would hurry her out. 'He needs time alone to mourn. That poor man,' she clicked her tongue, 'so much grief, so much worry, no wonder he's going to pieces, it's too heavy a burden for any man to carry.'

So. Violet wasn't enough for him. She pushed and she pushed but could find no way in through the coldness, through the stiffness. Even his shirts felt harsher and lost some of their smell as if his colours were fading away, like a dying flower or a dragonfly. His face was set with hopelessness. Perhaps he had really loved Sheena. Perhaps he suspected what Violet had done, her appalling accusation, perhaps he'd found out in some way and could not bring himself to confront her. Violet worried. If Daddy suspected, did anyone else? What would it lead to? Nothing so merciful as Kate's starched sheets and the nurses' tread but a cold, stone cell and a locked iron door, long sleepless nights behind that door until it pressed and pressed till she had to shriek, a dock before a staring crowd and— How long before the end, the long walk to the hangman's rope? Did they hang children? She didn't know. She picked great bunches of flowers, with Mrs H's help she cooked him his favourite scrambled eggs, she wrote him notes saying she loved him, she drew him drawings, she made him a raffia mat at school.

He stopped visiting Kate because he felt unable to bear it. His hands shook and his body jerked. 'Seeing her there like that, so wounded, so frightened, the poor child, and all because I hadn't the wit . . .'

Violet covered her ears. 'Stop it, Daddy, please stop it.'

'Her whole future ruined, her mother dead, because I was too damn self-absorbed . . .'

'Don't make me hear you say things like this.'

'And you noticed nothing odd either? You spent so much more time with her. Did she never say she was unhappy, did she never mention her fears to you, did you never talk together, share confidences?'

'Kate didn't like me,' said Violet flatly. 'So she wouldn't tell me that, would she?'

'And you, Violet? You liked Kate, didn't you? You two got on all right?'

'Oh yes. She was my very best friend,' said Violet sincerely.

'But you never accepted Sheena. You seemed to put up a barrier where Sheena was concerned, and nothing she did could get through to you. She tried, Vi, God knows she tried. Now if it had been you who pushed Sheena off the walls I could more easily understand it—'

'But it wasn't me, was it, Daddy? It was Kate, *and other people saw it, too.*'

Daddy shrugged weakly, his thinking disorganized, looking more confused than ever. 'I know, I know. It's all very hard to understand. It's all so difficult to come to terms with. Sometimes, sweet, I wonder if I ever will.'

'You have to get better. *You just have to.*'

'I will get better, I promise. Just give me time, that's all.' And round and round he went, his face drawn and fright in his eyes.

So that's when they stopped their visits to Kate. They learned of her progress through letters to Daddy, and to start with, of course, he paid the bills. But when the official investigations were over it was decided by those in charge that Kate was so disturbed she needed continuous care. The only place that could provide this adequately was Parkvale Hospital, a large Victorian asylum fifty miles from home, where there were doctors prepared to treat her and where there was a secure wing.

'Although the prognosis is not good,' said Daddy, reading the latest letter out loud with dismay. 'It's a crying shame there's no specialist care for someone as young and vulnerable as

Kate, it's a tragedy that she has to endure such a large, impersonal hospital, and one with such a Dickensian reputation.' He looked up, anguished, from his toast and marmalade. 'But there's nothing I can do. At least it's not Broadmoor. The Home Office are in charge of the case and although I will write and protest, it's most un- likely they'll take any notice. If there was a more humane establishment they would have taken advantage of it.'

'Poor Kate,' groaned Violet, listening to her crackling Rice Krispies.

Doubtfully he compressed his lips, afraid his wounds might suppurate afresh. 'Perhaps we should go and see her again.'

'But, Daddy, they already warned you that would undo all the progress you've made. Some- thing like that would bring it all back . . .'

'But I have a responsibility towards her. She was, she is, Sheena's daughter.'

'Now, Dr Lewis,' said Mrs H, bustling in in- dignantly at that very moment with Daddy's morning kipper. 'I hope I didn't hear right. I hope you're not entertaining the idea of visiting that dreadful place when you know it's right out of your hands and poor Kate is so confused she's not likely to know if you've been or not.'

'But I am responsible, Mrs H.' And he walked to the window and gazed out.

Mrs H drew herself up like a penguin and looked down her beak at Daddy. 'I don't want to hear that sort of talk. We know what that sort of talk can lead to . . .'

'But Kate . . .' he grappled for words.

'Kate killed your wife, Dr Lewis, in case you

need reminding of that. She killed her cold-bloodedly with her own bare hands. She might be a child, and she might be troubled, but you can't get away from that fact, and Kate has got to reap what she sowed as we all have to in this life. Nobody said it was going to be easy . . .'

'There's no rose garden,' said Violet, thinking about the desecration of Mummy's.

'But Kate's not bad . . .'

'No, she's mad,' said Mrs H conclusively. 'And let those best equipped to deal with such afflictions treat her in the way they know best. Fine intentions butter no parsnips. There's just no point interfering . . . that's what I say, especially when you're poorly yourself.'

And gradually Daddy got better, although his hair turned almost white. His dark thoughts ceased to permanently grip him, he ate his food with more relish, he pottered in the garden again and began to sleep well at nights. There were even times when his old happiness shone in his eyes once more and he smiled more readily at Violet.

Hey presto! The lights are on again! They've mended the line. There is electricity once more, hooray!

The Christmas revellers blink like owls. Machinery starts to whirr. The central heating shudders, the freezer sings with an easy buzz and the fridge dislodges another outsized wedge of ice before joining in more harmoniously.

It's like stepping into another world and Fergus's weary heart leaps at last, a ten-ton weight off his shoulders.

In the low-beamed sitting room the tree lights

gleam merrily, kidding that they were always on, the reds, blues, greens and silvers sneaking between the branches. The fire loses that primitive glare and fades to a respectable normality. Even the witchy crackling subsides, replaced by a more comfortable sizzle.

'Oh, what a relief!' cries Diana.

'Don't hold your breath,' Erin cautions, 'they might well go off again in a minute.'

'Come on, quick, let's play some music.'

People can stride so confidently when there're no candles to protect and carry. They are masters of the earth again, no longer the scurrying, fearful field mice of the dark, afraid of each disorientating shadow, skulking blindly through an underworld.

Just look at the mess they've left behind them, thinks Clover, revealed in all its squalor – dust and fluff, nutshells and tinsel, gift tags and sticky drink rings. How candid electricity can be.

'I'm off to milk,' declares Fergus, 'now we can see.'

'I'll come with you,' says Clover unexpectedly. 'I don't want to be in here when Granny wakes up.'

And it is this totally uncharacteristic reaction – Clover hasn't come with him to milk the cows since soon after they were married – that finally convinces Fergus that these hideous suspicions could well be true.

Twenty-three

Angels, from the realms of glory,
Wing your flight o'er all the earth . . .

It is late before the Tarbucks arrive and Valerie is almost too shattered by nerves to face them. So jittery is she that hardly have they sat down in the two chairs placed so carefully on the opposite side of her desk than she flies straight into attack, voicing her worst suspicions.

'And the only things I'm not sure of,' she follows up with almost a sob, 'are the reasons why Miss Bates was so important to you, what sort of sordid venture are you into, and *where that poor woman is now.*'

Jason Tarbuck, the red-faced man with the rheumy eyes and the bearing of a fifties gangster, sits there before her quite gobsmacked. His shoes are like golf shoes, white and shiny, and his camelhair coat hangs on the door and drips upon the carpet. Whatever he says, this man is a spiv, not to be trusted, or believed. While poor, retiring Miss Bates is a vulnerable victim of fate, and even though Valerie has opted to betray her, she will not be fooled by this man's lies.

His hard-faced wife, Mandy, not the most stoic

of women, forever living on her nerves and popping the Valium like there's no tomorrow, looks equally dismayed when she hears Valerie's wild accusations.

'Say that again,' says Jason.

'I'm not sure why I should agree to play this little game of yours,' Valerie sneers defensively, forcing her agitated knee to stay still. 'It's obvious to all of us here that your designs are on the missing papers which reveal a great deal about what has been going on these past two years. It was you who released Miss Bates from hospital, it was you who paid her at regular intervals, it was you who allowed her to stay here for nothing and took an unusual interest in the woman – I've frequently seen you leaving her room. All this extraordinary attention from two people who couldn't be less interested in the lives of any of your residents, and it has to be you who have spirited her away for reasons best known to yourselves—'

'Hang on a minute, hang on,' and the swaggering Tarbuck taps his cigar and leans aggressively forward. 'Now you tell me this. How the hell could we possibly benefit from paying this wretched woman?'

Valerie coughs and clears her throat while her cheeks flare and steam. If only she had rehearsed this, she sounds so naive. 'I know there's ways and means of laundering money, I'm not quite as thick as you might imagine. I know that to cream off the profits and hide them in some foreign account is one of the ways people like you function these days . . .'

'Profits? *What bleeding profits?*'

'The huge sums you must make from your illegal practices, and your mean-minded funding of this hotel . . .'

'Illegal practices? You daft cow!' And he brings his fist down on her desk.

'And there's no need to resort to that kind of language. What about your Jaguar and your posh house on Wellingborough Road? Explain how you pay for those . . . ?'

'Damn you and little interfering people like you!' roars Jason. 'We're up to here in debt, every damn thing we own is on tick, letters from the bank come every other goddamn day—'

'Miss Gleeson,' interrupts a heavily smoking Mandy, 'for God's sake, woman, *what d'you think we've done with Miss Bates?*'

'She was obviously no further use to you, so you either threw her out on her ear to take her chances, knowing her to be mentally unstable and thus more vulnerable than most, or you . . .' here Valerie hesitates, she can hardly bring herself to confront her worst, most abominable suspicions '. . . or you've done something far, far worse . . .'

'You think we've bumped her off!'

'*What?*' Jason whirls round to face his wife.

'Yeah, Jesus Christ, Jase, she thinks we did away with Miss Bates.'

'Disposed of her,' says Valerie more calmly. 'In some scurrilous way.'

'Shit!' gasps Jason Tarbuck, reddening.

Mandy forces another cigarette from her packet and snaps closed her patent black bag. She sticks the end between her red pouting lips and lights it delicately with a shaking hand, with a replica of the Eiffel Tower. 'Look here, sweetie, I dunno what sort of crap you read, or what sort of world you imagine you're living in, but it's a bloody sight more twisted and sick than the rest of us, believe me! You've got this whole sordid thing round your tits . . .'

Valerie draws herself up. 'You're here for the incriminating papers—'

'Yeah, too damn right we are, you bitch.'

Mandy lays a restraining hand on Jason's heavily cufflinked sleeve. 'Steady, love, steady, there's no point in ranting on like this.'

'There's every bleeding point. We're sitting here like a couple of turds being accused of murder no less. That's slander, that is, we'll get you . . .'

'*Be quiet, Jason.*' And Mandy gives him a hard look. She breathes in heavily and blinks her thickened lashes. 'Listen, sweetie. If you want to turn your snooty nose up at anyone, you can start right now and turn it up at that bloody retard.'

'*I beg your pardon?*'

'Miss Bates! Kate bloody Bates! That's who. That innocent little woman who wouldn't harm a fly, that's who. The one who's been blackmailing us for two bloody years, taking us for everything we've got and Christ knows that's not a lot . . .'

Valerie smiles coldly. She should have expected something like this.

'You self-righteous cow! And you're going to sit there and call us killers and all the while you were happy to go along with the scam.'

'I had not made up my mind,' lies Valerie.

'Oh yeah. Tell me another,' sneers Mandy. 'You'd do anything, go along with anything, to get that sodding father of yours off your back. You'd even look the other way when you thought we'd bumped the old lady off. It's you who's the moral vacuum, sweetie, not us.'

Alas, she is right. And she knows it. It matters not whether the awful Tarbucks are guilty of some diabolical crime. The real guilt belongs to her for condoning it and for what? What she says is quite true, Valerie would sell her soul to the devil to escape the crippling effects of Father, to weave anew some texture of happiness.

'*So what has happened to Miss Bates?*'

'You tell us,' says Mandy Tarbuck, shrugging her narrow shoulders. 'Your guess is as good as ours.'

Apparently the inquiry took place eight years ago, just a year before the Tarbucks, with Mandy's money, purchased the Happy Haven hotel. The inquiry that found Jason Tarbuck guilty of abusing the patients at Parkvale Hospital, the inquiry that dismissed him without notice or leave to appeal.

'It was pure luck that my dad died just when we needed the cash,' explained Mandy, 'or we'd have been in one hell of a mess. Well, Jason couldn't get a job, see, and I didn't earn enough. All I did was clean hospital floors and empty the fucking bedpans. God, it was a sodding awful place. They ought to have closed it years ago. All long echoing corridors and keys, rows of beds, high windows. If there's a heaven and hell that was the bad place. But Jason was the one with the qualifications and he'd gone and fucked that up.'

'We sold her dad's house,' says Jason, 'and put

a deposit down on this place. Worst decision we ever made.'

'And if you think we're making a bleeding penny from this sodding hole then you're out of your tiny mind,' adds Mandy.

'Ah. And you didn't need a licence to run a hotel,' says Valerie, with a cold dignity, imagining that awful hospital, the ruthless cleaning of colourwashed walls, the polished metal, the smell of ether and the maddening claustrophobia.

'No. Not like an old folk's home. I'd be had up for that. But still, if the relatives of all these old buggers who pay to keep them here out of their hair, if they found out about that blot on my copybook my time'd be up.'

'We got a letter from her, right out of the blue,' says Mandy, crossing her legs with a shushing sound. 'That evil bitch. I dunno how she found out about the hotel, but find out she did and that's when she started the blackmail. She had us by the short and curlies. We had to go and bail her out, take responsibility for her and satisfy the hospital authorities that we could provide a suitable home . . .'

'But surely the authorities knew you of old. They'd sacked you without . . .'

'Oh, they don't bother when it's a chance to shed an expensive patient, not these days, not when they're closing those places down, the paperwork's a shambles. Miss Bates's name had long ago disappeared from the limelight. She was just one more senile old bat they were eager to get rid of. She would have been released years ago but nobody would have her. I merely used the name of the former owner of Happy Haven, same

298

address, different name, nobody thought to check. They were just fucking grateful to see the back of her.'

'And who the hell could blame them? Vicious old bag,' adds Mandy.

'Was Miss Bates one of the patients you were accused of abusing?' Should Valerie offer a Christmas drink? No, he'll ask if he wants one, he is that sort of man.

'Abusing, my arse. If you don't give these people a nudge from time to time – a little push to get them in the bath or into bed – Christ, you'd never get anywhere. Some of them should be put down at birth. Jesus, you should see some of them. What's the point of them being alive, stuck there in cots, dribbling and drooling, jerking and pacing, not breathing the outside air from one sodding year to the next . . . ? But the worst ones, the worst bleeders of all are those with nothing fucking wrong with them.'

What a terrible man he is. Valerie is forced to lower her eyes. She cannot believe this conversation. 'But they wouldn't be in there if it wasn't necessary, surely?' she says.

'Don't you bloody believe it. There's wankers in there that've been there since they were kids, in the days when they were stuck in such places because there was nowhere else to go. You name it, they were there, your single mothers, your epileptics, your delinquents, even your sodding deaf. All the dregs of society at that time. Look at Miss sodding Bates. She'd done her time, she got lost in the system. Back in the fifties it was nothing. And nobody gave a toss about any of them.'

'Until now.'

'Yep. They're all crawling out of the skirting. The institutional ones, no idea of the world outside the hospital gates, can't even eat with a knife and fork, some of 'em. Can't even go to the bog on their own let alone catch a bus or buy a loaf.'

'And you were a nurse?' This seems a most unlikely occupation for Jason's unpleasant temperament and leanings.

'A state registered nurse,' he says with some pride. 'Went into it straight from school.'

'What on earth made you choose a hospital like Parkvale?' There is contempt in Valerie's voice, a contempt she cannot disguise.

Jason laughs sarcastically, aware of her disdain. 'Pretty grim, eh? Pretty depressing stuff? But an easier life than a straightforward medical job, and I knew all about that. Trained in a big teaching hospital and that was enough for me.'

'You hoped to get into the prison service, didn't you, love?'

'Get to rub shoulders with all the big names, Hindley, West, Brady, Nilson, the lot. Not at Parkvale, of course, that didn't deal with the criminally insane, but with experience I could have moved on up the ladder. Broadmoor, perhaps, or Rampton.'

Oh, what an odious lout. The finer thoughts of life do not trouble him. A completely conventional person, Valerie's nerves are on edge, so on edge she feels she can hardly take any more but she's going to get it anyway.

'That Bates cow was one of the worst. She changed her name from Lewis to Bates by deed poll shortly before she left, because she said it jarred the public memory. She murdered her mother, you know.' And Jason sniffs with disgust. 'When she was just a kid. Pushed her off the battlements of Harlech Castle. Jesus, crazy or what? If the woman felt the slightest shame we could have turned the bleeding tables, black-mailed her back. But she didn't give a damn about anything. If we'd threatened her with that she'd have laughed in our faces. Yes, in their great wisdom they declared her harmless. Harmless, my arse. I tell you, in that line of business you see 'em all.'

'She was a sharp one, she knew what she was doing all right,' says Mandy quickly.

Valerie draws herself up, shocked. Can what they are saying be true? *Miss Bates, a murderess?* This is quite astonishing. She offers the Tarbucks a drink, mainly because she suddenly needs a stiff snort herself.

'What have you got?' asks Jason. 'A rum and coke for Mand.'

'Nothing like that, I'm afraid,' says Valerie, striving for a casual indifference. 'Sherry, or there's a little brandy?'

The Tarbucks opt for brandy, so Valerie pours three. For the lack of suitable glasses she drinks hers from a china teacup. Finally, after three large gulps have fortified her sufficiently, she asks, 'So you'd say Miss Bates was still insane?'

'She was bang on target, mad as a hatter. But cunning with it, believe you me. She knew what she was doing all right. If she could make life a misery, she would. If she could cause trouble on the ward, she would. She'd goad the more dis-turbed patients, she'd constantly complain, she'd mix up the drugs if she could, she'd get them all up in the night . . . I tell you, that one, she was the bane of my fucking life.'

'But then that Mrs Ball went and died on you,' says Mandy impatiently.

Jason has the decency to hesitate. 'Well, that was just unfortunate. Sod's law.'

'But the end?'

'The end of my career, that's for certain.'

Valerie's heart is beating so fast she hardly dares ask. 'Mrs Ball?'

'She was half dead anyway. And that gave them all the excuse, all those little creeps protecting their own backsides, they couldn't squeal more loudly if they'd fucking well tried.'

' 'Cos it wasn't just you, Jason, was it?' whines Mandy, nodding her head in encouragement. 'Tell her. Tell her how it was.'

In a voice breaking with self-pity, Jason tries to explain. 'Everyone was as bad as each other. Anyone could have killed that old woman. She was frail. She had a bad heart.'

'But they blamed you?' asks Valerie weakly, sitting forward in her chair to hear. At this point, although it is warm in her office, she can't help shivering.

His eyes light up angrily and Valerie is immediately and horribly aware of how dangerous this man could be. 'Well, they needed a scapegoat, didn't they? And yours truly fitted the picture.'

'She refused to get out of the bath,' says Mandy simply.

'And not for the first time,' says Jason.

'There was an accident. They said she'd been held under. The post-mortem said she could have

302

been deliberately drowned. And she was bruised all over her body. But nobody could prove it, of course.'

'She did that to herself, lots of them did that,' says Jason, with the nerve to chuckle.

And now the stream of Miss Gleeson's being converges into one channel and flows full and tranquil and free. Miss Bates was blackmailing these two people, they need the envelope that implicates them, she will give them the envelope but keep a copy. If ever the Tarbucks renege on their promises to shelter Father for free, she will have no compunction about taking over Miss Bates's task and threatening them with an exposure they so justly deserve.

But Mr Tarbuck rambles on. 'From the moment we were forced to collect the cow from Parkvale she has been a thorn in our side. First it's the odd hundred quid, then the odd thousand, money we just haven't got to spare, and all the while she held the threat of closing us down over our heads.'

'We thought there might be something in her room that would give Jason's background away to the pigs.'

Now Miss Gleeson nods knowingly. She takes the copy carefully out of her drawer. 'There's nothing, really,' she says in some triumph. 'Only some old photographs, Miss Bates's release form from Parkvale, a rather disturbing photograph of herself and her sister. As you see, nothing that would have incriminated you, nothing so important as to make your recent offer to my father worthwhile.'

She watches with pleasure as Jason's florid face

takes in the exasperating truth. He's gone and hung himself with his own petard. He had no need to make these confessions to Valerie, no need to offer that wretched man a refuge for life. What a fool he has been, opening his great mouth, it was Mandy's fault, she felt sure there would be more evidence, the agreement they had signed with Miss Bates for a start, the newspaper cuttings that dealt with the inquiry, all sorts of stuff that would alert the authorities to their vulnerable situation.

And now Miss Bates is out of their hair their fate lies in Valerie's overlarge hands. He fumes and beats a foot.

He knows he is stuck with her father for a start.

'I must say,' says Valerie placidly, freed from her usual timorous caution, 'I find it quite surprising that you did not harm Miss Bates, bearing in mind the circumstances. After all, you had no qualms about poor Mrs Ball . . .'

Jason's eyes flash, but he is defeated. All he can do is twirl the stem of his empty glass. Maybe it would be a good idea if she was left uncertain, give her a little respect, put a bit of the fear of God up her. If they could do away with Miss Bates Valerie might be the next. But no, if she believed that she would go straight to the law, father or not. She wouldn't put her own life in jeopardy. No, dammit, they are stuck with the fact that they have played right into Miss Gleeson's hands. They are at this pale woman's mercy.

'I understand why Miss Bates picked you as her salvation. After all, you were the only ones prepared to take her on,' Valerie carries on calmly. 'But it seems as if she had a sister down in this part of the world and I wondered if you knew any more about that side of her life.'

Jason accepts another drink. The first was too small to see, let alone taste. 'Yep, she had a sister. She never stopped ranting about her bloody sister. Not a real sister, a step-sister is what she said. She hadn't seen her for years and had some score she wanted to settle.'

'What sort of score?' Miss Gleeson's mind is now fixed on the mutilated photograph.

'She never said,' says Mandy, lighting up again and breathing in deeply. 'But I'm hellish glad I'm not her sister . . .'

Valerie's mind is wandering as another thought leaps from the confusion. 'What I can't understand is how Miss Bates, if she is the person you are describing to me, could have fooled Miss Kessel for so long. Miss Kessel thinks she is wonderful, a truly beautiful person . . .'

'Not hard,' says Jason easily. 'That woman has perfected the art of deception. She's spent her whole life acting. Remember what sort of life she's had, no privacy whatsoever, always under special observation, reports to the Home Office, punishments for the slightest offence, and for how long?' He thinks for a while. 'At least sixty years behind bars. She could fool anyone with her eyes closed.'

All those cold, clean heartless corridors. 'Yes, I suppose you're right.' How shocked the trusting Miss Kessel would be if she knew the awful truth. 'Perhaps,' says Miss Gleeson significantly, 'Miss Bates has found her long-lost sister! Perhaps she's there, safe and sound, sipping sherry, even as we speak.'

Twenty-four

The holly and the ivy,
When they are both full grown . . .

Eureka. There is light. And the light is good, as
the story goes, and He went on to separate the
light from the darkness so there was evening and
there was morning.

Now it is evening but my goodness what a difference the light makes out here in the farmyard.
The cows are gathered in the yard where the ice is
melting. Here, amongst the churning hooves, the
snow never managed to grip. The beasts slip and
slide in the sloshing mud, but now, in the fierce
glare of the lights, not a wisp of straw, not an
ear-tag, not an impatiently flicking tail can go
unseen. Their warm, huge bodies seem to boil
here, great black and white pieces of flesh
bubbling round and round in a rank, steamy stew,
as they wait for their twice-daily relief. At last
Fergus can move the tractor away from the
parlour and use the much stronger, much more
reliable power from the mains. The pulsing, sucking sounds are more regular, oh yes, there is such

relief in receiving power from the outside world once again.

In all this squelchy slime it is best to walk with your arms outstretched for balance. It's worse than an ice rink. Children playing aeroplanes. Clover hoses the parlour for Fergus – if everything's wet the shit won't stick, so it has to be hosed before each milking as well as after. So here in the parlour it is clean and wet, cement clean, and water drips from the clusters, the pipes and the jars. She watches the water playing off the walls. With hands frozen from the icy cold she grips the hose, she won't give in. The feed clangs into clean tin troughs. When the cows trail in they will bring their filth with them, they will trail their brown muck all over the floor.

On the rare occasions when Clover helps Fergus on the farm she refuses to don overalls, preferring to work in jeans and a sweater and then wash them afterwards. To Clover, so defensively angry, overalls are the uniform of defeat. Clover does not enjoy coming to the parlour at night, but tonight, with the threat of death like a stigma, she'll do anything to stay near Fergus, for he is her knight and protector.

What on earth is going on inside Clover's head? After years of little enmities, Granny is finally triumphing over her daughter-in-law, but only up to a point. The final campaign will be won by Clover when she watches her erstwhile enemy carted off by ambulance, because even Fergus is now convinced of Granny's unstable and dangerous state. But how peculiar that Violet should suddenly, one Christmas, quite out of the blue, come true to form and behave with such a murderous cunning, such vicious attacks, not the sly and devious mental slights with which she used to be satisfied.

Clover might have considered her malevolent, but certainly not in a physical sense. The truth is as much of a shock to her as it is to everyone else.

Knowing that Granny is mentally ill has not softened Clover's attitude one jot. She has put herself in this mess, nobody else has put her here. The thought of poor old Violet confined in some no doubt expensive mental home does not evoke the slightest pity for the woman who, over the years, has made Clover's life a misery as far as her domestic vocation has always been concerned. Right from the time of that first burnt offering, duck, to the gods of misfortune. No, all she can think of is will the sale of Ocean View, a desirable residence with stunning vistas of the sea, bring in enough to cover the fees? And will this mean that at dear last Fergus will legally own the farm?

Such a base and disagreeable opportunistic attitude.

Her heart is as deep and as cynical as sin and she deserves to be punished.

In the quiet of the granary Violet Moon, all trussed up against the cold and lying under the straw beneath the muck-spreader, looks scruffy and travelled as a bag lady.

She looks like someone who has been without a home for too long.

She plucks at her fingers as bag ladies do and her head sways dreamily backwards and forwards. Her tired eyes roll towards the ceiling, to the sounds that assail her from above, from the harshly painted yellow machine like the belly of a crusty whale singing its sea-songs above her. Somewhere she has mislaid her torch and it's dark in here, and hugely empty. The granary echoes like no other place on the farm and Violet remembers the time it was built, under the expert direction of William.

'*Oh, William my dear, where have you gone?*' she cries in vain. No tears will come. He might be absent but she isn't alone. Her coach-party curls peep out from under her scarf, her face is apple-red and cold, the boots she picked nearly swamp her and she feels like a small child again. She sings the song softly, '*Roses whisper goodnight 'neath the silvery light*,' for reassurance as she did then, and her clear voice rises as far as the great iron rafters, over the mighty grain bins, out through the roof corrugations and higher, higher, to the dark of the moon.

Sheena had warned her never to break the ice on the goldfish pond. 'They have all the oxygen they need in the water itself, so they're nice and warm down there. If you crack the ice they are likely to die from the cold.'

But Sheena told so many lies, Violet had stopped believing her. She'd gone and stamped on the frozen surface, making a satisfying zig-zag crack that sounded so clean and pleasing, and the crack spread from one side of the pond right across to the other. There were good, thick chunks of ice then, ice that she could pick up and move in order to let the poor fish breathe. Under the ice the water was dark and oily-black. She prodded about with a stick but could find no signs of the fish, just crusty weed and slimy snails.

'Violet, was it you who broke the ice on my pond?'

'No, it was Kate.'

And Kate said, 'Mummy knows it was you, Violet. She knows I wouldn't do a thing like that. She knows it was you. Why do you always tell lies?'

Yes, Sheena knew who it was and punished her for it. And here is Sheena once again, not dead, of course, but worrying about her pond again and Violet has another chance to crack the ice if she dares, she'll put the blame on Kate again, she doesn't care if Sheena believes her or not. So there.

Granny struggles to her feet. The singing that comes from the belly of the spreader is so loud she has to cover her ears. It feels like cold, she wishes she'd put cotton wool in her ears before she came outside, but she thought her scarf would be protection enough. It's not, the cold screams right through her eardrums, turning her dizzy with the sound of pain. The inside of her head reels, leaving her sick and dazed.

Where is that pond? She must find it, and quickly.

'I'll show you,' says Kate's voice. 'Follow me.'

But can she trust Kate? That is the question.

Granny sets out with eyes that are curiously blank. She leaves the granary and crosses the yard, heading straight for the parlour.

'We'll go round it,' whispers the traitorous Kate, 'because we don't want anyone to see us. We'll creep through the cubicles and out to the pond that way.'

Granny knows they are up to no good and that Sheena will probably be watching. This could be a trap set by Kate. So she creeps, well bent, with her head down. They enter the long, low cubicle building, avoiding the milking parlour itself. They creep all the way down it, ignoring the few cows who are dry and have therefore been left in here undisturbed. The animals ignore them but wander around listlessly from cubicle to cubicle, searching for the rations of which they have been cheated. E64, Daisy, is one of these. Since her fall her milk has dried up, probably temporarily, Fergus says, it is the shock and who can wonder at it? 'We don't want to put her under too much pressure so we'll let her rest for a bit.'

Kate turns round and whispers, 'We're nearly there now. D'you remember?'

But no, Violet cannot remember this place. Sheena's garden was quite different. It was neat and tidy and clean. Sheena abhorred nature. She fought it with trowel and fork and killer sprays.

Violet shivers because it is winter and terribly cold.

Back in the farmhouse the children are down their separate end catching up on the soaps. As far as they know, Granny is still asleep, and a jolly good thing too. Let's hope she sleeps soundly all night and most of the morning. If the thaw keeps going she could be removed tomorrow. Jonna keeps trying to phone for help – nothing. So everything's not back to normal, not yet.

The twins will go out to help in a minute, they don't like to miss the milking. Diana and Jonna are settled in chairs beside the fire and Jonna feels guilty, as usual. As a man, as an extra pair of strong arms, he certainly ought to be out there but he must stay near in order to keep an eye on Granny. She cannot be left to range free all alone. What if she bursts in wielding a hatchet, or tries to set fire to the farmhouse, or removes one of Fergus's guns and rampages about on a killing spree? He will stay indoors to protect Diana, to protect Fergus's children, so he ought not to feel guilty, because his is a manly role.

And Diana? How does she feel as she sits by the fire pondering fate and fortune? What makes her shudder so? Is it the sound of melting ice, the irritation of the drip drip drips from the window-sills, like Chinese torture? Is it the wind which scours away at the night? Is it the sight of Jonna, who even now inspects his mug to make sure it is sufficiently sterile to drink from? Who excuses himself for his wimpishness by trying to make out he is minding Granny? Or is it some impulse of light or noise that travels the ether from some-where outside and invades her wicked thoughts? She twitches, animated, almost happy. Poor Diana, people must say, married to a man who is not a man, a man with a cleanliness fetish, who is constantly regrouting the bathroom tiles, pettily on his knees scrubbing the lavatory bowl, scouring coffee-stained mugs with salt and spending hours in the bathroom on personal hygiene quivering with a nervous intensity. Waging war against silverfish. And so caught up in that news-paper of his he hardly bothers to come home any more. Either tired, ill or unhappy, never a practical man, Jonna can't mend cars, he won't decorate. When she married this was not part of the deal. No, Diana's shudders and twitches are not caused by the cold.

The worst mistake she'd ever made was to turn down Fergus and opt for Jonna.

On top of all this her last two years have been aggravated by her best friend's disgruntled and selfish attitudes. She is so tired of listening to Clover's grumbles. Clover, silly Clover. She always was the silly type, young for her age, impressionable. If it wasn't for her closeness to Diana, she would never have bagged Fergus. Life has always been simpler for Diana. Back at the time of her almost-engagement to Fergus she had used her head, not her heart, and Jonna's expectations had seemed, then, so much more realistic than Fergus's, with his dominating mother and his prehistoric father and their terrible habit of eating in the kitchen. And city life was far more appealing, especially the wife of a newspaper man, opening fêtes and doling out prizes, charity work, civic functions, immersed in the life of the county. So much more agreeable than sloshing through shit in wellies. So much more likely to end up with an MBE.

Diana had been surprised when Fergus turned round and proposed to Clover. Cheated, if you like, and a little hurt, perhaps? And her two admirers stayed friendly.

Diana frowns at the thought. Foolish, naive Clover, constantly expecting Diana to listen and sympathize. Dear God. Why the hell doesn't Clover just leave him? Why does she play all these childish, dramatic games? What Fergus says is true, it has to be the change of life. OK, so she's fearful of hurting Fergus, and Diana can understand this for Fergus is a decent man, although hardly over-sensitive. Dammit, if he'd been a tad more sensitive Clover wouldn't have grown so desperate.

And then there was always the farm excuse. 'I can't leave him while Violet owns the farm. If I left him now I'd get nothing.'

Clover, her friend. Her best friend. Diana both likes and despises her. If only she would stop whining. Clover doesn't know she is born. Free to do exactly what she likes, spend what money she likes because Fergus is never critical, yet Clover fails to appreciate just how lucky she is. Clover is in clover. But Clover doesn't care about clothes, or furnishings, or new cars. What does Clover care about? Herself, and that's the truth. She stumbles around in her own self-pity, in her newly acquired ideas of injustice, a latent kind of feminism from where the rest of the world has moved on. Like a late convert to Catholicism, like a newly born non-smoker, these are the fiercest fanatics of all. She lives in such an idyllic setting, most people would give their right arms for that, but Clover isn't a country lover, she yearns to live in a town. She should have thought of that earlier. She is a spoilt and petulant woman full of imagined grievances, who needs to be taught a lesson.

'But if you no longer love him . . .'

'Christ, Diana, what's love?'

'And now you sound like Prince Charles.'

By rights all that Clover has, all this that Clover enjoys, is Diana's natural inheritance.

Clover was already pregnant when they spent

that fateful weekend at the croft, she was pregnant and tired and demanding as usual. Friends from childhood, Fergus and Jonna were used to sharing and perhaps that is why Jonna so naively waved Diana and Fergus off together. Cheese and lettuce sandwiches. He'd even prepared their picnic. She remembers the intoxicating smell of those baby tomatoes to this day. How could she ever forget? It was the intense heat of them, as if they'd been baked on hot stones.

They were young and innocent spirits.

The Highland air played its treacherous part.

They sailed away in a currach, a weedy punt full of corks and nets.

They fell down together in the lonely glen, in the springy, spongy turf and nowhere a soul to see them. They ate the picnic ravenously, and his eyes moved above the lip of his cup and caught hers. On their left the granite boulders lay tossed among the gorse, an occasional grey-black sheep nibbled the turf on the slopes behind. The great lake below them, slate grey, was fluted by a breeze that brushed its surface like a bird's wing.

She feigned a laugh but her voice trembled as Fergus drew her in his arms and she went to him willingly. She rested her head on his shoulder for a while while he stroked her cheek and neck, she kept her eyes closed and her lips slightly smiling. But when he felt for her breast she said, 'How can we . . . ?'

But he persisted gently until abruptly she turned to him and drew him down, with her eyes closed again and the same faint smile on her lips.

Welcoming him as he thrust his procreative loins.

Locked in copulation he was more of a man than Jonna, by Christ. Far more earthy. A man of the soil.

Nine months later came the twins.

The farm is the twins' true inheritance.

She felt brazen and embarrassed. Her own dreadful guilt kept her silent, yes, even in the face of an almost certain knowledge that, over the years, Jonna and Clover have carried on a discreet if irregular relationship of their own. This never threatened her marriage, Diana knew that, because Clover would never leave Fergus, her need of him was too great. And how could Diana complain, bring her flighty husband to book, when the fruit of his loins was not his at all but belonged to some other man?

But Diana kept stirring this cauldron of wrath, savouring its bitterness and bringing it to the boil. Because Fergus was a decent man, as distressed by his faithlessness as she was by hers. They never again referred to it, out of total remorse. Better if it had never happened.

But Fergus isn't happy, have you noticed?

How could he be with such a wife? Poor man. So sorely tried.

She hadn't planned a thing. It had all developed quite naturally and is now, even Diana admits, getting uncannily out of hand, carried by the force of itself. It need not be said, or emphasized enough, that this bizarre behaviour is quite alien to Diana's nature. It's as if some malevolent outside force has stirred the bitterness to a bubbling boil. The game of Trivial Pursuit on the stairs had seemed such an obvious ploy, something to shut Clover up, give her something real to think about instead of all these imaginary slights. Diana was shocked when she heard Clover fall so heavily and she saw the bruises, the damage done. But immediately the blame was directed on Granny, who had innocently crept upstairs with a candle, trying, in her irritating way, to be helpful. The consequences were fairly amusing – all the fuss they made of Clover, wrapping her up in cotton wool, lying her down on the sofa as if she'd been seriously injured. And wow, didn't she lap it up? How she played up to Fergus and how, as usual, he fell for it, the great protector, the dependable one.

Only Diana noticed the tick of annoyance that played round Fergus's mouth.

Diana fulfilled her role as best friend and encouraged Clover's manic suspicions. Sadly Granny was off her head. Granny – who wouldn't hurt a fly.

She was at the sink in the kitchen when Sam came in with the glass of chlorate. 'Dad's been fussing about the sink, so Fergus sent that,' was all he said. Jesus! Jonna making waves again and Granny in the way fussing over the damn chestnut stuffing. They were all in desperate need of a drink. It was she who suggested it, Diana, so tense she felt like screaming.

Granny got out the glasses and went shuffling out of the room, dismissed. It was left to Diana to pour. Impulsively, quite undaunted and unafraid, in a kind of mad exultation, she reached for the glass of chlorate on the fridge and in the blink of an eye she tipped it in Clover's gin. Calmly she took the other glasses into the sitting room on a tray and left Clover's where it was, as instructed.

The next thing she heard was the screech of pain and far from the horror and guilt she expected all Diana could feel was that some discord in her life had finally been resolved, as though a jumbled kaleidoscope had been given the correct turn. Oh, she never expected the act to be fatal, nobody could drink more than a mouthful of what must be such vile-tasting acid. But it was right and proper that the acid should hurt. Not only did Fergus seem sickened by this, but Jonna, too, looked fed up with Clover's OTT performance. And there's absolutely no doubt about it: both men wondered secretly if this was a put-up job. So Clover was punished in some way, some way she deserved. Now she can complain with good reason.

Again the drama was blamed on Granny. But Granny, so strangely abstracted this year, was never accused of the crimes and had no opportunity to deny them.

The sliver of glass in Clover's pudding was an added touch that just kept the adrenalin going, kept boredom at bay. What would Clover's reaction be this time? As expected, the men buzzed around her, a woman who naturally attracts protection. Diana had found the broken glass in the bin, a glass which failed Jonna's hygiene test and therefore had been discarded, a glass with the tiniest chip in the rim. She pushed it into Clover's bowl as it made its way down the table. There was no need for a conjuring trick, it was so dark it was simple, she had the sliver in her hand and just tipped it in when the bowl went past.

It was interesting to note Clover's reaction.

318

This time she was more cautious. This time she confided in Jonna. She used Jonna to approach Fergus on her behalf and convince him that his mother was mad.

Good heavens above. But what does Diana hope to achieve with this dastardly behaviour? Apart from the entertaining aspect of watching her rival's suffering? Well, maybe there are ways of wearing Clover down so completely that she will leave Fergus at last, especially when he takes such convincing that his mother is at the root of the evil. Perhaps she will feel so unsafe at the farm that after Christmas she'll beat a retreat and leave the way clear for Diana who, when all's said and done, is doing her friend a favour. Giving her a nudge in the right direction.

Leaving Jonna won't worry Diana. Any love there was died a long time ago. If Fergus wanted her she'd be his tomorrow, his soul-mate, a proper wife, willing to dirty her hands and toil beside him in the earth as she should have done years ago. But Fergus will never look at another while Clover remains his wife. For him, that one fateful fall from grace in Scotland was enough.

Alas, but now matters have gone too far. There's talk of nursing homes for Granny, deep discussions of Alzheimer's disease. With Granny securely out of the way the farm will legally revert to Fergus, and Clover, so emotionally demanding, will somehow persuade him to sell up and go.

Diana has been a fool to herself. The twins and their mother can wave goodbye to their earthy inheritance for ever. Unless . . . *unless* . . .

*   *   *

'Now the lights are back you can see those spiders' legs in the saucepans again. I do wish Clover wouldn't keep them in that cupboard on the floor. It can't be hygienic.'

Where is the sympathy he expected to see? Now, when Jonna looks at his wife, he sees only withering scorn.

Twenty-five

Once in royal David's city
Stood a lowly cattle shed . . .

E64, commonly known as Daisy, rocks herself on her spindly legs and stares at the weak place in the fence with a red and rolling eye.

'Hurry them out of the yard, will you, Clover? They're creating a blockage outside the parlour door.'

Yes, he always treats her like a navvy the minute they get outside into his own manly domain. He shouts at everyone when he is milking, Jonna, the twins, Blackjack, Marvin. And they all accept it with a meekness that Clover detests. He's intent on everything moving smoothly, efficiently and fast. Who the hell does Fergus the farmer think he is?

But crushed into unnatural obedience by her own fearful needs, Clover runs up the passage behind the parlour and shoos the cows with slaps on their backs. She peers into the dimly lit distance. Away from the bright parlour lights the cubicle house is softly lit, like a long, thin hospital ward divided by metal beds. Who is causing this logjam? The cow called Horny is trying to reverse,

refusing to accept her meagre share of the good-
ies. She believes she deserves more, not wise
enough to know that there's no going backwards
to cheat this failsafe system. To do that you'd
have to start at the beginning and even then
you'd most likely be spotted.

Spryly Clover climbs the gate and wanders
across to the cubicle house. She gives Horny a
hard slap and stings her own hand. The cow
jumps and gives her a dark look. The rest scatter,
frightened. There in the distance, outside the
yard, Clover sees Daisy eyeing the fence to the
slurry pit. My God, not again. Fergus is meant to
have mended it, but has he had time to do a good
job in the confusion of the last two days? Clover
will have to take a look. She is, as you see, a
farmer's wife at heart, after all. She can't just
return and report her concerns because cows can
act impulsively, you can never be sure with a cow.
And Clover does not like the eager look in the
silly animal's eye.

Perhaps it strikes a chord.

From deep in the shadows of the cubicle house,
Granny watches Clover. There she is, across
the yard, staring into the deep black depths of the
slurry pit, wobbling the fence with her hand to
test it, turning back anxiously to check on the
cow.

Granny creeps through the shadows and
crouches. Nearer she goes. And nearer. Like a fox
after chickens, that's how she moves and all the
time the piercing sounds in her ears nearly block
the sight from her eyes. She writhes with the
shrieks in her head . . . Oh, where do they come
from?

'When the dawn peepeth through they will wake them and you . . .'

This place is so blessedly familiar. All her happiest years with William, and Fergus, small, bigger, growing. William and Fergus belonged to her until that one, Clover, came along insensitively barging her way into what had been a perfect family. William and Fergus belonged to her just as Daddy belonged to her again after Sheena and Kate went away, he was all hers, loving her again, loving her only. And it was Mummy that made that happen, so is Mummy here now? Is Mummy trying to make the pain in her head go away as she had done all those years ago high up on the castle walls?

She'd never intended to leave Daddy, no, not until he died. He belonged to her now, and it was her duty to care for him. But Daddy's work took him away, the late hospital hours, the conferences that lasted a week, the weekends he used to work while Violet was left with Mrs H, cooking and telling stories.

Perversely, she was frequently tempted to confess the deed to Mrs H. She'd like to tell someone, and sometimes the need to find that relief frightened her, and she turned to Mummy for consolation. At least she could talk to her in the dark, although as the years went by Mummy's presence seemed to pale.

For a while little Violet had nightmares, the obvious nightmare of Sheena's revenge because Sheena was a spirit now, and presumably as capable as Mummy of contacting the dear ones on earth. Sometimes, dreaming of this, she woke up screaming and gabbling in the night. But in spite of Violet's worst fears, Sheena never did come through, and Violet could only suppose that communications from hell were well-nigh impossible. Perhaps, along with the fire and brimstone, this was part of the punishment.

'D'you believe in life after death, Mrs H?'

'Well, there's a question.' The toffee had not set right, it stuck to Mrs H's spoon. She attacked it viciously with a hot knife.

'What about ghosts?'

Mrs H referred to her recipe book, spattered by the mixtures of ages. 'I know there's people swear they've seen 'em, but I'd have to see for myself. Same as all this Buddhist stuff. We're supposed to come back as something else and I'm not at all sure I'm too happy with that.'

'I talk to Mummy sometimes.' There! It was suddenly out, the impulse to tell was overpowering. 'And she helps me decide what to do.'

Mrs H turned sad eyes on the child, bless her heart, such a strange little mite, Daddy's girl, and how easily she had accepted the tragedy that had befallen them all. But there, children are robust little creatures, and life is so simple when you're eight years old. 'Of course you talk to her, darling. It's a jolly good thing that you can.'

'I only have to turn on my musical box and she's there.'

'Pass the toffee tin over, dear. And are you sure you greased it properly?'

'She takes care of me. She watches me all the time. Mummy was lovely, wasn't she, Mrs H? Everyone says.'

'Oh yes, she was a lovely lady. And it's very sad that she died so young. But then you had a new mother! And a new sister too, didn't you?' Such a little chatterbox. Dr Lewis had advised Mrs H that talking things through was good therapy, but Mrs H herself wasn't so sure. Best not to dwell on things, to put horrors like that behind you and get on with your life.

'But when Sheena came, you went away.'

Mrs H sniffed. 'Mrs Lewis had her own ideas.' She paused and turned round in astonishment. 'Hey! I told you to break that toffee, Vi, but I didn't mean you to attack it with a hammer as if it might leap up and bite you! Look, you silly-billy, you've smashed the lot to smithereens.'

'I like it better like that,' said Violet.

William was the first boyfriend Violet ever had. Rigid, plain, clean and orderly, she disliked boys and their rude intentions. In her opinion they were rough and silly, she was looking for someone as admirable as Daddy. So she never bothered to tart herself up or learn to dance to the latest records, she didn't care if she was the only one in her class to openly admit her lack of interest.

'I'd rather have dogs,' she said, bristling with defences. 'And anyway, who wants to get married?'

She'd rather go to the pictures with friends, or stay in and listen to the wireless, or walk for miles in the country. She drooped round the house, careless of her appearance, preferring her own company.

And then she met William. It was really rather romantic, like a story. A hot summer's day, and it started to thunder, and there was this tractor and a lonely man toiling beside it, frantic to pick up the last bales of hay before the laden sky burst open. She could hardly pass by without offering to help.

They hardly exchanged a word.

And then he came into work one day, dressed up in suit and tie so she hardly recognized him as the lad in the shabby dungarees under that hot and threatening sky. He walked into the council office where she worked as a receptionist. He came to pay the annual rent on his farm and Violet happened to be at the desk at the time. Then there was coffee and a bun at the little place opposite, no particular conversation other than William's farm, and Violet was fascinated by his singleness of purpose, his determination to succeed against all the odds, something she understood very well.

It went on from there, just as if it was meant.

William was not a complicated man. But he was decent and honest and hard working like Daddy, although his hands were red and hard where Daddy's were soft and white. There was nothing petty about him. William had a dream, and his dream was so enormous it dwarfed everything else in his life. One day he wanted to own his farm. This kind of dream, a kind of diffuse eroticism, is precisely what Violet needed, at dear last somewhere to put her own tormented energy, and she was overcome with joy when she learned that he was prepared to let her share his enterprise.

'Daddy, this is my friend William.' How fresh and young he looked.

Daddy would be sure to be jealous. They had

been together for so many years with nobody else save Mrs H.

Daddy and William shook hands. 'So this is the boy that has taken my little girl's fancy.'

Daddy seemed pleased to meet him, or a better actor than Violet thought. She'd imagined there would be some resentment, some sadness and regret at the thought that their routine existence might be disrupted, Violet leaving home, perhaps, marrying William and sharing the farm. But Daddy's was the opposite reaction, even though he'd be alone and abandoned by the person who loved him most.

And then she'd imagined Daddy would be concerned with William's lowly status, a young farmer starting out with hardly a penny behind him. He'd always wanted Violet to train for a profession, a doctor like himself, perhaps, and was openly disappointed when she opted out of school in favour of going to work.

'I only want you to be happy,' Daddy would say, with a strangely sorrowful look in his eye.

Pity he hadn't thought about that when he went and married Sheena.

He didn't seem even slightly concerned by the fact that his son-in-law to be was a lowly tiller of the soil, a hard and thankless world which his precious daughter intended to share. But the thought that was most disconcerting of all was that Daddy seemed pleased to be rid of her.

There never seemed any reason to tell William about Sheena and Kate. As far as he was concerned, and he wasn't overly interested, Violet's mother, Wendy, died when she was a child. Violet left it at that to save unnecessary complications.

So she never told William where she was going the day she set off to find Kate. The matter had gnawed at her mind for so long she had to go and satisfy herself. It was after Daddy's death, quite recently, really, only ten years ago, and Daddy had left Kate a small bequest in his will. She could only assume that her step-sister was in the same hospital, and if she'd been moved the authorities at Parkvale would have informed her.

It was with some trepidation that she drove up the winding drive, suddenly overwhelmed by the size of the imposing building which overlooked the car park. She flinched. So what were her intentions? Was she going to introduce herself to her long-lost sister? Enquire as to her health? Take her through the photograph album page by page, pointing out various highlights in her life – her marriage, Fergus's birth, Fergus's childhood, the many shows attended by herself and William, the precious rosettes and cups he won for his animals? Hardly the most sensitive approach, when you consider it.

Violet had no intentions. Only a mawkish curiosity.

Outside, in the gesture of a garden, an oval patch of grass and flowers, a few patients in ill-assorted garments shuffled or marched round a pathway of paving stones. They shuffled round and round until weary of the monotony of it and all the while the sunlight made deeper hollows beneath their eyebrows and cheekbones, turning them into a sad little circus of lost souls. The high hospital walls were pierced with rows of little barred windows. This was an asylum little changed by political thinking, one of the few remaining to cater for those too disturbed to survive in the outside world of community care.

She introduced herself at the desk, then dutifully followed the arrow heading for Livingston ward, followed the long, empty corridors devoid of all gentleness, or pity. Occasionally she asked for directions from a scurrying woman in white.

And suddenly there was her step-sister Kate. Fifty years older, with a grim, set mouth and ageing eyes which turned neither right nor left and certainly did not bother to study the visitor who, after the door was locked behind her, slipped quickly into the small glass office which offered some slight degree of concealment.

Violet was resolved to feel no emotion. The texture of subdued silence in the ward was broken by an occasional jarring cry.

'Well, you'll want to see her yourself, my love, after all these years!'

After the damning pause Violet said, 'Er, no! I doubt that that would be wise.' She couldn't feel more uncomfortable. 'My reason for coming was really to sort out this small bequest and make sure my sister received it, and for that we require a signature on this document I brought with me . . .'

The nurse had trouble with her spectacles as she attempted to read the document and study Violet at the same time. 'But you'll want to spend some time . . .'

'I'm afraid that won't be possible.' She caught a glance of Kate again and her skin flushed to the roots of her hair.

The nurse listened with knitted brows as Violet strove to explain. 'It's not quite as simple as that,

329

you see. I only wanted to assure myself that Miss Lewis . . .'

'Kate, surely? Why the formality? After all, she is your sister.'

Violet moistened her lips. 'Oh, yes, of course, that Kate was well and—'

'Happy?' the nurse interrupted accusingly. 'Is that what you were going to say? Miss Lewis hasn't had a visitor for as long as I can remember and I've been here more than five years. If only someone would come forward and accept some responsibility for her Miss Lewis could leave Parkvale tomorrow. She's no need to be here any longer, but because she's an old Home Office case there's rules that must be followed, unfortunately . . .'

The drumming of feet. The odd laugh from the underworld. Then Kate lifted her face and saw her. She did not smile but only stared, before she looked away again. Had she recognized her? That's doubtful. Kate stood, first on her right foot, then on her left. Sometimes she sighed, sometimes she withdrew her hands from her pockets and fiddled with her fingers, sometimes she passed a hand over her greying hair.

Violet fled and the door clanged behind her. She would never see Kate again. She should never have come here. There was no further satisfaction to be had.

She hears Mummy's song again, the song of the musical box, but there's a difference about the voice tonight, there's something savage and rasping. Could it be somebody else pretending?

Granny closes in. Softly. Slyly. That one – she

was never any good, not for Fergus, not for anyone. She is one of the women who take love away.

'*See her, Chickadee. She's the one, look, see, watch, wait until I tell you, steady, steady, steady, NOW, CHICKADEE, NOW.*'

But the horrible shriek that follows her action, the devilish, sinister laugh, is not at all like Mummy's laugh. In fact it sounds more like Kate's.

Oh, the nauseating horror of this, oh, the singing cold. She feels naked, she is icy and wet and the stench of it clogs her body so she can't move, she's held tight in a grip of odious slime and she can't lift her limbs, they are dream-weighted.

'*FERGUS! FERGUS! FERGUS!*'

SHIT. *Where is he?* Why doesn't somebody *do* something? For Jesus' sake, can't they hear her? Clover won't be able to scream for much longer because the glutinous muck is not only reaching her mouth but slipping inside it, clogging her throat, invading her nostrils, she tastes the sour stench of it deep in her stomach. From high above, from the comparative safety of the yard, Daisy observes her. Her big, bemused eyes are wide with understanding. She flicks a shit-tasselled tail and she munches. For a terrible, gurgling second their eyes meet knowingly. The fetid bubbles in the stinking manure burst and rise and grip around her until Clover is totally helpless, not even one arm is free and she's clamped as high as her neck. She is not built for floating, not round and bloated and buoyant like a cow, and she hasn't the long, muscled neck. She is little and thin and quick and she strikes out too wildly for her own good, the reeking, sticky, putrefaction covers her nose and mouth like a foul and malodorous gag. If only she were more of the accepting type, more bovine, then perhaps she would not sink quite so quickly.

'*FERGUS!*' And Clover can taste the word. It slips down her throat and burns like acid.

What a way to go.

The slime boils with its own sour sound as it reaches her ears and fills them. But over this she can hear something else. As the bubbles reach the sky in her head, as they fade, she hears a lullaby she knew in childhood and recognizes this moment as the one that heralds death, part of the lifetime that's supposed to flash before you before you see that beckoning tunnel.

A filthy black layer of darkness slides over Clover Moon's head. Granny stands there, toothless and mesmerized while somebody else's shadow scuttles back into the night.

Twenty-six

We all want some figgy pudding,
We all want some figgy pudding,
We all want some figgy pudding,
So bring some out here.

'Good god, Mother,' yells Fergus Moon in a voice choked with outrage, tall and stark and fixed in alarm against the parlour door. *'Mother, what the hell are you doing standing there? For Christsake what have you done?'*

Can't he move just a fraction faster in order to save the life of his wife? He urges every muscle and sinew, blood pulsates frantically through wooden limbs as he moves with a speed he's never achieved, and yet he feels he's being pressed back.

He is quite unaware he is screaming.

Is he too late? *Dear God, no!* In seconds he's at the edge of the pit, it takes milliseconds to heroically fling himself in, with nothing but a rope of binding twine between himself and a final, sticky extinction.

With the strength of the maddened he gropes for his wife, flailing, calling, this way and that, plunging his life-giving hands into months of accumulated dung, fermented dung so good for the soil. And all the while he shrieks, 'Clover! Clover! Hang on, hang on . . . Clover, *fucking well grip my hand if you can . . .*'

With his spare hand he clings to his slither of twine, one piece among hundreds that decorate the metal surrounds of the pit, and that hand has already been sliced by the thinness of the twine and the force of it as it cuts his skin. His violent struggles are exhausting, a flailing wasp in a full tin of treacle as he beats and he flutters and he strives for some useful movement.

'Oh God!' Fergus shouts to a darkening moon. '*Oh God oh God oh God help me.*'

He is up to his neck already, well in danger of choking, and only one hand remains free, the one that connects him to life on earth by one fragile strand. But dammit he'll never give up. With the strength of will of an athlete he endeavours to search the muck with his legs, just one touch, that's all Clover needs, just something firm to cling on to and, if she's any strength left in her body, she might be able to claw herself free.

Fergus kicks out savagely, as helpless, now, as a newborn infant. He can hardly move his legs at all. In his rage, in his tormented grief he cries out, 'Clover! Clover!' Dear God, she must have sunk right under and the pit is deep and at its fullest. It will not be emptied until the spring when the vast muck-spreader comes into its own.

Above him an excited audience gathers.

Jonna manages to throw him a more reliable rope. His words hang like fog over water. 'FERGUS! FERGUS! Try to stop thrashing about. I got through to Ernie Wakeham and he's on his way here with his crane. He'll batter his way through if he has to . . . and Erin's dialling 999 . . . so hang on, Fergus! *Hang on!*'

'Clover's in here!' Fergus weeps, his blackened face slick with noxious slime, like the festering marks of a plague, and his desperate eyes enormous. 'Clover's in here, dear God . . .' and then, with all strength ebbed away, he sobs wildly like a child, *'What are we going to do?'*

'Just don't panic, old man, all is not lost, not by a long chalk, we'll get you out of there and then we'll have machinery and men . . .'

'Christ, Jonna! Sodding hell! How long d'you think she'll survive in this?'

'I know,' calls Jonna, whey-faced and fearful, at his most inadequate. Hell. What do you say to a man whose wife has just drowned in a pit of shit? 'But whatever we do we won't give up hope . . .'

Fergus dangles. He can do nothing else. He dangles on the end of the rope, not enough power left in him to hoist his way out of steaming mire. This is truly a living nightmare and all his attempts are futile.

'Daddy! Daddy, don't drown!' calls Polly, foolishly, her breath caught on the edge of her tears.

'I won't drown, darling.' Even in this bizarre situation the practical, sensible Fergus tries to reassure his child. He knows what has to be done. His brain begins to function again. 'Don't you worry.'

Diana hovers beside them, nervously watching, biting her lip. So far, apart from Fergus's initial outcry, nobody's looked for the cause of the disaster. It's far too soon to turn to that, she supposes, but the way it was done means there won't be a problem. No doubts will linger in anyone's mind. Perversely, for a moment back there, it looked as if Granny might do the deed for her. Perhaps there's some truth behind extrasensory perception. She was certainly acting most strangely, creeping around in the dark and watching. And even now she is standing there, gaping on the sidelines in headscarf and boots, rubbing her hands like a Lady Macbeth, shaking her head in bewilderment as if she is really the culprit.

If all things are equal, at last Diana is set to succeed, the wrongs in her life have been turned to rights and it only took one mighty shove. All the actors were in their positions, it only took a little direction. But this, this is grotesque.

In the middle of this sad disorder it is now decided that Sam and Dan should attempt to hoist poor Fergus to safety. They cannot wait for the crane to arrive, Fergus is weakening by the minute and the gripping cold won't help.

Slowly, like a wreck from the fathoms, shedding several skins of shit as he goes, Fergus is raised. When his second arm comes free there's a feeble cheer from the watchers, because now, at least, he can transfer the rope from his wounded hand to the other. Jonna's face, while hopeful, is underlined with disgust. For him, with his cleanliness fetish, just to sink one arm in this muck would be sufficient to induce hysterics.

With a dreadful certainty Fergus knows Clover is dead. But he feels he is abandoning his wife, and his groans are despairing, he tries to vomit but nothing will come. Although he was achieving nothing down there, merely risking his own life, the thought of leaving her there on her own –

Clover, so nervous, so dependent – sickens and enrages him. Yes, he has finally failed her, and if only he'd repaired that weak fence properly . . . if only he'd heard her cries earlier he might have averted the catastrophe, but the noise of the milking machines . . . What the hell was she doing so near the edge anyway?

And Mother?

In one terrible flash he sees it all clearly. And to think he'd never truly believed in Clover's wild accusations.

The twins' strong arms haul him to safety while Jonna, haggard, steps back a hasty pace.

'There's no point me pullin' if I've nothin' attached,' says Ernie Wakeham thickly, scratching his head. 'And if 'ers bin that long in the pit I doubt we could reach 'er anyways.'

Fergus hears the man out and then says in a terrible voice, 'So what are we to do, then, Ernie?'

'He'll have to be emptied, I'm afraid.'

Fergus grates his teeth, thwarted by the man's vacant face. 'Good God, man, that'll take hours.'

'Carn be helped. Carn see an alternative.'

'Mummy! Mummy!' screams Polly in agonized terror, the first sign of any attachment she's shown to her mother in years. 'No, Mum, no! DO SOMETHING! *Do something . . .*'

'Take her inside,' commands Fergus groggily. 'Nobody should be out here. Come on, boys, let's get that pump going. Dan, start up the tractor.'

'You should go indoors, you're going to freeze to death and you know there's not much point any more,' says Diana tearfully, softly. 'Please, Fergus, think of yourself.'

'*And leave Clover in that?* The idea is grotesque.'

'The fire brigade is far more likely—'

'If they manage to get here at all. Sod the fire brigade,' he says throatily.

Diana hesitates. She continues calmly. 'And what about Granny? She shouldn't be standing out here, either. Shall I take her inside?'

Fergus, a man with a knack for closing his eyes to anything he'd rather not see, is suddenly aware with appalling shock of the presence of his mother, the woman directly responsible for this whole heinous horror.

'Do whatever you like with her, she's of no concern to me.'

'Oh, Fergus, this is all so dreadful, I'm so sorry,' quavers Granny in a state of shock.

'Take her away!' shouts Fergus in fury, his eyes gleaming wickedly. 'I never want to see her again. She's sick, she's evil.'

'*But, Fergus . . .*' she whispers frantically, crouched like a cornered animal. Is this a bad dream?

'Take her away, Diana, please,' and Fergus turns away abruptly, struggling with his anger. He wipes a trickle of shit from his mouth, 'before I do something I might regret.'

One hour later the emergency services arrive and find little left to do. The stinking pit is a quarter empty, revealing poor Clover's head and shoulders, fermented in vile brown liquid.

'Best to take her away,' says Diana. 'Considering the state she's in. No, no, I'm quite sure Fergus wouldn't want her in the house. The

338

family, understandably, are quite upset enough.'

And then there's the shock of the body in the spreader. It is Jonna who takes the police to one side. Fergus, beyond consolation, has been encouraged upstairs for a shower. He refused the paramedics' advice to go to hospital for a checkup.

Jonna describes exactly what happened. 'And we kept it quiet from the others,' he says, 'because of unnecessary distress. Huh, after all this that idea seems bloody funny.'

'And you've never seen the woman before?' asks the officer, tall and lean as a telegraph pole, perched on the edge of the spreader and gently folding down the sacs. What is this place? Some sort of nut house?

Jonna shakes his head, exhausted, yearning for home and sanity. 'And God knows how she got here.'

'You've had quite a Christmas, haven't you, sir?' He murmurs into his walkie-talkie.

'You could say that,' Jonna groans.

'You won't forget it, anyway.'

But Jonna can't be bothered to answer. This is no time for platitudes and the farmhouse itself reeks of dung, it's all been trailed up the stairs, dropped there by Fergus. Jonna's not sure how he's going to cope and he doubts if Diana will have tackled it.

The bodies depart by ambulance, Granny, a wildeyed witless creature, in the back of the police car. 'An ambulance would be more suitable for the old lady but with the bodies already inside . . .'

'Quite,' says Jonna. 'Not quite the thing.'

'And there's no doubt in anyone's mind . . . ?'

'No doubt at all, officer. My wife, Diana, is a witness. Mrs Moon made several attempts on her daughter-in-law's life before she finally succeeded, and all of us can testify to that.'

'And yet nobody took precautions?'

'We thought we had taken precautions. But clearly she was too cunning for us. We had a great deal on our minds this Christmas, what with the weather and the electric and the farm to run, no help available . . . it's not so easy.'

'No, sir. I suppose it's not.'

The officer glances at Granny with interest. The old lady's face is a greenish white, her knit-up mouth moves out and in and her eyes protrude in a set horror as the eyes of a fish protrude when it finds itself on dry land. Every now and then a shiver rents her. 'Happily, at her age, this sort of occurrence is very rare.'

'They never hit it off,' says Jonna. 'This must have been festering in her mind.'

'Rather hard on Mr Moon.'

'Too early to say how he'll take it.'

'Yes, well, we won't disturb him today, but tomorrow, I'm afraid, we'll have to start the ball rolling.' The policeman turns towards Violet, hat in one hand, and extends the other to help her. 'Come along, then, Granny, let's go.'

Compared with the size of her escort, Violet seems wizened and helpless. Jonna, rendered speechless, feels there is something he ought to say, something appropriate for times like this, a polite 'Good luck,' or, 'See you soon,' or, 'Keep your pecker up.' Instead of defending herself against the several allegations from the beginning,

340

apart from scratching and fidgeting, Violet's response has been meekly accepting. Perhaps, in the face of Diana's strident attitude, she felt there was no point in fighting. Perhaps, crazed as she was, she was merely relieved it was all over and out in the open, her macabre ambition achieved at last.

As far as Jonna is concerned, he has not had time to gather his emotions, to gauge the depths of his grief over the death of Clover, his lover. With Fergus temporarily out of the picture it is he, with Diana's help, who has had to deal with the whole damn mess. No doubt, as time goes by, the pain will come in with the sense of loss, as much the loss of his youth and virility as the loss of the loved one. For Jonna, this is the end of an era.

He nods towards the departing Granny. 'Where will you take her tonight?'

'She'll have to be charged and statements taken.'

'I doubt she's of sound mind.'

'Don't worry, we're used to that. And then she'd probably spend a night at the station before we take her to court in the morning.'

'She'll want to plead insanity.'

'Naturally. We won't argue with that.'

'And then what?'

'I suppose, after that, it will be very much up to the doctors whether they think she should be hospitalized, which I'm sure they will, rather than some penal institution at her age. I should imagine, if Mr Moon is willing, he will have the opportunity to pay for the extra little comforts his mother might require . . .'

Huh. At the moment Fergus would be happy to see poor Violet hanged. But in time, perhaps, his attitude will soften.

Clover's buxom daughters are bereft, but appear to find the ministrations of the twins a comfort. Before going to bed, fortified with suitable medication, they spend some time consoling each other, sharing their loss and great distress.

'I'm never going to get over the way poor Mummy died.'

'She wouldn't have known anything about it,' says Fergus absentmindedly, smelling fresher now, scrubbed, with clean clothes, but Jonna would rather not sit too near.

'There's no point in lying, Daddy, of course she knew, that's what's so awful.'

'She must have called for help, in vain.'

'Nobody heard her.'

'She died alone. And struggling.'

'Listen, this isn't going to help us,' Fergus says finally and firmly, gritting his teeth and tasting sewage. 'Somehow we've all got to cope with the horror, and at the moment I can't help myself, let alone you two. But I do know that dwelling on the more morbid aspects of Mummy's death,' and he spreads out his hands to the room in a gesture of despair, 'well, we're just not ready for this yet. We've all got to be very grown up and realize that this is going to take time . . .'

'And we'll be with you,' whispers Diana.

'Sorry?'

'Well, Jonna. I'm certainly not leaving them on their own. You'll have to go home tomorrow because of the paper, but Sam and Dan are determined to stay here with me, so they can help Fergus all they can. And I'm going to stay for as long as I'm needed . . .'

'There's no need for that, Diana.' But Fergus's hands are trembling, his jaw fallen, his eyes staring. The poor man has been through enough.

'Fergus! I wouldn't hear of anything else. Of course I'll stay. For as long as you need me.'

'I would feel better if Sam and Dan were here,' murmurs Erin.

'Erin and Polly are going to need all the support they can get,' says Diana briskly, not prepared to brook any argument. 'Not only have they got to cope with the death of their mother, but the frightful circumstances of that death, their own granny at the root of it, and by tomorrow the press will be swarming all over the place with their cameras . . .'

'I hadn't thought of that,' says Polly, but there's a tiny spark in her eye. 'We'll be famous.'

'Well, I wouldn't go that far. But someone'll have to man the phones and keep an eye on the gate.'

'We'd be very grateful, if you felt you could stay and help,' says the anguished Fergus politely. 'As long as it doesn't disrupt your own lives too much.'

'Oh, it won't last that long,' says Jonna brightly.

And Diana gives him a well-honed look.

Twenty-seven

Jingle bells, jingle bells,
Jingle all the way . . .

The cold releases its bony grip like a madman's hand unclenching. There's a thaw overnight and, warm in her hotel bedroom, Valerie Gleeson dreams soft dreams of warmer climes, palm trees, thatched bars beside blue lagoons, and Jeffrey Vincent, barefoot without his trainers, running across the sand towards her.

Boxing Day at last. Christmas is almost officially over. Oh, its legacy will drag on in various intrusive little ways, she'll find pine needles on the hall carpet well into next month, the ham will appear till it turns blue and the cheeseboard will put in many more appearances than puddings. Those wretched tins of biscuits will linger until somebody finally realizes nobody's going to eat the pink wafer triangles at the bottom, that they could even be packaging. But it will pass as Christmases do until there's gradually nothing left of it, and she will gaze back at the time as if she is browsing through photographs, surprised to find she was really there. And did she ever look like that? What happened to that skirt she was wearing?

But for Valerie, this Christmas has brought her the gift of freedom, a casket of pure gold compared to the usual myrrh. It's like a re-birth. She's never felt properly born before. She can now leave her old self behind like a crusty, dry cocoon. Far from exploiting the Tarbucks, she convinces herself she is doing them a favour because as soon as Father is installed she will leave and they will find peace. She herself will be far away, will have ceased to care, will have reunited with Jeffrey.

She wrinkles her face, bites her lip when she remembers how close she was to scuppering her chances when she tried to share her suspicions with the sergeant on Christmas Eve. Mercifully she'd kept quiet. Father's aspersions were quite correct and she was being ridiculous. How strange she has that cantankerous old man to thank for that golden moment of doubt. The police have nothing on the devious Miss Bates. They can search and search and still be unlikely to reveal her true background. She never visited doctors or dentists. Thanks to the well-meaning Miss Kessel they have no previous address, no bank accounts, not even a photograph. Nothing that might give away her distasteful past. All they know is that she stuffed birds for museums in London, not the most reliable of clues, one of Miss Bates's peculiar lies. Even if they find the wretched woman dead in some ditch, they will conclude that she was a timid recluse, the resident of one of the many hotels catering for such people in Torquay.

And if, by the remotest chance, Miss Bates has found her lost sister, if that's where she spent the Christmas holiday, too thoughtless to inform the hotel, now that Valerie knows all about her blackmailing campaign, Miss Bates won't have a leg to stand on. No, for once in her life it is Valerie Gleeson who holds the best cards, she's only got to play them properly.

So it's to the hot, coffee smell of Boxing Day morning that Valerie wiggles her toes in bed. Her heart flutters with hope and excitement. She is safe at last. Her boat has come in and all is well with the world.

But Sergeant Andrew Pollard does not feel so positive this morning. The great black bags under his eyes make his nose look longer and give him a haunted look. He has had one hell of a Christmas with his wife's terrible family and he's back at work with a hangover. Something has been niggling him for the last two days, something to do with the missing resident from that sad hotel. What was it the manageress had said?

Boxing Day. And the first thing he has to deal with this morning is the missing Miss Bates. With difficulty he tries to remember. He'd paid proper attention, hadn't he? Or had he been concentrating on the order he'd been supposed to pick up from the off-licence before it closed, or Darren's new mountain bike hidden in next door's garage, or the fact that his car was un-licensed? The weather was dreadful that night. It had been hard to hear what Miss Gleeson was saying and he'd been keen to get away.

'We'll call in,' he says to Tom, his partner, lighting his first cigarette of the day and coughing it up all over the car. 'I'll only be a moment. I want to check up on something that woman said.'

346

'It looks as if your missing Miss Bates could be the one they brought in last night, drowned in the cellar of a farmhouse. It might be worth you radioing in for a description.'

It only takes a few minutes, parked up outside Happy Haven, for Sergeant Pollard to be convinced that this drowned corpse could well be the missing resident. 'I'll see if the manageress will agree to identify the body. You wait here.'

The police car draws up outside the Happy Haven hotel just as Jason and Mandy Tarbuck arrive, just as Miss Gleeson's unlocking her office, just as Miss Kessel comes mincing downstairs, her colossal knitting bag hung on her arm and seeming to drag her sideways with its weight.

With a thumping heart Miss Gleeson steps forward and greets the sergeant with a quick smile. 'Oh, Sergeant, it's you again. Do step inside.'

'Any news?' enquires Jason Tarbuck, eyes narrowed and fiddling with his bracelet.

'Nothing definite yet,' says the sergeant, 'but as I said before, it's early days. We've circulated the description you gave us but it's difficult without a photograph . . .'

Miss Gleeson bustles him into the office and the Tarbucks follow him through the door, which is quickly closed behind them. There aren't enough chairs for everyone and nobody wants to share the put-u-up with the sergeant. Mandy and Valerie take the chairs, Jason perches on the edge of the desk and Sergeant Pollard sits well forward, overlong legs outstretched, letting his hat slip through his fingers, round and round, round and

347

round. The black and white band turns to silver as Valerie Gleeson watches it. Like a cat with a bird she watches it.

Sergeant Pollard hesitates, cursing his slip of memory. What did this woman say, or try to say, that evening as they stood on the porch in the freezing cold? Christmas stands between him and his memory, and Christmas can seem like a year. There is always the feeling that life as we know it might not carry on after it. It is all too simple to start believing this, and get careless.

This is not the time to mention the body.

'If I remember rightly, Miss Gleeson, you mentioned the fact that you were worried. You said that you felt all was not well here at the hotel, that there were things going on . . .'

Miss Gleeson could be a girl again, the way she throws back her head and laughs. It is too light and impulsive a gesture, not one that sits easy on such a broad face, such closed features and such a heavy mass of red hair. 'Oh, good heavens, Sergeant Pollard, of course I was worried, I'm still worried, we're all worried . . .'

'We certainly are.' Jason's frown is most concerned, and Mandy has started to slap her gloves against her handbag again, a habit that shows she is ill at ease.

'Only it's strange,' Pollard goes on, 'that we have so little information about this missing person. We expect there to be much more, an elderly person living like this, her few belongings neat and tidy, there certainly should be something else . . .'

'We have long ago ceased to try and fathom out the little idiosyncrasies of our more senior

348

residents,' says Jason, coughing nervously. 'Haven't we, Mandy?'

And Mandy Tarbuck, desperate to smoke but afraid it makes her appear untrustworthy, twitches her bright red lips and closes her eyes for a fraction too long.

Tap tap. Tap tap.

'That must be Mrs Thompson,' says Jason Tarbuck edgily, unable to prevent himself from checking his watch. 'At this hour? She's gone and got it wrong again. I didn't realize she started this early. I thought they were all having breakfast. Mrs Thompson's a touch confused, you see.'

He slaps his knee and tries to make a joke of it, but nobody laughs. The sergeant, making space in the room for somebody new, sits back and pulls in his legs.

Only Valerie knows that this knock is not Mrs Thompson's, because Mrs Thompson's timing is invariably correct. One tap for morning, two for the afternoon. She is now so very nervous she finds it hard to cross the room without stumbling clumsily. She must try and open the door with a nonchalant calm. But if she tries to stand up straight she might well fall down again, and her jaw has started to tremble. She's not really up to this sort of deception, unlike the Tarbucks, and it shows. There is even a tremor behind her right eye. Can everyone see it, or is it that she feels they can? She has led a calm and boring life, she is not used to this kind of stress from anyone but Father. Now she suspects that the slightest wrong move is going to give her away and she's very aware of the Tarbucks watching her, depending on her to stay calm and reasonable. She is also wildly aware that she's brought this visit upon herself by opening her silly great mouth. Oh yes, this is all her fault.

Somehow she manages to open the door.

'Yes?' She sounds too impatient.

'Good morning, Miss Gleeson.'

The tick thumps behind Valerie's eye. She almost sways when she says, 'Can I help you, Miss Kessel? Or can it wait until afterwards? As you can see, I'm rather busy just now.'

'It's about poor Miss Bates, isn't it?'

'Well yes, it is. The sergeant is here to report on his progress. I'll have a word with you when he's gone.'

Agitated and quick, this wretched old woman is dangerous as the flailing end of a skipping rope. Miss Gleeson attempts to close the door but Miss Kessel's inquisitive face keeps it open. For how can she close the door on that face without being openly rude? And that pale, thin but inquisitive moon is swinging like a pendulum, shaped like a pendulum, ticking like a pendulum, right left, right left, trying to see in, trying to see behind Miss Gleeson, and the eyes are startlingly wide, determinedly aware.

'Oh, but I have important information to impart,' says Miss Kessel, loud enough for all to hear. For this is Miss Kessel's confession voice.

Miss Gleeson's smile, given back to the room, confides to them all that Miss Kessel needs treatment, that she's not in her right mind. The smile leaves her face when it meets Miss Kessel's again. She says warily, 'We're really terribly busy just now. As I said, I'll come and find you afterwards and perhaps we can have a cup of tea and talk about this . . .'

'But this is imperative.' Miss Kessel will not give up. 'I must speak with the sergeant immediately.' And she slips into the room underneath Miss Gleeson's large arm, delves into her knitting bag, of beiges and browns, and draws out the envelope, her copy of the envelope. But Miss Kessel can't find exactly what she seeks, and so intent and eager is she that she drops her knitting bag onto the carpet and falls to her knees beside it, delving, rooting and calling, 'I know it's in here because I put it in here last night. I won't be a minute. I know I'm being a nuisance but bear with me a few more moments . . . Ah . . . here it is! I knew I had it. It's Miss Bates's Christmas card to me. She must have posted it on the very day she disappeared, the day before Christmas Eve. And I didn't consider it important until I read the address on the back. Here, you can hardly see it, but look at this: Southdown Farm, and the name on the top is Violet Moon, and I happen to know that Violet Moon is the name of Miss Bates's medium. So perhaps that's where she is now! At Southdown Farm. Spending Christmas with her medium. Miss Bates and I have an agreement. Wherever we go we like to let the other one know where we are. That's why she scribbled this address on the back of the card, and the name of the person involved.'

Miss Kessel, from her place on the floor, holds out both the card and the large brown envelope like a dog doing tricks for the sergeant. And he takes them from her in the selfsame manner, holding the items aloft as if to display them to an audience.

'You see, she remembered me,' says Miss

Kessel, with a sob in her voice.

'Well, what a sweetie,' says Mandy Tarbuck, sweeping her tired eyes round the room and letting them rest briefly on everyone in it.

'What else is in this envelope?' asks Sergeant Pollard politely. 'Is there anything else of interest in there, Miss Kessel?'

She starts to stuff her knitting bag again, gathering up rolls of rainbow wool. 'Nothing you haven't already seen.'

'I haven't seen anything yet,' he replies.

'But you have the original envelope, surely?' She pauses in her task. 'Mine is only a copy because Miss Gleeson gave you the original. And after my silly behaviour I wanted to tell you myself that I'm sorry.'

The sergeant merely holds out his hand to help Miss Kessel up off the floor.

'So let me get this quite straight. You both bribed Miss Gleeson here to keep quiet about the hospital inquiry and your subsequent dismissal. And you, Miss Gleeson, were perfectly happy to accept Mr Tarbuck's bribe, a free place here for your father for life, even though you knew that an elderly resident involved in the matter had suddenly gone missing?'

Valerie remains rigid and silent. She listens with gazing eyes. She is the damned and everyone else is the blessed.

'You succumbed to temptation. You must realize,' the sergeant goes on, soft voiced, unimpassioned, 'that this also amounts to blackmail.'

Lord have mercy.

'Sergeant! We have done nothing wrong,' whines Jason Tarbuck in wounded dignity. 'We are the victims here, the victims of blackmail, and all we ever tried to do was keep our heads above water. Christ, all we want to do is survive. I know it looks as if we have withheld important information, but our hotel was on the sodding line, our bread and butter . . . It's Miss Bates and Miss Gleeson you want, not us.'

'And any one of you would have found it to your advantage to dispose of Miss Bates. We will have to see what the post-mortem says.'

The game is up and everyone knows it. Mandy Tarbuck breaks down and sobs. Sergeant Pollard uses the phone while everyone sits and waits. And it looks as if they have found Miss Bates.

'Valerie! Is that you?'

'Not now, Dad, *not now*.'

Valerie Gleeson puts on her mac and accompanies the sergeant to the hospital mortuary. She is not repelled by this macabre identification process. She knows what is expected of her. In her line of business, unfortunately, this is one unpleasant role she has to fulfil only too often.

Valerie enjoyed her brief two days of wickedness, but now it's all over. A fair cop.

As the damp corpse is run out and the sheet is pulled back, all she can see is Father's face. Father's face and Happy Haven under new management, herself out of a job. Father getting older and iller until Valerie can no longer leave him by day and try for some kind of menial work, but has to stay home in a nursing capacity, a nursing capacity, *a nursing capacity* . . .

She starts to laugh. The policeman and the mortician glare at her in disgust. She tries to pull herself together but she can't. She just can't. A frightened and unhappy bird that beat its wings to escape into an air it could breathe and failed. She shakes and she roars with unpleasant laughter and all the expressions she's saved up for years and never dared use, never dared display, they are here playing all over her face.

And it is amusing, in its way, there's no getting away from it. She is thinking of what Father would say if he could see her in these circumstances. 'Spit in the wind, Valerie, and it'll come slap back in your face.'

Spit against the wind, what a horrible image, but yes, she supposes that's just what she has been trying to do. Strange how it sounds so disgusting, because Valerie would call it playing with a dream.

And now look, it's a lot worse than spitting, she's been well and truly shat on by the devil's own satanic herd.

Twenty-eight

Slowly, as the years passed by, the world as she had so briefly known it fell away.

When Mummy was blown off the ramparts sixty-four years ago, the shock, for Kate, was compounded by Violet's wild accusations. Over the years only one nurse had taken the patient's bewilderment seriously, and she soon left and took a job in some other part of the country.

'It sounds to me,' said Nurse Higgins sagely, 'that your step-sister is suffering from delusions born from guilt. Perhaps she genuinely imagined you killed your mother that day, or she deluded herself into thinking it was her and was desperately trying to avert the blame. Whichever, from what you tell me it sounds as if Violet is a straightforward case of schizophrenia and I'm quite surprised that illness hasn't been diagnosed by now.'

'Because of the voices?'

'Yes. You say her voices told her what to do.'

'She only heard one voice,' said Kate. 'And that was her mother's. She didn't even consider it odd, she thought everyone was the same as her. She was quite surprised when I told her nobody spoke to me.'

And although, many years later, Kate fought hard to try to persuade more professional doctors to take up her case, although she read up the symptoms of schizophrenia, presented well-thought-out case studies, insisted on being heard, nobody else bothered to act, although some people displayed a vague interest.

The problem lay with her own original shocked reactions. There she was, alone on the battlements (Violet had gone inside because her ears were hurting as usual), when a sudden gust of wind caught Sheena's coat, she was standing perilously near the edge, and with a small cry and a flapping of arms, she disappeared into the void.

For a child of eight this was beyond comprehension.

The next thing she remembered was Violet shrieking, she couldn't remember what she'd said, or what her pointing finger meant. All she knew was that Mummy was gone and she was terrified, dumb, incoherent.

When they conducted their various tests she responded like a robot. So awful was that moment, that shriekingly stark, tormented moment she'd never forget, that she'd say anything, do anything, rather than cast her mind back. It was only much later that she was able to recall her mother's death coolly and calmly.

But by then it was far too late.

The authorities in their great wisdom had made their decisions and nothing she did or said could change that. Because she was a child she was sent to Parkvale Hospital, which dealt with a broad range of afflictions but, although there was a secure wing, it was not for the criminally insane.

There was no need to move her when she reached maturity.

Even her step-father, normally such a gentle and fair-minded man, could not, or would not help her. They said he was suffering from shock himself. He could not even risk his own fragile state of mind in order to visit her, let alone relive the whole horrific nightmare, see it through a fresh pair of eyes.

But why, dear God, oh why, did Violet despise her that much? Was it possible that an eight-year-old child could harbour so much resentment towards a mere child, as much a victim of circumstance as herself?

Kate was not short of time to think. It must be as Nurse Higgins suspected. Violet was so deluded by voices she merely behaved as she was directed. Or the only other alternative was that she sincerely believed it was she who had committed the awful crime. If only Kate could confront her, beg her, force her, torture her until she agreed to tell the truth, the truth that only the two of them knew, that nobody pushed Sheena, the whole grim affair was an accident.

The most sinister part of all this was the way those two witnesses on the scene confirmed Violet's story. But Nurse Higgins had an answer for this. She said it was merely the power of suggestion in such highly emotive circumstances. She said that tests had been done that proved that some people were easily impressed given certain powerful conditions, and the conditions at Harlech Castle on that fateful day were certainly highly charged.

Kate's only hope was that one glorious day the

healthy part of Violet's brain would break through. That she would come to face the reality, tell the truth and release Kate from her sterile incarceration. Until then she was condemned to live among the dead.

When she was younger she raged and screamed against the injustice, turning her anger and indignation, her awful powerlessness, on herself with razor blades, drugs and knives. This only confirmed the authorities' view that her mind was badly damaged. Many times Kate applied to the Home Office for release – her sentence was open-ended, left to the wisdom of those in charge of her. And every time she did so the newspapers got hold of the story, the drama was re-enacted in newsprint, the public threw up their hands in memory of the vicious child-murderess and it was not in the interests of any Home Secretary to show any degree of mercy.

Merely her name, Katherine Lewis, seemed to cause a mass shudder.

So many appeals for clemency. So many highs and lows, in the end she found the mix of hope and the desolation unendurable. For her own sanity's sake it was best to accept her destiny and make the most of her grim existence. This hatred drained her of energy and split her head, but nothing she did could dim the glow of pure loathing that flamed whenever she thought of her step-sister, Violet.

Daily despair and inertia. Her temples beat, her limbs shook, her heart played tricks and her eyes began resting on objects without seeing them. Surrounded year after year by the mad, eating and sleeping, dressing and bathing, singing and screaming, to keep a firm grip on her own sanity was a daunting task and how could she possibly judge whether she succeeded or not? How can anyone ever be sure, especially when influenced by various series of drugs prescribed and altered according to popular medical trends.

Someone said there could be no hell, because in ten days you would get used to it and it would cease to be hell any more. But Kate never got used to the intolerable sick despair – the slow, monotonous movement of days and the even longer nights, and the realization that this was for ever, left her a jaw-dropped idiot. Thought became passive, comatose, active at two points only – her fury and loathing of Violet and the dimming yet sustaining hope of release one day. She would set her teeth, clench her fists and hold herself together for as long as these powerful images took her.

Curious to be alive yet know she'd never see freedom again. She ate her meals, but what for? Footsteps might be heard, the clatter of keys, the voices of nurses coming on duty, the cries and the laughter of fellow patients, but the sounds she wanted to hear were of birdsong, the rustle of leaves, the sound of her running feet through the grass, the conversation and gossip of friends. She passed her time helping the nurses, cleaning the ward, knitting, playing cards, dominoes and draughts, reading or watching TV. She spent long hours composing letters to various authorities, protesting her innocence, bringing her plight to their attention, but in those early years even the charity MIND was sympathetic yet unable to help such a notorious killer.

She made what friends she could among an ill assortment of patients, some came and went, some remained on the ward till they died. Rose Ball was one, poor Rose, the victim of a campaign of cruelty led by a staff nurse they all despised and Tarbuck was his name. Oh, most of the nurses were decent, overworked people trying to do their best in difficult circumstances, but every so often there'd come a man or a woman with a different shine in their eyes, a resentment, a bitterness that a little bit of power would magnify.

Staff Nurse Tarbuck was such a man with the power to infect his colleagues, and the long-term patients on Livingstone ward recognized this difference about him immediately and were wary, they trod softly around him. He picked out his victims with cunning, mostly those too ill for friendship, too incoherent to complain, the weak, the maimed, the ugly, the old. It was always shocking to see with what ease these bullies influenced the most ordinary characters around them, turning them into accomplices who often went further than they did with their petty spite and malicious games.

His friends soon deserted him when poor Rose Ball was found dead in the bath. They were quick enough to condemn him then, and to support the patients' complaints. Hah, Staff Nurse Tarbuck was left to carry the can on his own and life went on after he left in disgrace, all memory of him sucked under as the stagnant pond of life on the ward closed over.

But Kate remembered. She'd been fond of Rose, lonely, silly, confused old biddy who loved Rowntrees Fruit Gums.

On the day that Violet arrived on the ward, Kate was given no warning. Perhaps Violet had not told the hospital she was coming, perhaps she acted on impulse, or out of curiosity. Who knows? The reason for her visit was connected with Dr Lewis's will. He had left Kate a thousand pounds, and there was some question about whether she'd be allowed to have it.

She recognized Violet instantly. Her face had never been far from her mind. Kate managed an iron calm, an astonishing self-control. The shock of it came later. It left her near to breaking down, in an agony of confusion, despair and dismay when she realized that her step-sister's visit was nothing to do with her release. It had taken her fifty years to visit. She hadn't even bothered to see her. When she signed the document Kate was in such distress all she remembered of it afterwards was the one word, Torquay.

So she hadn't moved far from her childhood home.

With Kate's thousand-pound bequest the Parkvale Hospital League of Friends purchased two hardwood garden benches.

Fate.

It wasn't until ten years later she saw the advert while flicking through an old magazine brought in by a visitor.

TORQUAY

'*Happy Haven Hotel*'. *Personal hospitality in small, homely residential hotel in the centre of sunny Torquay, licensed bar, conservatory and sea views. Proprietors: Jason and Mandy Tarbuck.*

Hello! Staff Nurse Tarbuck's wife was called Mandy, she'd worked as a hospital cleaner. The coincidence was worth pursuing, but only with great caution.

So Kate wrote a careful letter.

Dear Mr and Mrs Tarbuck.
Having seen your advertisement in The Lady, I am writing to enquire about the availability of a single room in your residential hotel. At present I am a patient at Parkvale Hospital, and forgive me if I am wrong, but I seem to remember you yourself had connections with this institution approximately five years ago.
I look forward to your reply.
Yours sincerely.

To her overwhelming joy the reply that came back was the one she wanted. The Tarbucks suggested a visit. The point of her letter had gone effectively home.

Three years ago the overworked doctors had decided Kate was harmless. Her long-lost freedom merely depended on finding suitable sheltered accommodation. Not quite so easy as it sounds. The young went first. The young and the completely do-lally. Kate waited and waited, unable to discharge herself without a responsible carer. Unlike some, she had nobody in the world to come forward. The hospital was large, patients like her were shoved to the end of the queue. Luckily for her, MIND and various pressure groups were busily campaigning for patients' rights, the public were rightly appalled that such a diabolical place still existed.

The Tarbucks, terrified of losing their livelihood, were easier to convince than she'd imagined. And after these wasted years, all the struggles, all the hardships, the end was almost simple. Yes, they'd agree to sign her release if she kept quiet about the inquiry. And yes, if she insisted, they'd give her a room at their hotel, free of charge. She had them in the palm of her hand and what is even more extraordinary was that the hotel was in Torquay, the one precious word she had to connect her with Violet.

Two years ago.

And she changed her name from Lewis to Bates.

There was much rehabilitating to do, let alone spend time searching for her sister. Freedom was hard to handle. Everything required such an effort, letters, dressing, shopping, talking. The outside world was a dangerous place, she began to appreciate the benefits of the hospital but never, never to regret her escape.

If she'd known Violet's married name she'd have found her much more quickly.

It wasn't the hours of research she put in at the library. It wasn't the scouring of newspapers or the intense scanning of directories. It was Miss Kessel, her room-mate, such a kindly soul, who seemed so keen that Kate and her sister be re-united. She wished she'd confided in her before. Miss Kessel told her to go through the marriage certificates, and once she'd found her sister's name she could discover her present whereabouts by a simple scan of the voters' register.

It seemed so obvious. But when you've been out of circulation for over sixty years these problems are not so easily solvable.

Violet Moon. And a Torquay address, exactly as Kate had expected.

Of course, sod's law, soon after that she was in a café passing the time with a cream horn and a newspaper when Violet's name came up. In the crowded café the two women asked to share her table. They were discussing spiritualism, of all subjects. Kate should have known Violet would be dabbling in something like that. Kate joined in. One of the women, Nora Bunting, described the seance she'd just attended in a bungalow on Wideacre Road. Shamelessly, Kate Bates expressed an interest and wondered if she could accompany Mrs Bunting on her next visit.

But would Violet recognize her? Kate wasn't ready to be recognized.

She'd only seen her ten years ago, through glass. They'd recognized each other then.

No, not only had Kate changed her name from Lewis to Bates, but since her release everything about her was different. Her hair was neat and held back tightly, she wore spectacles, her clothes were subdued and smart, money had been no object to her since she'd moved in with the hapless Tarbucks. And surely, on top of all this, a seance would not be held under the brightest of lights.

So she took the opportunity and went. Who dares wins. Violet actually touched her, she took her mac and hung it up in the dimly lit hall. Kate left as soon as the seance ended, shattered to discover Violet's preoccupation with voices. Did none of these poor fools recognize her for what she was? She went another twice after that until she decided what she must do. She would visit the night before Christmas Eve, when Violet would likely be alone. Christmas Eve, the evening of innocence, was an unsuitable night to confront her sister with the horrendous truth. To shake her, to slap her, to scream at her with all her nightmares, to tear her apart if necessary until she woke up to the monstrous evil she had done.

Kate had long ago ceased to care about the consequences of her actions.

But the bungalow was deserted.

It took Mrs Fitzhall, from the house next door, a while to answer her ring.

'Oh no, dear, Mrs Moon's not here. She's gone to stay with her family over Christmas, she always goes and she won't be back for a week. Oh dear,' she looked at the threatening weather, 'I hope you haven't come far. You should have rung her up first. What are you, one of those clients of hers?'

'Just a friend.' It was hard to sound normal, in this awful passion of disappointment.

'Well.' Mrs Fitzhall scratched her head and the smell of swede came wafting out of her kitchen. 'I don't know how I can help you.'

'Do you know her family's address?'

'I do happen to know that, yes, if you'll just hang on a moment. I've got it somewhere by my phone. Her son, you know, he insisted,' Mrs Fitzhall lowered her voice, 'in case anything should happen. We're none of us as young as we were.'

Eventually, with the address in her hand, Kate Bates walked the mile from Wideacre Road to the gale-torn front. She passed a postbox on her way to the taxi rank and suddenly remembered she had Miss Kessel's card in her handbag. Maybe she should tell Miss Kessel where she was going, just in case she encountered some hostility, or got herself lost, which is more than likely. Miss Kessel, the nervous, motherly type, might be concerned if her friend did not reappear for a day or so. So she posted the card after scribbling the address on the back with a small stub of pencil – she hoped Miss Kessel would be able to see it – and walked on. White, haggard and shaking by now, she picked up a taxi. It was sleeting hard already and snow was on the way.

The skies were black and heavy.

'You'll not get back in all this, my lover.'

'Never mind.'

'If this snow starts now we'll be lucky if we get anywhere tonight.'

Miss Bates remained silent.

They drove through the violent weather, creeping along the flooded lanes, where low-lying branches beat the roof and slapped at the windows as they went by. It seemed to take an eternity. Finally they arrived at the name of the farm and the posh sign that twisted and blew above it, Southdown, an accredited Friesian herd.

'I'm not happy leaving you in the middle of nowhere on such a night, but I don't think I'll make it down that track without getting stuck in the mud. I'll be lucky to get back home tonight.'

Kate, struggling in the dark in her smart handbag for her money, stayed silent. Did something about her demeanour disturb him?

'Let me take you back to Torquay. Once this snow starts falling nobody's going to go anywhere tonight. It's your last chance, midear.'

'This'll do nicely, thank you.' And Kate battled hard to open the door.

'Well, I hope they're expecting you,' said the driver, making one more friendly attempt.

'Oh yes, someone's expecting me. I expect they've been expecting me for years.'

Barmy. Aren't they all? And the driver shook his head and drove off.

Early evening but already pitch black and no friendly guiding light.

She carried the accumulated anguish of a lifetime. Massive and overwhelming, it weighed her down. It tired her out but still she blundered on through the rain and the wind, up to her ankles in frozen mud. She was not in control of her breath and she gulped and spluttered as she went. She knew she had finally reached the house when a ribbon of yellow radiance came from beneath the kitchen door. She thought of homely fires burning on so many Christmas nights while families sat round together in love, all those Christmases she missed.

'*Silent night, holy night . . .*'

She liked the savagery of this weather, the curious beauty of it all and the dismaying terror. Every step forward felt like a wound. Her anger and revulsion had triumphed. At last she was ready. When she met her sister she would kill her.

'*All is calm, all is bright* . . .'

She saw the great door hanging off its hinges and the steps that led down . . . to where? To a spirit of order lying somewhere beneath the house, behind the riot? There might be another way in, a way that made it possible to avoid the needy knocking at the farmhouse door, the surprised enquiries of strangers. With a dead heart, Kate stumbled on to investigate. The icy waters rushed past her and gathered pace . . . gathered depth . . . she put out both hands to steady herself, felt the roughness of the walls, sensed the chasm of nothing below her at the same time as she lurched to one side, smashing her head against the door-frame.

Such intolerable memories.

The blackness as the flood water claimed her was almost a relief.

A happy release.

Epilogue

There is a stillness and there is waiting. But this is a different kind of stillness, a gasping kind of waiting.

'Is there anyone there in spirit?'

And the airy feel of a modern ward, painted with colours chosen deliberately to meld with the senses. The day room curtains are a lively print in pastels, and the view from here is of the quad, a specialized garden designed for the occasional slow promenade, with seats set in shady places and a therapeutic fish pond filled with enormous carp.

'Is there anybody there in spirit?' The medium's attitude changes uncannily, from endless patience to sudden, sharp insinuation as the idea that some of the spirits are messing about and leading her a merry dance, as they tend to do when they're in that mood, strikes her.

Sometimes they are so infantile.

In a shrunken, communal cardigan and large, ill-fitting lace-up shoes with American tan popsox wrinkled round her ankles, nevertheless, when she is in communication the medium's image is commanding. Her legs are uncomfortably stuck to the seat of the upright, plastic chair, and when she shifts them the skin squeaks as it is released, only to stick once again.

Her curiously pubic curls, originally designed by Audrey, are shorter and more startling since she allowed her friend, Isla Mott, to practise on her last Saturday. She won't allow Isla to cut it, of course, the visiting hairdresser does that, and after this mishap of a perm she won't allow Isla to touch her hair again.

There are no rings on the medium's fingers because jewellery is not allowed here. Theft, or more likely absentmindedness, is rife, and relatives have naturally complained. It does seem a shame, as wedding and eternity rings can be part of a person's persona, a living reminder to others, particularly the staff, that they were loved ones once, worth a diamond or two in their day.

It is visiting time on Mandela ward. Up this end of the day room the lights have been left off, and anyone who trespasses gets frowned upon. Even those who display a serious interest are quickly moved on by Godfrey. Two Formica-topped dinner tables have been pushed together to accommodate the gathering, and over the mottled pink the medium has thrown a white sheet with hospital initials in denim tattooed on one corner. Apart from the medium herself, there are four hopefuls here today, three women and a man, and they perch on wipeable, upright chairs with their feet on sticky lino. Unfortunately candles are not allowed due to the fire regulations.

A nurse passes and smiles sympathetically, a bedpan under one arm. A patient comes up and attempts to present tomorrow's menu to Mrs Moon.

'Not now, Betty.'

She pauses for an irritated moment.

'Is there anybody there?'

It wouldn't be surprising for any spirits tempted to join this little band to be turned off by the unsuitable atmosphere, but there's no other choice. Mrs Moon put in a request for the psychiatrist's room, she explained the problems she faced quite clearly, but, after a ward meeting at which everyone gave a view, it was decided that if they allowed Mrs Moon permission it might be the thin end of the wedge. The next petition might come from aerobics, or the basket-weavers, or the stained-glass window-painting class. They couldn't permit one and not the other.

Mrs Moon didn't bother to argue.

The wait for contact with the other side takes patience and endurance but the earthly listeners are used to this, they have been here before. There was a brief lull around Christmas, when all that trouble flared up and poor Mrs Moon was accused of murder and labelled too insane to plead, but it would take much more than that to influence her regulars. They soon discovered where she was and approached the hospital authorities discreetly. It wouldn't do for the press to find out. Luckily one of their number, Gladys Carter, had influence with the local authority, and finally managed to swing it.

However, it was thought unwise for the group to accept new members. Concerned relatives might disapprove, if patients, already confused, came under such controversial influences.

Joining hands like dancers performing a jig round their dead, these four present make disconcerting bodily contact, one of the little familiarities one has to get used to, these days, as Nora Bunting points out; last time she went to Christmas Eve mass she was shocked to be forced to shake hands with the person next to her in the congregation.

BANG.

CRASH.

WALLOP.

'Gracious!' And their hearts all leap together. 'What on earth?' 'Good grief.' 'Christ almighty.'

'It is merely a patient fitting,' says Mrs Moon complacently, frowning at the jerking body being carted away by stretcher. 'Must be somebody new. The dosage not quite strong enough. It's one of the many little upsets one gets used to. Now, if we could try to concentrate harder, perhaps we could carry on.'

Violet ought to have recognized Kate. She came to the bungalow three times before her fatal visit to the farm and on every occasion Mrs Moon was disconcerted, but no more than that. The change in her step-sister was uncanny. The last time she had seen her was in the ward at Parkvale, a downtrodden, nervous shadow of a woman with no spirit in her. In contrast, the woman in grey seemed very together, smart, self-controlled, but of course there was the warning sign – she'd had no aura.

That was the clue that should have alerted Violet.

Never before had she failed to sniff out an aura.

She was lucky, they told her, that Miss Bates had the self-control to postpone her malign intentions until she could catch Violet 'off duty'. She could easily have pounced during one of those seances she attended, Violet being at her most vulnerable during the times she is 'under'. That kind Sergeant Pollard took the trouble to visit Violet and explain. 'There is no doubt Miss Bates was out to harm you. Poor misguided woman. Apparently she never accepted her guilt over her mother's death, blamed you, said you'd set it up out of spite . . .'

'What nonsense.'

'Well, of course, she should never have been released from Parkvale.'

Mrs Moon sniffed. 'It's appalling, it's happening so often these days.'

He looked at her narrowly. 'And now you yourself . . .'

'You're saying it runs in the family? Might I remind you, Sergeant, that my sister and I were not blood related. Might I also remind you that a vile injustice has been committed. I never touched my daughter-in-law no matter what they say.'

'So you're denying your involvement yet again, Mrs Moon, just as you did all those years ago. You swore then that it was your sister, Kate, who pushed your step-mother off the battlements. Later, when she was over the shock, Miss Lewis denied her involvement. You were the principal witness against her.'

'There were others,' sniffed Mrs Moon, affronted.

'Oh yes,' said the sergeant, tiredly. 'As you say, there were others. And it was those others who inadvertently prevented justice from being done.'

'I hope you are not accusing me of that unpleasant murder.'

'There's really no point any more, Mrs Moon. It happened a long, long time ago and now Miss Bates is dead. I'm just interested, that's all. Call it a policeman's little fetish.'

A voice across the ether. A voice from the dark, drifting icily across the day room. 'Hello! Good afternoon!'

At last the medium smiles. Aha, Caster again, usually the one to come through in the end, a most dependable spirit guide.

'Good afternoon, Caster my friend. I'm so glad to hear you. I do hope it wasn't too hard to get through, bearing in mind the unsuitable conditions.' There is anger behind the apology, they should have offered the psychiatrist's room, this sort of effort takes it out of the spirits and their commitment should be applauded.

'Have you anyone waiting there with you today? Anyone with a message, or merely a jolly greeting? As you see, we are using the hospital day room again so I hope nobody's finding this too distressing. This is now our regular meeting place, unfortunately, hardly conducive to our purposes but the only available space, I'm afraid, and, as such, we must just try to surmount the obstacles.'

The earthbound ones are game for anything. This is it! *Here we go!* There's an excited lift in the atmosphere, shoulders hunch, eyes widen, toes curl up under sensible shoes and Godfrey can already feel the sting of tears behind his eyes. Nothing can beat this experience, no amount of money can buy the exhilaration they feel on these Tuesday afternoons, the knowledge that death is not the end, that one day they and their loved ones will be reunited.

Contrary to accepted beliefs, life *is*, in fact, a rehearsal. So it doesn't really matter how you waste it.

The feelings of Mrs Moon's clients post-murder and insanity accusations are mixed. Godfrey doesn't believe a word of it. He is her most avid fan, she is his glorious conductor of souls without whom his sister Minnie would have been lost to him long ago and he would have been unable to live with the guilt of surviving her. Gladys Carter, the one in the hat, is into crime and grisly deaths and comes for the drama as much as anything, and the recent accusations about Mrs Moon (she's sure she did it) merely enhance her enjoyment of the whole uplifting experience. Nora Bunting, the woman in the café through whom Miss Bates was introduced to the sessions, doesn't care whether she did it or not, she cannot release her grip on her dearly departed George, and it is only through Mrs Moon that she can keep him beside her for ever. And the fourth contender, not yet mentioned, a hippy-type alternative person, decorated with pendulums and various pieces of meaningful stone, believes nothing she reads in the press but prefers to go with the flow. She never realized, before she started attending the seances, that so many of the blessed dead were concerned about her welfare. People pop up from nowhere.

'My dear friends in spirit,' cries Mrs Moon, sweeping her hands from the table to her chest, causing some alarm to the unsuspecting visitors at the other end of the room, 'please don't keep us waiting any longer. For some of us the suspense is killing.' She does not blanch at the use of what might be a somewhat unfortunate word.

At dear last here comes the familiar voice of spirit guide, Caster the Eskimo, again, as cool and icy as ever, bringing them hope from the vast avalanche of the other side. 'Dear friends on earth, have patience, although we do understand that in your little scheme of things such a virtue is hard to realize. Ours, of course, is eternal, something which, one day, you yourselves will come to understand. We are gathered here this afternoon just as you are now, eager to speak with the loved ones we left, grieving, so far behind.'

Suddenly Mrs Moon's eyes bulge, she leans forward and takes a swig of water from a plastic beaker. (Glass is not allowed, same as any sharp instrument which might enable patients that way inclined to inflict damage upon themselves.) Just as violently she lurches back and closes her eyes again, licking her lips and smacking them pleasurably. Yes, she decides to go with the force, to hell with restraint. Any eavesdropping visitors who might find this alarming will just have to put up with it, or leave the day room and sit somewhere else. She did ask for the psychiatrist's room . . .

Who will come through first? Will it be Minnie, Godfrey's dear little sister? The henpecked George, or one of a number of regular callers who are made so welcome by Mrs Moon's little troupe?

To Godfrey's joy it is little Minnie, the child

who drew the weeping angel, but what is the matter with Minnie today? She sounds frightened and short of breath, she doesn't bother with her usual greetings but hurries straight into her message. In the high-pitched voice of the child Mrs Moon's words are strangely garbled. 'Godfrey dear, I'm sorry but I can't stop, this is awful, like when Dadsey used to hide, d'you remember, and jump out at us in the dark . . .'

Godfrey's spectacles steam up and his face turns a ghastly white.

The medium is gibbering. 'It's getting closer, Godfrey, and I don't know what to do. I wish you were here to look after me like you were when Dadsey had too much to drink and you put me in the blanket chest . . .'

Eyes starting from his head, trying to hold the terror at bay, Godfrey stretches out trembling arms to fight off the maddening pressure. He mutters, 'Oh God, give me strength,' as he tumbles into some blinding desolation where nobody earthly can reach him. A despair too complete for tears. Minnie's terrible scream, by way of the medium whose limbs tremble and shudder with the force of it, is the last thing he hears before he passes into blessed unconsciousness.

By now the whole day room is silent and staring as Godfrey slides to the floor.

Mrs Moon tears herself from her chair and beats her head with her fists. Quick, short gasps come from her body. Gladys Carter stands up and looks around for professional help – so the court was right, after all. The other two women are shocked and frightened out of their wits because this spectre is too appalling. The medium's eyes are being forced from their sockets.

Is it Minnie? Or has poor Minnie fled in terror?

Nobody notices the premature twilight or the chill draughtiness of the spotless room with its ruthless cleanliness of colour. From the floor Mrs Moon sobs like a child, unseeing, unhearing, her lips moving violently, her fingers plucking stupidly at her mouth. The words she spits out are full of wrath and savagery. 'Chickadee . . . Chickadee . . . yes, yes, YOU.' The venom is almost a living thing. 'At last I LIVE and I'm waiting, sister mine.' The medium pauses and gasps. 'Mummy's not here, my darling, and nor is your sweet William, they were your private voices. So many voices. You are sick, Violet, very sick.' Mrs Moon grabs at her throat. 'And you'll get a lot sicker, believe me. Violet, listen, after sixty years of sleeping I AM HERE AND I'M NOT GOING AWAY, even unto death, *do you understand what that means?*'

Eternal damnation.

Goodness me. This is an utter disgrace. Why is nobody rushing across with a suitable hypodermic? Dear God, this is too much, you don't expect this sort of thing when you come bearing grapes and magazines on an innocent afternoon visit, everyone knows what sort of ward this is, but, heavens, you'd think they'd keep the more disturbed patients drugged and in bed while visitors are on the ward.

'Nurse! Nurse!'

There's an urgent rushing of feet and a garble

of voices. 'If you'd all leave us to cope with this and move back to give the patient some air . . .'

'She looks like she's dead to me.'

'She is not dead, I assure you. This is quite normal . . .'

'Normal? Well . . .'

'Whatever she was doing, and I saw her behaving strangely, she should never have been allowed . . .'

'There should be more supervision.'

'And look, that poor old man's fainted.'

'I'm not surprised. It must be the shock. Or is he a patient?'

'No, I'm sure he was a visitor. What were they all doing, anyway, sitting round two tables holding hands . . . ?'

'Up to some hocus-pocus, no doubt . . .'

They can't get out of there quick enough.

No more tea and sandwiches.

It is not their habit to resurrect the afternoon's experiences. Well, death is embarrassing, more tasteless to bring up at the table than sex and when you add insanity . . . And again their flushed faces and careful eyes suggest that they have been taking part more in an orgy than a spiritual happening – and maybe they have. No, they like to avoid the subject of what they have been up to behind the hospital swing doors, over the beige and brown carpet tiles that lead to the day room.

They'd rather not be seen together, especially after this, and poor Godfrey is still feeling shaky. The pool of warmth in which they are used to bathing now seems shameful, a little obscene, it feels as if they've exposed themselves and their hopelessness to each other and now they must pay for their folly, each one solitary and vulnerable. Disgraced by their morbid needs.

Wrapped in their own embarrassment, so nobody notices the woman in grey. She stands on the other side of the road, half hidden behind a car parking sign, the mac that smells of stale water clutched tight round her and her face turned towards the wind. She watches the hospital with tired, dull eyes while above her the gulls scream their agony.

THE END

UNHALLOWED GROUND

The gripping new novel
from Gillian White

One

Once upon a time, it is said, the devil walked in this valley. His progress was marked by a straight line of hoofprints, black two-legged tracks on a light dusting of snow, over shippen and stable, stone wall and stile, through graveyard and frozen furrow.

No detours.

Legend has it that Millie Blunt, a silly wench, recovered his codpiece from the bough of an oak while searching there for mistletoe. The hapless girl spirited it home believing it held all manner of powers. She slept with it under her pillow one night – it must have been uncomfortable – when the moon flooded her attic room through her little casement window, and she never spoke another sane word from that day until she died, poor soul.

Though why the devil should choose a valley such as this for a survey, or a gathering of souls, was always far from clear; there were such few souls, even then no more than twelve, in the hamlet of Wooton-Coney, and the few there were were undoubtedly Christian and safely hidden behind shutters on howling nights such as those. As pious and God-fearing a community as any. The church itself, and the graveyard through which the devil walked, collapsed way back in the seventeenth century, and only rubble and lichened old gravestones remain to mark the spot. At some un-recorded moment in history the weathervane from the crumbled church spire was rescued from the debris, and for the last 200 years that bent tin cockerel has swung round on its rusty perch on the gabled end of the Buckpits' barn.

Centuries later, and Georgina Jefferson is as opposite in character to the blighted wench in the fable as it would be possible to get. Educated and cultured, she is sane, *she is sane*. Where Millie Blunt was free with her favours and considered something of a halfwit from the start (the preacher rapped hard on the pulpit and disclaimed her in church, called her child the devil's spawn), her teachers wrote in her termly reports that Georgina could go far. There is nothing melodramatic about her, unlike the troubled Millie with her wild tangled hair and her flashing eyes and her lies. When her child died she swore that the devil had come in the night and smothered it. In character Georgina is solid as a rock, not morbid or sentimental, not given to the flights of fancy in which so many of her friends indulge. So when she first heard this devilish tale it certainly did not unnerve her, although she did think, as a professional, that poor Millie's predicament would be more mercifully dealt with these days. She wouldn't recognize a codpiece if she saw one, she would probably think it was some piece of saddlery. Practical and sensible, Georgina does not overindulge. She sits and watches while lesser mortals get rat-faced and make prats of themselves at parties, she is the one with tomato juice and a dab of Worcester sauce, the complete one, the one who drives.

Boring perhaps? A shade too cautious?

Certainly not. Not a bit of it. She is glad she is not one of these irresponsible folk; their lack of control shocks her, for she cannot bear to relinquish it, not in bed, not in the kitchen, and thus her meals (and her sheets) tend to be dry, with each taste a neat and separate daub on the plate. She would rather do without gravy, or too many dangerous spicy sauces.

So we can see that Georgina Jefferson, forty-two, slim, dark and attractive, who shops for her clothes at Marks & Spencer, sends Lifeboat cards at Christmas, is a solid, dependable person, concerned, right-thinking and busy. She knows who she is, believes that virtue carries its own reward and is satisfied with that.

And that is why it is such a worry for her to believe, like poor Millie before her, *that she is gradually going insane.*

And, like Millie, there's no help to be had.

It was autumn, a thick juicy one, when she first saw the figure on the hill. The air was rich with the smell of fungal decay and winter had started to breathe on her mornings. She walked straight towards him and frightened him away, or that's what she thought she had done.

Amused by her own curiosity, living where she did it was easy to forget the outside world and that everything wasn't strictly her business. She saw him through the softly stirring curtains of her opened kitchen window, through a blue pall of bonfire smoke, between the crooked branches of the ancient apple trees twisting and heavily hung with clumps of crab apples, bleeding with wasps.

A rural encounter.

At first she thought the Buckpits must have put up a scarecrow, so still and so stark did the dark figure stand. But hang on a minute, it was more substantial than a scarecrow, and why would they put a scarecrow on a small triangular flag of a field that was only good for grass, and poor grass at that?

Georgina stared on meditatively, inhaling watery lemon and her Marigold hands foamy with bubbles. A few towels flapped fresh on her line and tugged at her ears with the sounds they made, and the old wooden wheelbarrow, half full of logs, eyed her muddily from a tangle of grass, a reminder that she had not yet finished the first task of the morning.

Whichever window she chooses to look out of Georgie is forced to look up, because Furze Pen Cottage is down in a dip, a small coin dropped at the bottom of a coarsely woven patchwork purse, an envelope of moorland. Her skyline is unfailingly interesting, copses and boulders and low scudding clouds make vibrant colour changes and act as barriers against the outside world from which she has fled. Her horizons cast nothing but gentle shadows.

Has she fled? Everyone seems to think she has fled.

Or has nothing more intersting than fate brought her here?

Certainly, in her sensible, practical way, she was glad of the bequest when it came.

But back to the figure, this rambling will not do. It was the stillness of it which grabbed her attention. Nevertheless, she finished washing up, taking pleasure in the sparkle of the glasses . . . her life was solid enough, composed enough at that time to allow for pleasure from simple things, so that even changing the sheets on the bed was becoming a kind of sweet-smelling joy. She had been right about coming here. The effects of her rural retreat were already beginning to work.

Was it the distance which made him so dark or was he wearing black? It was rare for tourists to stray this far, mostly they miss the lane or see it and consider it far too steep, so they carry on along the road across the top towards the village one mile on, where they can have lunch at the Blue Bull Inn and peruse the slate etchings and metallic bird engravings in Mrs Morgan's gift shop. The lane, with its scatter of reedy grasses and its manure-splattered, rutted appearance, gives the impression that it leads to a farm, and people are nervous of finding themselves trapped by a pack of sheep dogs.

And what if the farmer is unfriendly?

The figure was not a Buckpit, not a Horsefield or a Cramer, because none of those would stand still for so long, and there was no gun on its back.

So Georgina went to the back door and sensibly slipped on her boots. She walked through her acre of rustic garden, ducking and bobbing to avoid the branches, ignoring the rush of her pecking hens. On reaching the fence at the end she hitched up her skirt and stepped over. Wading through her own small stream, looking back from her place on the boulder, she whistled softly for Lola.

The spaniel with careering ears, dewy wet on the fringes, outwitted once again because she likes to announce such outings by barking – she prefers to lead from the front – snapped at a few drunken wasps as she set off after her mistress.

There must have been something very wrong because the man had been standing for half an hour.

A diminutive figure, head down, arms crossed, Georgina started up the incline, no threat to man or beast, just a slender woman in a flowing skirt and a cotton smock with a hood. The sun was a hazy yellow as it filtered through the corn chaff. Every now and then she raised her eyes to check how far she had come. She'd grown used to climbing by then; wherever she goes she is forced to climb, and it had taken a while to acclimatize after living so long on the smooth flat streets of London. To climb properly and with purpose means adjusting the breathing so that it doesn't run out. There was no fear then – nothing to what came later – merely interest and a slight unease. A reporter who had managed, somehow, to dig her out of her hole? To expose her? To drag her back to the tabloid pages? The past sliding into the present? God forbid! Maybe he was lost and needed help. Maybe he was a hiker, or an artist, or a man from the Min of Ag come to do something about the water?

And yet she knew he was not.

Screwing up her eyes against the sun, Georgina felt the lines in her tanned skin pull and imagined she felt her age coming through. The figure (she could not see his face from here, no definable limbs, no neck, no hair) was no more than a smudge, a dark stunted tree trunk, and yet she could sense the furtiveness of him.

He must have been able to see her coming and Lola was charging about, driven wild by the scent of rabbits. She would be friendly and polite, she would ask him what he was doing.

That's all.

She stopped when she heard the sound of the whistle. It was soft, on two notes, like sailors piping a captain aboard, or how a shepherd might whistle to his dog. It was after she moved her eyes away, just for a second, while she eased herself through a crumbled gap in a wall, that she saw the figure had disappeared . . . into the copse . . . there was nowhere else. No other cover. No hiding place.

A feeling of outright panic gripped her. He must have moved very quickly.

An orange shadow came out of the clouds, swinging from one horizon to another and casting a horribly accurate spotlight over Georgina's fear. Because it was at that moment that she first sensed the violence, and yet pushed it away from her consciousness – *Oh God, was she so in tune with violence that she could smell it from 500 paces?* Surely her reaction was nothing but imagination, and imaginations can become vivid when you live all alone, buried amongst such desolate, lonely countryside. Even for someone as sensible as she.

The shadow of a buzzard followed her home, and the sound of a distant tractor. Lola followed sorrowfully – the walk had been too short for her liking – and made an attention-seeking pass at a hen as they strolled back through the garden towards the silence of Furze Pen Cottage.

The incident was over. That first sighting was as strange and as simple as that. But frozen by the experience, for the first time since Isla and Suzie had left the previous weekend, Georgina wished that they were still there because she would have liked to discuss the matter. Isla and Suzie were the last of the summer visitors who were all kindly trying to put off the awful hour when Georgina must adjust to her new life and endure, alone, the oncoming winter.

'But I am not alone,' she used to tell them all, wearing that brave wooden smile of hers, attempting to reassure herself with that well-rehearsed argument: 'My neighbours live close by, almost within calling distance when the wind's in the right direction.'

'Neighbours!' Isla gave a derisive snort. Her lips curved mirthlessly. 'You might live next door to them,

Georgie, but they're freaks, from some other planet. They are hardly going to provide you with the most stimulating company during the long evening hours.'

'Isla. This isn't fair. You're supposed to be trying to cheer me up.'

'I'm just wondering how you imagine you can depend on them, for anything.'

'They're polite enough.'

And here Suzie smiled in the same disbelieving way as Isla. 'Oh, yes, they mutter the odd miserable good morning when you meet face to face and there's no avoiding it.'

'Oh, that's silly,' Georgie snapped. 'They just believe in minding their own business; they probably think I don't want people nosing, prying into my affairs. They probably think I'm like my brother, a recluse, an artist, an eccentric who wants to be left alone. I bet Stephen bit their heads off in the past.' And she could feel that annoyance which itched whenever the conversation got too close for comfort. 'Anyway, what choice do I have? I've made my bed, as my mother would say.'

Isla met her stare, sifting through a dozen responses to find the most suitable one. In the end she said in a weak, troubled voice, 'You should never have come here in the first place. Out of the frying pan . . .'

'You think I'm a bloody fool, don't you?'

Isla looked away and picked up her drink. She lay on the messy sofa, surprisingly comfortable despite its amorphous nature, next to the crackling fire that winked on her overlarge tortoiseshell spectacles. 'I think you over-reacted, yes. I think you are punishing yourself as usual. God said, "On all their heads shall be baldness and every beard cut off," And you, my dear Georgina, secretly want to be bald.'

Not funny. Georgie wound a curl around her finger and rubbed her sloppy socks together – curiously nervous gestures for her – as she stared thoughtfully into the flames. She suddenly felt an urge to lean forward and arrange a few untidy sticks in the enormous hearth. A cold draft spun down the massive chasm of a chimney. Crossly she reminded them both, 'There wasn't much time for thinking! Not then, dammit. This place felt like a refuge then, a friendly lair in a hostile world, *but why am I wading through this shit again?* You know how it was. You were there for God's sake. You know what it was like for me then.'

'It was bloody hell,' agreed Suzie, as frizzy-haired as a freshly gathered fleece, her complexion smooth as a china doll's with cheeks painted a soft pink and a cold nose bright and shiny. The evenings were already chilly and Suzie was almost entirely cocooned in a baggy, knee-length purple fleece. 'But even so, you could have used the cottage as a temporary hideaway and put it on the market in the meantime. Nobody dreamed you'd end up living at Furze Pen, Georgie, nobody thought you'd take it this far.'

No, neither had Georgina, but she'd never dreamed it would get that bad.

'If I'd put it on the market I would have had to be here all the time to show the punters round. And I couldn't have faced all those strangers. I couldn't put that sort of false smile on my face or cope with anything so fake. Hell, Suzie, I couldn't put my mind to anything like hoovering or dusting or sorting out the garden.'

'That is ridiculous.' Isla, on the sofa, pounded the limpish cushions and rearranged them behind her back. A feathery aura of age and dust floated into the atmosphere. 'The solicitor would have sold it for you;

391

you had an offer right at the start. They'd have had no problems selling this as a holiday cottage, bang in the middle of Dartmoor; it would have made a fortune, untouched, original beams, original windows, flagstone floors . . .'

'No central heating,' Georgie interrupted, shivering slightly as she crossed the small sitting room to the even colder, more primitive kitchen to add mushrooms to the stew. She felt like a piece of lettuce walking into the salad crisper. Perhaps she should not have chosen whitewash, a warmer shade might have done wonders. The cheery rugs did help a tad, and the paintings that covered the walls, of course.

From her place by the fire, Lola snored loudly and woke herself up.

'And we're just very concerned you're going to feel terribly depressed and lonely, way out of your depth, surviving like this in the winter,' Suzie called through the narrow doorway with a meaningful look in Isla's direction. 'All your perceptions of the world are fuddled. It's not as if it's too late.' You could come back to London with us, put this place on the market and start searching for something more practical.'

Georgie, chewing on her fingernails, watched the hypnotically floating mushrooms, allowing the steam to caress her face, enjoying the hot smell of the stew, taking comfort from the warmth and the feeling of something well made with love. Since she'd been down here her cooking had developed a wetter, more mixed consistency . . . so much free fruit, so many vegetables . . . it was easier to use only one pot because of the cramped kitchen. Home-grown potatoes from the farm and a home-made apple pie with fresh cream to follow.

Yet everything Isla and Suzie said made sense,

while every argument she put forward fell apart full of holes. And if she was trying to prove something by standing out and being so stubborn, then for God's sake what was it?

She had been so frightened, so intimidated by everything. But most of all by the way she had, in a few short months, been so easily destroyed, shattered, all confidence gone, the confidence she had built up over forty-two years, melted away in a moment. Until she felt, as she lay in bed night after night weeping, that all the time there'd been nobody there, that Georgina Jefferson was a 'let's pretend' person from childhood, a face miming with nobody behind it. As unsubstantial as soap worn to a frightening slither, gargling off down the plughole.

Was she so naive as to believe that by enduring life on her own for a while, a hermit existence with only Lola for company, she would find herself again? Could she grow large and firm again as simply as that?

I will lay me down in green pastures. She wanted her soul restoreth.

Oh, I am a strong and sensible person . . .

Well, this was what she returned to her friends in the sitting room and told them. And they said, tipsily, that they did understand her motives, they saw how easily a person could be demoralized and torn apart under such attack from every quarter.

'Even people I'd trusted as friends turned their backs on me,' she wailed, tormented by an alien self-pity. '*Can you honestly imagine what that's like?* Ringing people up – oh yes, feeling bad enough about ringing people up – o damn needy, hands in a sweat, heart aching, so desperately wanting reassurance, and being told by quiet, polite voices that they weren't in, they'll ring you back, they were away when you knew they were not.' She played with Lola's soft ears as a child might play with a comforter. The dog opened one eye. It was soft and brown and liquid with love. 'And all the while, to add to the horror, the newspapers crucify you.'

'It could have happened to any one of us.'

'*Don't tell me that one more time!* I can't bear hearing that! I'm sorry, I'm sorry, I know it could have happened to anyone, but it didn't, Suzie, did it, *it bloody well happened to me!*'

And Georgie wanted to shout that, above all, she needed time on her own to mourn for the child with the wise grey eyes who had ended up in a grainy frame with shaggy hair on the front pages of all the papers. The child that had depended on her for its life. The child she had, through her own ineptitude, betrayed and allowed to die. But such a protest would have been unnecessary because Isla and Suzie knew that very well, and yes, as social workers, it could have happened to either of them, and it would happen, again and again as it seems to, every few years, and every time it would be equally terrible . . .

'What should I have done,' had become such a wizened old question that she had stopped asking it, even of herself. If only she could have taken time back. But what was the use of any of this? She had known there was violence at that wretched flat, it oozed out through that cold yellow front door with the thin metal letter box through which she had stuffed note after note, time after time, through which her lips had called so often. Hopelessly. Tiredly. Fearfully.

And back then, as she leaned forward from her sunken chair that even in late summer smelled of damp, wringing her hands and sharing her feelings with her friends, aware of her secret resentment, she would have liked to have screamed, And I am grateful for your continued friendship, can you sense that, dear God? Because that meant that their friendship, once on equal terms, once as honest as friendships could be, was flawed, even though they would have rceived this as an afront and answered, 'That is absurd.' Yes, that resentment, that bitternes, it was there now and nothing could alter it. And what would they have thought if Georgie had screamed across their cosy pink drunkenness, as she longed to do, *This outrageous, diabolical thing did not happen to either of you, but my God how I wish that it HAD*. I wish it was me sitting where you are giving advice and sympathizing. I wish I was you and that either of you were over here in my position.

Yes, she was giving them too little and they were giving her too much.

She re-embarked on her train of thought. She said, 'I wish I'd been able to go to court and stand trial. It would have been fairer, and they were trying me anyway.'

Wretched. Despairing. *And guilty.*

'No, they were not. The inquiry never expected to find you guilty, Georgie. Nothing is that simplistic. You did all that was humanly possible. You are not a fortune teller. The inquiry found you blameless.'

'Blameless? *Jesus Christ!* A child is murdered and how can any of us be blameless? And I could have done more. It is always possible to have done more.'

Isla removed her dramatically circular spectacles and rubbed the lenses on the arm of the sofa, as if to polish them and study Georgie simultaneously. 'You can't stop dwelling on all this, can you? Punishing yourself over and over? I can see you doing it. One minute we're talking normally and the next you sink into yourself, clam up, your expression changes, you go miles away.'

During this terse exchange Georgie attempted a stoic smile, her teeth must have looked like false ones, clenched so rigidly, in a jar. She tightened her hands in her lap. 'How the hell can I get this out of my mind? Five minutes is the longest time I've been free of it so far, and at night I have such nightmares about it.' She might as well admit it. Yes, yes, punishing herself over the smallest details, all those ifs and buts and if onlys, any device to add to the torture.

'What on earth is that rank smell?' Thank goodness the subject was changed.

'There must be a dead rat in the wall.'

'Last night, in bed, I thought I heard scratching. Maybe one of your more experienced neighbours could put some poison down.'

So you see how uncomfortable Georgie felt with her visitors, some of them colleagues from work, some old friends who went back to Toby, others picked up, like most friends are, while thumbing their way along the hard shoulder of life. They came in a steady stream, like memories, so that, incredibly, there had been no complete week from June through to September when she had been alone for longer than forty-eight hours. They kept her busy. They entertained her. But at the end of the day it did not matter how hard they worked with her on the cottage, it made no difference what fun they shared as they laboured in the sunshine repairing the fences, patching the thatch, turning over the rock-hard soil or unblocking the stream. It mattered not what picnics they shared or how many bottles of wine they drank, she could not overcome that grim stumbling block however hard she tried.

They were the blessed, she the damned. They brought car-loads of supplies, they worked with a will, paying their way, but they overdid the kindness bit. Their visits were of condolence, of support in her hour of need, just as hers would have been if the boot was on the other foot. They pitied her and her sad predicament. They thanked her for her hospitality, they thanked her for their holiday, but they were being kind and *Georgie was grateful*. And that put something unpleasant between them, something she found hard to deal with. Poor old Georgina, psychologically standing up while everyone else remained sitting down.

Perhaps she was oversensitive, but she could suddenly easily understand why the troubled resent do-gooders so. And there's only so much support you can get before you see yourself as a cripple.

In some perverse way their well-meaning presences prevented her from healing herself. And yet, look at this, one week after their departure and already she wanted them back. She feared for the roots of her being. She thought she was going mad.

The shaking first started . . .

It was Roger Mace who broke the news that Angela Hopkins was dead. Over the phone for God's sake, a most personal call. The ringing woke her in the morning – mental alarm in her head – she heard the freezing-cold news in a hot crumpled bed. 'Georgie. I'm so sorry. I wanted to tell you myself.'

She had to know, shoulders hunched to guard breathless conversation. 'How did she die?'

'They're not sure yet . . . a blow to the head . . .'

'When?' She hugged the duvet to her stomach. She could feel death's proximity. Her ankles were white as bleached bones, thin as a child's, thin as a skeleton's.

'Last night.'

'And Patsy and Carmen?' She spoke with deliberate, polite calm.

'There's a place of safety order, but no sign of abuse so far.'

'What will happen?'

'Well, I'm no expert, but the case will be given a high priority. There'll be an enormous public impact.'

Her hair fell forward to hide her face. 'I'll come straight to the office.'

'No, Georgie, stay where you are. There'll be time for all that later.'

A warning kindly given. A glimpse of the scalpel of scrutiny. She hadn't asked for an explanation. And then it was suddenly *déjà vu*, she'd always known this was going to happen and what would happen next. Oh God, let it not be true. *She had always secretly known and yet done nothing about it.* Guilty as that bastard, Ray Hopkins himself, the man with the bullet-shaped head and the earful of sleepers, who lived behind the yellow door and swore blind that his five-year-old daughter had fallen down the stairs.

She sank on all fours, her lips trembling, her eyes welling. She pressed one hand to her mouth and squeezed her eyes closed. And she thought, At least it was quick, dear God, at least the end came quickly. She would not let herself think more of the child, no, not at that time. She blocked little Angela out, and that was another small betrayal.

As if she had never known her.

And that's how the dreadful story began.

**Read the complete book – out
now in Corgi paperback**

THE WITCH'S CRADLE
by Gillian White

Barry and Cheryl had become famous. Desperately poor, living in a tower block with their two small children, they were possibly the most famous family in the country after the Royals. Their fame had come, not from wealth or success or glamour, but from the attentions of a television company, who had made them the subject of a fly-on-the-wall documentary.

Cheryl was prepared to do anything – *anything* – to be a media star. She thought that the public loved her – and, indeed, for a while it seemed that the nation had taken this simple, gutsy, poverty-stricken couple to its heart. But then it all starts to go horribly wrong. Cheryl has a third baby – and is transformed in the public's eyes from a plucky but unlucky trier to a profligate sponger on the state. She desperately wants to be loved – and then, mysteriously, all her three children go missing. Have they been abducted? Murdered? Or is there some even more sinister explanation for their disappearance?

'This fast-paced tale explores the ruthlessness of the media when transforming real life into drama'
Good Housekeeping

0 552 14765 6

A SELECTED LIST OF FINE NOVELS AVAILABLE FROM CORGI BOOKS

14496 7	**SILENCER**	Campbell Armstrong	£5.99
14497 5	**BLACKOUT**	Campbell Armstrong	£5.99
14646 3	**PLAGUE OF ANGELS**	Alan Blackwood	£5.99
14775 3	**THE EXORCIST**	William Peter Blatty	£5.99
14586 6	**SHADOW DANCER**	Tom Bradby	£5.99
14115 1	**WYCLIFFE AND THE GUILT EDGED ALIBI**	W.J.Burley	£4.99
14661 7	**WYCLIFFE AND THE REDHEAD**	W.J. Burley	£4.99
14578 5	**THE MIRACLE STRAIN**	Michael Cordy	£5.99
14604 8	**CRIME ZERO**	Michael Cordy	£5.99
14654 4	**THE HORSE WHISPERER**	Nicholas Evans	£5.99
14495 9	**THE LOOP**	Nicholas Evans	£5.99
13991 2	**ICON**	Frederick Forsyth	£5.99
14719 2	**THE PHANTOM OF MANHATTAN**	Frederick Forsyth	£5.99
14525 4	**BLIND DATE**	Frances Fyfield	£5.99
14526 2	**STARING AT THE LIGHT**	Frances Fyfield	£5.99
14597 1	**CAUGHT IN THE LIGHT**	Robert Goddard	£6.99
14601 3	**SET IN STONE**	Robert Goddard	£5.99
14538 6	**A TIME TO DANCE**	Kathryn Haig	£5.99
13699 9	**HOTEL**	Arthur Hailey	£5.99
14623 4	**THE RETURN**	Andrea Hart	£5.99
14584 X	**THE COLD CALLING**	Will Kingdom	£5.99
14603 X	**THE SHADOW CHILD**	Judith Lennox	£5.99
14736 2	**THE HEART OF DANGER**	Gerald Seymour	£5.99
14734 6	**CONDITION BLACK**	Gerald Seymour	£5.99
14391 X	**A SIMPLE PLAN**	Scott Smith	£5.99
10565 1	**TRINITY**	Leon Uris	£6.99
14563 7	**UNHALLOWED GROUND**	Gillian White	£5.99
14564 5	**VEIL OF DARKNESS**	Gillian White	£5.99
14409 6	**HARD FROST**	R.D. Wingfield	£5.99
14778 8	**WINTER FROST**	R.D. Wingfield	£5.99